Jessica Adams is an international *Vogue* and *Cosmopolitan* astrologer. She is also a team editor on the *Girls' Night In* series in aid of War Child. Her novels include *Single White E-Mail, Tom, Dick and Debbie Harry, I'm A Believer* and *Cool for Cats*. Visit www.jessicaadams.com.

www.books

Tom, Dick and Debbie Harry

'*Tom, Dick and Debbie Harry* is a book you take everywhere: in the bath, on the bus, and to bed . . . Jessica Adams' witty, understated style feels exactly like a bunch of mates chatting to you. Clear-eyed, compassionate and very funny'   Victoria Routledge

'Jessica Adams has written an engrossing and utterly original tale which is both funny and frequently very touching'   Isabel Wolff

Single White E-Mail

'She gives Nick Hornby and Helen Fielding a damn good run for their money . . . thoroughly enjoyable'   *Daily Telegraph*

'Sexy, funny, smart. For any woman who has ever been single' *Cosmopolitan*

'A blissfully refreshing treat. I found it very, very funny and quirky enough to be really original. It was *Muriel's Wedding, Sex, lies and videotape* and *Ally McBeal* all rolled into one, and I defy any woman of my age not to relate to Victoria'   Fiona Walker

'Fresh, frenetic and fun'   *Elle*

'A very funny novel for the 90s woman – read it and recognize yourself'   *New Weekly*

'A modern classic'   *19*

'Smart 'n' sexy'   *B magazine*

'Recommended . . . the e-mail of the species is deadlier than the male'   *Marie Claire*

'Meet Australia's answer to Helen Fielding's star character Bridget Jones'   *Sydney Morning Herald*

THE SUMMER PSYCHIC

Jessica Adams

BLACK SWAN

THE SUMMER PSYCHIC
A BLACK SWAN BOOK: 0552772577
9780552772570

First publication in Great Britain

PRINTING HISTORY
Black Swan edition published 2006

1 3 5 7 9 10 8 6 4 2

Copyright © Jessica Adams 2006

The right of Jessica Adams to be identified as the author of
this work has been asserted in accordance with sections 77
and 78 of the Copyright Designs and Patents Act 1988.

Set in 11/12pt Melior by
Falcon Oast Graphic Art Ltd.

Black Swan Books are published by Transworld Publishers,
61–63 Uxbridge Road, London W5 5SA,
a division of The Random House Group Ltd,
in Australia by Random House Australia (Pty) Ltd,
20 Alfred Street, Milsons Point, Sydney, NSW 2061, Australia,
in New Zealand by Random House New Zealand Ltd,
18 Poland Road, Glenfield, Auckland 10, New Zealand
and in South Africa by Random House (Pty) Ltd,
Isle of Houghton, Corner of Boundary Road & Carse O'Gowrie,
Houghton 2198, South Africa

Printed and bound in Great Britain by
Cox & Wyman Ltd, Reading, Berkshire.

Papers used by Transworld Publishers are natural, recyclable
products made from wood grown in sustainable forests. The
manufacturing processes conform to the environmental
regulations of the country of origin.

For Jane Pirkis

ACKNOWLEDGEMENTS

Huge thanks to Diana Beaumont for her sensitive and savvy editing, to my copy editor Shauna Bartlett and to Larry Finlay and Bill Scott-Kerr – and all at Black Swan – for seven happy years. I would also like to acknowledge everyone at Curtis Brown in London and Sydney for the most incredible support and friendship. Special thanks to my fellow editors on the *Girls' Night In* and *Kids' Night In* series, which hit its sixth volume while this was being written. Cheers to Maggie Alderson, Helen Basini, Imogen Edwards-Jones, Nick Earls, Chris Manby, Carole Matthews, Sarah Mlynowski and Juliet Partridge.

CHAPTER ONE

I am interviewing an Australian psychic named Jim Gabriel when he stops the tape recorder and tells me we will be married by next summer.

He is peering into a bucket full of sea water when he gives me the good news. Apparently this is how Nostradamus saw visions of the future too. Though obviously not with one half of a bucket and spade set.

Do I believe Jim Gabriel? Of course not. But the more he gazes into the water, the more he sees.

'Your middle name is on our marriage certificate. It's Margaret. You were named after your mother's doctor.'

'How do you know that?'

'Well am I right?'

'Tell me how you know.'

'I saw it in the water.'

Oh my God. I know it's unprofessional, but suddenly I'm longing for a cigarette.

'Oh, and I've just seen something else,' Jim interrupts me before I can ask. 'We'll be married here,' he nods at me, 'in Brighton.'

'Interesting.'

I try to forget about the packet of Benson & Hedges in my handbag, and fail.

Jim Gabriel's bookshelves are as strange as he is. A large crystal ball is at one end, next to a plastic dragon, a copy of *Zen and the Art of Motorcycle Maintenance*, a pack of tarot cards, a solitary yellow flip-flop, and some incense.

It's the middle of winter, but Jim is still padding around in bare feet. He is also wearing white cotton trousers, a baggy white cotton shirt and a woolly brown hat. And he has a fish tank in the corner of his office – I suppose I can call it an office, though it's actually the back room of a strange New Age gift shop – and a surf board leaning against the wall.

The shop is called Cornucopia and it's tucked away in the Lanes. There are no Christmas decorations in the front window, but there is something called an Orgasmatron, next to a poster of a unicorn sticking its horn through the middle of a rainbow.

There is a bakery next door selling mince pies, and Jim has a half-eaten one on his desk, another one in a paper bag and the rest down the front of his shirt. He looks like he eats a lot of them. He also looks like he's spent too much time in the sun. He has a permanently faded tan, like a lot of travellers who chase summer and end up here.

'You've had one serious relationship,' Jim continues, frowning. 'I can see two signposts. One says London, the other says Brighton. Did your ex move from London to Brighton?'

'Yes.' Who hasn't round here?

He interrupts me. 'No, hang on. Your ex-boyfriend died in London, but his ashes only just came to Brighton. He was cremated in London, but his parents wanted the urn down here. There was a disagreement.'

I have been polite and smiley up until this point, all tolerance and good humour, which is my standard Monday morning journalist pose. But now I find my face has stopped moving.

'How do you know?'

Andrew's ashes only went back to his parents last

12

weekend. They've been arguing about it for months, with me – and Dan, his older brother. There is no way Jim Gabriel can possibly know any of this, unless he has just hired a private detective. It's like the fact that I was named after my mother's doctor. How could he know that?

The thought occurs to me that if Jim was right about my name and right about Andrew, then he must also be right about our impending nuptials. God help me. Am I really going to spend the rest of my life married to a professional bucket reader?

I want a cigarette again. No, I *need* a cigarette.

Jim frowns into his blue plastic bucket. The matching spade, I notice, is on top of his bookshelves.

'Actually, can we get back to the interview? For the paper?' I ask him, switching on the tape recorder.

I wonder if I am the kind of woman who Jim Gabriel fantasizes about marrying. I suspect not. And I am still upset that he has talked to me about Andrew – how the hell did he know about that? – but I'm not going to let it show.

'You smoke,' he smiles as I finally succumb and find my lighter.

Then he looks in the bucket. 'You'll give up cigarettes,' he tells me. 'You wouldn't give up smoking for Andrew, but you'll give up for me.'

I stub out the cigarette on the side of the rubbish bin and turn the tape recorder off again.

'You look a bit taken aback. Sorry.'

'To be honest with you, this is one of the oddest interviews I've ever done.'

'Am I freaking you out?'

'No,' I lie. 'But . . . do you just want to keep going with this future marriage thing? Because if you do, I'll keep this turned off. It's not that I'm not . . . flattered, but I don't really want the story to be about me. It's supposed to be about, you know, the year ahead. Jim

13

Gabriel peers into our global future, that kind of thing.'

'Sorry,' Jim shakes himself and gets up from his chair.

I sneak a look at his back while he puts the kettle on, and, nope, I still don't fancy him. He reminds me of a lion. A great, big, shaggy, golden lion. His billowing white trousers look like part of a fat bloke's cricket uniform.

If he is my future, it's not a future I want. Andrew – now there was a husband waiting to happen. Nice, normal, funny Andrew.

I suppose this small, cold room used to be the kitchen, in the days when Cornucopia was somebody's house. It is crammed into one of the darker sections of the Lanes, where the rents are lower and the rising damp is higher. Despite the radiator, the smoky incense and the glowing pink candles on the desk, the room still feels gloomy, and it smells stale and nasty, as if too many people have cooked cabbage in it.

I try to picture Jim living with me in my flat, and fail. I don't believe in Zen, or the art of motorcycle maintenance. I am terrified by tarot cards. I don't like the look of unicorns. I haven't been to church since the 1980s, and even though they say one in three people in Brighton is a Buddhist, I'm not one of them. And Orgasmatrons? I wouldn't know where to put one. I'm about as spiritual as . . . I don't know. A plank.

'The funny thing is, Jim,' I tell him, 'you don't seem particularly interested in the fact that you've just found your future wife. I suppose I am going to be your first wife?'

'Oh yeah,' Jim gives me a lopsided smile.

'I mean, you've just seen all this marriage malarkey in the bucket, and you seem . . . I don't know. Strangely underwhelmed.'

'Sorry,' he rubs his face with his hands. 'I zone out

14

when I'm doing readings.' He is miles away now, staring at his fish tank as if he's just seen something very important inside it.

'So what brought you to the UK then?' I look at the surfboard propped up against the wall. 'It can't be the weather. Don't you miss the beaches?'

'I felt it,' Jim touches his chest. 'I had to come.'

'All right then. Can you tell me how you first knew you were psychic?'

'Long story—' Jim sighs. Then he changes the subject.

'You're my teacher,' he says. 'I'm your student. And then it changes. I'm the teacher. You're the student. I can see us with university gowns on, switching them around. It's symbolic. And you're not my usual type. And I'm not your usual type. But we're meant to be together, and we will be.' Then suddenly, he turns away from the fish tank and frowns at me.

'Do you eat meat?'

'Oh yes,' I own up. 'Lots and lots of it. I just had a sausage for breakfast. Actually, two sausages, in a roll, with some tomato sauce and onions. Sorry.'

He shakes his head from side to side, as if this is the worst thing he has ever heard.

'And,' I cut in, 'I'm not going to give that up either. Not even for you, when we're married.'

But my sad little joke falls flat in the cold, dark room, and already Jim is miles away again. I turn the tape-recorder back on, suddenly worrying that my breath smells of sausages.

'Um. Given that this is your chance for instant fame, Jim, what can you tell us about 2005? What's in store for the readers of the *Brighton & Hove Courier*? And can you make . . . twenty predictions?'

'Why twenty?' Jim looks at me curiously.

'It's my features editor. He likes things to be in lists of ten or twenty. And in chronological order if possible. Sorry. I'm sure the future doesn't organize itself like that.'

Then finally, Jim Gabriel looks at me properly and laughs.

'It's pretty funny', he says, 'that I've never predicted world events' – he makes quotation marks with his fingers – 'in my life. And now I'm being asked to make twenty of them?'

But before I can say anything else he's off, gazing into his blue plastic bucket and leaning forward into the tape-recorder so I can hear every word.

'OK then, let's make a start. The first thing is 1987 and 2005 are connected. Prince Harry went to school for the first time in 1987, and it's like he's being forced back to school in 2005. But it's the school of life. And there's more, in 1987 a hurricane ripped England apart. In 2005 there's another hurricane, but it's in America. In 1987 the stockmarket crashed in London. In 2005 it's going to happen again. In 1987 England won the Ashes. In 2005 history will repeat itself. England's going to beat Australia. I see the lion wrestling the kangaroo and the emu, and the lion wins.'

Jim is breathing harder now, and he seems to have forgotten I am there.

'In two weeks from now, I see foxes, hare and deer – and a dog turned away,' he says. 'And I see a famous dancer too – she dies in the bath. Then there's a train. It's the queen of the sea. It drowns in the waves – on Boxing Day. There's an English schoolgirl – they should listen to her, but they don't. And then,' he takes a deep breath, '2005 starts with a funeral for Nelson Mandela.'

'He's going to die?' I interrupt him. This is exactly what my editor wants.

'Not him. Someone close. It's a lesson for Africa about AIDS. Then I can see a shark. It's a £7 million shark. And then a desk. I see a shark and a desk, around Valentine's Day. The shark's eaten the desk too. Weird.' He shakes his head. Then he takes another deep breath.

'Al Qaeda want Russell Crowe's head. Bill Gates is knighted. Then after this, the King of Chess is free at last. Then I can see mugs – with Prince Charles and Camilla Parker-Bowles on the front. The message is, buy the first mug, as well as the second one. And keep them. Then I can see the world's biggest plane taking off – and the French word for seven. And Tony Blair, a victory for him.'

Jim swirls the sea water around in his bucket and takes another deep breath.

'Australians are taken into Indonesian jails. And New Zealanders celebrate in June. They've captured a tiger. Then I see two men married in Canada, with a diamond ring. Then London celebrates in the summer, in Trafalgar Square, but weeps tears of blood the next day. I can't see why . . . Madonna's on stage then, too – she's holding hands with Africa. Then she's on a horse, but off the horse. Then after that, I can see a fireworks display. A famous writer is blasted into the sky and a famous film star pays for it . . .'

'Well that's twenty predictions.' I stop him. 'In fact, I think it's more than twenty.'

And of those, I think, I can understand very few – but I'll have to ring Jim back. He looks exhausted.

'There's more,' Jim holds up his hand. 'I'm being shown the years to come, on a wall calendar. 2006. 2007. 2008. 2009. Each sheet on the calendar is peeling off. And what happens to us all in 2014 is the end result of what happens when the sun swallows the moon, in 2006. And then in 2008, the first big global corporation crumbles and falls . . . make sure your pension is safe.'

'It's OK, Jim,' I try to stop him. 'Honestly. We just

want 2005, for now. We can come back to that later.'

A knock on the door interrupts us. It is Courtney, the girl who was behind the counter when I came in.

She is pretty, like a Goth Barbie doll, but she speaks with hard South London vowels, like a cabbie.

'Your editor's on the phone,' she tells me. 'He says it's urgent.'

She shows me to the phone, on the front counter. It's next to a candle shaped like a skull, a row of sickly strawberry-scented pink candles and a rack of turquoise crystal bracelets, all claiming magical powers.

'Guy?' I pick up the phone.

'Katie! Switch your mobile back on. I need you back here.'

'But I've got two more psychics to interview after this one.'

I glance over at the little back room, where I can see Jim's legs and bare, tanned feet stretched out on the floor, and the back of Courtney's head. She has long, fox-red hair down to her waist, like a Shakespearean princess. Or a Shakespearean witch.

'Well we're wanted in a meeting. You've got fifteen minutes.'

'Any particular reason?'

'I think they're going to close us down. Not sure.'

'What?'

'Molloy's called everybody in,' Guy sighs.

'But how can we close at Christmas?'

Guy makes a hmph sound. 'Anyway,' he goes on, 'forget the psychics – unless they can give you some good news.'

I hang up and catch sight of my face in one of Courtney's strange, Gothic mirrors. I look worn out and pale, and my hair looks like it needs a good cut. Suddenly, I look and feel unemployable. What the hell am I going to do, if they shut the paper down?

I owe about £100,000 on my mortgage, £2,000 on my credit card, and I still haven't paid my TV Licence, or my Council Tax. And there are no jobs for journalists in Brighton. None – ever. If they close us down, I'll have to move to London.

'I'd better go,' I tell Jim, collecting my tape-recorder. 'Thanks very much for that. It was really interesting.'

'Thanks for your time.' He nods politely.

And with that, I bid my future husband farewell, and all his weird visions – honestly, there's more chance of me taking vows with the giant octopus at Brighton Sea Life Centre – and walk back past the pier.

I wonder what I could sell if I lost my job tomorrow, and realize that even on e-Bay, a total sale of the contents of my flat would barely cover my salary for a month. Andrew was always the one with the money.

I buy some chips on the way back to the office. They taste of vinegar, and rain. As usual, I have come out without my umbrella, so I'm soaked by the time I get back to the office, where I find Guy staring at a large white stain on the window.

'That seagull out there', he says, 'should play for England.'

'Really?'

'It can bend it like Beckham. I've never seen any-thing like it. After it lifted its leg, the crap actually seemed to turn around in mid-air and hit the glass at a right angle.'

'So when are we having this crisis meeting with Molloy then?' I ask him as he smokes out of the window.

'We just had it. You missed it. Sorry, Katie.'

Without leaving his chair, Guy pedals himself over to the air conditioner, points the remote control at it and wheels himself back to his desk again.

'I give management full marks for the heating, even more marks for our new wheelie chairs, and no marks at all for anything else,' he says. 'And basically, we need 50,000 more readers – or 25,000 more readers, and a lot more ads – or that's it. They'll close us down in six months.'

I realize I'm breathing again. Six months. Well, that's all right, then. Sort of.

Guy fiddles with his signet ring. He claims it is his family crest, though as far as I know his father was only knighted for having a fax machine company and giving a lot of money to Mrs Thatcher.

'Which brings us to you,' he says, not looking at me.

'What did Molloy say?'

'He said syndicated features are cheaper than you are.' He sighs. 'I'm sorry.'

I try to take this in.

'Am I definitely sacked, then?'

'Not sacked,' Guy sighs. 'Warned. We need about a zillion more female readers fast, and at the moment they're not reading you, they're all reading the London rags. Everything, in fact, except your stories about cats up trees. I know it's local news, Katie, but try to make it sound a bit more important. Focal.'

Focal. Guy's favourite word. I try to ignore the bit about cats up trees. I've never written a story like that in my life.

Guy pulls a container of chicken-liver paté out of his desk – his favourite snack food – looks at it, pokes it with a plastic spoon and then puts it back in the drawer again.

'My grandfather worked on this paper,' I say. And, oh God, I'm starting to cry now.

'I know,' Guy shakes his head as if he cares, but I can see he doesn't.

'Is this about the conversation we had a year ago?' I ask. 'About me getting some real stories for a change?'

Guy smiles at this and blows his cigarette smoke out of the window, whereupon a howling gale blows it straight back in his face. His ash lands on the window ledge.

'I was dragged here all the way from London by Molloy to take the readership up, and it hasn't happened. And I was hired to get a certain kind of story out of the staff, including you, and that hasn't happened either. Now, you tell me. What's it going to take to make you find us an interesting piece, Katie? Or even to find us a boring piece and make it sound interesting?'

I can feel my heart hammering now, the way it did when I was at school and the teachers used to tell me off.

'Pete Oram lives in your building doesn't he?' Guy asks.

'I went to school with him.'

'His girlfriend's just walked out on him and taken their kid as well. Go and find out why. He thinks the story's going to be about his New Year's Eve concert, though, so lead him in gently. And get the drugs angle.'

'Just because he's a musician doesn't mean he takes drugs,' I say automatically.

'Oh, come on, Katie. He plays guitar. He sings in a band. He lives in Brighton. What's not to take?'

'And what else do you want?' I hear myself challenging him. 'Is it all going to be about scandal and sex in our paper now? I mean, he's my neighbour. What do you want next? The size of Pete Oram's penis?'

'That'll do nicely,' Guy wheels himself back to his desk in his chair, laughing at me.

Amazingly enough, though, the first thing that happens when I arrive back at my block of flats and knock on Pete Oram's door is this – he points to his fly and tells me his penis is shrinking.

He also has a large pink sugar mouse tied to the zip

on his fly; its long string tail is holding his trousers up.

'Sorry about the trouser situation,' he apologizes, leading me into his flat. 'Me fly broke. Nothing fits any more. Do you know, since Polly left me I've lost half a stone? And that includes my manhood?'

Then he offers me a glass of red wine, which ends up being served in a mug, because apparently Polly has taken all the glasses, and we sit down on the floorboards.

'I know who you are,' Pete nods. 'You're Katie Pickard.'

'Yes, I'm still Katie Pickard.'

'You did me for the school magazine. When I was in that band.'

'Yup.'

'You asked me what my motto was. I didn't have a motto, did I?'

'No. But you told me your favourite food was jam sandwiches.'

'Jam sandwiches.' Pete looks around the room and shrugs. 'Sorry there's not much furniture. Polly took most of it.' He obligingly switches my tape-recorder on for me.

I sneak a look at him while he rolls himself a joint – I suppose that's Guy's drugs angle taken care of in the first two minutes, though I'll refuse to write it up.

Although I've seen him around the flats, this is the closest I've ever been to him since my embarrassing interview with him for the school magazine at the age of sixteen. He was always miles away from me then – in different classes or on the other side of the playground, smoking, and taking other girls' bras off when I was queuing up for the bus.

Today he has a dark three-day growth, shaggy, black curly hair that needs a cut and an ancient denim jacket. And he's having the same effect on me that he had back then, when he was in his first band and I

22

used to stand in front of the speakers in the school gym, risking deafness just so I could be closer to him.

'Here,' Pete takes off the denim jacket and puts it on the floor, like Sir Walter Raleigh putting his cloak over a puddle. 'Sit on that. I've noticed you round here for ages. You should have come up to say hello. Polly used to get jealous. I used to say, "Who's that girl who looks like she's out of the nineteen fifties?"'

'Me?' I say stupidly.

'With all the flowery dresses and ponytails and that.' Pete waves a hand.

I never think about the way I look these days, but Pete has just forced me to. And is it a good thing, or a bad thing? Suddenly, it really matters. Do I look as if I'm out of the 1950s?

His flat is like mine in a Spot the Difference competition, although he has extra rooms and a bigger kitchen. Where I have photographs on the walls, though, Pete has guitars. And just a single picture of Polly and their son taped to the wall. There is almost nothing else, though.

'You've got cracks in your walls, too,' I tell him, looking at one which begins halfway up the ceiling and disappears behind one of the hanging guitars.

'Crap flats, aren't they?'

'Yes, but you can see the sea, if you squeeze yourself behind the loo and turn your head 180 degrees.'

Suddenly I think of Guy – and the story I'm supposed to be writing.

'Can you tell me about the show you're doing on New Year's Eve?' I ask.

'Nope,' Pete rubs his face and smiles at me. 'I can't tell you anything. I'm not feeling too clever, Katie, to tell you the truth. Do you want the heater on?' Pete nudges me. 'I can get it out the bedroom. I got it yesterday. Put it under my coat at the shop and walked out with it. The woman must have been a fan. She didn't say anything. Me central heating's not working, I don't know why. Probably haven't paid the bill.'

When Pete nudges me, I register the nudge for a full five minutes after he has touched me. I wish I wasn't wearing my most boring brown skirt. I wish I looked better. I wish I was a more interesting version of myself. While he goes and gets the stolen heater, I reach for my make-up bag. But it's too late, he's back before I can even put my mascara on.

'I was almost married once,' I hear myself say as he plugs the fire in.

Pete nods thoughtfully.

'He died two years ago.'

I have no idea why I'm telling him this. And the wine is horrible – sour and cheap – but Pete's knocking it back like mineral water. He smells of warm skin, aftershave and old denim, and . . . I realize it's been far too long since I had sex. It's the kind of smell you can become drunk on, never mind the wine.

'This is Tracey Thorn,' Pete tells me, springing up to put a CD on. 'Do you like her? This was her first album. Cost her a hundred and twenty quid at university. Who needs a record company?'

We listen to the music for a while. I had just left school when I first saw Pete Oram play in a pub, play-ing guitar with his school tie threaded through his jeans, like a belt. His dad was a policeman, which is probably why he got away being under age in a bar. God knows how I got away with it – maybe because of my make-up, which I remember used to be slapper-strength.

Since then, I have seen Pete in his Johnny Marr phase (Raybans and quiff) and Oasis phase (hooded top and trainers). He's had many incarnations in Brighton over the last fifteen years or so, but despite everything, none of them have ever made him rich or famous.

Nevertheless, Pete Oram is still the man you most hope to run into, even though he does have a few wrinkles these days. And look, he's single again. Maybe Polly had him locked up in the flat all this time, kept well away from all single, eligible women.

'Polly had someone else in London,' Pete explains after we've been listening to Tracey Thorn for a while. 'He's got money,' he continues, 'I haven't. I should have gone out with you instead, when I had the chance.'

'Sorry?'

'You used to come and see us play,' he grins, tapping the side of his head as if it will help him remember. 'You and your mates were always at the front, by the speakers.'

'Yup.'

I can feel myself becoming properly drunk now as he fills my mug again. Semi-stonkered, in fact. It feels like a long time since my vinegar and chips on the pier.

'You won that poetry contest.'

'I can't believe you remember that.'

'I entered it too. Didn't win. I didn't double space me entry. Your poem was fantastic. I cut it out of the paper. Is that how you got the job?'

'Did you?' I shake my head. 'No, I got the job on the paper because of my grandfather.'

'Grandfather,' Pete says in a posh voice.

'It's just what we always called him. He got me a holiday job in the paper's reference library and I just stayed.'

'Let's put Slade on.' Pete smiles at me. He sings the opening lines of Merry Christmas. 'I feel like getting drunk and shouty.'

He has an amazing smile. Or do I just have my red-wine goggles on?

The something I'm feeling is definitely not love, and it's certainly not at first sight. It makes me feel paralysed with shyness and stupidly excited all at the same time, and it develops over the course of the next Tracey Thorn song, and during the next three or four minutes we spend listening to Slade.

Pete jumps up and puts on more CDs. When Barry White begins booming through the speakers, he gets up in his socks and starts pointing at imaginary ladies in the audience, including me.

His singing voice, like his speaking voice, is gritty, warm and unbelievably sexy. He sounds like he's been drinking honey and smoking cigars all at the same time.

When Barry White finishes, he puts on Roxy Music. 'Love is the drug,' he says, putting his head on one side and looking at me. 'Or in my case, drug is the drug.'

Then he plays something I don't know, which he tells me is Teenage Fanclub. 'Scottish romantics, man,' he says.

Then he tells me he has just seen an Australian psychic, to find out if Polly and Ben would come back to him, but instead the Australian psychic told him he would have a number one hit next year.

'Make sure you get that on there,' he points at my tape-recorder. 'That's interesting, isn't it?'

'I bet it was Jim Gabriel. I just interviewed him. Was he in that shop in the Lanes?'

'Yeah. Jim Gabriel. He was good,' Pete shakes his head. 'He knew everything about me. And he said' – Pete stares into space and makes woo-woo gestures with his hands – '"You will be at the top of the charts in 2005, have your first number one hit and become rich and famous. And then she'll be sorry she left you, the bitch." '

'Did he see it in his bucket?'

'Yeah. The little bucket of sea water.'

Pete Oram is ridiculously good-looking, I decide, as he passes me the joint. Just like some proper paid-up rock star from the Sixties or Seventies – the kind who used to come on a poster with staples in his middle, with dark eyes and sideburns and suede boots.

Maybe he's someone's love child. A lot of famous bands used to end up in Brighton. Perhaps he's the off-spring of a stray Rolling Stone and some local hairdresser.

Then, two bottles of red wine later – I am nothing if not professional, because I have nobly let him drink most of it – I realize I have a long and rambling con-versation about music on my tape-recorder, which Guy will probably hate – because there's nothing much about either drugs or Polly on it – and a vague feeling of itchy excitement that I will be seeing him again.

'Come round again,' he says, bowing at the door. 'I won't be such a prat next time. And I'll even take this mouse off me trousers. I'll see if I can find your poem, Katie.'

Despite the rain and everyone in Brighton wanting a taxi, I manage to flag one down, but before I can tell the driver to take me back to the office, I switch my mobile on, only to find a message from Guy asking me to interview Courtney, the girl from Cornucopia.

'WHAT ABOUT?' I text back.

'WITCHCRAFT,' he texts back.

I ring him straight away.

'Guy, that's three interviews in one day. I know the paper's in trouble so I have to work harder, but honestly . . .'

A pause. 'Katie. Are you drunk?'

'A bit. I had to have some wine to keep up with Pete Oram. Why do I have to interview a witch?'

'Because she's unbelievably fit, according to the photographer. He's just come back from doing your Aussie psychic. Why don't you spot these things, Katie? This is the kind of piece we need for the paper. This is a young, local, sexy, gorgeous, weird, hot, strumpetty witch.'

'Sorry,' I stare out of the taxi window as a seagull the size of a cat glides past. Then I make the driver stop at Starbucks so I can buy a large black coffee and sober up.

When I arrive at Cornucopia, Courtney puts the Closed sign on the shop door and drags a chair out of Jim Gabriel's reading room for me.

'He's gone home for the day,' she says, 'but he said to say thanks again for this morning.'

I get the details. Her name is Courtney Creely, she is 25 years old and lives in Hove with her flatmates, who are also witches. They are in a coven together and they work skyclad, or stark naked, on the South Downs.

'What, in this weather?' I try to joke with her, but Courtney is having none of it.

'It connects us to our female power,' she says seriously. 'Wicca is the old religion. We don't need clothes to work our magic.'

She blinks at me with big, round eyes, carefully lined in black pencil.

'Right,' I humour her.

I look around the shop, still feeling slightly muzzy and drunk from my afternoon with Pete, while she rambles on about spells. I wonder how much money Cornucopia actually makes. There is a kind of desperation about the way the owner has crammed almost everything onto the shelves. From Brighton rock to tartan novelty dog coats, it's all here. Along with the books on astrology and the decks of tarot cards, of course.

Then she swears and I see a man knocking on the door, trying to get in.

'Landlord,' she explains, tutting. 'I'll be back in a tick.'

I look through the glass as she glances round, then steers him expertly into a dark alleyway full of restaurant bins. The Cornucopia landlord looks like he's in pursuit of his rent – and he doesn't look happy.

I pick up all the books on the shelf behind Courtney's counter and flick through them, until I come to one bound in faded brown leather and inscribed with her name in violet ink. Courtney writes like a schoolgirl, with circles over the i's instead of dots, and little Elizabethan scrolls under the last word in each sentence.

The spell book is full of old seagull feathers, dead leaves and strange doodles. And then I see a long recipe list for an incantation which begins with a handful of broken glass and ends with shit.

I look through the window, but there's no sign of Courtney and the landlord returning.

The spell, I gather, is to make sure that any woman who gets between her and Jim Gabriel meets a sudden and nasty end.

It is illustrated with a pentacle, with the words WEALTH, SUCCESS, SEX, POWER, JIM & ME on each point. She has also sketched a little picture of him at the top of the page.

I quickly replace the book on the shelf before Courtney comes back and pick up her newspaper instead. Strangely, for a witch, she has tried to do the crossword. Or was that Jim? Surely if he's psychic he'd know all the answers?

'Sorry about that.' Courtney smiles sweetly when she finally returns. Then her phone rings.

'Hello?' she answers, flicking her long, red hair away from her face, 'Cornucopia?'

I find myself watching Courtney closely. She's one of those people it's hard not to stare at. She has long, immaculate, plastic fingernails painted dark purple and decorated with glitter. I've already decided I want to forget all about her book of spells. Even the cover felt repulsive to the touch, like toad skin.

Courtney is wearing high-heeled velvet boots and black fishnet stockings. And she smells of patchouli, mixed up with some other strange, slightly bitter, herbal smell I cannot identify.

'Yeah,' she nods and chews on her pen. 'Yeah, yeah, course I will.' Then she puts the phone down and tells me Guy has just asked her if she will pose for a photo shoot.

'He said he wants to do a thing on alternative religions at Christmas.' She stares at me. 'I like that.'

Then she looks in her desk drawer and finds an old local magazine – it used to be free until it closed a few years ago – and shows me a picture of herself straddling a chair, wearing a lacy red bra and suspenders.

'See, that's nice.' She nods approvingly. 'That was a Valentine's Day thing. I didn't get paid, though. That's what I showed your photographer this morning when he came round to take the picture of Jim.'

Then she laughs. 'Your editor just said he'd pay me two hundred pounds if I let them take some photos of me for the paper. So that's not bad, is it?' Then she traces a shape on the desk with her index finger, and I realize she's drawing a small, five-pointed star.

Later on, at home, I find my journal. After Andrew died, my bereavement counsellor told me to buy it, so I could express some of my feelings. The only blank notebook I could find in the shop had a polite Edwardian lady on the front, with a pink parasol, and somehow it's always put me off. Whatever it was that I had to write down after Andrew died it wasn't polite.

Folded inside the back cover are the counsellor's notes from a couple of years ago. She has drawn a balloon with my name inside it, and another balloon with the word 'FEELINGS' coming out of it with arrows.

We both had high hopes that I would find a few in the six months I spent seeing her. But I never did.

There, too, in her notes is another instruction: 'TRUST PEOPLE. LET THEM IN.'

Well, she would be pleased with my progress today, I think. Trusting Jim to tell me all that stuff about Andrew. Letting myself tell Pete how I nearly married him.

Maybe they can be my new projects. Jim and Pete. Or . . . maybe they already are, and they've just snuck in without me noticing.

I think about how long it's been since I made a new friend, and then I think about how long it's been since I slept with anyone.

I should really write something about Andrew, I suppose. His name's come up a lot today, after months of not speaking about him at all. It's a perfect chance to work on my FEELINGS balloon.

But there, you can't have everything. I go to bed with the names Jim Gabriel and Pete Oram scrawled at the top of my page, like a work list I have to complete, and as usual a journal full of blank pages where the emotion should be.

CHAPTER TWO

A few days after this Pete is going through my CD collection while I let him dry his washing on my radiator. Christmas is a few weeks away and he says Polly won't let him see Ben, who will be five in January. Consequently I have let him occupy my flat for most of Sunday afternoon because I feel sorry for him.

Well, that's my excuse anyway. I had my first dream about Pete a few nights ago, and it was – how shall I put this? – Fantastic. A dream to hang on to.

'Hey, and you've got vinyl as well!' Pete discovers a box of old records.

'I should throw those out.'

'Were all these your boyfriend's?' Pete examines an old Prince record. 'I used to do that too. Write my name on the front of everything with a felt-tip pen. Andrew Hamblin,' Pete recites. 'Funny writing. Like a girl.'

'I didn't want much of his stuff when he died. Just those, really. And a few books.'

Pete gives me a long, thoughtful look.

'Andrew had a car accident,' I tell him. It's what I tell everyone. And it's true, I suppose. If you keep the car bit, and leave out the accident part.

'You should get an iPod,' Pete pats the box of records. 'Shall I get you one?'

'Where would I put it? I'm not hanging it around my neck.'

'Put it in your 1950s pockets.'

'I still don't understand why you say that. I've got two flowery dresses. That's it. Look at me today.' I look down at myself. 'Jeans, jacket, boots.'

'Yeah, I like those boots,' Pete says, 'but you need to wear them over, not under.'

'What, tuck my jeans in? That's a bit too fashionable for me. Sorry, Pete.'

'Here.' He bends down on the floor and smiles up at me as he starts to push up one leg of my jeans.

'Stop it.' I kick him away and he laughs.

'Make fashion your friend, Katie.' He waggles his eyebrows at me. 'Come into the year 2005. Don't be scared.'

'You can talk.'

Pete is wearing a black coat today – he calls it his Echo and the Bunnymen coat. He's had it since he was at school. I'm impressed that it still fits. Like most of Pete's wardrobe, it seems to have been with him for-ever. A lot of his clothes appear to have been acquired in Manchester, where he and Polly lived for a while. And like his Manc-acquired accent, which he lapses into occasionally, the clothes show no sign of leaving.

'I'll get you an iPod,' Pete tells me as we watch the rain come down outside the window, 'and then I'll put all your songs on it. And all of mine. So she shall have music, wherever she goes.'

Then he stares at my mouth.

'We've got the same lips,' he rubs a finger over his and looks at mine. 'I never noticed that before. Sort of rosy and smiley. I don't like people with thin lips. Do you?'

'Oh no.'

For every moment that Pete embarrasses me, he also makes me want him more. But I have already decided how I'm going to manage the Pete crush situation. I'm going to manage it by simply not thinking about it.

I don't mind the trust thing, or the letting people in thing. But a relationship with Pete Oram? Forget it. The knickers may say yes, but the brain says, 'Throw yourself off the pier first.'

I think back to my journal – amazingly, I have managed two entries in the last fortnight – and the plans I've been making for myself.

It's Christmas. I have two party invitations propped up on the mantelpiece between now and Boxing Day, and there's a New Year's Eve party in London as well. There are dozens, even hundreds of men out there, waiting with mistletoe, and possibly even condoms, who I know will be better for me than Pete.

'I know it's a bit corny.' He shrugs. 'The gift of music, and all that. But I know you've bought me that jacket, and you know I'm broke, so that's the best I can do.' He sighs.

I have, of course, already bought him a present, despite the fact that I'm absolutely not interested in him and am absolutely never going to sleep with him.

Pete and I were walking through one of the shopping arcades in town when he saw it – a vintage striped jacket that reminded him of John Lennon circa 1967, and subsequently became an object of desire.

It's under my Christmas tree, now, wrapped in silver paper, along with presents for my friends and my parents. I can't believe he's already had the nerve to peel off the wrapping and have a look; it was supposed to be a surprise.

I told Mum about Pete a few nights ago on the phone. My new friend in the flats. She thought it was big enough news to tell Dad, who then e-mailed me about it a few days later.

They can put their new boyfriend radar away,

though. And anyway, a sugar mouse is holding up his trousers.

The rain is pouring down, now, bouncing off the windows at the corners.

'Did you see anyone about your central heating?' I ask him.

'I'll put "Unfinished Sympathy" on your iPod first,' Pete says, ignoring this boring but necessary question. 'It's a rainy sort of song. Do you think you ever got over it when your boyfriend died?'

'Andrew?' I say stupidly.

I think about my journal entry the other night. It was supposed to be about Andrew asking me to give up smoking and it ended up as a ten-page rant, which I finished by pushing my pen down hard into the page and slashing the paper.

'I've never had anyone close to me go.' Pete grimaces. 'Polly leaving and taking Ben is the worst thing. Shall I tell you what I played, about a hundred times, when she took him?'

'What was that?' I wish he'd stop talking about Polly.

'"There Is A Light That Never Goes Out". I'll tell you what, Katie, I'll put that on your iPod as well when I get it.'

I wish I knew more about music, but it's never really been my thing. It was Andrew's, a bit. But if you asked me to name half the songs I hear on the radio, I couldn't tell you, and on the two occasions I've been to Glastonbury, both the people and the event have felt like another world to me. I felt the mud, but I didn't feel much else.

Suddenly I remember Andrew's tent and his sleeping bag. What happened to those? I suppose I must have given them to Oxfam, but I can't remember.

Pete reels off more songs for my iPod. 'Fool's Gold'. 'Come On, Eileen'. Kate Bush.The Kaiser Chiefs. Franz

Ferdinand. 'Maggie May'. I wonder, childishly, if the songs are some kind of code for how he's feeling – or even how he feels about me. Then I remember that he's a man and they're just not that complicated.

I think I have already worked out where I fit into Pete World, and it's somewhere between a nice neighbour and the kind woman at the cash register who let him walk out with a stolen radiator under his coat.

Since he told me I was like a 1950s girl, I have been inspecting myself and my wardrobe from all angles in the mirror, trying to work out what he means.

I have an awful feeling, though, that what he means is I'm straight. Nice, conservative and very, very straight. A kind of brown-haired Doris Day.

There is a small tabby cat which sometimes lurks around our block of flats and it rubs up against everyone it sees. Because the cat is careful to do this when nobody else is looking, though, everyone who is on the receiving end of its affection thinks he or she is the only one in its feline existence. Consequently the cat gets several dinners a day.

I think the cat probably learned everything it knows from Pete. I've never seen him being charming to any other woman yet, but I know it happens, just as I know that at some point he'll start rolling himself a spliff and suggest he goes downstairs to get us a bottle of wine.

'Shall I get us a bottle of red, then?' he offers when the rain finally stops.

'We can finish mine if you like,' I say, knowing that the bottle on my kitchen table has only enough wine left for two small glasses. The less alcohol I consume with Pete Oram, the better.

'I had a phone call from my old manager,' he says as he gets up to go to the kitchen – half-dancing and half-skidding on the floorboards in his black socks.

'I'm listening,' I say, putting some music on. It's a horrible old second-hand Pink Floyd CD that I only bought a few days ago to impress Pete, but have already decided I'm going to pretend I've owned for years. I'm fed up with him laughing at my music collection.

'Me manager says there's a label called Parrot in America who are interested in me,' Pete yells over the top of Pink Floyd, booming through the speakers. Then he comes back, holding two wineglasses in one hand and a lump of my cheese in the other.

I can tell by the casual way in which all this information is being delivered that the phone call might mean more than he is letting on.

Then I realize something else about Pete. It feels like I've known him for about six hundred years.

How did he do that? I mean, I know I've let him in – as per the Edwardian lady journal instructions – but how did he get this far in, this fast?

Pete sits down on the sofa next to me, and I sense his leg, almost next to mine. As usual, we are almost touching – but not quite. I get on buses in Brighton all the time and people squeeze this close to me; needless to say the proximity of their thighs never has this effect.

'I thought the name of the record company was a bad omen.' Pete pulls a face. 'Polly used to get called Parrot at school. But then, the man told me they're signing people up for twenty-five grand a time.'

'Great!' I think of all the unopened bills Pete throws straight in his rubbish bin.

I re-light a candle which has died on my mantelpiece. It's supposed to get rid of cigarette smoke and appease my non-smoking friends, although I don't know why I bother when Pete travels with his own personal dope cloud.

'I like that candle – great lemon smell,' Pete muses.

'When I get rich, I think I'll have a lemon tree. Then I can make me own lemonade.'

He's wearing a striped pyjama top over his jeans this afternoon, and I can see the dark hairs on his white chest below. I've seen the weights on his bedroom floor, too – one of the few things Polly didn't take with her – and I can tell he uses them. It's probably his only discipline, apart from his guitar. All I ever think about recently, I realize, is him holding me – and then him taking me to his bed. And it's got to stop.

'Do you think I should take my old manager back?' Pete asks thoughtfully.

'Was he any good?'

'He was a good dealer,' Pete pulls a face. 'Half of London was coming to him for their Marvin K.'

I have no idea what he's talking about.

'Don't put that in your story, though,' he says.

'I won't.'

I'm still writing the feature about Pete, of course, because it gives me more excuses to see him. Pathetic is not the word for it.

'Marvin K,' Pete explains, 'is two parts E, one part Ketamine. My old manager's brother is a vet and he's married to a doctor. The whole family's in on it. He makes a fortune.'

'Have you tried it?' I ask.

'Nah.' Pete sniffs. 'I'm not having that, on the back of a key.'

He leans back on my sofa and closes his eyes, and I realize he's absorbing the music.

Guy could send out a photographer to get a great shot of him now, I think. Even though he still looks pale, the exhausted look I saw when I first knocked on his door has gone. He just looks like – I try to think of a better word and fail – a star.

Then I wonder if I'm being biased, but decide I'm not. I have been at the paper for almost fifteen years, working

38

my way up from filing cuttings to where I am now. I must have seen thousands of faces in thousands of photographs in all that time. And I know Pete is different. Never mind the fact that I am obsessed by him.

'So anyway.' He sniffs again, opening his eyes. 'Have you finished my soul-baring interview yet?'

'Almost.'

'We should do it again,' he says, 'now I know I can trust you. What do you want me to say?'

I take a deep breath.

'My features editor said he was going to sack me if I didn't make my stories more interesting.'

'What does that mean?'

'It means tricking people into saying things they don't want to say. And making things up when they don't give you what they want. And going behind their back to ask other people about them. And then, when they ask you not to print something, putting it in anyway.'

'Right then.' Pete rolls up his sleeves and strikes a mock-serious pose.

'Katie. I'm going to give it to you straight. I'm a struggling musician who can't afford to give my beautiful partner and son the time and money they deserve. She was me childhood sweetheart. It was an unplanned pregnancy. And she left me because she met a bloke in London with his own car, his own business, his own house and a nice little holiday flat in Spain. She also left me because I drink too much and, if I see a bill, I chuck it out the window, which is why we ain't got no central heating. I've been a terrible partner to her, and this record deal is the first good thing that's happened to me in a long, long time. I don't want to end up as Brighton's biggest failed rock star.'

He winks at me.

'Will that do for you, Lois Lane?'

'Pete. Come on. I hate doing this.'

'Well, it's not like you're telling them the real truth, is it?'

'And what's that?'

'Polly's only agreed to go off with this bloke in London because he likes tying her up, which is all she ever wanted of late. My doctor told me if I don't stop drinking I'll end up with a dodgy liver, just like me fat, beer-drinking mum. When Polly started an affair with the bloke in London, I went home with one of my fans – who also happens to be married with children. I've been trying to make it for nearly twenty years, since the day I walked out of school and gave the teacher the finger, and if that psychic's wrong and I don't make it next year, I'll probably put bricks in me pockets and walk straight into the sea.'

The rain starts again and we listen to the end of the Pink Floyd album while the candles send their sharp, lemony smell around the room. Pete catches my eye and smiles.

Then he finds a packet of chocolate biscuits shoved down the side of the sofa and offers me one, while he relights the spliff with his other hand.

'So just write down the first thing I said and we'll both be happy,' he concludes. 'No need to make anything up. No need to trick me. No need to go behind my back. Is that really how it works?'

'Molloy, my editor, thinks the paper is boring and that's why it's not selling. So does Guy – he's my features editor. He's the one who wanted the story on you.'

'Are they from round here?'

'Molloy is. He grew up in Brighton. Guy isn't. He's from London. But he's got a big flat up on Marine Parade. They headhunted Guy to come here and get the sales up on the paper, but it hasn't worked.

Probably because of me.' I shrug. 'Apparently, I'm rubbish at being entertaining.'

Pete smiles and meets my eyes.

'See,' he says, 'we do have exactly the same lips. That means we're all right, you and me. Not like everyone else. I don't want to read shite in the paper. Nobody does.'

'Guy's all right.'

'They're the worst. It's always the all right ones who are the devil in disguise.'

'I think they're putting everything on Guy's shoulders. Molloy drinks too much.'

'They should sack him then.'

'He's been there for years. And he's friends with the people who own the paper.'

'Aha.'

'So, it's down to Guy to make it work. Or . . . that's it.'

'He doesn't have to work on a paper.' Pete closes his eyes. 'He could get an honest job. In a fish and chip shop. More people round here buy the fish and chips that are wrapped in the paper than buy the paper to read.'

Eventually, Pete goes. I don't want him to, of course – it feels like the biggest wrench in the world – but I know that Guy is expecting my story on Jim Gabriel tomorrow, and I also promised Jim that I'd e-mail it to him before I send in the final finished version.

I put the kettle on, trying to forget that Pete is downstairs in his flat – I want him so much it's like constant background noise – and try to concentrate on the computer screen instead. Then I press the send button.

AUSSIE PSYCHIC PREDICTS BUCKETING FOR AMERICA – Australian-born psychic Jim Gabriel (38) is unlike most Brighton clairvoyants. Working from his office in the Lanes, he uses a bucket full of sea water instead of a crystal ball. But we were still stunned by his predictions for 2005.

A DEVASTATING HURRICANE for America

AN ASHES WIN at last for England

NELSON MANDELA to face horrific personal tragedy

A STOCKMARKET crash in London

RUSSELL CROWE to be slaughtered by Al Qaeda suicide bombers

Modern-day Noztradamus Jim says he's using gazing – a technique pioneered by the original Nostradamus – but all we know is he's got a reputation for spot-on psychic spookiness, despite the bucket and spade/ ENDS.

So there it is, or the beginning of it anyway. And it's all Guy Booth's own work, because if there was ever anything of me in the story, it's disappeared now. I suppose I wasn't making Jim sound interesting enough.

I attach the page to my e-mail, and send it to Jim, then I move onto my other e-mails, most of which are from my cousin in Canada (who is excited about Pete) or other far-flung friends and relations (who are, embarrassingly enough, also excited about Pete.) Clearly, my dad has been on the internet a lot this week.

Then, suddenly, a reply from Jim comes back. The subject header is PLEASE CANCEL STORY.

'Dear Katie, that's not the kind of story I would like to have written about me, and it is not a story that is worthy of you. What's wrong with the truth? Please cancel. Sorry. Jim.'

So. What now? Two years ago, when Guy first arrived, I remember him warning me never to give anybody the right to see stories before they went to press. And now look. Jim has talked me into letting him see it, and suddenly I don't have a story any more.

I e-mail him straight away.

'Dear Jim, I promise you this is just a rough version. Best, Katie.'

Well, it will be a rough version, if I can make Guy change it before it goes to the printer.

But then, no matter how long I sit and stare at the computer screen, nothing comes back.

I call Jim's mobile. No reply. Just a slightly tired-sounding, twangy Australian message.

Then I give up and call Guy. He's not going to be happy, but the story is due at 5 p.m. tomorrow.

'Why the bloody hell did you show it to him?' is the first thing Guy says when I ring.

'Sorry,' I say.

'Did he say what he objected to?'

'Probably being called Noztradamus. I wish the subs wouldn't fiddle around with things like that.'

'But he's from Oz! I came up with it, Katie, and it's bloody brilliant!' Guy dismisses me.

I flick the television on with my remote control from my desk in the sitting room while Guy gives me a free lecture on the art of giving the people what they want.

I stare blankly at the news. It's the cricket in Australia. It looks wonderfully hot and sunny. I wish I was there, not here. In fact, I wish I was anywhere, even the Outer Hebrides. Then I think of something.

'Guy, can't we just make it a story about England winning the Ashes next year? Or the stockmarket crash? All that 1987 and 2005 business?'

'No.'

'I think Jim might be worried about the Russell Crowe thing you wrote, too.'

'He said it. That's his problem.'

'But he didn't say that at all. Jim never said Russell Crowe was going to be killed by suicide bombers.'

'And I'm going to run a shot of Crowe nice and big, from *Gladiator*, looking suitably petrified, so don't argue. I've already got the headline sorted out.'

'Guy. Please. We've taken Jim's words out of context.'

'So what do you want us to do? Print a whole lot of waffle about foxes and hares, English schoolgirls, Madonna on a horse and Prince Harry learning a lesson? All that stuff about the sun swallowing the moon?'

'But I saw the way Jim was working. It was like a stream of consciousness. I think it needs to be pieced together. If we give him time I'm sure he can do it for us.'

'And another thing,' I hear Guy say as I gaze mindlessly at the news. 'I bet the Ashes thing was a set-up. That's something he could have found out from any of his Aussie mates. He's probably got inside information. You know the cricket's rigged.'

The news ends, only to be replaced by a repeat of *Porridge*. I am freezing, I realize, and then I see that I've left the curtains open. The rain we've been having lately has been replaced by sleet and slush on the streets.

'So you think he's a fraud?' I ask Guy.

'God help me, Katie, of course he's a fraud. But Jim Gabriel has taken up large amounts of our time and I am going to get my money's worth. End of story.'

The following day, while Guy is still listening to the tape and tinkering with the story – he has taken it out of my hands, he says, because he wants me to focus on the Pete Oram feature instead – I call Jim again.

He's at Cornucopia when I ring and he sounds miserable.

'I trusted you,' is all he will say, and instantly I think of my own instruction to myself in my journal: trust.

'Don't worry,' I lie. 'Guy's really experienced. I'm sure he'll do something good.'

'I never should have agreed. I've never done

44

anything like this before, Katie. Big world predictions – it's not my thing.'

In the end, I decide to go round there, and use my lunch hour to take Jim a few conciliatory goodies from the bakery next door.

Mince pies, I think. Mince pies and slices of Christmas cake and a stupid cake that looks like a frog. That should do it.

When I walk into the shop, though, Courtney tells me Jim is reading for a client and can't see me.

'He's busy.' She smiles, sitting on the counter and swinging her legs. Today she looks less like a Goth Barbie doll and more like a Russian princess. She's wearing a long, patchy rabbit-fur coat and a pair of tapestry boots, along with the obligatory miles of cleavage, short black skirt and striped tights.

I wonder if Jim has told her about the reading he had with me, and the fact that he saw us being married next summer, and decide that he hasn't. If he had, I'm sure she would have picked up the little knife she has lying on the counter and pointed it at me by now.

I saw the knife the last time I was here. It gives me the creeps – almost as much as she does, with her big, vacant eyes.

Then suddenly Jim emerges from the back room, pushing the door wide open, and I can see that he's been sitting in there by himself all along. I suppose Courtney has been trying to protect him from the evils of the press – namely me.

'Sorry,' he gives me a tired smile, ignoring a pointed look from Courtney. 'I thought it might be you waiting out here. Come in, Katie.'

Then he closes the door behind us, and the last thing I see is Courtney staring straight through me, still swinging her legs on the counter.

'I really, really need you to stop that story,' is the first thing he says.

'I can't. I'm so sorry. Guy's got it marked up for the inside front cover. He's working on it himself, you see.'

'I don't know' – Jim flaps his hands helplessly – 'English law. Can I get an injunction? What about the . . . do you have a press complaints organization?'

'More to the point, can you afford a lawyer just to stop the likes of us? And honestly, Jim, never sue a newspaper, or shop them to Press Complaints. They'll just bide their time if you do, and then when they finally get you, you'll never get up again.'

He sighs and rubs his face. 'What happened the other day was crazy. Even I don't know what it all means. So how can your editor possibly hope to interpret it? I mean, I was seeing way into the future.'

'But some of it was specific.' I catch myself playing devil's advocate.

'I saw Nelson Mandela at a funeral. That could mean anything. It could be symbolic. I saw a shark eating a desk. What does that mean? Nothing. It's like the vision I had of us getting married next summer.'

I blush, despite myself.

'See?' Jim gestures, 'That's crazy. Insane. I was having an off day.'

'Well, you'll be pleased to know the wedding is still our little secret anyway.' I try to make a joke.

Then Courtney knocks on the door.

'Can you mind the shop, Jim?' she asks, looking – unusually for her – happy and excited. When she smiles, though, I realize, her eyes are always somewhere else.

'Sure.' Jim nods. 'When will you be back?'

'I'm not sure,' Courtney says breathlessly. 'It's a modelling job. I just got it. For a sales catalogue they're doing for a shop on Ship Street.'

Jim nods again. 'OK.'

Then she turns to me.

'Jim said it would happen. He's amazing.'

I nod politely.

'He can do anything,' she tucks her arm through his.

And then she is gone. She wears too much patchouli oil and not enough deodorant.

'Sorry. Are you together?' I ask Jim, trying to make it sound like a professional enquiry.

'No.' He shrugs.

'Brought you lunch.' I change the subject, opening up the bakery bag.

'Good call,' says Jim, opening the mince pies first. If anything, he looks bigger than the last time I saw him.

I wonder if Jim and Courtney were ever a couple, and decide not. The body language between them is all wrong.

'So I'm doing a story on alternative religions at Christmas now,' I tell him. 'Did Courtney tell you? We're doing Islam, Buddhism, and Paganism—'

'Courtney would prefer you to call it Witchcraft, I'm sure,' Jim smiles.

'I want to know more about that knife she's got hanging up in the shop,' I say.

'She found it in a shop in the Lanes.'

'And do you approve?'

'Is this a "you" question, or a newspaper question?'

'A "me" question, I suppose.'

'I spoke to her about it.' He shrugs again. 'She goes her own way. That's cool.'

My phone rings. It's Guy. He says he has some news I'll like and some news I won't like.

'What's the news I'm going to like, then?'

'Upstairs took one look at the story and called it off. They think it's bollocks,' he says. 'Actually, the word Molloy used was drivel. They hate the Russell Crowe photograph; they say everyone's seen it a million times.'

'Oh,' I breathe out, flapping a hand at Jim and miming a look of reassurance.

'The bad news is, it's going to mean more work for you. We're going to make more of this alternative Christmas religions thing,' Guy goes on. 'So you'll be working this weekend. But I don't want anything ugly, all right? I don't want some old Buddhist monk who's as bald as a badger. So find us a good-looking Moslem girl or something. And listen, we do want a bit of woo-woo in there, too. But nothing as woo-woo as your Aussie. OK?'

'I'll try,' I tell him, suddenly relieved on Jim's behalf.

'And while you're at it,' Guy continues, 'find out if Courtney is single.'

'Why, for the story?' I say stupidly.

'No, because I keep hearing how fit she is,' Guy tells me and then hangs up.

After this, Jim goes off to make a cup of tea, and I'm left staring at his bookshelf. The crystal ball and tatty copy of *Zen and the Art of Motorcycle Maintenance* are still up there, but he has also added a row of white candles, which is the most Christmassy thing in the shop, apart from the mince pies on his desk.

I wonder if he gets homesick for Australia at this time of year, and his family – if he has a family. Then, when he returns with two mugs on a tray, I tell him the good news about the story, just in case my miming on the phone hasn't allowed Guy's message to fully penetrate. Then I catch myself thinking, if he's so psychic, he should have known Guy was going to cancel the story anyway.

'I can't see everything, all the time.' Jim smiles when I ask. 'I'm not some master of the universe.'

'Do you just switch on and off then?' I ask.

'But I'm picking up that Guy wants Courtney,' Jim interrupts.

'How?'

'I saw it.' Jim replies. 'In the fish tank.'

'Of course you did.'

'And Courtney and Guy are fated to be together,' he continues.

'They are?'

'Oh yeah,' Jim shrugs again, finishing his mince pie in two large bites.

'Because?'

'Because Courtney wants to go where the power is, and even in a small town your editor's got power,' he says.

Later on, I go for a walk along the seafront and see a group of teenage girls queuing for fish and chips. They all look like junior Courtneys – long hair, striped tights, black eyeliner and black fingernails.

If Courtney is fated to be with Guy, then she'd better hurry up and fall out of love with Jim. It's the worst case of unrequited love I've ever seen.

Then I think about the spell in her book and wonder if she actually is a witch.

CHAPTER THREE

Despite everything, Jim's bucket is right and Courtney walks into our office for a lunch date with Guy a few days later.

Almost immediately, Claudia – who works in advertising and has been chasing Guy for ages – bolts behind the coffee machine and starts sending furious text messages.

I don't know Claudia all that well, except that she's always asking me to sign her petitions for Amnesty International or sponsor her on endless fun runs.

Claudia is not the only woman in the Guy Booth fan club, of course. She is part of a triumvirate from advertising and accounts who follow him wherever he goes – from the pub, to the gym and back again.

Courtney looks incredible today. She's wearing a sunshine-yellow frock over a pair of tight jeans, with a huge silver and turquoise necklace and big gold rings on her fingers. Her pale white breasts are, as always, pushed up around her collarbone, like a Jane Austen heroine.

'They lent all this stuff to me on the photo shoot,' Courtney tells Guy when he asks about the rings and necklace. 'You know that shop called Fifi on Ship Street? I did their summer catalogue.'

'You must be freezing,' he says, glancing at her breasts.

'Oh, I'll put my coat back on in a minute.' Courtney smiles. 'I just thought I'd take it off to show you all the jewellery they'd lent me. It's beautiful, innit?' Her Sarf London vowels return.

Then they're interrupted by a freelance writer who needs Guy to sign off his expenses, so Courtney folds her arms and waits, watching Claudia from the other side of the room as carefully as Claudia has been watching her.

I calculate that Guy was a teenager when Courtney was being born – if indeed she was born to a human mother at all, and not concocted in some naked ceremony on the South Downs. I have seen him go out with a lot of different women since he started the job here – including poor Claudia, who is now looking genuinely stricken – but Courtney is easily the youngest of the lot.

'Sorry about that,' Guy apologizes once the freelance writer has gone. 'So where do we feel like for lunch?' he asks Courtney. 'I can probably get someone to book us a table at the Hotel du Vin. We're still quite early.'

Courtney, I can tell, is equally impressed by the sound of the Hotel du Vin, which even broke local Goths must know about, and the fact that Guy can ask someone in the office to make the booking for him.

And then there's his silver BMW, I think, which he will no doubt steer around the front of our office in a minute, the better to beckon her in, in front of the passing lunchtime crowds.

If Guy loses his job next year, I realize, the BMW will have to be sent back to the hire firm. But maybe Courtney can cast a spell for him, involving badger's excrement or eye of newt, and save the day.

Guy is wearing his favourite suit, which is the same suit he wore on his first day at work here. It's a funny plum colour, and it immediately began rumours that he was gay. It didn't take us long to work out that he was just vaguely posh instead.

'Katie?' Guy barely looks at me as Courtney leans her head forward, pouts, licks her lips and adjusts her turquoise necklace. 'Can you have the rest of that Pete Oram story to me by the end of the day?'

'Absolutely,' I promise him, although I've barely made a start on it. And then I watch him steer Courtney out of the foyer, taking her coat with one hand and frantically texting with the other. It's sad, but the junior, junior secretary he is now asking to book him a table at Hotel du Vin is probably the same woman he bedded at last year's Christmas party. She and Claudia were both neck-and-neck in the Guy Olympics for a while.

Claudia beckons me over.

'Katie, can I have a word?'

She makes a huge fuss of getting me a cup of instant coffee from the machine, and then organizing change for a packet of salt and vinegar crisps. Then I realize she is trying not to cry.

'Oh, Claudia.'

'Sorry,' she takes a deep breath. 'Can you tell me anything?'

'I'll tell you everything I know,' I say, as I realize she is so rattled that she has swiped the plastic cup away from the coffee machine too early and it's only half full.

'That girl who was here to see Guy nicked my cat,' Claudia says, frowning. 'I'm sure it's the same girl. She had long red hair, just like that. It was a couple of years ago. She was hanging around with a group of Goths in this big VW van, which was parked near my street. Then one day my cat went missing, and a few weeks later I was going for a walk and I saw it, in the van. They had it on a string, tied to its collar.'

'Sorry?'

'She nicked my cat, I'm sure it was her. Or they nicked my cat and she helped them.'

I tried to drink the disgusting coffee and failed.

'OK.' I take a deep breath. 'Well. She's a witch. Maybe that's got something to do with it.'

'What?'

'I interviewed her the other day. She works in a shop called Cornucopia in the Lanes. She's twenty-five. Though she might be lying about her age. She's nuts.'

Suddenly Claudia looks hopeful. 'Do you really think she's nuts? I can't believe Guy would go out with her.'

'She's a lingerie model.' I try to let her down gently. 'She does catalogues. Free magazines. Stuff like that.'

'I shouted at them, about the cat, but they just drove away,' she says, and now she really is close to tears.

'Did you tell the police?'

'I couldn't even get the police to come round when I'd been burgled,' she says helplessly. 'How would I ever get them to sort out my cat?'

I take in Claudia's watery eyes and try desperately to think of something that will make her feel better. 'I'm sure your cat's all right,' I say. 'Maybe it was a different cat. Maybe that wasn't even Courtney you saw in the van. A lot of girls round here look like her.'

But they don't, I realize as Claudia departs, taking her gloom and coffee away, and that's the whole problem. Courtney Creely doesn't look like any other woman Guy's ever met, which is exactly why he's interested.

I wonder if Courtney's got what it takes to become Queen of Guy's harem, and decide she will win, unopposed. She's like some exotic tropical fish which eats everything else in the tank. For all her niceness and blondeness – and Guy has always had a weakness for nice blondes – Claudia simply cannot compete.

I go back to my desk and read this morning's epic ten-page memo from management.

It's been signed by Guy and Molloy, along with a few of the people in sales and marketing, and then copied to all the people at our parent company in London. Oh God.

As promised, the newspaper will be shutting down next year unless we can increase our circulation massively, or at the very least slightly less massively as well as selling thousands more ads.

There are lots of graphs attached, which I avoid, as most of them show our sales figures going off the end of a cliff, and endless amounts of market research that I have already seen before. There is also a chart showing sales and circulation of the *Brighton & Hove Courier* compared to the *Daily Mail*, the *Sun*, the *Daily Telegraph*, *The Times*, the *Guardian*, the *Mirror* and other south coast papers – I stop looking at that point. I'm sure they could compare our sales to the local Anglican church gazette and we'd still be bottom of the ladder.

Then, to my utter horror, I see some of my stories have been included in the memo as examples of the kinds of articles we have to drop.

Children putting Christmas presents inside shoe boxes for children in Romania. A battle to save a Victorian church hall in Kemptown by the Old Brighton Preservation Society. A new recording studio on Sydney Street offering cut-price rates to help local bands. Gone, gone, gone.

Molloy writes in block capitals – the rumour is that he left school at fifteen and never learned to read and write – and I can see his scrawl over everything I've written. I suppose he came back from a long lunch at the pub; even for him, the writing's unusually shaky.

Oh, and they've made a photocopy of my Steve Buxted story too.

I wrote it just after Andrew died. It was supposed to be on the front page. Steve Buxted was a drunk driver who had taken his best friend home after a party, driven into oncoming traffic and killed him, though he survived. In the end my story was shoved back to page five.

Guy and Molloy wanted to rename Steve Buxted as STEVE BASTARD, capitals included. The idea being, as Guy explained, that the man who died was about to become a father for the first time, so Steve had effectively widowed his best mate's wife and the mother of his unborn child. Ergo, Steve Buxted was a total Steve Bastard.

They sent me to see him, and when I arrived at his house his mother couldn't even look at me. And Steve? He was just lying on his bed, staring at the wall, as he had been for weeks.

I didn't get the story, of course. Then Guy sent me to the funeral with a photographer with a long-range lens, and I didn't get a story then, either. Too many people were in tears, and I was the last person they wanted to see – everyone knew I was there from the paper, and nobody was fooled for a minute, despite my big black hat.

And now, it seems, everyone who works on the *Brighton & Hove Courier* can learn from my amateurism.

According to the memo, it seems I didn't put enough B, S, T and B in it, which is a favourite phrase of Guy's – blood, sweat, tears and bullshit. And it also seems I ignored one of Molloy's golden rules: turning people into local heroes or local zeroes. Apparently it's the only way to sell papers.

I take the memo and drop it in the bin. I feel trembly and strange, as if some of Claudia's panic has rubbed off on me. Then I laugh, because I've just seen another one of my stories, also photocopied in the memo,

55

but Molloy's given this one three big ticks and a star.

It's about a grandmother of three, who caught a 28lb carp in a gravel pit. She brought it into the office in a suitcase, plonked it on Guy's desk and kissed it repeatedly on the lips for our photographer, until he had to ask her to stop. I'd forgotten about the amazing carp-snogging granny until now.

I decide to go for a walk along the seafront, to blow the day away. It's something my parents taught me to do when I was a child, and even now, if there's any kind of crisis, it's the first thing they always suggest.

I think about ringing them, to tell them about the horrible memo. They're in Canada for Christmas, visiting Dad's sister. She went to see them in France last year, so they're returning the favour this year.

After Andrew died they kept offering to move back here, so I'd have some support. But, as I said to my bereavement counsellor, unrecorded in my Edwardian lady journal, sometimes it's not support you need, it's space.

When I finally make my way out onto Marine Parade, I get stuck in a gale which is blowing so fiercely that it reminds me of one of Andrew's long-standing tricks – pretending to walk against the wind around Brighton, like Marcel Marceau.

I miss him. I really, really miss him. He was one of those people who know they're not funny, but try any-way, because they know they're being so crap, that's funny all by itself.

'What's the joke?' people used to ask when they'd see us out together with our heads down, laughing, but I could never explain.

We were never like those horrible couples who snog in the queues for taxis, or paw each other at dinner, or go on and on about each other. And we were never that other awful thing either, 'partners'. What we had was more like a stupid secret society. We didn't have a secret handshake, but we did have great sex.

I'm going to cry. Unbelievable. Where did that come from?

Then I hear someone shouting behind me, in the gale, and I realize it's Jim Gabriel.

'Katie!' he yells, running with his head down in a flapping sheepskin coat.

I nod in the direction of the pier, so he'll know to follow me, and turn on my heel with my hair whipping around my face as he catches up, striding to the shelter of the boardwalk shops.

Then he yells something that sounds like bath dancer or dancer bath, but is lost in the wind.

I follow him into the amusement arcade at the end of the pier, while gigantic gulls struggle to stay on course around us.

'I thought you'd be around here,' he pants when we finally find a seat at the café and sit down.

'Well you are supposed to be psychic,' I pant back, though it's strange that he's tracked me down.

'The dancer in the bath I saw, was Dame Alicia Markova. I just found out she died last week,' he says at last.

'Oh.'

He nods. 'But I got it wrong. It wasn't a dancer in the bath. It was a dancer from Bath – that was where Alicia Markova died.'

Jim gets his breath back in the cold air.

'The foxes, hare, deer and a dog turned away was the House of Commons,' he goes on. 'It was the hunting ban. So what I was seeing was right. Or at least I was on track. Which means the rest of the predictions must be on track as well – maybe even everything I saw.'

'What, like us getting married?' I hear myself blurt.

And then he goes very quiet and neither of us say anything for a minute – me out of embarrassment and him out of . . . I don't know.

'Sorry,' I say as the amusement arcade machines ping around us. 'I have no idea why I said that.'

'You were thinking about Andrew,' he states as a waitress finally appears. 'You nearly married him. He was the closest you ever came. That's why you said it. All this stuff is probably on your mind.'

'Don't,' I tut, shooing him away with the menu. But there, Jim Gabriel has done it again – he has gazed off into space, with those strange, pale blue, translucent eyes of his and managed to see into my soul.

Then I think of something.

'Is Andrew talking to you?' I ask.

Jim shakes his head.

'Sorry, but no.'

'Are you a medium?'

'Yes. But I've had nothing from Andrew. I'm sorry.'

'No, don't be sorry. I wouldn't want to hear from him.'

I look around me and realize how much of an Andrew day this is becoming. First the wind, which would have been perfect for one of his deliberately crap Marcel Marceau moments, and now the café in the amusement arcade – we used to spend hours in here, operating those miniature cranes which drop every fluffy toy they pick up.

'Let's get drunk and not be able to pick up toys,' Andrew used to say. And we did. For hours.

Then . . .

'You can trust me,' Jim says out of nowhere.

'Funny you should say that.'

'You can let me in.'

'Oh God.'

I look sideways at him.

'What?' he looks worried.

'Have you been reading my diary? Letting people in was something my counsellor told me to do after Andrew died.'

'Right,' Jim nods.

'Though at this rate I'm beginning to wonder if I should,' I look pointedly at him.

'You can trust me.'

'Yes, but it feels . . . I dunno. You know things about me that are private. Can you just back off?' I paused. 'Sorry.'

'All right. But . . . this is me. If you want to be friends with me, this is the way I am. I can't help it. I see the whole picture.' Jim makes a circle with his hands. 'It's like being a scuba diver or something. Other people swim on the surface and they don't see anything. I get the whole vision.'

'Maybe I'd rather not be your new friend then,' I tell him, and then I see I have hurt him.

'Another wall goes up,' he says after a while.

'Sorry.'

'Give me a chance. You'll be giving yourself a chance. All right?'

'All right, I give in.' Then I remember Guy and Molloy's letter.

'I had a nasty memo today,' I tell Jim. 'It was for all of us, but I got singled out.'

'A pot of tea, please,' he tells the waitress in his twangy Australian accent. Then he turns back to me.

'It was about a story I got wrong,' I explain. 'Sort of, what not to do if you work on this paper. But I've just realized, the reason I probably did the story all wrong was Andrew. Because it was about a car crash.'

'Your boyfriend killed himself,' Jim says flatly, staring through the café window out to sea.

I follow his gaze, as if he's seeing something I can't.

'They were different deaths,' Jim goes on. 'But it still upset you. Andrew committed suicide. The story you were asked to do was about a drunk driver who accidentally killed his best friend.' Jim narrows his eyes, gazing into the distance again, then he turns back to me. 'They should never have asked you to do it. It's not your fault.'

'Jim. You're being scary. Stop it. And don't tell anyone. Nobody knows it was suicide. Just me and Andrew's brother. We haven't even told his parents about the note.'

Jim sighs. 'Sorry.'

'Andrew drove to Kent at three o'clock in the morning, where he bought a bottle of vodka, a bottle of brandy and drank both of them, went up to eighty miles an hour and hit a telegraph pole. He left Dan, that's his brother, a note, but when the police asked him about it, Dan lied.'

Then I check myself. 'It sounds wrong, calling it a lie. It was a white lie. Dan covered up the note for Andrew's sake. For everyone's sake. I was the only person he told.'

'I'm so sorry, Katie,' Jim looks out to sea again, through the window. 'It must be tough, hiding it.'

'It's just like remembering to brush your teeth before you go to bed, or remembering to deadlock the front door. I've trained myself to cover it up.'

'Cry if you want to,' Jim finds a packet of tissues in his coat pocket and hands them to me.

'I don't want tissues.'

'What then? How can I help you?'

But despite myself, he has made me cry.

'If you ever hear anything from Andrew' – I can barely get the words out – 'can you let me know?'

'As soon as I can. As soon as he lets me, Katie. It's OK.' Jim puts his hand on top of mine. It's warm, even though it's cold inside the café, and I see that he has a scar on his thumb.

'How did you get that?' I touch it.

'I came off my surfboard on a beach called Hungry Head in a little town called Urunga.'

We sit watching an assortment of local chavs play

with the machines for a while, while I dab at my eyes with his tissues, then we watch them giving up as they run out of money, and letting a group of teenage Italians take over. One of them is eating a dressed crab with a plastic fork and the smell wafts over to our table.

'Do you wish the interview with you had run after all?' I say, thinking of the fox hunting and Dame Alicia Markova. 'What if England beats Australia in the Ashes as well? You'll be famous.'

'Your newspaper's not the right place for me,' Jim shakes his head. 'Everything's so woooah! Oooh! Aaaah! And,' he finishes waving his hands around, 'I'm not so sure I want to be famous. The story you did was just a favour for the guy who owns Cornucopia. To get more people in. To help us pay the rent. The shop's in trouble.'

'Despite Courtney's spells.'

'Yeah.' He smiles.

'Do any of them ever work?' I ask him, thinking about her horrible book.

'Never asked her.' He shrugs.

'Well, I think Guy seems bewitched. But then again, anything ten years younger with tits tends to bewitch him.'

'Guy.' Jim frowns, playing with his name, as if he's never heard it before. 'Guy's a desperate kind of guy. Is that true? I see him with a chequebook. He's signing cheques, but they fly away from him. No, they bounce.'

'Probably.'

'You're feeling like you want to give up your job,' Jim says thoughtfully. 'You don't feel appreciated. You feel hurt. You've been working on the newspaper for a long time. It's your life. It was your grandfather's life as well.'

'Do I just agree with everything you're saying?' I

tackle him. 'Because it's all true. I mean, what do you want me to say?'

'Nothing.' Jim shakes his head. 'But I knew there was another reason for me to find you now. It wasn't just to tell you about the reading, the dancer in Bath, or the prediction about the foxes and dogs. It was about Guy.'

'What about Guy?' I prompt him but he's miles away, staring through the window again, as if he's watching a film.

'He lives on the top floor of one of the most beautiful houses in Brighton, built for a man who bought and sold tea, and then after that, by an actor – a lot of actors. It's his home and castle. His father gave him the money for the deposit, and the bank lent him more money than he could afford to borrow because of his father's name.'

I nod.

'If he loses his job on your newspaper, then he loses his home as well. That's why he's being so hard on you. Try to understand.'

'Ha!'

Jim gazes up, then to the left, then back to me. His eyes look incredibly blue today.

'I keep seeing an English schoolgirl,' he says. 'She's looking at the waves. And she's right, while everyone else is wrong. Every time I look at the sea I see her. It's driving me crazy.'

I shrug. 'I don't know, Jim.'

We finish our tea, and I make a bad joke about Jim successfully predicting which fruit machine he's going to win on, but he waves me away as if he's heard it all before, and I suppose he probably has.

'I've got to get back to work,' I tell him. 'Guy wants me to finish that story on Pete Oram.'

'Number one,' Jim says thoughtfully as we weave our way out of the amusement arcade and back onto the boardwalk.

'Are you sure?' I shout in the wind.

'It's his time,' Jim yells back. 'I can tell you that much.'

Then he stops to buy some chips and we huddle in the shelter in our coats while the gale which blew the seagulls north starts blowing them south.

'I love the way they cruise like that,' he nods, offering me a chip. 'They just go with the flow, you know?'

'But there's no way Pete Oram's going to have a number-one hit,' I persist.

'You're throwing out bait,' Jim smiles and looks across at me.

'Am I?' I say innocently.

'You know you are. I never discuss my readings with other people. Especially not', Jim narrows his eyes and makes a stern face, 'women of the press.'

'The thing is, though,' I tell him as we work our way through the chips, 'Pete's been trying to make it for fifteen years. There are lots of people who think he's too late. He says his ex-manager's got some American label interested in him, but it still doesn't sound very promising. The sort of stuff he does isn't even fashionable any more. His songs go on for hours. The radio would never play them.'

Jim pulls a woolly brown hat out of his coat pocket and jams it onto his head, still smiling.

'He's already had two chances,' I tell him. 'He had one record label at the start of the Nineties, and another one at the end of it. They both threw him off. And he's hopeless on television. He showed me his one and only video the other day. Live, he's fantastic. I mean sexy as.'

Jim catches my eye.

'But on TV? No. Pete's hopeless.'

And still Jim stares out to sea, as if he's not listening to me, and smiles to himself. It's infuriating, I decide. But I am enjoying talking about Pete. And it reminds me, after all these years, that this is what happens when you're falling in love with someone. All you want to do is talk about them, even to people you don't know very well.

'I've got to go,' he gets up. 'It was nice to see you again, Katie.'

I watch him walk away, pulling his sheepskin coat around him as he strides off, worrying that I have talked about Pete too much, and then worrying that Jim Gabriel knows everything about me, including the contents of my dreams. I suddenly realize I can't wait for Pete to open his stripy jacket on Christmas morning. He's already said he's going to pack it in his case, so he can take it with him to his mother's flat.

He's still banned from seeing Polly and Ben. He told me about it this morning, at 6 a.m., when he knocked on my door with a pot of coffee.

I think about Andrew, and I think about Pete, as I walk back to the office. An objective outsider would find parallels in my attraction to both of them. Andrew needed saving, although I couldn't do it, and so does Pete now that Polly has gone.

I think about Andrew's note to Dan, asking him to look after me and throw his ashes into the Thames. And now look. Andrew's urn is back in Brighton after all, destined for the family plot. And despite everything at the funeral, Dan's hardly called me since. All that effort Andrew put into his final letter and . . . nothing.

I don't blame Dan. We only met two or three times when Andrew was alive, why should he take me under his wing now?

Perhaps if I asked him for help, I suppose, but I haven't. All I've wanted since the day the police came is to be alone.

And now look, I'm writing in my Edwardian lady journal and people are coming in again.

64

I check my watch and try, unsuccessfully, to stop missing Andrew. It's too early to go back to work, and it's the last place I feel like being.

There is a sheltered spot down near the cafés at the bottom of the flagstone steps that take you from the pavement under the pier. In summer you sit there to get out of the sun. It's hard to believe it ever gets that hot here but it does. In winter, it's protected against everything, even the wildest hail storms.

In the Sixties, there was a famous palm reader here called Petronella. She had a little red-painted hut exactly where I'm sitting now. There have always been psychics in Brighton.

I think about Jim and his dancer in Bath, Dame Alicia Markova, who I remember now was 94 years old when she went. Even if we'd printed the story, though, it wouldn't have been enough for Guy and Molloy.

Pete says he's written a song for me. No, better than that, he says I have inspired a song and that he will record it in the studio once Parrot pay for his new album. He says he's hearing music in his head again now that he's got to know me.

I hug this information to myself as I retreat further under the canvas awning overhead. I've been doodling Pete's name all week secretly on my notepad at work. He makes me feel as if I'm at school again and he's on stage, with his striped tie threaded through the belt of his jeans and his hair combed into a neat Smiths quiff.

I decide that Jim's bucket visions are right, but the wrong way round. It must be easy to get confused. The dancer in the bath was all mixed up, so maybe Jim's confused about my impending marriage as well. Perhaps it's Pete Oram after all. Saved by me, in the aftermath of his painful break-up with Polly. Rescued by his muse, the woman who single-handedly got him writing great music again.

I manage to make myself laugh – I knew I would,

eventually, if I tried to be enough of a wanker – and then I get up, and battle my way back to work, against the howling gale.

There's an envelope on my desk when I finally get back to the office, though there's no sign of the person who left it or of Guy either – I suppose he is still rubbing his Hush Puppies up against Courtney's ankle.

There are two photographs inside – one of Pete, obviously taken a few years ago, with sideburns and a parka, during the early stages of Britpop, and another one of him and Ben, playing on the beach.

I realize that up until now I've never thought too hard about the fact that he has Ben. It's like Polly; out of sight, out of mind, and the less I have to think about it, the better.

But there he is, Pete's only child. I turn the photo over. Ben looks incredibly like him. Same messy dark hair, same browny-black eyes. Then I see Pete's hand-writing – or Polly's? – on the back. Benjamin Marc Harley Joe Oram. I take a calculated guess and decide that Pete has named his son after three of his musical heroes – Marc Bolan, Steve Harley and Joe Strummer. I already know that Benjamin is from Benjamin Zephaniah, the poet.

I look for a note with the photo and find it folded neatly into an impossibly small square, shoved in the corner of the envelope.

'Polly gave me this for the paper,' it says. 'Proper family dinner for us tonight! Luv Pete.'

I read it again. Polly gave him the photograph for the paper. When? Today? Did she drive up from her parent's place? And what does he mean, a proper family dinner for us?

I realize that most of the muscles in my body have just gone tight. I am wrapping my leg around the chair as if it was stuck there in a mantrap. The fear and jealousy are awful.

'All right, Katie?' someone from the art department walks past and gives me a little wave. I suppose they've read the memo about me, too. Can this day possibly get any worse?

I strain to recall all my different memories of Polly. They are usually mixed up with my memories of Pete, because they were such a public couple in Brighton for such a long time.

She used to wear short shift dresses and black leggings with pixie boots. That was when her hair was cut into a blond quiff to match Pete's, when he was first starting out with his band. She had a hippie phase, too, when she grew her hair so long she could wear it in plaits. That was the beginning of her eternal summer phase, I seem to remember, when every time you saw her she was brown and white-blond. How could I ever compete with Polly?

I try to sort out what has upset me most today – the photograph of Ben, the note about the happy family reunion dinner, or the memo from Molloy, Guy and all the other faceless men and women from upstairs.

Then I realize the answer is blindingly simple. It's none of the above. It's thinking about Andrew, after all this time, that has really upset me. And I suppose I should have been expecting it. When Dan and I hand-delivered his ashes to his parents, I couldn't have been better behaved. No tears. No drama. No trauma. And now? It's all back with me again, as powerfully as if the police had just turned up at my door.

Even now I am embarrassed to remember the way I spoke to them. A man and a woman came, and I was so irritated by all her questions (he was writing it all down) that I swore at her. And I think – I'm pretty sure I did this anyway – I got up out of the chair, stormed over and took the notebook off him – the idea being that I would do a better job of the interview about Andrew if they just let me get on with it by myself.

Then I had a mad idea that they might think I'd murdered him or something, and I panicked so much that I threw up the scrambled eggs I'd had for breakfast.

Enough. Enough.

A few days after this, Christmas arrives. I do what I always do if Mum and Dad aren't around and spend a few days with my friend Linda and her hotch-potch group of friends, random children and stray ex-boyfriends. Linda is an old punk who has her own DJ night in Brighton. I met her years ago, when I first started doing the listings guide on the paper. She runs an open house from Christmas Eve to the January sales, and it's one of those places where you just turn up with a bottle of wine and never leave.

I had thought Pete might have wanted to come along a few days ago – it might have seemed a better offer than a day in front of the television with his mother – but that was before the photo of Ben and the sudden reappearance of Polly. I've rung, but he hasn't rung back. And I've knocked, of course, but there's nobody home. So I try to work myself back into a pre-Pete frame of mind instead, and buy lots of reindeer-antler headbands for everyone at Linda's and promise myself I'll ring up everyone I know in the world on Boxing Day to cheer myself up.

But then, as December 26th turns into the 27th, Jim Gabriel's visions come true again, and instead of wasting my time on Linda's sofa – her mad friend Gwynnie has decided my reindeer-antler headbands make good suspender belts – I find myself being called into work.

'I need you in here.' Guy calls me while Linda and I are in our dressing-gowns, watching the tsunami on the news. 'Or to be more specific, Molloy said anyone without families or partners has a duty to be here.'

'I have got family,' I say, gritting my teeth. 'They're called parents. They just happen to be away.'

'It's terrible,' says the relief receptionist when I finally turn up at work, 'isn't it.'

But she means the devastation we have to cover on the front page, of course, not the fact that Molloy has chosen to discriminate against those staff members who lack husbands, wives or children this Christmas.

A few days after this, I read my transcript of Jim's tape at my desk. 'Then there's a train,' I read, and it gives me chills. 'It's the queen of the sea. It drowns in the waves – on Boxing Day. There's an English school-girl – they should listen to her but they don't.'

The train is in Sri Lanka. The schoolgirl is in Thailand. The name of the train, in direct English translation, is Queen of the Sea, and it is swamped by the waves, killing almost everyone on board. And nobody, except a lucky few, listen to the schoolgirl, who recognizes the early signs of a tsunami from a school project and tries to clear the beach.

'Jim?' I answer immediately when I recognize his number on my phone.

'I can't sleep,' he tells me. 'Can't sleep, can't think. And I need to see you, Katie? Sorry. Merry Christmas. But I don't know what's happening to me any more.'

'All right then,' I say, suddenly feeling responsible. 'Do you want to come out for a cup of tea or something? I know a couple of cafés in Kemptown are open.'

'All I have to do is walk past a rock pool on the beach and I see more,' he says helplessly. 'I think I'm seeing the whole century flash in front of my eyes, Katie.'

Then he asks me to take the tape from Guy's drawer.

'What?'

'Please, Katie.' Jim is insistent. 'Just get the tape. It's really important. I need to hear what I was saying to you, in every detail.'

'You can't remember?'

'I never remember psychic readings.'

'I can sort of remember.'

'I need to hear the exact words. There might be other warnings in there – I know I could see a hurricane coming.'

'Yes. I remember the hurricane, too.'

'We've got to get this information out there. And not in your paper. I'll find another way.'

I take a deep breath. 'OK.'

'Can you get the tape?'

'He'll know I've taken it. Who else would want it?'

'Please.'

A post-Christmas journal entry, written in the gold felt-tip pen I used to write on the labels for my presents. And for once it's not about Andrew, or the things I believe I should be doing to help me get back to normal after Andrew's death. It's just about . . . life.

DECEMBER 27 2004

Jim Gabriel has managed to scare himself, as well as me (for a change.) A train got destroyed by the tsunami, just as he saw, and he even got the name right. He also got the bit about the English schoolgirl right. Now he's worried there might be more predictions of world disasters on the tape. So am I. There was definitely something about a hurricane on there, and a stockmarket crash as well. I'm also worried that Guy and Molloy will try to flog it to the tabloids in London. Jim hasn't been sleeping and neither have I. HELP!

P.S. The other reason I can't sleep is Pete. HELP! Again. Am I ready?

70

CHAPTER FOUR

New Year's Eve comes and goes, and still I don't hear from Pete.

I successfully put him out of my mind for a couple of days, and then I walk into the Top Shop sale as if I'm under hypnosis, in my lunch hour, and buy two bags' worth of clothes I think he would like.

None of them are very me – lots of black and lots of stripes – but all of it's very Pete.

'They look good on you,' the girl in the shop says when she sees me in a pair of over-tight black trousers.

Do they? I don't believe her. It's not true what they say about bereavement, it makes you eat more, not less, but . . .

'They look good with your boots too,' says the girl, and I have to believe her. Part of me, I suppose, just wants Pete to get down on his hands and knees and tuck me in again.

Guy runs the feature on Pete on a single page in our weekend section, but it seems to get lost, along with all the tsunami stories. I read it, and then re-read it, to see if Pete will like it or not, and then I realize I have no idea.

This is a man who carries most of Enid Blyton's Secret Seven books in a plastic shopping bag so he can have something to read on the train. He has a skull and crossbones tattooed on his arm, he puts peanut butter on his ginger-nut biscuits, and he once told me his favourite thing in the world was sitting on radiators and giving himself scorch marks.

So . . . really. How would I know what Pete Oram likes or doesn't like?

Courtney turns up in the paper in the alternative Christmas religion story, together with some non-bald Buddhist monks that our photographer has somehow managed to find, and undoubtedly the most gorgeous teenage Moslem girl in Sussex. But even this story is lost against the only real story of the New Year.

The subs are usually immune to big disasters, but as more first-hand accounts of the tsunami come in they increasingly start working with their face in their hands, unable to process the awfulness of what they are reading.

I go to my big New Year's Eve party in London, see nobody I fancy, attract nobody in return, and catch the 4 a.m. train back to Brighton, dossing down on the seats along with everyone else, until the guard wakes us up at the other end. I obsess about Pete the whole way home.

The following afternoon I email selected friends and tell them he was a false alarm, at which point, inevitably, I get some of those 'I-didn't-want-to-say-anything- but . . .' emails.

Then Linda takes me out to the pub one night and tries to break it to me gently. It seems Polly was hanging around backstage on the night of Pete's big New Year concert. And they were together, as in, *together*. So . . . my life is complete. Is the start of a New Year ever fun for anyone?

From my Edwardian lady journal:

JANUARY . . . date? I don't know and I don't care.
Shit, shit, shit. What's the point in letting men in if they just bolt straight out again? SHIT.

Entry ends.

'Sorry,' Linda rubs my arm when we go back to the pub a few days later. 'You know what they say. It ain't over till it's over, and all that. I think it will take Pete and Polly a long time to break up. It's like all those music couples. They're all mad.'

I shrug. I can't think of anything else to say about Pete and Polly because I feel as if someone has just punched me in the stomach, so I people-watch instead.

'But don't worry. You're better for him than her anyway,' Linda tries to reassure me. 'You know what I mean. And you're looking good, Katie.'

'I need a haircut.'

She ignores this.

'You look happier and men notice that. Come on, Katie, sooner or later someone's going to snap you up.'

Then Linda pulls an agonized face as someone puts some hip-hop on the jukebox.

I have never met anyone like Linda – except perhaps Pete – whose entire mood can be dictated by the music playing in a room. And she hates anything that isn't old punk. Or at least profoundly, deeply British indie. I've even seen Linda throw a drink over someone who tried to put Eminem on the jukebox.

The lines between gay pubs and ordinary pubs are blurring these days, so that Linda and I keep on wandering into theirs, and they keep on wandering into ours. She and I have been drinking at The Dove for years, and I don't think it's ever occurred to the landlord to hang a rainbow flag outside the door, but still. The place is packed with men in pairs.

'Pete's just an idiot crush,' I tell Linda as the hip-hop on the jukebox dies away. 'I think it's because I never got him out of my system when I was at school. I'm just reliving my lost youth, really.'

Linda nods.

'He's an epic talent.' She sighs. 'He's always been the boy most likely. Of course, Polly held him back.'

'Really?'

This shouldn't make me feel so happy, of course, but it does.

'It's scary when someone makes it,' Linda says. 'It's like they've just moved to a foreign country. When I lived in London I saw it happen a lot. Their girlfriends get paranoid about other women and start pulling them back. They know if they get successful they'll start sleeping with groupies or end up with some rich rock star, so they sabotage them.'

'Right.'

'Have another drink dear, have a spliff, don't worry, everything will be OK.' Linda puts on what she imagines is the simpering voice of a musician's girlfriend.

'And then it isn't,' I agree with her.

'And then it isn't.' She nods wisely. 'But in the meantime, you can bet the girlfriend will have forgotten to take the pill and churned out a baby. That's Polly all over.'

We sit for a while with our bottle of wine, amused as two men with matching goatees get up on the dance floor and start solemnly waltzing around in their leather jackets to the Pet Shop Boys.

A *Big Issue* seller comes over, with his badge slung over his back and his hair blown sideways by the wind.

'Is that your last copy?' Linda asks, handing over a five-pound note without looking at him. 'Keep the change.'

Then she pulls a horrified face, as some syrupy female ballad wafts over from the jukebox.

I wonder, again, if Pete is wearing the stripy jacket I gave him. I'm sure he is. Apart from anything else he doesn't have that many clothes. Then I worry again that he's seen my story in the paper and hated it, which is why he won't return any of my calls.

'Stop thinking!' Linda brings her hand down on the top of my wineglass.

'Sorry.'

'So, any other blokes on the horizon?' she asks. 'What about that big Australian?'

In the middle of yet another panic session over his predictions, I asked Jim to come round to Linda's house so he could sit down, have a slice of Christmas cake and get back to normality, or at least as normal as it ever gets at Linda's house.

I shake my head. 'He's definitely big. And he's . . . too weird, too big, too everything.'

Linda wrinkles her nose, thinking about it. 'Maybe.' Then she laughs. 'I would, if he asked me. I've never had a psychic boyfriend before. Imagine the sex!'

We watch the men with goatees finish their old-time waltz and, along with the rest of the pub, clap them off the floor. Then Sheryl Crow comes on, which draws a long moan of distress from Linda, and some girls in jeans and tiny tops get up and start the kind of dance that makes you think they're on a machine at the gym.

The tiny-tops thing was just starting to come into fashion when Andrew died. He used to think they looked like hankies, so as a joke he bought me two Dad-style hankies, one for each breast, with my initials embroidered neatly in the corner.

It was one of the red herrings that led me astray, before he killed himself. It made me think he was still himself and still happy and that everything was OK.

He got his hair cut at a new, expensive hairdresser's in Brighton two weeks before he died. He ordered a box set of *The Office* from Amazon three days before he died. I still haven't watched it. I can't.

'Katie!' Linda pulls my wineglass away. 'We've

come out here specifically to stop you thinking. And I forbid you to think. Is that clear?'

'The thing is,' I tell her, suddenly feeling tired, 'I think I'm still looking for someone who can replace Andrew. And nobody can. Not Pete, not Jim' – then I think of all the boring men at the New Year's Eve party in London – 'nobody.' Then I contemplate telling Linda about Jim's marriage prediction and decide against it. It all seems too . . . I don't know. Mad.

Linda gets up to take over the jukebox – I knew she would eventually – teetering slightly in her stiletto-heeled leopardskin boots. Nobody in Brighton actually knows how old Linda is (it is one of the great mysteries of Sussex, like the fire which destroyed the West Pier) but even if she is very, very ancient indeed, she still manages to pull fascinated looks from all the straight men in the pub, and a few of the gay men too.

Linda rides everywhere on her bike, so she has the kind of bottom people can't stop looking at. I have made no resolutions for the New Year, of course – have I ever? – but if I have to force myself to do anything new, it might just be to buy a bicycle.

Jim could use a bike, I think. For someone who claims to have spent most of his life surfing on Australian beaches, he's really given in to the Great British lard thing. He looked enormous the other day in his big white woolly jumper and flapping white cotton trousers.

Summer is now officially six months away. So he has about twenty-four weeks in which to persuade me to marry him. Alternatively, the world has twenty-four weeks before the final countdown to nuclear armageddon.

My mind drifts back to Pete. If Polly and Ben move back in with him then I may have to let out the flat and go somewhere else. I'm not sure I could stand having him so close but so far away.

I wonder if Pete played the song he was writing for me at the New Year's Eve concert. And I wonder what Polly would have said about it. Then I think about the iPod Pete said he was going to program for me.

And then Pete walks into the bar in his long black coat with – I can't quite believe this – the beginnings of a big black beard.

'You didn't come to the show.' He pats my head, holding two glasses in his hand, and sits down.

'I had a party in London,' I say, still registering the pat on the head as I watch Linda teeter back from the jukebox. 'I rang you. Have I got the wrong number or something?'

'They hated me.' He waves me away. 'Did you hear about it?'

I shake my head. He looks washed out.

'There were three people from Parrot there. And my old manager. And I stiffed. As soon as I played a song that went over five minutes I almost got a glass through the neck.' He blows his nose, sounding as if a cold is descending. 'I got slow-handclapped. The people from Parrot buggered off before the end so they wouldn't have to talk to me afterwards.'

Before Linda and I came out tonight I left Pete a note on his front door, just in case, telling him where we would be. It was the last desperate measure I allowed myself. Linda moaned at me for holding the taxi up while I searched for a pen, but . . . oh, how glad I am now that I made her wait. It feels ridiculously good to see him again. Even with the beard he remains the man in the world I most want to sleep with.

Because she's an old friend, as well as a good friend, Linda stops halfway to our table, makes an 'Oh' face, jerks a thumb at the door, gives me another thumbs-up for good luck and then staggers off towards the exit as if she'd never been there at all.

Pete hasn't even noticed because he is too busy

downing the two double vodkas he's just lined up.

'Chug, chug.' He catches my eye. 'Don't worry. I'm not drinking. This is like mineral water for other people.'

'Whatever you say.'

He rubs his chin and I find myself staring at his beard. 'You can't stand this, can you?'

'It reminds me of something, but I can't think what.'

'Paul McCartney, straight after he broke up with The Beatles in 1970.' Pete shrugs. 'See, this is my break-up beard with Polly.'

Immediately I want to dance around the bar to all of Linda's jukebox songs and do victory laps, picking up random gay men to waltz with as I go.

'Did you see the story in the paper?' I ask eventually.

'It was fantastic.' He gazes into my eyes. 'What you did for me was fantastic. You're a good friend, Katie.'

'Well, you gave me everything they wanted.'

'But you wrote it with heart. And people really liked it. Even me bloody mother liked it.'

He pushes his fringe out of his eyes and I see he has a sticking plaster on his head.

'How did you get that?' I touch it.

'Someone threw a can at me.' He says casually.

Then he gives me my iPod, unwrapped but with my name written on the front in black felt-tip, encircled with flowers.

'I lost the phone when I went back up to Polly's.' He sighs. 'And her parents won't let me use theirs.'

'I only called to see if you liked the jacket.'

'I loved the bloody jacket.' He looks at me intently.

'And are there songs on this?' I look at my new present.

'She shall have music wherever she goes.' He finishes his drink.

And then 'Brimful of Asha' comes on the jukebox –

Linda must have put it on – and he stands up, bows like an idiot and takes my hand.

'I've always wondered what it would be like to dance with you,' he says.

'I can't dance.'

'Yeah, you can. Coom on, nineteen fifties girl.'

'No, it's really weird, I know everyone else can dance, but I can't.'

'Don't you like the song, then?'

'No. It's not that. I do.'

'Come on, Katie. Just a little dance.'

And then he gives up and sits down, while people at the bar, who were looking for a moment, look away.

'So how was Christmas?' I ask, but Pete holds his finger up, which he always does when he's really intent on listening to music, and I give up and go to the bar for another drink.

I decide I'm going to get Pete a water and a single vodka, which should cancel each other out and leave him exactly where he was five minutes ago. And me? Well, I'm tempted to bring back a bottle of red wine, just so I can get drunk and dance with him after all. But I know if I do that it's the point of no return. And it's the wrong time. Wrong time, wrong place, wrong everything.

He is making my emotions slosh around like sea water. Yes, no, yes. Every time he comes near me, Pete Oram spins me around.

When I finally return to the table the music has changed and – this must be Linda again – 'The Hounds of Love', by Kate Bush is on the jukebox.

'Fear of love,' Pete holds his finger up in the air again as if he's giving me a lecture. 'It's an epidemic. Worse than flu.'

'Is that what this song is about?'

'You should listen to Kate more, Katie. The hounds of love can rip you to shreds. Nobody wants that. So we all run away from it.' He pulls a face, which I gather is supposed to be me. 'Can't dance, won't dance.' Then I realize the face is meant to be Polly. 'Scared of loving someone and being loved.'

Pete shakes his head and finishes the vodka, ignoring the water.

'You're the first happy person I've ever met who didn't like dancing,' he says.

I feel quietly pleased that he thinks I am a happy person, even though I'm ashamed of the not dancing.

'Me mate found a seal,' Pete suddenly remembers. 'On the beach. He's an' – he licks his lips, 'advanced marine mammal medic. His name's Trevor. The medic, not the seal. He got some lovely photos. He's going to be in a Hollywood film.' He raises one eyebrow at me and gives me a meaningful look.

'I don't know if Guy wants me to write stories about lost seals, if that's what you mean.'

'He's a very, very nice seal indeed.'

'I'm sure he is.'

'He's three foot long. A pup. He had a cut on his flippers but he was all right. I think Disney are auditioning him.'

'Disney?'

'Yeah, them. Or maybe the other one. Steven Spielberg. Anyway, there's a new film coming out next year. Big Hollywood budget. Half animation, half real. And they rang up Trevor and said, when his seal's better, can they borrow him? They wanted a real rescue seal.'

Bells start ringing in my head. I think I've even read about this somewhere, in one of the London papers.

'I told Trevor he had to give you' – he makes a dramatic face – 'the elusive seal exclusive.'

'Is it all right if I make a phone call?' I ask him.

I already know the headline Guy will want.

BRIGHTON HOLLYWOOD 'SEAL' OF APPROVAL. Fnar, fnar. I ring him.

'Katie, have we found someone on the council in an advanced act of buggery? Because if we haven't, I'm not home,' he says.

'Sorry. I know it's late.'

'What, then?'

'Someone found a seal pup on the beach. It's going to star in this big Hollywood epic they're doing next year.'

Guy thinks about it. 'Who else knows?'

'Nobody. Pete Oram's friend Trevor is a mammal medic. He rescued it.'

'Find out who owns the seal legally and see if we can adopt it,' Guy thinks quickly. It's hard to believe he can still function like this at 10 o'clock at night. 'We'll go up to two hundred pounds for it. Better still, get it free. I've got sardines in the fridge. It can go in my spa in the meantime. Get a contest going, so the punters can give it a name. Katie, is it a sexy seal? I don't want something with dirty great dents in its head.'

'I honestly don't know, Guy.'

'Brilliant!' he spits into the phone, not listening to me. 'Brilliant!'

I give Pete the thumbs-up. 'And to think he wanted to sack me a few weeks ago,' I stage whisper so that Guy can hear me.

'We'll get it to sign an exclusive contract with the *Courier*,' Guy goes on, 'with its flippers dipped in ink. Get the snapper to take a shot.'

'Its flippers dipped in ink? I don't think ink washes off, Guy.'

'Course it does. Get the mammal medic,' Guy instructs me. 'Where are you?'

'At the pub. At The Dove.'

'Get him there and tell him £500 the lot. Has he got photos of the rescue?'

81

'Yes.'

'Don't move. I'll be there in fifteen minutes.'

And then I hear a woman's voice complaining in the background – it sounds like Courtney – and he is gone.

When Pete rings Trevor he immediately tries to raise the £500, until it becomes clear that some ancient mates-only favour from years ago is also involved.

'I know you could probably get more money if this seal's going to go to Hollywood, but you won't get as good a story from anyone else but Katie,' Pete says solemnly.

The jukebox works its way through Madonna (this must be the point at which Linda's money ran out), Michael Jackson and Mariah Carey (people at the bar start yelping along in outright mockery at this point) and then the Pet Shop Boys (more waltzing from the bearded men), another Madonna song and (all together now) 'Angels', by Robbie Williams.

I want to cry. Why do I want to cry? I don't even like Robbie Williams. But . . . that's how it's been all the time lately. Random, unprompted, uncalled-for, unwanted tears.

To stop myself, I think, I've got Pete to myself again. He's here, he's real and he's not going anywhere – at least until closing time.

Then Trevor the marine-mammal medic arrives in a big anorak and gloves. He looks strangely like a marine mammal as well, thanks to his nose, which is pure sea walrus. Pete, meanwhile, is happily rocking backwards in his chair, looking smug at his powers of organization.

Guy arrives. I don't know if he's done a line of coke in between his departure from the house and arrival at the pub, but he's talking faster than any man has a right to, and with such excitement you'd have thought Flipper had washed up on the beach at Brighton, in the loving arms of the Loch Ness Monster.

'Trevor, hi, good to meet you,' Guy shakes his hand and pulls up a chair. I think it belongs to the man who has just gone to the loo, leaving his fags and paper behind, but there's no point in saying anything because Guy is on a roll.

'Is the seal trained?' he interrogates Trevor. 'Can it hold a tea tray?'

'I don't know.' Trevor tries to be helpful. 'It's at the vet. I'd say it's wild. We had a hell of a time catching it.'

'This is front page.' Guy offers me a cigarette. 'This is seal fever in Brighton. This is Hollywood comes to Hove.'

Then he ushers me to the bar with him, ostensibly to help him carry back the drinks but principally to talk shop.

'Everything goes in threes!' he jabs me with his arm. 'I had photos of Paul McCartney and Heather on their bikes delivered to me this morning. We found the art gallery flasher last night. And now this: a film-star seal.' He clicks his fingers three times in rapid succession. 'We're back in business, Katie. I can feel it. It's the turn. I rang a mate of mine – if we play our cards right we can sell the rights on from here to bloody LA and make the total spring advertising budget in one hit. I heard a rumour that the kid from Harry Potter's going to be in this seal film. Do you realize what we've got here, Katie?' He nearly, but not quite, hugs me.

After this Guy proceeds to fast-talk Trevor through a story and photo deal that I know will give the *Brighton & Hove Courier* all the rights to syndication and serialization worldwide, and give Trevor no money whatsoever. I can only hope the favour Trevor owes Pete is worth it, especially if the seal really does become a global superstar and end up with its own Disneyland ride.

The conversation goes on. Pete puts my new iPod headphones on and shuffles from one track to another with his eyes closed. I wonder which songs he's chosen for me. Maybe he's trying to educate my musical tastes. And then I remember Linda, slamming her hand down on top of my glass and telling me to stop thinking so much.

The first bell clangs for closing time just as Courtney Creely walks in, looking more like a Russian princess than ever. Then I realize she is wearing her rabbit-fur coat over a pair of pyjamas. And wellingtons.

She stands near our table with her arms folded while Guy bangs on about the seal, ignoring her.

'Oi!' she says at last, pulling at his sleeve.

'Sorry, darling,' Guy breaks off from his conversation, and then he catches my eye as the 'darling' escapes from his mouth. Guy is not a darling kind of man. Unless you are sleeping with him, of course, or close to it.

Pete takes his iPod headphones off and smiles broadly at her.

'I'm Pete,' he shakes her hand. 'Are they not listening to you?'

I feel a jealous twitch and try to ignore it.

'Nobody listens to me.' Courtney pouts. 'Especially him.' She points at Guy.

And then – nobody can quite explain it afterwards – two empty glasses next to Guy's elbow fly off the table. One remains intact, but the other flies so fast, and so far across the pub, that it smashes on the carpet.

'This is the second time you've fucked off without telling me where you're going, Guy, and it's the last time,' she says calmly, staring at him with her big, grey Cleopatra eyes. I'm impressed that she bothers with make-up 24 hours a day. She must spend hours putting on her mascara and eyeliner.

'Glass of white for you?' Guy presses a ten-pound note in her hand.

But Courtney is having none of it and pushes it back.

Pete fits the iPod headphones back on his ears.

'Relax,' Guy stares back at her while I watch one of the bar staff cleaning up the broken glass.

'If you had more respect for yourself,' she tells him furiously, 'you'd have more respect for other people as well.'

Guy tries again.

'Come on, have a glass of wine.'

'No!' Courtney screams suddenly, and then she pulls a knife out of her pocket – it's the knife from the shop – and holds it up in front of him. 'It's over. As of now. You're over.'

Then she turns on the heel of her wellington boots and leaves, replacing the knife in her pocket. I suppose they were in bed together when I rang about Trevor. Maybe they're even Guy's pyjamas.

At work the following day I am rewarded for my amazing Hollywood seal discovery by a casual walk-past from Molloy.

'Nice find,' he says while people look my way.

'Thank you.'

I sometimes wonder if he's colour-blind. Today's unbeatable Molloy ensemble? A grey suit with mustard yellow tie. And as usual he smells of beer and is charging around with a handful of Post-it notes.

Post-it notes. I swear they hold the newspaper together.

'Seven cats have gone missing,' he says, sticking one on my desk, 'all from one street.'

I see that he's written down a list of names and phone numbers for me. I suppose he thinks I'm in charge of all the animal stories now.

Why does nobody ever remember my award? I won an award once. It was on the restoration of The Royal Pavilion. There were loads of entries from all over the country. And I won. Me. Me, me, me, me, me.

I ring the first phone number. A croaky man answers and I switch onto *Brighton & Hove Courier* autopilot.

'Hello there, my name's Katie Pickard, I'm a journalist at the *Brighton & Hove Courier*. I've just heard that your cat might have gone missing.'

'Yes,' he says usefully.

'Could I ask who I'm talking to, please?'

'No,' the croaky voice says and the phone is slammed down.

The next number is a dud – there's no answering machine and nobody is home. Then I strike lucky with the third number, which belongs to someone called Julie Stevenage but she seems secretly pleased that her cat has gone missing – because it is her daughter's apparently and has clawed her sofa to pieces – so I give up.

I do what I always do when I am going nowhere fast with a story and switch to something else. Not before I finish the last quarter of my carefully preserved Christmas Crunchie, of course.

'I don't know how you can do that,' says one of the subs, looking across his desk at me. 'I ate all mine before we'd even got through dinner.'

The sub, it seems, has heard all about my amazing seal exclusive.

'The thing is,' he sighs, stretching his arms above his head, 'Molloy will come back drunk from the pub and hire someone to shoot its flippers off before Disney can even audition it. Then we'll have a Seal Carnage story and a reader appeal to pay for a frigging flipper transplant to get it to Hollywood.'

I laugh.

Then Julie Stevenage rings me back. She didn't want

to tell me before, she says, because she didn't think it was what I wanted for my story – but now she feels guilty so she has to tell me – after it went missing, the cat was returned safely in a cardboard box.

'Well that's a relief.'

'But it had all its fur cut off,' she continues. 'As if someone had taken a pair of scissors to it. I wasn't going to say anything, but then I rang my daughter just now and she said I should tell you.'

Then she says something which gives me chills.

'It's a spell-fixer, isn't it?' she goes on. 'Our auntie said she remembers it from when she was a little girl in Rye. They had covens and all kinds of things. If the first spell didn't work, they used to fix it with a dead cat. Auntie says they used to hang the cats by their necks from the trees.'

'But these aren't dead cats,' I point out. 'Yours came back in a box.'

'No,' Julie's voice trails off.

Then, just as I am taking the rest of Julie's details and getting to the end of my Crunchie, a real story comes in – and missing cats are the last thing on anyone's mind.

'That's sad,' the sub clicks his tongue. 'Nelson Mandela's son has died of AIDS. He's just given the statement.'

'God,' I think of Jim. Then I count his predictions in my head. The hunting ban. Dame Alicia Markova. The tsunami. And now this.

'Did you see Guy this morning?' I ask the sub.

'Nope,' he turns away, still reading the statement about Mandela's son.

'Is he out doing the seal story then?' I ask.

In reply the sub makes 'Arf! Arf!' noises and flaps his hands together. Then he turns back to the Mandela statement and starts pencilling notes.

I have already decided I'm going to pinch the tape

from Guy and tell him Jim's had a sudden revelation about his predictions, which he will only confide in me, and that he needs to listen to the tape all over again. It's the best thing I can come up with.

I'll tell Guy I left it on the number 9 bus. I'm always leaving things on the number 9 bus, so I might just get away with it.

Then I'm going to delete my transcript of the Jim interview from our shared documents file. I'm always having trouble with computers. That's another useful flaw of mine, along with my amnesia on public transport.

I still have no idea why I'm going to these lengths for Jim Gabriel. I must be mad.

Part of me believes in him and his predictions, part of me doesn't. There, I've said it.

Oh, I don't mind letting him in and trusting him. But every now and then a thought knocks me sideways, like the giant foot in Monty Python: this is mad. He's mad, this is mad and I'm mad for going along with it.

'Just getting a tape,' I tell Guy's PA who's on the phone.

In the first drawer I find a red bank statement which is Guy's final warning on an overdraft. Then I find a stapler, a half-empty bottle of expensive mens' cologne, some chewing gum, a broken cigarette and a scrunched-up tissue.

I keep looking. In the second drawer there are two tapes, neither of which are Jim's, but one of which is marked 'SHAME OF TOWN'S TRAFFIC WARDENS'.

Guy also seems to have forgotten that he owns a peppermint tea bag from Fortnum & Mason, so I seize it, in the interests of public health and safety, while his PA flicks through a magazine.

In the last drawer I find a porn magazine, a solid silver paperweight in the shape of a pig – which I'd guess his rich mother gave him and he's too embarrassed to use it – and, ta, da, Jim's tape, labelled in my handwriting.

Later on, when I have slogged through a day of follow-up pieces about AIDS and more stories about missing cats – not to mention hacked-off cat fur – I smuggle the tape home and slot it into my recorder. Then I fast-forward it to hear Jim's familiar deep, twangy voice. 'There's an English schoolgirl – they should listen to her but they don't. And then 2005 starts with a funeral for Nelson Mandela . . .' After this I settle into an armchair and call Jim. Then maybe, just maybe, after I get this last job out of the way, Pete will come home and I can reward myself by taking him to the pub.

'Katie?' Jim recognizes my number on his mobile.

'I've got the tape.'

He sighs. 'Thank you.'

'But you already knew that.'

'Yeah, funny.'

'Sorry Jim,' I apologize. 'I don't know why I always say such stupid things when we talk about this . . . stuff.'

'It scares you.'

'All right. It scares me. But Jim, Nelson Mandela's son just died of AIDS.'

'Makgatho Mandela. I heard.'

'So what do you want me to do with this tape, then?'

'Do I own it?'

'No. Well, I think you do, of course, but Molloy would disagree. I've already worked out what I'm going to tell Guy. I'm going to pretend I had to take it because you wanted to talk to me about it, and then I'm going to accidentally on purpose leave it on the number 9 bus. I've already taken the transcript off the computer.'

'Katie . . .'

'It's all right. You can't lose any more sleep over this, Jim.'

'Katie. Thank you.'

A journal entry – I'm getting better at them – written after another boozy night at the pub with Linda.

Jim Gabriel is losing weight and I'm worried. I don't think he's eating or sleeping. It must be horrible being him. I wish he'd just get a normal job or something. He said he used to take people out scuba diving, in Australia. Maybe he could do that over here. Even if all we've got is manky cod to look at.

P.S. Had wild sex dream about Jim. What's all that about?

CHAPTER FIVE

Guy has just remembered Jim's prediction about Nelson Mandela's son. But he is not impressed.

'Anyone could have predicted he was on the way out,' he tells me, wheeling backwards in his chair. 'It's like the Prince Harry thing the other day. Why wasn't he more specific? Why didn't he just say, "Prince Harry's going to be caught wearing a swastika, instead of all this going back to the school of life bollocks?" You can't be half right about things, Katie.'

Nevertheless, Guy admits he has already placed a large bet on England beating Australia in The Ashes, at Bobby the Bookmakers in Kemptown.

'It's to make up for my other bet,' he shakes his head, 'about Germaine Greer winning bloody *Big Brother*.'

Then he asks me where Jim's tape is.

'Molloy's changed his mind about the Aussie psychic thing,' he says. 'He wants us to do something on him, and the sooner, the better. He thinks the Mandela prediction is enough, even if I don't. So the word is, lots more Jim. Lots and lots more Jim.'

I take a deep breath. 'I left the tape on the number 9 bus. Sorry. I had to get it out because Jim said he had some more stuff for me and he needed to hear it again.'

'No he didn't.' Guy stares at me. 'No *you* didn't.'

'And I was mucking around with the notes on the computer,' I take a deep breath, 'and I accidentally deleted them. Sorry.'

'Yes,' Guy says coldly. 'All right. But really, Katie, did you have to steal the tape as well?'

I stare out of the window, willing one of the seagulls to crap on the glass again and create a diversion.

'You're lucky I haven't let anyone know about this.' Guy smiles, but his eyes aren't smiling, and I can feel whatever Brownie points I had left disappearing fast.

'Anyway,' he moves away from my desk, 'I don't need the tape. Or the transcript.' He taps his head. 'It's all up here. And I got a quote from him anyway.' He smiles broadly.

'You spoke to Jim?'

Guy gets up from his own chair, then finds another empty swivel chair, abandoned by one of the subs, and sits down in it, wheeling himself backwards and forwards.

'I could swear the subs have nicked my chair,' he complains. 'This feels much more like it.'

'So what did you say to him?' I persist.

'I rang him up just now, and asked if it was true that a shark was going to wash up on Brighton beach on Valentine's Day with seven million quid in banknotes and a desk in its stomach. Whereupon he said "I don't want to talk about it," giving me the finisher for the story. The art department's done a lovely job on the shark, by the way.'

'So what did you put in exactly?' My heart is pounding.

'You'll see.' Guy grins. 'Every other bastard's going to have a free love songs CD on the cover on Valentine's Day, but we'll have Jaws.'

As soon as he's gone back to his desk, I ring Jim.

'It's OK,' he says before I can deliver the news. 'It's

not your fault. I shouldn't even have picked up the phone when he rang.'

'Jim, how many people know your address?'

'It's no secret.'

'The whole world's going to be on your doorstep once you're in the paper and this shark turns up.'

'Maybe.'

'Well, what's your bucket telling you?'

Jim laughs. 'My bucket is telling me to put on my wetsuit and head for the Marina with my board. I was out there when the sun came up and it looks like the only place to be.'

'What, now? It must be freezing.'

'Yes, now. If you go before ten o'clock you've got the place to yourself. Plus, I spent all last weekend waxing my board and there's a north-easterly gale. How can I not go?'

At lunchtime, I catch a bus to the Marina, with my sandwiches, to see if there are any surfers apart from Jim left in the water. It's fun watching them take on the knee-high Brighton waves, even if they do spend most of their time falling off.

I'm joined by a small group of French school-children, who are also fascinated by the surfers bobbing around in the waves and who appear to have escaped their teacher's supervision, because they're all passing round a full packet of Benson & Hedges.

Then a figure walks towards me in the distance and I see that it's Jim – with a board under his arm, sopping-wet tennis shoes and a tight black wetsuit that seems to have made him shrink.

'You've lost weight,' I tell him.

'I know. Lovely weather we're having.' He grins. And at that moment I realize I've never seen him look happier.

He shakes his head like a wet dog while the French

schoolchildren shout at each other, their voices blown away in the wind.

'Let's go to the beach huts,' I suggest. 'There's a bit of shelter up there.'

'Funny you should say that.' He shakes himself again. 'I've got a beach hut.'

I'm impressed and amazed at the same time, because Jim Gabriel is one of those people you can never imagine owning anything.

I follow him along the path as the waves crash far too close to us on the other side of the iron railing. Judging by the wet tidemark on the concrete they have been reaching up as far as the cliff face.

'I was left the hut', Jim explains, 'in somebody's will.'

'Did you give her an amazing psychic reading or something?'

Jim shrugs and nods.

'Lucky you,' I tell him as we walk as close to the cliff face as possible. I've always wanted a beach hut in this part of Brighton. In fact, I've always wanted a beach hut anywhere. Next to my cottage-by-the-sea fantasy, my pink beach hut comes a close second.

Then, before I can say anything else, a wave over-reaches the iron railings and slaps me neatly in the face.

'Oh God,' Jim says, seeing my wet hair. 'Sorry.' Then he feels for my hand and makes us swap places so that he's facing the water instead of me.

Then another wave hits and we quickly pull ourselves into the cliff face.

'Let's go back.' Jim squeezes my hand. 'You can see the hut another time.'

But every time we try to weave our way back to the Marina, another huge wave threatens in the distance – so in the end, the best we can do is make our way back to a concrete bench, chopped in half, tucked away in a cavity in the cliff face. It's the only shelter for miles.

'I've been meaning to say,' Jim stares out to sea, 'again, please, once and for all, forget that thing I said.'

'What thing?' I realize we're still holding hands.

'The marriage thing. It's getting in the way of' – Jim gestures awkwardly – 'the friends thing.'

I nod as the seagulls wheel and squawk in front of us. His hand feels warm inside mine and it reminds me of something. And then I remember my Jim dream from the other night. The one where we suddenly found ourselves on a beach in Fiji. Not that I've ever been to Fiji. I just drink the mineral water.

'I don't know many people round here.' Jim nods at me. 'You know? So, friends would be good.'

'Oh well,' I say, suddenly feeling as embarrassed as he looks.

We sit and wait and watch as the sea roars ahead of us, and he drops my hand. I'm glad he did it first.

'I have to go back,' I tell him. 'I'm going to be soaking wet anyway. Come on.'

As we make our way back to the Marina I realize that in his wetsuit, and without the baggy white trousers and big knitted jumpers, Jim seems taller as well as lighter on his feet.

I wonder how long it's been since he had anyone in his life, and decide that he should try harder with the women of Brighton. Someone out there would be positively thrilled with an Aussie surfer type (and he's not unattractive now) who owns his own beach hut. Even if he does read buckets for a living, Jim must be a catch for someone, despite the fact that Courtney's magic spell has already cursed any woman who gets near him.

I wonder if she's still in love with him and decide that she must be. Courtney Creely is an obsessive. Girls like her don't just drop their passions overnight, even if they do have Guy throwing his charm and credit card around.

I don't believe her passion for Guy for a moment. He's probably just the pointy money bit on the left-hand side of the pentacle in her spell book.

'What's Courtney up to these days?' I ask.

'She's started doing power yoga three mornings a week. She wants me to do it as well.'

'Will you?'

'Not sure.'

Then Jim remembers something else and clicks his tongue.

'I was supposed to go to the theatre with her this week; she said she had free tickets for something in London.'

'Oh well.'

'She was lying.' Jim half smiles at me. 'She paid for them.'

'Did your bucket tell you that?'

'My bucket did.'

'I think she's got a bit of a crush on you,' I hear myself say. 'Are you going to do anything about it?'

But all Jim Gabriel will do is shake his head and look the other way, staring across the sea towards France.

We walk in silence for a while, then I remember something. 'Oh, one of Linda's friends wants to have a psychic reading with you. She's a book publisher. From London.'

'OK,' Jim nods as we carefully pace our way around the line of the undercliff.

'Her name's Sue. Do you remember her? She was around on Boxing Day. After you left Linda's place she asked me for your phone number.'

Then we are caught by another huge wave, though the spray hits Jim in the face this time, and we tuck our heads down, and try to walk faster.

'Wrong shoes,' he says, staring at my black lace-up boots.

'Absolutely the wrong shoes,' I agree.

Then at last we reach the Marina and the safety of the bus shelter. I am sopping wet and will be amazed if the driver lets me on, but if I stand all the way and try not to drip too much, I might just get away with it.

'I'll walk back,' Jim says. 'If I go surfing again I'll call you. Then you can see the hut.'

'Brilliant.'

'I can tell', Jim raises an eyebrow, 'that you are very impressed with my hut.'

Then, all in a rush, before the bus can wobble towards us, he tells me that the day he spent with me and Linda and her friends, after Christmas, was the best time he'd had since he moved to Brighton.

'Well then,' I tell him as I watch the bus pull up, 'we'll have to sort something out. And I'll give your regards', I say meaningfully, 'to Linda.'

When I get back to the office half an hour later, I am immediately bollocked by Guy while everyone watches.

It seems his Hollywood seal story has fallen through – the word from London is that the film has been postponed indefinitely because of budget problems – and consequently Guy's mood has changed from slightly iffy (at a quarter to ten) to downright dark (at a quarter past two.) And I have overextended my lunch hour, of course, and am sopping wet – none of which helps.

'I rang lost property,' he says coldly, 'at the bus depot. Not one tape handed in. Lucky I'm a gentleman or I'd tell Molloy about this. But if it happens again . . .'

'Sorry,' I peel my coat off and squash it into a plastic bag, which is more diplomatic than hanging it on the back of my chair. 'Yes, you are a gentleman,' I say, which I know is all he secretly wants to hear.

I'm dying to take my boots off as well, but I'm afraid Guy will pick one up and throw it at me.

'Where were you?'

'I was watching the surfers at the Marina.'

'Spot any stories?'

'It was my lunch break.'

'Of course you didn't spot any stories,' Guy folds his arms and sighs heavily. 'The Mayor of Brighton could die naked in front of you, with the cast of *Big Brother* dancing a conga line at the rear, and you'd still be looking the wrong way.'

'Thanks.'

Guy finds a spare chair from the subs' desk and wheels it over to where I'm sitting, kicking a rubbish bin out of the way.

'Find out if Jim Gabriel won £1,000 on the football. On a £10 stake.'

'What?'

'Courtney tells me, in good faith, that he won £1,000 betting on an Everton game when he first got to Brighton.'

'But why would Jim tell me anything like that?'

'Because you're matey with him.' Guy sighs. 'By the way, I've had a snapper following him around all day. Well,' he stares at me, 'I could have saved us all the trouble, couldn't I, if I'd known you were going to meet him for a nice time at the beach.'

Guy sniffs and looks disdainfully at my soaking-wet feet.

'The snapper just rang me. We should have just given you the camera and told you to get on with it, Katie.' He wags his finger at me.

'But why are you so interested in him?' I cringe, thinking about Jim taking my hand on the undercliff while one of our photographers sat in his car with a long lens. I know how they work – they park the car just out of sight and sit there for hours with their lenses resting on the window until they get their shot.

'Because Molloy smells something special about Jim

Gabriel.' Guy shrugs. 'And so do I. In fact,' he casts a look at the subs' desk, 'so does everyone else around here. So find out about the £1,000 and I'll ignore the fact that you've stolen the tape. It's newspaper property.'

I ignore this.

'What if Courtney is wrong about the bet?' I ask.

Guy shakes his head. 'She's an impeccable source.' He grins.

'So you've made it up with her, then?' I say, thinking of her hysterics in the pub.

'Katie, my career in the mee-jar has always been distinguished by the fact that work stays out here,' Guy pinches his fingers in the air, 'and my private life stays over here.' He pinches the air again.

'But you still want me to use my friendship with Jim to get some kind of quote.'

'If you'd done the story on him properly in the first place, it's the kind of thing we'd have got anyway.' Guy sighs. 'And we'd have got full access so I wouldn't have to send some turnip out there with his Nikon to get a fuzzy photo.' He rubs his eyes. 'I'm trying to keep the paper afloat here. How do you think that happens? Nobody cares about endangered buildings, Katie. Nobody gives a shit about Romanian orphans getting Christmas presents in shoeboxes, but they all want to know about a psychic who saw the future and won himself a thousand quid betting on the football, and a shark on Brighton beach.'

'How do you know that's what they want?'

In reply, Guy picks up a pile of newspapers lying on the corner of someone's desk, licks his finger and flicks through them, beginning with the *Sun* and *The Times*.

'Now, let's see what's happening in the real world, shall we? Oh dear, not much news here about the last Molesey versus Hastings game.' He tuts. 'Nor is there a great deal of in-depth reportage on last week's nail-biting quiz-night final in aid of World Mental Health Week.'

That was my story, about Mental Health Week. Guy sighs and blows his nose.

'Do you feel like a coffee? I can't talk about all this' – he flaps a hand – 'in here. And if you're really lucky I'll drop you at your flat so you can get some dry clothes. You look like a drowned rat.'

I agree, more because I am fed up with feeling damp and cold than anything else.

Guy arranges several copies of the paper on the front seat of his car, for me to sit on, in case I leave water marks on the BMW upholstery, and we drive past the station, where most of his favourite cafés and bars are, after stopping at my flat so I can change into some dry clothes.

I automatically think about Pete as I open the front door, then I automatically tell myself not to.

'I'm on a budget that *The Times* would use for its crossword puzzle,' Guy sighs as we drive off again, shunting past an annoyed taxi driver. 'We have six months to increase our sales by more than fifty per cent, and I'm working with the kind of expense account the *Sun* would throw at a losing contestant on *Who Wants to Be a Millionaire* just so they can get his bloody baby photo. We go up against the London papers every day and we lose.'

'I know money's tight, Guy.'

Then his mobile rings.

'Courtney!'

In a second Guy's face changes from bloodhound-gloomy to ridiculously pleased.

He falls into the kind of cryptic conversation I recognize of old, mainly because it's happened so many times before, with Claudia and all the other women in his harem at work.

It sounds like a kind of mysterious rap, with a chorus that goes, 'Yeah, mmm, yeah, mmm-hmmm, OK, yeah, mmm.' And in between, there is the patented Guy Booth Charming Laugh. And once again I recognize it of old. I've heard him using it so often I can practically fake it – in fact, a lot of the subs can too.

When Guy first arrived at the paper to take up his job as Features Editor, we sniffed around each other for about a nanosecond. It seemed like the natural thing to do. He'd been hearing a lot about me and I'd been hearing a lot about him. And we were both single, so I suppose there was a build-up.

Then Guy invited me to his new penthouse flat for a drink after work. He turned the spa on just to show me how powerful it was, and then he got out a bottle of vintage red wine – and lectured me about it – and after that he told me how much his property had gone up in value since the day he'd bought it.

And then came the heavy references to his family, and more particularly his father's knighthood, and that was that. I left his flat thinking I would rather gnaw my own arm off than go anywhere near Guy Booth.

I suspect Guy's turn-off point with me came rather later. But still, eventually it came – probably on the night Claudia persuaded Guy to donate to her sponsored charity swim and showed him her new bikini, all at the same time.

Without realizing he is doing it Guy checks his face in the rear-view mirror. He's like a peacock, I think. Captain Peacock. When he showed me the view from his balcony on the night I had a grand tour of his flat, he even strutted around like one in his brown Hush Puppies.

Guy finishes talking to Courtney, puts the phone down, and focuses his eyes back to the road. I've never seen anyone drive quite so much on autopilot in my life.

Then I notice the birds – dozens of large seagulls, wheeling and crying in front of us.

'Bugger off,' Guy honks his horn.

It reminds me of something, though I can't think what. Then it comes to me. On the day that Courtney was arguing with the landlord in the alleyway outside the shop there were seagulls flapping around the door.

I've lived in Brighton all my life and I can honestly say I've never notice'd one stupid gull from one day to the next. But this is the second time I've noticed the birds behaving weirdly.

Then one of them craps on my side of the window.

'Oh for God's sake,' Guy tuts.

Then . . .

'I think I may have arranged another date with fate,' he muses as we're honked by the car behind.

'With Courtney?' The seagulls are still circling around us.

'Yup. Here.' Guy reaches over my knees to open the glovebox. 'I've even got some of the reject shots of her from the Christmas shoot. That's how smitten I am, Katie.'

I examine them. The photographs show Courtney looking sulky, Courtney looking innocent, Courtney looking sultry, and Courtney looking wildly excited. She has nipple erections in all of them. I open Guy's glovebox, which contains yet more bottles of his favourite posh mens' cologne, and put them back.

'So what was the reaction, exactly, to our alternative religions at Christmas story?' I ask once we are out of the car and inside one of Guy's favourite cafés. The birds, thank God, have disappeared. 'I mean, I did give up two weekends to work on it.'

'Don't be like that.' He lights a cigarette. 'You know the tsunami stuffed everything.'

'So why are we here,' I watch the waitress and beckon

102

her over, 'so you can actually sack me properly this time?'

Guy laughs. 'No, since you ask.' Then he succeeds where I have failed with the waitress, and she finally takes our order.

'It's like this,' Guy says in a low voice once she's gone. 'I want to know about Jim and Courtney.'

'They work together,' I say automatically. 'That's all.'

'Courtney says you're friends with him.'

'Yes.'

'Well he must tell you things. Is he interested in her?'

'No,' I shake my head.

'Was he ever interested in her?'

'I have no idea, Guy. He doesn't seem to care about her one way or the other.'

Then I realize I'm hearing something new in his voice, and it's good old-fashioned jealousy. Whoever would have thought it?

'I'm just doing some groundwork before I get too involved.' Guy drags on his cigarette.

'Are you in love with her, then?'

'I don't know.' Guy shrugs.

'I bet you are.' I take one of his cigarettes. 'And I bet it's the first time ever, isn't it?'

'I don't know,' Guy repeats.

'Are you sleeping? Are you eating?'

Then, like a drowning man who has seen a lifeboat, Guy tells me the story of his life since C-Day – the name he has given to the day he met Courtney. He can't have too many friends to confide in, I realize, as he pours his heart out to me.

'I can't stop thinking about her.' He puffs on his cigarette. 'First thing in the morning, last thing at night. And all through the day as well. I'm obsessed. If she told me to jump in the sea, I would. And she won't sleep with me.'

'Really?'

'Nope. I've bought her all the stuff she wanted – over two hundred quid's worth of underwear – and nothing. Here ' – Guy pulls down his shirt and jacket to show me the top of his shoulder – 'And I got a tattoo.'

Please God, I think, don't tell me he's paid to have her name tattooed on his arm. If so, it's one of the worst mistakes of his life.

'It's a witchy thing,' Guy explains. 'A pentacle. It's her sign. Her symbol. She and her friends watched me, while I had it done. Bloody painful, too.'

'You, with a tattoo, Guy?'

'I know,' he puffs his cheeks out, almost proud at the fact that he has sunk this low.

'What about Claudia?' I ask, but he's already waving me away.

'Courtney talks about Jim a lot,' Guy returns to his subject. 'But she won't tell me anything. You must know. Come on. What's the story there?'

'No story,' I lie.

I can't explain why, but I have no desire to talk about Courtney's book of spells to anyone. It's like Pandora's Box, I think. If I open the lid, all the bad things will get out.

I don't know if Jim takes her witchcraft seriously or not, but I do. She travels with her own private black cloud.

Suddenly I feel sorry for Guy. An hour ago I wanted to kill him, for all his smugness in the office, but now I recognize the look in his eye – and it's me, a few years ago, when I first fell in love with Andrew and was driven mad with jealousy by one of his irritating ex-girlfriends who wouldn't go away.

'Anyway,' I take a deep breath. 'Sorry to change the subject, Guy. But I've actually got a story for us.'

'Oh yes?' Guy says, taking the coffee as the waitress finally delivers it.

'You don't have to sound quite so enthusiastic.'

'Katie. I'm listening.'

'Pete sent me a text a few days ago. He and some of his mates are organizing a benefit concert for the tsunami.'

'Not another one,' Guy sighs, flicking through the menu.

'But those were all in London. This is local. It's virtually every musician on the coast. They've got sponsorship, free advertising, the lot.'

'Marvellous.' Guy nods, but I can see he's miles away, probably in bed with Courtney. I've seldom seen him so distracted.

'Pete's modest,' I say, 'but that American label, Parrot, picked him up. It's really well known. They think he's going to be huge,' I exaggerate. 'You know he's got a cult following around here.'

'I'd get another tattoo for Courtney too,' Guy sighs, ignoring the information about Pete, 'if she wanted me to. Can you believe that, Katie? Is that the act of a rational man?'

There should be a new 0800 number, I think, as we finish our coffee and leave the café. It should be a number where you can ring up anonymously and pay a pound a minute to bang on about the man or woman who is your current obsession. Then Guy could talk about Courtney and I could talk about Pete. We'd both be doing each other a favour.

Later on, when I'm at home in bed, I count the nights that Pete's lights have been out, telling myself I will wait until the third night so I can give myself the sweet relief of a phone call, just to hear his voice. I have no idea who invented the three-day/three-night rule, but they should be shot.

Somewhere between the second night and the third morning, though, Pete knocks on my door. It's half-past six when he does so, and as usual I'm in my spotted pink flannel pyjamas and my decidedly unglamorous pink woollen dressing gown.

'I made you a pot of coffee,' he says hopefully, waving it around in the doorway. 'Are you up?' Dawn is Pete time. I worked it out ages ago. And no, I don't mind. Though if it was anyone else I'd kill them.

I keep meaning to buy a decent nightie, or at least a reasonably alluring dressing gown, because of Pete's early-morning wake-up calls, but as usual Pete looks like a rock star and I look like – I don't know – somebody's boring unmarried aunt.

Pete has shaved off his beard and he smells of lots of lemony soap, this morning, and even larger amounts of toothpaste.

'So did you just get home?' I ask as he follows me into the flat.

'The concert's going to be great,' he explains. 'We've worked out all the songs, all the encores, and the whole running order. We've been at it all week.'

'So have you been staying on someone's sofa then?' I push him as he puts the coffee pot down on the dining table.

No other human being has the right to look as good as Pete Oram at this hour of the morning. Maybe it's the caffeine.

'What time is it?' he asks, without waiting for an answer. 'Sorry, you know I never know what time it is.'

'It's the crack of dawn and it's January the 16th. I wish you'd buy yourself a clock, Pete.'

'What you been doing then?' he asks me when he returns from the kitchen with two mugs.

'Working.' I rub my eyes. 'You know what it's like. Christmas turns into New Year's Eve, and then before you know it, there's Valentine's Day ahead of you. And then we had the tsunami in the middle of it. Oh, that reminds me, Guy says we'll do something on your charity concert.'

'Valentine's Day.' Pete snaps his fingers at me. 'I knew there was something.'

'I don't want to think about it,' I say automatically, feeling myself go red.

'Well, let's not think about it together then,' Pete says, stirring sugar into my coffee for me. 'Cos I hate it too. So you and me, we'll not buy each other a card, and not buy each other a box of chocolates, and not buy each other a bunch of flowers. And we won't take each other out for a candelit dinner, either,' he promises.

'Whatever you say.'

'Feelings don't run on a timetable.' He says with a shrug. 'My heart's not run by Hallmark Cards. Is yours?'

'I like that,' I say, half wanting him to go on like this and half terrified at where he's taking me. 'Did you just make that up?'

'It's from a song I wrote.'

Then Pete puts down his mug and walks over to my sofa, taking his boots off as he goes.

'Can I sleep here?' he asks. 'I'd feel better if I could sleep here.'

Then I realize that his fly – the sugar mouse fly, still not fixed – is coming undone, and I have to force myself to look away, instead, at some extremely un-interesting candlesticks which have been on my mantelpiece for ever.

'Feel your feelings on your own timetable,' he says, turning sideways on the couch and pulling my blanket over him.

'I will.'

'Look at me,' he says with his voice muffled by my cushions. 'Polly's been gone for eight weeks and three days and I already want someone else. That's not supposed to happen, is it?'

'I expect you want lots of someone elses,' I push him. 'You probably feel as if you've been set free.'

Then I realize this makes me sound bitchy about Polly and clam up.

'Oh yeah,' Pete suddenly sits up on the sofa with my blanket wrapped around him like a cloak. 'Freedom's the thing. But it's because of the girl upstairs.'

I cannot speak, so I just look at him instead.

'The nineteen fifties girl upstairs has had a most interesting effect on me,' he says.

And then I go over to the couch and he pulls me on top of him – at last, at last. And that is the beginning of the end – or the beginning of the beginning of the beginning, as Pete says later.

I think of all the walks next summer that Pete and I could take along Brighton beach, and I smile to myself inside his jacket. Then I fall asleep, with his hand tucked safely on top of my breast under my pink pyjamas. I know I have to be at work in a couple of hours, but I never want to leave this sofa again.

CHAPTER SIX

A few days later Pete is thrown off Parrot.

'Fook it,' is all he will say when I ask him about it.

We've been together every night and every morning since we slept on my sofa. I check my phone every hour for his texts and listen religiously to the radio on the bus, with my headphones on, in case one of the local stations decides to play one of his old songs. I hop around on my chair at work until I can go home and I doodle his name on any spare scrap of paper that crosses my desk, like some sad fifteen-year-old.

Number of pages taken up by Peter Oram in my Edwardian lady journal? Oh, about half the book. I'll have to buy a new one soon.

'Did they throw you off because they changed their mind, or because of your manager, or—'

'I didn't co-operate.' He shrugs. 'I'm not being photographed with me shirt off, running around on the beach in the middle of winter, like a ponce.'

Then he sits down at the piano in his flat and plays something which starts out like some old Rolling Stones song – 'Angie'? – but turns into something long and beautiful and strange, which I have never heard him play before.

The piano is one of the few things that Polly left when she moved out. In fact, thanks to Polly, I can take a precise inventory of Pete's possessions, and consequently his life, just by walking round the flat.

He owns a second-hand piano, a stack of music magazines and weeklies that could support a bed – and in fact is, on one corner – and some tinny-looking second-hand lamps. He also has a fine collection of burned-out candles, a wing-backed blue armchair with a red-wine stain and a wardrobe rack full of black, denim and leather. And piles of books. Kurt Cobain. Janis Joplin. John Lennon. Jimi Hendrix. Almost any dead musical genius, in fact.

'Are you sure this time, Katie?' one of my friends emailed me about him, this morning.

To which the answer has to be, as sure as I'll ever be. I've done the sensible love thing. I did it with Andrew and look where it got me. So, Pete seems like the next best bet.

I am back to anger with Andrew. I felt it after the funeral for a couple of months, and I stamped on a framed photo of him twice with the heel of my boot, then I picked the whole thing up with rubber gloves and threw it in the bin.

After that, nothing. But now the rage is back. The more time I spend with Pete, the more I want to kill Andrew, even if he wasn't dead already.

After a few glasses of wine I tell Pete about smashing Andrew's photo and – inspired – he decides to burn his contract with Parrot, which he has neglected to sign anyway, over a candle flame.

'Always read the small print,' he announces as it burns. 'Well, I never do. Can you believe I'm going to be number one this year?'

I hesitate, then I remember his reading with Jim.

'I'm still working on that song about you.' He smiles. 'Maybe that's it.'

I smile back at him, but here's my awful secret. I have heard the song and I don't like it. It's too long, too rambling, and just too . . . weird. How's that? I am one of the very few women in the world to have a song written about them and I cringe every time he wants to play it.

And here's my other awful secret. I don't like what Pete's put on my iPod either. I shuffle and shuffle, and still I can't find anything I like. And I know it's only music, but . . . with Pete, it's always more than that.

I think about some of the Christmas photos he's shown me, of Polly and Ben. Or, to be honest, the Christmas photos he deliberately didn't show me. I found them in the pocket of his stripy jacket instead. They show the three of them with their arms around each other, looking happy for the camera.

And I found the drugs in his pocket, too, as if I was ever going to avoid them.

Pete sells ecstasy up and down the East Sussex coast. He has done for years. Linda told me about it a few days ago, and her friend Nathan – who runs a club in Hove – backed her up.

Then yesterday, after Pete had gone out, I found it all in the inside pocket of his jacket. Enough pills to get us both arrested, stuffed inside an electricity-bill envelope inside a small clear plastic bag.

Pete comes over to kiss me.

'What do you want to hear?' he says without waiting for the reply. ' "Goodbye Yellow Brick Road"?'

'I know you think it's naff.'

'No,' he insists, 'you're changing me and I'm changing you. It's good.'

And then he plays 'Goodbye Yellow Brick Road' note for note, singing it line for line. When I sing I always have to stop. I either run out of words or the song suddenly seems too high or too low for me. With Pete, you never want to stop listening.

'Nothing ever changed with anyone else,' he holds my hand when he has finished. 'But what's the point of that? The reason people come together is to move each other on, isn't it?'

'What about Polly?' I ask, pushing my luck.

'She left me as she found me.'

And perhaps she did, I think later, as I do the washing-up – Pete has gone off for the final rehearsals of the tsunami concert.

I have already made up my mind about their relationship. She was a fan, she indulged him and she never let him grow up – or grow in any direction at all. And if there is any other version of the truth, please don't tell me. I refuse to be the intermission in the continuing story of Pete, Polly and Ben.

And here's another thing. He never married her. See? See? He could have, when she had Ben, but he didn't.

The next day Jim invites me to his beach hut for lunch.

'You won't get blown away today,' he promises. 'I'll meet you at the Marina and we can walk up.'

'Well I've already ruined these boots, so I suppose it doesn't matter.'

He's wearing his sheepskin coat and brown woolly hat when I arrive, and the tennis shoes – plus a new addition: a pair of dark sunglasses. They make him look like some weird kind of Sixties detective.

'I heard I was photographed by your paper.' He shrugs. 'I'm wearing these for a while.'

'Bloody Guy,' I say as we make our way along the undercliff towards the huts.

And then he tells me something amazing. Sue, Linda's publisher friend, wants him to write a book. His life story, about being psychic.

'I gave her a reading,' he says, shielding his eyes as the sun comes out over the sea. 'And then I gave her sister a reading. And a few of her friends from the

112

publishing company. And then they rang me up, and I told them about Dame Alicia Markova and Nelson Mandela and the tsunami – and they asked me if I thought I could write a book for them.'

He unlocks the door of his hut and I peer in. There is room for a pile of cushions, a rug, some incense, a camping stove, a packet of herbal tea and not much else.

'But I can't write to save my life, Katie,' he continues. 'I can't even spell. So I was wondering if you'd . . . do it.' He looks at me and adds, 'You know.'

'Be your ghostwriter?'

'You could help me make sense of everything.' Jim takes off his woolly hat and shoves it in his coat pocket.

'Well thanks. I mean, thanks. But I've never written a book before.'

'You'll be fine.' Jim smiles. 'And before you ask, yes, that is a bucket thing. I saw you writing the book in my bucket. Could even, I dunno, change your life.'

'You might be famous,' I tell him as he searches for a packet of biscuits in the depths of the hut.

And then the following day he is, though not in a way he ever wanted, because Guy decides to run his story on Jim on the front cover.

The art department have, as promised, done an amazing job with Photoshop, superimposing what appears to be a shark on the beach below the pier. They have also airbrushed a cross-eyed, puzzled look on its face, and a school desk has also been dropped into the shot.

The headline is JAWS! And below it in red capitals, LOCAL PSYCHIC PREDICTS HUNGRY SHARK. Then there is a photo of Jim in his wetsuit, taken with a long lens – thank God they've left me out – and another photograph of him from the original story that Molloy dropped. I read the piece.

113

Brighton and Hove psychic Jim Gabriel is our very own Noztradamus. Aussie Jim claims to see visions of the future, which other soothsayers miss. And now gambling-mad Jim, who friends say has already made a fortune from his £1,000 footy predictions, claims a *giant shark* is poised to turn up on our beaches on 14 February, as a Happy Valentine for locals. And not only that, our own Brighton Junior Jaws will be hungry. Professional spook Jim, 38, says it will have eaten a whole desk and *seven million* quid by the time it gets here!

Then there's a series of red ticks in a box. Jim Gabriel was *right* about the tsunami (tick.) *right* about the death of Nelson Mandela's son (tick.) Will he be right about the Brighton jaws that's worth a fortune?

I try to be objective about the front cover. Would I, as a local person, buy it? Would I buy it ahead of the other newspapers? I walk around the table, looking at it from all angles. Is it true? Is it fair to all concerned? Is it in the public interest? Is it, in any way at all, in the spirit of what my grandfather taught me all those years ago about being a professional reporter?

Of course it isn't. But even my grandfather would know it's a sell-out cover. Even if it is pure fiction.

I am terrified for Jim, and reach for my phone, then stop instinctively. He has probably thrown his phone in the sea by this stage. I expect everyone in the world, never mind Brighton, has been ringing him.

At lunchtime I decide to go back to his beach hut, on the off-chance that he might be there. I eat my sandwiches at my desk to throw people off the scent, just in case they want to send out another freelance ferret with a camera, then I slip out at half past two, after I hear from one of the subs that Guy has gone to a meeting upstairs with Molloy.

I have a cab voucher, which I'm supposed to save for

the missing-cat feature, but I decide to use it on Jim instead. It's the least the *Brighton & Hove Courier* can do.

The driver drops me at the top of a flight of flagstone steps, which twist and curve all the way down to the beach. I can see Jim's hut in the distance – it's a bright, summery blue, like the piece of turquoise he sometimes wears on a leather cord around his neck.

And then I see him, out in the water. He is paddling further and further out to sea on the gentlest of waves, but it looks as if he never wants to come back.

I sit and wait. And then I realize he's waving at me, from a spot just in front of the rocks which all the locals call the Wash.

I wave back, waiting, until he finally swims back to shore and half-jogs, half-walks along the undercliff to meet me, with his board under his arm.

He shakes himself hard, and then I look at his face and realize he is furious.

'I should never have let you talk to me,' he says.

'Jim! I came here to see if you were OK.'

'I'm too trusting. Fuck it,' he says.

'Guy literally made that all up by himself. It had nothing to do with me. He patched it together from what he could remember from the first story, the one Molloy ditched. You know how these things work. Come on, Jim. It wasn't anything to do with me.'

'I'm human,' he shakes all the water off again. 'So this is me, being human. And Courtney told him about the football thing too. Fuck it. Katie, are you going to stand here and tell me you tried to stop it?'

And with that he strides off, and I am left alone, staring at his back as he vanishes along the curve of the cliff face.

I spend the rest of the day at work, ringing up people whose cats have gone missing.

Guy returns from his meeting with Molloy just as

the office is gearing up for its afternoon tea break. He has already chalked up two regional television interviews at lunchtime, all thanks to Jim.

'We've sold out.'

'Jim's devastated.'

'Did you hear me?' he taps his ear. 'We've sold out.'

'He never said the shark would appear in Brighton. Nor did he say it had seven million pounds in its stomach. For God's sake, Guy.'

'Katie. He talked to us. He posed for us.'

'He didn't know. He didn't understand that this is what it would be like.'

Guy calls Molloy.

'Got BBC Southern Counties in the can,' he says, almost panting. 'It's going to be their funny end bit. I got the producer to promise me.'

I roll my eyes, and then catch him noticing me.

'Katie, come on.' Guy does a little jig in his designer shoes. 'We've sold out. We're back in business. We can do it. We've sold out.'

And then he tells me he has sacked his PA and is going to hire Courtney part time, to help Molloy meet his new stripped-back budget.

'Oh. So you've really made it up with her.'

'It's going to be great.' He grins, waving me away.

'How are we going to manage editorial if she's only part time?' I ask.

'She wants to keep her job at the shop.' He shrugs. 'And the modelling.'

'Has she ever actually worked on a newspaper?'

'She's been a PA.' Guy dismisses me. 'What is it really at the end of the day? Answering the phone?' Then he gives me a meaningful look. 'Stopping the staff from going through your desk?'

Then Guy says he has to talk to Molloy about another story they're doing (something big, apparently, because it's making him rub his hands together and fiddle with his signet ring) and he finally leaves me in peace.

I wonder what would happen to my life if Courtney moved in with Guy? I'm sure she is working on it. It's probably the final phase of her weird black magic rituals.

Throughout the Claudia period – and indeed the *Brighton & Hove Courier* harem period – Guy kept up a relationship with a woman in London called Sophie. I met her once. His mother's best friend had introduced them, apparently. She was a ponytailed blonde with a beautiful white shirt and thin, thin legs in ironed, clean jeans. She had a permanent tan, from all her permanent holidays, and tiny pearls in her ears.

In a word, she was Claudia, but in a parallel universe, with a public-school education and money. I was gobsmacked when Guy told me he'd dumped her, but now I think it might have been the other way around.

I try to imagine Guy and Courtney living together, or even Guy and Courtney publicly having dinner together. It seems impossible, like hearing that Prince Charles has just gone off with . . . I don't know. Britney Spears.

Later on Claudia stops at my desk.

'So we sold out.' She nods.

'The story was nothing to do with me. It was all Guy and Molloy.'

'Was it rubbish?' Claudia asks, looking tired.

'Total rubbish.'

'Bloody Guy.' Claudia sighs. 'Maybe I should talk to him.'

'Do you think so?' I try to put her off. I wish she'd give up this idea that she still has any influence on Guy.

And then Claudia tells me about Guy's old PA, Alison.

For over three weeks Alison's block of flats has been covered in pigeons. She's been finding dead birds lying in front of her balcony door, and her windows have been covered in so much pigeon shit, that she has done nothing but scrub it off. Birds keep banging into her bedroom window and dying on the spot, and it starts just after dawn and doesn't stop until dusk.

And Alison's flat smells, as well, Claudia tells me. And it's not even a dead-pigeon smell – more like a foul stench, a dead body smell. She had to fake a sick day off work in order to deal with it. Then Guy found out and sacked her.

'And Alison's got ringworm too,' Claudia tells me. 'But it's not like normal ringworm. It's only down one side of her body. The doctor says it could be from picking up the dead pigeons, but he's not sure. It's like red circles all over her skin.'

'Is she all right?'

'Not really.' Claudia shakes her head. 'She thinks she's going mad.'

'Birds,' I hear myself saying. 'They're not behaving normally at the moment. Have you noticed?'

'Why?'

And again, although part of me wants to tell someone about Courtney Creely, another part stops me. It's the Pandora's Box thing again, I realize. There's a superstitious side to me which believes that if I tell people what I'm thinking it will release all the nasties which are currently being held in.

I am giving myself the creeps. The story about Alison is horrible. Awful.

I catch myself longing for Pete. His dopey half smile, and the way he rubs my back when I'm tired, and his 'Any requests?' on the piano, and the smell of his soapy skin – I have never known anyone take so many baths.

Drug problem? What drug problem?

I'm aware that I have already filed the ecstasy dealing away, in the same place I file Polly and Ben – a dim and conveniently distant spot at the back of my mind. It's where I put Andrew two years ago.

Pete and I still haven't had sex. He says he wants to wait until it's the right time. But today I don't think I can wait any more. So once Claudia has gone – I am still trying to forget the pigeon story – I decide to go to his rehearsal rooms, on the Western Road.

He's playing the piano when I arrive. It's 'Eleanor Rigby', but with a twist I can't quite describe. A Pete twist. When he sings it sounds as if he's talking to you. When he plays the sound goes straight through you.

'She's here! She's here!' He leaps up from the piano when he sees me, and he grabs me in front of an assorted group of musicians and their girlfriends.

'Like your new coat. Nice soft leather.' He nods.

'It was just in Oxfam. Claudia works there on Saturdays; she put it aside for me.'

'Love it.' Pete squeezes my arm.

'Your phone's out of range,' I tell him, embarrassed by the fact that people are staring at us.

'That's 'cos we're in a dungeon,' he whispers in my ear.

And then he tells me that they've decided to play a night of Beatles tributes for the tsunami concert after one of the local radio stations promised to give them a series of free advertisements.

After this, he sits down at the piano and finishes 'Eleanor Rigby', while two musicians step forward with a violin and a clarinet to accompany him.

Suddenly I understand the appeal of being a groupie. There's a lot to be said for sitting on the floor, cross-legged, gazing admiringly at your man while he unleashes his genius on a room.

There. I've called him my man. How pathetic is that?

Pete, who cannot pay electricity bills and who will not co-operate with his record company, is in sole command of everything that happens in the rehearsal room over the next hour, like a monarch with his courtiers. Talent wins, I suppose. It's probably the only thing in here that anyone respects.

He keeps playing. Guitarists step in and out. A version of 'Strawberry Fields' which I think is astonishing is deemed not good enough by Pete, who starts it all over again, and then he plays 'Imagine', and almost, but not quite, makes me cry.

'Coom on,' he hustles me into a corridor when he finally takes a break from the piano.

'Where are we going?'

'In here,' he pulls open the door to a dark, cold storeroom filled with cardboard boxes and vacuum cleaners, and guides me inside.

And then he shoves a rubbish bin against the door with his foot, pulls me down on top of him and tells me that all the time he's been playing the piano, he's been thinking of me.

'Slow songs, fast songs,' he whispers. 'Slow or fast? Which one?'

'Fast,' I give in as he pulls off my new leather coat and then my tights, and finally my pants, and moves in while they are still bundled around my knees.

'Oh God. Oh Katie,' he shuts his eyes as we move together on the floor.

And then about two minutes later, when I am brushing the dust off my leather coat, 'God, that was fast. Part two at home, Katie. And I'll look after you properly, I promise. Nice and slow. All right?'

'All right,' I say, feeling woozy with longing.

'That was rock 'n' roll sex. Sorry.'

I shake my head.

'And I want to live with you,' he says, sliding his hand inside my underwear again. 'Can I? Because if I live with you, we can do it all the time. For hours.'

'You want to live with me?' I repeat like an idiot, feeling his fingers stroking the edge of my pants.

'If you do.'

I nod.

'I've thought about doing it with you for so long, Katie. I don't know how I'm going to get back behind that piano . . .'

And so that is how Pete Oram moves into my flat. And into my life, properly, at last, with his collection of lamps, his books on dead rock 'n' roll stars and his wardrobe rack of black, leather and denim.

A few days later, on February 14th, after another build-up in the paper about Jim's prediction, I am sent to the beach as the day ends to make one last attempt to look for the shark with the desk in its stomach – and seven million quid. Dozens of people have been milling around on the shore all day, apparently, waiting for the miracle. 'Or even just a desk,' Guy says desperately, as he continues to search all the beaches in East Sussex to see if anything has washed up. 'Or even just a few five-pound notes.'

He's had snappers on standby since sunrise, just in case any of the London papers or TV crews have decided to turn up and cover the story too – though wisely, they haven't – and now he's beginning to lose hope.

Just as every branch of the media catches a rash at the same time, it also gets the collywobbles at the same time. Nobody's ringing. Nobody's emailing. Suddenly, nobody wants to know.

'Charlatan,' Guy says flatly, shoving his desk drawer shut as if Jim's head is inside it.

'He was right about everything else. You know he was. The name of the train in Sri Lanka. Nelson Mandela. And lots of other things.'

'Lucky guesses.'

I look across at poor Alison's empty desk, which has been cleared for Courtney's impending arrival.

'The shark might turn up tomorrow,' I say, although I don't think it will.

Guy cracks his neck. 'I've got a headache which isn't responding to aspirin. I'm going home.'

From my Edwardian lady journal . . .

FEBRUARY 2005
Happy Valentine's Day to me after two years of nothing at all. Pete's moving in. So I'm going to have to find somewhere safe to hide this diary. But I'm in love again. Not what I expected . . . but totally fantastic. What's that song Pete sings about not looking back? That's exactly how it feels. And I'm not faking it, for once. I actually mean it. DO NOT LOOK BACK.

Later, Jim calls with his new, secret address. He has quickly packed his bags and left the studio he was renting in Brighton, and has decided to slip quietly into a new flat in Hastings an hour down the coast.

A friend of a client found it for him after seeing all the publicity in the paper, and has promised him a safe haven, for a while.

His flat is in the Old Town, at the top of a steep incline, where he says he has discovered a thing called twittens – narrow old pathways which connect all the houses together.

'And if you know your way around the twittens,' he tells me on the phone, 'you'll know how to get away from anybody. Even someone from your newspaper.'

I take the phone into the bath with me and keep the water running while Jim talks. I have a choice of two Christmas present potions – one is honey and vanilla, and the other is something blue with seaweed in it. In the end I pour both of them in as the steam rises.

'The thing is,' I manage the tap with one hand, and the phone with the other, 'Molloy and Guy have this theory about our paper. In their view, you're either a local hero or a local zero. So what they've been trying to do is build you up as a local hero.'

'And now there's no shark, I'll be a zero,' Jim concludes.

'It won't be that bad,' I lie.

Then I think of something else, as the bubbles begin to froth in the water and a sweet vanilla smell fills the bathroom.

'What does your bucket tell you? Have you looked?'

'Nothing. No.' Jim sighs.

'Don't you want to?'

'It's not that. I just see what I'm shown,' Jim explains. 'It's not on tap the way people think.'

'You'll have to find yourself a nice local girl in Hastings now you've moved,' I say, changing the subject in a silly, bright voice. It's all I can think of to cheer him up. The thought of Jim, alone, hiding in a town where he doesn't know anyone, is suddenly more than I can bear.

'Oh yeah.' He half laughs. 'Women. Another thing I'm not seeing in my bucket. Or at least—' he stops himself, then starts again. 'Not since the last time.'

Then a few days after this, one of the subs is working his way through a selection of syndicated features when he makes a strangled sound, rather like a football fan watching a goal being scored.

'Garr!' he yells as he comes over to my desk waving a piece of paper. 'Got it!'

'Got what?' I ask. He's a part-time staffer who we hardly ever see, except when we're working on the Sudoku section.

'It's all in the way you see it.' He folds his arms. 'And in the way you say it.'

'What is? Clear as mud. Sorry.'

'The shark ate the desk on February 14th. Is that what this psychic guy said?'

'A seven-million-pound shark.'

' "The Physical Impossibility of Death in the Mind of Someone Living", by Damien Hirst,' the sub reads out from a press-release fax. 'A four-point-three metre shark preserved in formaldehyde, sold for seven million pounds by Charles Saatchi, who paid fifty thousand pounds for it in 1991. And the desk was sold just after Valentine's Day. It belonged to John F. Kennedy and it was engraved with his monogram. It sold for a lousy four hundred and fifty-two thousand, eight hundred US dollars. So' – the sub smirks at me – 'the shark ate the desk. By several million pounds. It ate it alive.'

I stare at him. They don't bring him in to sort out the Sudoku for nothing.

Then I call Jim immediately, but his phone is switched off.

He was right. Wrong, but right. And I am dying to let him know.

CHAPTER SEVEN

Russell Crowe tells an Australian magazine that he was targeted for kidnapping by Al Qaeda when he was filming *Gladiator*, *A Beautiful Mind*, and *Master and Commander*, and was given FBI protection. Bill Gates is given an honorary knighthood.

Thus, Jim is a sad old local zero in the paper one day (after what Guy and Molloy are calling the Shark Debacle) and an amazing local hero the next. He's in, he's out, and then he's in again.

It makes no sense. But then, nothing in our paper has added up, either for me or anyone else, for ages. Teenage single mothers are the devil incarnate on Tuesday, and brave battlers with sick kiddies on Wednesday. George Bush is a warmonger, George Bush is saving the world from terrorism. Chips are bad for you, chips are good for you. No wonder, looking at Guy's face these days, I get the distinct impression I could shake him and watch his pupils rattle around in his head, like one of those children's birthday cards.

At least Molloy has an excuse, because he drinks. But Guy?

'Where is he?' he asks me excitedly as soon as I get to work. 'Where's Noztradamus, Katie?'

'Not sure,' I lie.

125

'I can forgive you the tape, and the shenanigans with the computer, if you'll just do the right thing, Katie,' Guy makes a bored, tired face, 'and tell me where he's gone.'

'I don't know.'

'Yes you do, and I don't need to tell you this is gross disloyalty. Look, maybe we were a bit heavy-handed with him before, but we're looking at a different story treatment for him now. Molloy and I were rather impressed with the Russell Crowe thing.'

'How can Jim trust you now?'

'He's done all right out of all that publicity.' Guy draws himself up.

'No he hasn't. He didn't want it in the first place. He only did the interview to help the shop get more customers. You and Molloy made him look like an idiot with all that stuff about the shark with seven million quid in its stomach. And for your information – though why Courtney can't tell you this I don't know – the shop's sacked him. They don't want someone who looks like a fraud.'

'All right, all right.' Guy backs off, finally leaving my desk. He doesn't so much hover around it these days as strut around it, as if he's on parade.

I'm sure the only reason he hasn't sacked me yet is because he thinks I know where Jim is hiding.

But . . . I'm not telling. Despite the fact that there is a part of me – the old journalist part – which feels like standing over Jim with a tape-recorder, there is another, saner, part which is content to leave him where he is, tucked quietly away in Hastings with a window that looks out over all the rooftops, across to the sea.

Jim described his new life to me from a phonebox on Hastings seafront last week and it sounded idyllic. If it's choppy on the water he has an early-morning surf in his wetsuit as the sun comes up, and then home-made organic vegetable soup on the stove as the sun goes down.

In Hastings, that funny little fishermen's town, Jim seems to have found some kind of sanctuary. Peaceful walks and cobbled lanes, meditation and long baths, currant buns from the bakery, and a chance to get his bearings back after the madness of February.

And . . . he needs to get the visions in his bucket back again, too. Jim says they've stopped since the shock of Guy and Molloy's story.

In the meantime, there are other news stories to finish. I continue teasing out my notes on the missing cats, widening the circle of people I'm speaking to, knocking on doors as far away as Newhaven and Lancing. There are plenty of animals involved, but so far not one person will go on the record, or remarkably, even off the record, and talk to me about local witchcraft.

I play with the idea of confronting Courtney, and then intuitively let it drop. There is something about Courtney Creely that flashes warning signs every time I think about her.

I tried writing something about her in my journal a couple of nights ago. When I looked up from my book I saw a pigeon knocking itself against the window.

I ripped out the page and closed the book.

Pete's tsunami concert money has finally made it to Sri Lanka, in the form of three trucks with food and medical supplies on board, but when I try to pitch it to Guy as a follow-up story, he just rolls his eyes and tells me everyone's fed up with the tsunami and I should be trying harder.

Then, for good measure, he makes me accompany Courtney to the Paradise Bingo Club, who are running a frozen chicken promotion as part of their March Madness month.

A freelance photographer who doesn't get much

127

work comes with us. The idea is to snap Courtney in her finery, waving a winning bingo coupon in the air, while a man dressed as a chicken, and looking suitably mad, hands her a fistful of fifties.

It's the third time Courtney has acted as an unofficial model for the paper since she started working as Guy's PA. So far, we have been treated to Courtney jumping up and down in the air wearing an extremely tight Brighton & Hove Albion football strip, and Courtney reclining in a bubble bath with two slices of cucumber over her eyes ('Get Gorgeous For Spring!')

The bingo hall is half empty and smells vaguely of spilled beer and wee. Then the man from Paradise Bingo appears, wearing one of the worst ties I have ever seen, and tells us we can all have a free game while we wait for the snapper to set up his lights.

I haven't been here for years. A group of us used to turn up on Friday night sometimes in a self-conscious, studenty way. But it was never much fun. There were too many sad old people spending their pensions and taking their losses and wins far too seriously. And too many mad people standing by themselves, queuing for the cheap chicken and gravy in the cafeteria.

Courtney is wearing a low-cut green T-shirt with daisies on the front today (nipples, as always, on standby for the photographer) and green shorts. It's all been borrowed from the boutique in Ship Street, she tells me, and if she asks nicely they might sell it to her for half the price afterwards.

The regular bingo players start staring when the three of us troop in, and I expect they'll still be staring after us hours later. Fast reactions don't seem to be their strong point.

The man in the chicken costume cannot speak English very well and has to be steered by the elbow – or rather the wing – whenever our photographer wants him to do something.

And because nobody actually seems to know his name, and he doesn't seem able to tell us with his giant feathery head, he is politely referred to as Chicken Man for the rest of the shoot.

'Over here, please, Chicken Man,' says our photographer, steering him towards a vacant table. Then he mimics what he wants him to do, which is, rather bizarrely, hold a forkful of roast chicken and gravy up to his beak.

'But that makes him a cannibal,' I say.

'House!' yells Courtney with her mouth wide open, waving her coupon. 'House! House!'

She has every number that has been called. The lot.

'Goodness,' says the day manager, quickly stepping behind her shoulder to check. 'Well, you're connected through to Power Bingo at the moment – that's the national competition as well. So that's fifteen thousand four hundred and twenty-five pounds and seventy-five pence.' He checks it again.

'Faark,' Courtney opens her mouth again, sounding not unlike the man in the chicken suit should be sounding. 'Faark me.'

The first thing I think is, it's rigged. Set up for us, probably by Guy, and the day manager should win an Oscar for best performance. But the next thing I think is, nobody ever, ever wins at Paradise Bingo. Especially not £15,000. And especially not for some crummy piece in our paper.

Courtney hugs the form to her chest, which makes her breasts bulge out again in the tight green top. Our photographer, who has momentarily stopped shooting, starts clicking the shutter again.

Then Courtney calls Guy, while the chicken man takes his head off and makes a great show of panting with his tongue hanging out. His fringe is plastered down on his forehead. He looks East European, and I don't think he has the slightest idea what's just

129

happened – probably just as well. How much do you get paid for dressing up as a chicken these days? Certainly not £15,000 a minute, which is what Courtney has just earned.

Her chest is heaving now – I think she may be genuinely hyperventilating with shock. And then finally Guy answers.

'Babe. Babe. Baby!' she squeals. 'I just won fifteen thousand quid on the bingo!'

Twenty minutes later Guy arrives.

He is breathing heavily, as if he has just run all the way here in his Hush Puppies. Which he probably has.

Courtney throws her arms around him, and part of her left leg too, and Guy automatically snaps his eyes shut, as if by not seeing us we are not seeing him. He looks embarrassed and pleased all at the same time.

'I won it,' Courtney shows him her circled bingo coupon while the day manager hovers, like a proud parent, with a queue of staff gradually trickling in behind him to see the winner.

'Of course it's not the biggest afternoon jackpot this year,' he tells Guy. 'We had someone take fifty thousand at the beginning of January.'

Lying toad. But then, maybe it's time that Paradise Bingo had a bit of luck too, as well as Courtney. Once this is on our front cover – the chicken man, Courtney's green shorts, the huge wads of cash – people will be fighting to get through the door.

'I'm going to fly you and me to Paris,' Courtney gazes into Guy's eyes. 'How would you like that, babe? We'll go on Friday night and come back on Monday morning, shall we?'

Guy jingles the change in his pockets, looking like a schoolboy who has just been told his tuck box has turned up. From the expression on his face I gather that Paris means sex – finally – and consequently he is having difficulty standing upright.

Then I think about all the missing cats, and the pentagram spell with money written on one corner, and I wonder if that's how Courtney has just secured her bingo win. But that way madness lies, and it's best not to think about it.

The following day, Molloy secures a warehouse full of dried sage and onion stuffing. The warehouse is in Newhaven and it belongs to an old friend of his who has three shops along the coast which sell everything for 99p.

The biscuits in our tea room often come from the 99p man, and the ingredients list is always in Arabic. They are vile, but there a lot of them.

I'm invited to a mini-meeting with Molloy, Guy and some of the people from marketing and advertising, to discuss the dried sage and onion stuffing plan.

'Synergy,' Molloy declares, smelling of Scotch as usual, as he pushes the shots of Courtney and the Chicken Man around the table. 'The idea is, we'll give you the sage and onion stuffing if you turn up to the bingo and bring home the free chicken.'

'Genius,' someone says, almost sincerely, and almost on the spur of the moment.

'We've got the girl,' Molloy slaps one of the newly printed shots of Courtney in her shorts, 'we've got the girl and the big cash win, and now we've got the freebies.'

God, Molloy reeks. And the peppermint humbugs he's always sucking just make him smell worse.

'So,' Guy puts on his serious face. 'How's this all actually going to work for us in practical terms?'

'The synergy is,' Molloy leans back in his chair, 'the punter turns up to the bingo on Saturday night with three coupons from the paper from Monday, Wednesday and Friday, gets his free chicken, and then a gorgeous girl gives him the free stuffing to go with it,' he smirks, 'so to speak.'

On Monday morning we go out with a big red cover splash on Courtney with Monopoly notes stuffed down her bikini top (nobody in the art department is either willing or able to go to the bank and get real money.) Plus there's a last-minute stroke of genius from Molloy – a packet of instant mash, as well, for the first hundred people in the queue on Saturday night. We'll be buying the mash ourselves, apparently, but Molloy thinks it will be worth it, and his wife has seen it on special at ASDA.

On Monday evening, Molloy rings circulation with a smile on his face, anticipating the best, because he's already heard we have sold out all along North Street. 'Result,' he says, trying to look cool about it and failing. 'We were all out, everywhere, by half past four. A stampede on sales to the over-sixties, apparently.'

'We're back in business,' Guy keeps telling anyone who will listen. 'We're back in business!'

'With pensioners,' one of the subs adds under his breath, but Guy can't stop grinning.

Then on Saturday afternoon, when Pete is at rehearsal with his band, I put the tape in my pocket and take the train to Hastings to try and find Jim, who has not been answering his new mobile phone.

The sun is shining in Hastings when I arrive and people are out on the streets without their coats for the first time in ages – two girls in short denim skirts have even daringly covered themselves in fake tan. I take my time walking along the seafront. And then I pick up a map from the tourist information centre, looking past the adventure golf, mini golf and crazy golf to try and find Jim's flat.

The smell of fish and chips is driving me mad, so I give in and buy some chips, drenching them in vinegar. Then I go into a second-hand clothes shop on the high street and mindlessly try on a red bobble hat that makes me look deranged, then I wander out as the sun disappears behind the clouds again.

I finally find Jim's flat and press the buzzer. He lives in a small block of four flats, tucked away at the end of a narrow, winding pathway.

'You're in love with Pete Oram,' is the first thing he says when he opens the door.

'Nice to see you too,' I try to joke, but he's having none of it.

I have seldom seen Jim look so serious.

We go inside the flat, which is full of someone else's furniture – I can't imagine Jim owning so many beige velvet cushions and books about gardening – and I sit down on the sofa while he settles into an armchair in front of me.

'Be careful with Pete,' he says at last.

'Is this a bucket thing, or just your opinion?'

'How much do you know about his life?' Jim sighs.

'A bit.'

'He's going to be rich and famous,' Jim explains. 'I mean *seriously*. Are you ready for that?'

'So you keep saying. It was great that you told him that, by the way. I think it keeps him going. He got thrown off his record label.'

'I warned him that would happen if he wouldn't do what they wanted,' Jim stretches out his long legs in the armchair.

'Did you?'

Jim shrugs and gets up to put the kettle on. 'One thing I want you to write in this book', he says, 'is the myth about psychics being all powerful. Do you want to know the truth? Nobody ever listens to you.' Jim sticks his head around the kitchen door and smiles at me. 'Nobody listens. Especially to the hard bits. At the end of the day, Katie, all anyone wants to hear are the good bits, the easy stuff.'

I think about Pete for a minute. I'll be home soon.

He'll be waiting for me and I'll be home. Despite everything Jim is saying, I can't wait.

'So how's your love life anyway?' I coax Jim when he brings back two mugs of tea.

'Oh, great,' Jim puts on a deadpan expression. 'I had a cute blonde girl at the bakery interested for about two seconds, and then she came down with meningitis.'

'Really?'

'I was trying to get to the point where I could ask her out, and then when I turned up the next morning they said that was it. She was hospitalized overnight. Gone. And I didn't even find out her second name.'

I think of Courtney and her spell to keep Jim for herself, and push the thought away.

'And how's everything else?' I ask as chirpily as I can.

'I'm really going to need that book deal,' Jim says. 'The rent's due in two weeks and I haven't had a new client since Cornucopia sacked me.'

'What about round here?' I ask.

'I'm still trying to lie low,' Jim says. 'Until the shark thing goes away.'

Then he stands up, and I realize he has lost even more weight. The baggy white cricket trousers are hanging off him.

'I haven't eaten much since all that.' Jim looks at me, looking at him. 'Haven't slept much either.'

'Well, you look OK,' I say. And he does – like anyone on the coast who spends all their time on the water in the winter sun, he has even managed to achieve a tan.

Without realizing what I am doing, I find myself getting up from my chair to hug him. 'Poor you.'

'Thanks,' he says, hugging me back, and then he steps away and smiles at me.

We spend the rest of the day watching *Gone With the*

Wind on DVD, which the flat owner has left in a cupboard along with sticky bottles of liqueur, which we fantasize about raiding but leave alone, and a box of leftover Christmas biscuits, which we eat on the grounds that they are bound to go off.

'Come on,' I tell Jim. 'You've got to eat something.'

Then I remember why I'm there and hand him the tape.

'Thanks. I know they could have sacked you for taking this.'

'Oh yeah.'

'It means a lot that you did this for me.'

'My fault in the first place.' I try to make a joke of it.

'No really, Katie. Thanks.'

'I'd better go.'

'OK.'

For some strange reason I am still registering the hug from a few minutes before. I wonder if he is too?

'Take care, Katie,' Jim smiles as the credits for *Gone With the Wind* roll down the screen.

'When can I see you again?' I ask, suddenly thinking about the book he's asked me to write and hoping I don't sound too pushy.

'Any time.'

And then I go, but the hug remains with me all the way back to Brighton on the train.

When I get home, Pete is in the middle of packing up his flat and cleaning every centimetre of the bath. He is also naked except for a towel around his waist, which he says is the only thing to wear when you're scrubbing the bathroom from top to bottom.

'I thought you'd be at rehearsal for ages,' I say, once we have gone from the bathroom to my bed and back again. I think we lost the towel somewhere in the corridor.

'Couldn't wait to see you.' Pete kisses me. 'Shall we do it again? In the bath?'

But I don't want to do it again – not in the bath or anywhere else – because while we were on the bedroom floor just now, I saw another plastic bag full of pills under the bed.

I retrieve my bra and pants from the edge of the bath and put them back on, then I search for my jeans and jumper, which Pete has managed to hurl several feet outside into the corridor.

'What's wrong?' he stares at me.

'Nothing.'

'What?' he persists.

'I saw some stuff under your bed,' I finally manage to get the words out. I'm not even going to tell him about the ecstasy I found in his jacket.

Pete nods.

Then he wanders out to find a blanket, wraps himself in it and wanders back.

'I flog them sometimes.' He sits on the edge of the bath. 'It pays the rent.'

'Well when you're finally paying me rent –' I hear myself saying, 'not that I want it – it would be nicer for me, if the money didn't come from there.'

Of course we have not discussed money yet. Of course not. How can you possibly discuss bills when you're in love with Peter Oram?

But there it is. We have barely finished taking each other by storm on the bedroom floor, and now look. I'm ruining it all with my boring, practical nonsense.

'Just cover your share of the electricity and the phone,' I say, 'but not with drug money. All right?'

Silence.

Pete looks like someone who's been rescued from the tsunami, I think, as I watch him huddled in the blanket.

'I'm a disgrace,' he says.

'Yes you are.'

'Can I give you some good news?' he says at last.

'Sure.'

'One of the blokes who was doing the concert with me says he can get me a free website.'

'Great.'

'Don't be like that.' Pete sighs.

'Honestly, Pete, I'm pleased.'

'Well,' he pulls the blanket around him again, 'it means I can put all me music on there. Everything I've ever recorded. And videos.'

'Well that gives you a bit more freedom, then,' I say. I wish I hadn't talked to him about the drugs or the bills.

'He's not charging me anything because he's a fan,' Pete goes on, 'and he says he can have it up in a month. And a blog. And all the photos. So I can have songs' – he ticks the list off on his fingers – 'pictures, video, song lyrics, blog, the lot. It's the beginning of the beginning of the beginning, Katie.'

Then suddenly he gets up in his blanket, like a Native American chief, and strides out of the bathroom. While he's gone I check my face in the mirror. I still need a haircut. And my eyebrows need plucking. But for some reason things like eyebrows and haircuts have gone out of the window since Pete came into my life.

Too much sex, too many all-night conversations, too much wine, too much music. The fridge is empty and my hair is hanging in my eyes.

Then he comes back with a collection of small, transparent plastic bags pinched between his fingers. Without looking at me he places them carefully on top of the loo, then systematically flushes the contents away.

'Polly was telling me about a job that's going down at the Marina,' he says as if nothing has happened. 'They want someone to play the piano in the casino.

137

It's about time I introduced myself to the novelty of playing music for money.' He pulls a face.

'So when were you talking to Polly?' I try to sound casual.

'This morning.' Pete shrugs. 'Ben's been poorly. He broke a tooth at his new school.'

I think of the cost of a train fare to York, where Polly is now, trying to build a new life, and I think of the amount of money Pete probably has to find each week to cover the cost of Ben, and I immediately feel so ashamed of myself and my stupid bills that I start turning red.

'Sorry,' I say. 'I know you wouldn't have been selling stuff if you didn't have to.'

'Nineteen fifties girl,' Pete gets up and holds me.

'Just be with me,' I tell him. 'I don't need rent. Sorry. That's all.'

'Sore lips,' Pete says, stroking my mouth gently with his finger. 'Been in the wind.'

'I keep hearing that Kate Bush song, "The Hounds of Love", in my head,' I tell him.

'Must be sinking in at last then.'

'Bear with me, Pete. I haven't had anyone since Andrew. Not really.'

'I'll bear with you.'

And then he reaches behind the bathroom mirror – one of the few objects he hasn't packed up yet – and produces another clear plastic envelope, this time full of notes.

'You change me,' he says, 'and I'll change you. Now, this is how I'm going to change you. This is the money I got last night from selling the last of me stuff. Now I can either flush this down the loo as well, or I can use it to press enough CDs of me new songs to get myself back out there again. Alternatively,' he meets my eyes, 'I can tinkle away at the casino for the rest of the year pretending I'm Richard bloody Clayderman.

138

So what do you want your new boyfriend to do, Katie?'

Then he pulls me into his blanket, without even waiting for an answer, as if the conversation is now closed. And I suppose it is. Chased all the way up hill and down dale by the hounds of love again.

CHAPTER EIGHT

I have a bad cold for a couple of days, so I take some time off work and read the paper as if I wasn't working on it, for a change.

Guy has run a story on the chess champion Bobby Fischer in a single column in the sports section. After eight months' detention in Japan, he has been released and flown to Iceland.

'The King of Chess is free at last,' I recite to Jim on the phone, remembering his prediction.

'Yeah, I heard it on the radio,' he says.

'So what are you going to do about this tape then?'

'I don't know. Wait and see.'

'Did you play it all back?'

'Yeah. I scared myself. I don't want to do anything about the tape just yet. It's enough that your paper doesn't have it.'

I cough, and then I can't stop coughing.

'You sound awful,' Jim says. 'You shouldn't be talking, your throat sounds like sandpaper.'

'It's just a cold,' I explain through my nose. 'Pete's gone out to get me something from the chemist.'

Then . . .

'Let me try something,' Jim offers. 'Can you hang up and go back to bed for a while? I just want to see if this works.'

'If what works?' I ask, but I'm feeling too ill to argue, so I follow his mysterious instructions and retreat back beneath the blankets.

It's the kind of cold where you blow your nose every few minutes, and I am steadily running out of tissues and am now reduced to rolls of loo paper, which I keep losing down the side of the bed. I feel tired and achey, and my throat is sore.

I lie down, wishing Pete would come back with the aspirin and cough medicine from the chemist, and then I give in as sleep overtakes me.

When I wake up it's just after 2 a.m., and Pete is asleep beside me. How did that happen? I try to retrace my steps and realize the last thing I did was ring Jim, just after 4 p.m.

Then I realize something else. I feel fine.

I get up to go to the loo and look in the mirror. The back of my throat is no longer red. And I can breathe. My head doesn't ache any more, my nose is no longer stuffed up. I could probably sing the national anthem now if I felt like it.

Pete gets up too after this and follows me into the bathroom.

'Sleep's the best thing,' he says, rubbing my shoulders. 'I thought I'd let you sleep. You were out like a light when I came back.'

'Jim did something,' I hear myself saying.

'Did he?'

'Yeah, he did something – I don't know what – he just told me to go to bed, and now I feel OK.' I sniff experimentally. 'All clear. No sore throat. No headache. No cold.'

I go back to bed while I listen to Pete running the shower, and then he comes back in a few minutes later, rubbing himself with a towel.

The Oram body clock often works like this. Black coffee at 6 a.m, showers in the middle of the night,

141

fried bacon sandwiches at 3 p.m., Enid Blyton by torchlight under the bedclothes at 2 a.m. (recited to me, for no apparent reason, in a heavy Jamaican accent) and frantic sex during the 7 p.m. news.

'Someone recorded the tsunami concert we did and put it on the internet,' he says, yawning and cuddling into me as he tries to warm up again after his shower.

'Oh,' I try to sound sympathetic, though all I want to do is sleep.

'No, it's great,' he whispers in the dark. 'They've had twenty thousand downloads since Tuesday. All from Beatle-freak websites, mind, but it's a start.'

I think about this. Part of me is still trying to come to terms with the fact that I suddenly feel better. What on earth did Jim do?

'But you don't get any money from it?' I ask.

'Nah,' Pete spoons into me again. 'It's a charity thing. And it's all illegal anyway, from the fact that nobody cleared the songs in the first place, to the fact that it's now down to internet bootlegs.' He shakes his head. 'It's just the demand, that's all. People want to listen to me again. Twenty thousand of them, from all over the world, all wanting to hear me play "Eleanor Rigby" on me piano. I thought it was interesting.'

'Could be the start of something,' I offer. Suddenly I feel unbelievably, incredibly tired, as if I've just been anaesthesized.

'And I changed me mind. I took that job at the casino.' He holds my hand. 'So I'll have the money in for the bills. And I don't care what you say, I'm gonna give you the rent.'

'Did you? Do you want to?' I can feel myself crashing now, unable to talk any more.

'I did it for you, Katie,' is the last thing I hear.

'Love you,' I manage before I black out altogether. And even as I hear myself saying it, I realize it's the first time I have ever told him.

When I wake up, the curtains are drawn and the sun is up but Pete has gone. I look at the clock. It's almost 4 p.m.

I put a hand on my throat but it still feels fine. I count the hours, and realize I have been asleep for almost twenty-four of them in a row, unless you count the conversation with Pete in the middle of the night.

Then I look at my side of the bed and see one of my old teddy bears propped up next to a note.

'Sweet dreams,' it says. Followed by, 'Going away for a bit. Sorting my head out. Love you, Pete.'

What?

I read it again. I feel as if someone has just pulled off all the bedclothes.

There is a message on my mobile from Guy, asking me when I'm coming back, but I ignore it. All I can think of is ringing Pete.

Predictably, all I get is voicemail.

I look at the note again. What does he mean, going away for a bit and sorting his head out? Of all the stupid things he could have written, that has to be the worst. And the fact that he thinks he can get away with something so lame makes me even angrier.

When the phone rings a few minutes later, I almost drop it in my rush to take the call, but it's not Pete, it's Jim.

'I'm better,' is all I can think of to say to him.

'I thought so. I felt it,' he says.

'What did you do?'

'Nothing,' Jim replies. Then he corrects himself. 'OK. I asked the spirit people to help you get better.' He suddenly sounds embarrassed. 'I did it the other day as well. I had a headache. I asked for it to go away and it did. And then the woman next door to me had shingles. So I gave that some energy and . . . same thing. I feel as if they're working with me. It's like healing energy doubled, or something.'

'Right. Well. It worked. I'm impressed. Thank you.'

'Katie,' Jim interrupts me suddenly. 'What's up? What's happened?'

'Can you just mind your own psychic business, please?'

'It's Pete.'

'Yeah. All right. He's gone. He left a stupid note. I could kill him. It's such a cliché. Got to get his head together, needs some space, blah blah blah.'

'Oh.'

'Actually, Jim,' I hear myself saying, 'I'm a bit upset. So I might go. You know. Is that all right?'

'Sure, sure. But call me,' he finishes. And then he hangs up.

I go back to bed, try to read a book which someone gave me for Christmas, give up, go to the bathroom, splash my face to stop myself from crying, cry anyway, go back to bed again, get up again, have a ham sandwich, and then I get all my photo albums and curl up on the couch with them.

I suddenly feel very close to Andrew, almost as if he's here, though I know he can't be. Perhaps it's the combination of a sudden departure, a space on the other side of the bed and an unexpected note. Pete has brought it all back again.

The photographs of Andrew in my photo album begin, in chronological order, several months after we got together. Even though I was in love with him about ten minutes after I met him, I felt too stupid to take any pictures of him at the beginning of our relationship. Then he confessed to the same thing, and then we just went mad for a day, armed with disposable cardboard cameras along the seafront.

People always said how much Andrew looked like his father, but looking at the photographs now, I am only just realizing it for the first time. They have the same chin, same eyes and same slight stoop – they are both tall men.

Were tall men, I correct myself. I keep present-tensing Andrew and it's got to stop. He's gone. Gone, gone, gone.

I go through all the photograph albums and let myself cry.

Andrew had a habit of pinching me on the arm whenever the camera shutter was about to click, and after a while I knew it was coming, so all the pictures of us together show him looking deadpan and trying not to laugh, while I'm grinning like an idiot, antici-pating the pinch. In every single photograph I look stupidly happy.

And then there are the photographs he took of me at home, when he'd finally bought some wildly expensive camera. They are all taken using black and white film, which he was obsessed with for a while, and I look most unlike myself, although he always said he liked those photographs best.

When he killed himself I spent a lot of time trying to work out how he saw me. I suppose the answer is here, in these black and white shots.

I look as if I'm in my own little world, happy but self-contained. My own person. With him, but self-absorbed enough to be miles away, too.

If only I'd been in Andrew World, instead of Katie World. It was the first thing I thought of when I read the note he'd left behind.

You can see the self-absorption in my eyes, in all the photographs. I'm holding Andrew's hand, but my head is somewhere else. Living in the future. Dreaming about tomorrow, in the cottage with the roses round the door.

The jacket I'm wearing in one of the photographs is an all-purpose black suit jacket – it cost me a fortune – which I also wore to his funeral. I don't have it any more – I couldn't even bear giving it to Oxfam, so it went straight in the rubbish. I remember tipping half a can of baked beans over it.

I have almost filled up my Edwardian lady journal with Pete, but now all I want to do is write about Andrew.

MARCH 20, 2005
Jim cured my cold with the help of some spirit people. Every time he talks about them I wonder if Andrew is one of them. But he says not. If Andrew *was* here right now I'd ask him so many questions. Then again, maybe that's why he's avoiding me. In life, as in death, he never liked me interrogating him.

I think back to Andrew's annoying ex-girlfriend Philippa, the one who wouldn't go away.

That phase of our relationship involved weekly interrogations from me, with the result that Andrew shut down altogether and stopped speaking to me.

I think about the bad times, and the good times with Andrew, and compare them to Pete. There is no comparison, I realize. Not because Andrew is easier than Pete, or Pete is easier than Andrew. It's just that . . . I have to admit it. Andrew was the real thing, and I know in my heart that Pete Oram is not. There, I've said it. Or at least I've written it down, in my Edwardian lady journal.

I close the book. Then I realize how terrified I am, despite everything, that Pete will leave me and go back to Polly, or just disappear altogether.

The phone rings. It's Jim.

'He'll be back,' he says.

'For God's sake, Jim.'

'I nearly didn't call you,' he says. 'I don't want to mess around with your life. But I saw it just then.

Pete's coming back and he's got a present for you. It's like shoes, or boots.'

'What?'

'I was running the water in the sink,' Jim says patiently, 'for the washing up. And I saw his face in the water, then your face and then this shoebox.'

'Oh.'

And then Jim is gone.

I return to my photo albums. I feel calmer, I realize. And I wonder if that's down to Jim Gabriel with his new-found healing powers, or if it's because I've finally let myself look at the photographs for the first time since Andrew died.

My favourite photographs of Andrew were taken in a toy animal shop near the Lanes. It's where the teddy bear came from – the one that Pete has just used to prop up his note to me. Andrew found a ridiculous fluffy green python in there, and was mucking around with it before he knew I was taking a photograph, so he looks unposed and real – more like himself, in fact, than in any other photo I have of him.

They asked me if I wanted to see Andrew's body after he died, and I said no. I had a few nightmares about it, of course, but I have always been comforted by the fact that most of the pictures in my head must have come from gory late-night TV and not the reality.

His mother said he looked peaceful. I believe her. I expect everyone looks peaceful, once the professionals have done their thing.

I go back to the toy snake photograph now and stroke Andrew's face. He looks unshaven, tired and happy in the photograph – and all I ever wanted.

'Fuck you, Andrew,' I write in my journal. The demure lady on the front with her parasol and crinoline would be shocked. But there, I've put it down. Everything I've felt since he died in one neat sentence.

147

Then I cross it out, of course. I'm like that.

The next day, I return to work to find that Guy has framed the front cover featuring Courtney (and her nipples) in the green outfit, flanked by the chicken man, underneath the Paradise Bingo sign, and with the free stuffing headline. He has chosen a beautiful and no doubt highly expensive frame for it, and it's now hanging up on the wall, between the photocopier and the water dispenser.

'They'll be framing the loo paper round here next,' one of the subs says.

Guy and Courtney have been to Paris for what sounds like a weekend blitz of hedonism using Courtney's bingo winnings, and now, it would appear, they have also shagged.

I know this because Guy is smoking out of the window less and smiling more, and he is also freely groping her bottom at every opportunity, as if he suddenly owns it. There is also less frantic wheeling around in the swivelling office chairs. And Courtney is looking infinitely more superior than she did the last time I saw her.

Along with the framed front cover, I hear there are also three new additions to the social side of office life. Their names are Lou, Jan and Deb, and they are Courtney's flatmates, and members of her witches' coven.

It's the most exciting thing that has happened at the paper in a long time and everyone is talking about them.

'They turn up when the sky grows dark,' Claudia emails me from across the office, adding a smiley face with its tongue hanging out in disgust. 'It's just like Macbeth. The three witches and their mistress all go to the pub with us, then they disappear before the sun comes up.'

'Joining us for a drink later?' Guy asks cheerfully as

I manage to crawl through my first day back, finally laying the last of my dozens of unanswered emails to rest. By us, I suppose he means him, Courtney and the coven.

I think about it. On one level, I can't think of anything worse. But on the other hand I'm curious. So in the end, I get my coat and bag and sit on the edge of my desk, politely reading yesterday's paper, while Courtney and Guy flirt shamelessly as we wait for the others.

Courtney's flatmates all work in the same hairdresser's, it turns out – some place I've never heard of near the London Road station.

'You should get them to do your hair,' Courtney smiles sweetly, looking up at the top of my head as if it needs fixing. I suppose it does. But I'm not going to a bunch of witches for my cut and blowdry.

Then, finally, they arrive. Jan, Lou and Deb. Long red hair, long blonde hair and no hair at all – just a neatly shaved head and a few ear piercings.

I am introduced and realize I can't be bothered to remember who's who, although I suspect Jan will be the easiest of the lot to remember, because she not only bears an uncanny resemblance to Courtney, she also appears to be Guy's favourite.

'Hello, darling,' Guy raises his eyebrows at her, kissing her firmly on the lips before moving on to the other two, neatly pecking the blonde on the cheek and giving the shaven-headed one a long hug.

I stare and I stare. So do the other few remaining people who are left behind in the office. If Guy Booth's parents could see him now, I think, there would be serious discussions about the palatial flat with the English Channel views, the spa and the rather large mortgage. The signet ring would be seized and permission to use the family name denied.

Eventually we make our way out of the office and

down along the seafront to a pub called the Merchant Arms, which I last visited at some point in the late Nineties, when it was one of the many Brighton venues where you could count on seeing Pete play.

Pete. I have given him five seconds of headspace and now I'm dismissing him again. I try to focus on Guy and Courtney instead, and not far behind them the three witches, who are linking arms and giggling wildly, as their long, waist-length hair gets blown around in the wind.

Jan, the red-haired one who looks like Courtney – they must use the same hair dye – sidles up to me.

'Isn't Guy cute?' She nudges me. 'We were just saying what a cute little bum he has.'

I can't think of anything to say, so I leave the subject of Guy's bottom alone and hope she will go away.

'What about Courtney winning all that money?' Jan tries again.

'Yeah.'

Then Jan smiles and gives up, running back to join the others.

I wonder for a minute why you cannot be a witch and wear a nice white trouser suit, like a morning TV presenter. Or a big, draped pashmina and a pair of sensible flat-heeled shoes, like Guy's mother, whose one and only visit to the paper has never been forgotten by anybody.

I try to imagine Guy's mother being introduced to Courtney and her friends, and fail.

And here's another thing. Why do they have to cast their spells in the nude? And why do they have to be so over-perfumed, over-pierced and stripy-stockinged?

I suppose witches are the new rock stars. It had to happen. A bunch of nobodies trying to be somebodies, under the influence of a lot of bad American TV.

The most staggering thing about the Courtney/Jan/Lou/Deb combination, though, is their cleavage count.

Watching them bob around in the office just now was like standing in a field full of watermelons. I've already decided that the one with the shaved head either has silicon implants or balloons up her bra. You can't be that thin and have a chest that size.

I continue thinking ungenerous thoughts about them all, and then I realize something strange is happening above my head. I look up, because something is flapping in my peripheral vision. Then I see it's a collection of seagulls, flying dangerously close to my head.

I'm surrounded on all sides. There must be at least half a dozen of them. And then, without warning, the wind picks up – and at the moment I duck my head down, to stop my hair flying into my eyes, I'm splattered with bird shit, from the top of my left shoulder, down to the buttons on my shirt. It's wet, yellow-white and disgusting. And at the precise moment it happens, Jan turns round, catches my eye and laughs.

'Oh no!' Courtney yells in the distance, making a mock-horrified face, clapping her hands over her mouth. And then Guy shouts something too, but it's lost in the sound of their laughter.

I go straight to the loo when we get to the pub, and tear off long sheets of paper from the wall, trying to remove the stain.

Then I wash my hands and automatically check my face in the mirror. And I see two spots. One on my chin and one on the side of my neck.

I trace them with my finger. They weren't there before. And . . . I never get spots any more. I think I may even have forgotten what you do about them.

I decide to leave the spots alone, although they're red and sore-looking, and rejoin the others.

Guy has bought a bottle of champagne, and is waving it around as if he's just been made king.

Courtney is sitting next to him with her leg curled around his, and Jan is sitting on Guy's other side, twisting her hair. And although there is plenty of space around the table, for some reason the other two flatmates have decided to squeeze themselves in, like human bookends.

'Look at all this hair,' Guy lifts up Courtney's long red hair in one hand and Jan's in the other. 'So much hair for us to share. Isn't it lovely?'

I check my mobile for ancient text messages from Pete, which I have saved. Then I realize my phone has gone. I check my pockets and then my bag. And then I see the bald witch staring at me.

'Phone's gone,' I say to nobody in particular. 'Sod it.'

'Cheers,' Guy ignores this and clinks glasses with me. 'Here's to decent champagne again.'

'Guy got a bonus,' Courtney smiles at me and gives his hand a little massage. 'It's good news, innit?'

'Bonus for what?' I ask sharply. I can still feel the seagull crap all over my coat, even if I got most of it off.

'Just a general bonus sort of thing.' Guy shrugs and then turns his attention back to Courtney and Jan.

Suddenly I don't feel like champagne any more, even if it is Bollinger, so I make a show of checking my watch, and then I pretend I have to be somewhere else.

Well, I do, in a way. I have to be in a phone box on the sea front, so I can ring up Jim and talk to him urgently about this book we're supposed to be writing. I'm not sure I can last much longer on the paper if Molloy and the management are rewarding Guy for all his rubbish stories about chicken bingo.

It's wonderful to be outside again, even if it is freezing and starting to rain. I've never liked the Merchant Arms, and I like it even less with Guy and his gothic groupies in there.

I find a phone box and ring Jim.

'Birds,' is the first thing he says when I get through.

'Birds what?'

'Where are you, Katie? I can see birds. Someone's playing with you. Be careful. I'm worried.'

'A bird just crapped on me,' I start to say, and then I stick my head around the corner of the phone box, so I can check the night sky.

'OK?' Jim checks.

'No. Not OK,' I say. 'You're right. There's about a dozen seagulls flapping around really close to me. Yuck.'

'Wait,' Jim says as I close the door of the phone box.

'Can we talk about this book?' I ask him, backing off from the receiver – it smells terrible. 'I really, really need us to do this book, Jim. I don't think I can work with Guy and Courtney any more.'

'Wait,' he repeats.

And then, like magic – ha! like magic. As if I ever thought that phrase would come to have any sort of serious meaning in my life – the birds go away. I try to think if seagulls normally become this frantic and if they've ever behaved like this around me, and I decide that they haven't.

'If anything like that ever happens again,' Jim says, 'ring me.'

'So what's it all about then?' I ask, watching the cars shoot past the phone box.

'I'll tell you another time.' Jim sighs. 'But you know I'll protect you.'

'I think it's Courtney.'

'Maybe. Not sure.'

'Can't you see it in the bucket?'

'Don't be like that. Just remember, if you get the bird thing again, call me. I can help you.'

'Good. OK,' I say, feeling suddenly grateful. I've had just enough weirdness for one night.

'Anything else going on?' Jim asks suddenly.

'Apart from Pete vanishing, you mean?'

'He'll be back,' Jim reassures me again. 'That much I do know.'

'Well,' I tell him, suddenly feeling wonderfully and strangely calm – is it all in my mind or is Jim doing his thing? – 'The only other thing is my phone's gone. It got nicked tonight. Though I can't even remember putting it down anywhere. And – I just got two spots. Which is ridiculous, I know, but they literally sprang up.'

'Phone's gone for ever,' Jim says. 'Sorry, Katie. Get another one. And don't touch the spots: they'll get infected. It could get nasty.'

'So is this a witchy thing, then? Is that what's going on?'

'Kind of. Not serious. It's more that certain elements are playing with you.'

'What elements?'

'Think about everyone you ever wrote about in the paper who had an ASBO placed on them. Think about all the prank phone callers, con artists and sleazebags you've ever written about.'

'OK.'

'They exist on this side of life and they exist on the other side of life too. That's what these women are tapping into.'

'Well, it's horrible. How do I make it stop?'

'It already has,' he reassures me. 'Why don't you come to Hastings next week? Spring's on the way. It's going to be beautiful down here soon. We can pick up some food from the bakery, go up near the castle and have a picnic. Maybe we can go for a swim.'

'I'd like that,' I agree, suddenly longing for sunshine and salt water. Anything that feels clean.

Then I walk home, with no bus in sight, enjoying the wind as it pushes me further in the direction of the flat, taking me away from the pub, and Courtney and her awful friends, and Guy. Suddenly, I realize, I do feel like a bit of protection.

I go home, switch the bedroom light on, open up my journal and go to draw the curtains, then I see bird crap on the window. A long, green-yellow stain right where I can't get to it.

Fantastic.

What next, a toad on my pillow where Pete used to be?

CHAPTER NINE

Prince Charles and Camilla Parker-Bowles are supposed to get married on 8 April, but then the Pope dies and the funeral is planned for the same day, so the wedding date is moved to 9 April instead.

Buy the first mug, and the second mug, Jim said on the tape. Guy cannot believe it – and he is thrilled, of course, because despite all his sneering at Jim's royal predictions months before, the first thing he did when Royal Doulton issued the china was put in his order.

'I'm already being offered five hundred pounds for the first mug on eBay,' he gloats. 'But they can stuff it. I'm keeping both of them. Imagine if they get divorced as well! We're talking thousands.'

I am dispatched to Churchill Square in search of vox-pop reactions to the wedding, together with the photographer who scooped the front page with chicken bingo – or, as it's now being called in the office, The Chingo.

The fascinating thing about vox pops, and the reason I never mind doing them, is this: when you talk to people on the street, you realize how little anything you see in the newspapers reflects what real people think.

I go through all the papers, looking for inspiration about Charles and Camilla questions. In one of the tabloids, both their heads have been cut out with a pair of scissors, as if a child has been doing a school project, and plonked randomly on the page. It looks as if both Charles and Camilla have just been beheaded. The headline is, WEDDING 'SHAMBLES' SAY FRIENDS: A RIGHT ROYAL STUFF-UP!

There are long columns written by women who look like old bags calling Camilla an old bag, and men who aren't very bright accusing Charles of being not very bright. There are features telling Charles to cheer up, using old photographs of him where he looks miserable, and there are features telling him not to be so bloody happy about everything, using old photographs of him looking happy. Finally, there are photographs of Princess Diana, and the crashed black Mercedes in the tunnel, with the screaming headline LEST WE FORGET?

But when I stand on the corner outside Borders with the snapper for two hours, all I hear on my tape-recorder is this:

'Good luck to him!' Gary Radford, 32, Moulsecomb. 'I hope they'll be very happy after all this time,' Caroline Edwards, 42, Kemptown. 'I don't mind what they do,' Peter Toynbee, 58, Brighton. 'People should stop making a fuss and let them get on with it,' Harry Pearce, 47, Brighton. 'Go for it!' Rachel Mills, 22, Hove. 'I couldn't care less, but then I'm not a Royalist,' David Purvis, 26, Brighton. 'I'm as sick as a parrot; I fancied Camilla myself,' Norman Hewden, 61, Portslade.

Then, just when I'm begining to enjoy myself with Norman Hewden, who is barking mad but quite entertaining, my new mobile phone rings. It's Jim, and he has some bad news. Sue's publishing company has decided not to go ahead with the book. Someone in London heard about the shark story at the end of our local BBC news, and then they ordered all the articles on Jim in the *Courier* from a press cuttings agency, and that's it. No more book.

'Sue said it wasn't her decision,' Jim explains. 'But there are a million psychics out there at the moment, all with stories to tell, and nobody in their publicity department wanted some guy who'd just been exposed as a fraud. Or a total idiot, come to that.'

'But what about the Charles and Camilla prediction? Don't they care about that? What about the tsunami?'

'It's all right.' Jim sounds strangely calm about the bad news.

'But you saw me writing a book, didn't you?'

'Later,' Jim says patiently, 'If I saw it, it will happen. Hey, want to come down to the beach hut on Saturday? It's supposed to be a nice day. There's something on the tape I want you to hear.'

And with that he is gone, leaving me with Lindsay Fox, 28, of Durham, who is visiting Brighton for the day and would like to tell me that she thinks the media should leave Camilla alone, and that Prince Charles's free-range sausages are absolutely delicious.

On Saturday morning I wake up, still to an empty bed but also to a beautiful, warm, early spring day. Stupidly I think about the Easter egg I want to buy Pete, and then I try to get him out of my head. I have tried all forms of communication I can think of, from the internet (all my messages are ignored) to long texts, varying in tone from furious to hurt to forgiving – and still nothing.

When I walk down to the beach huts I see that Jim is not the only owner in residence; there are couples setting up barbecues, children with bikes and one impossibly tanned man with white hair and tartan shorts asleep in a deckchair with a book over his face.

'Hi,' Jim waves and beckons me over. 'The billy's just boiled,' he says, pointing proudly to his camping stove as he stirs a teabag into two tin mugs.

'So what about this tape then?' I ask.

He shuts the doors of the beach hut, so I have to pull my knees up to my chest – the whole place is about the size of my kitchen – and he presses play on an old-fashioned tape-recorder.

'What I want you to do is listen between the lines,' he advises. 'Try to hear between the cracks in the tape, if you can, and just tell me what you hear. You've played this back before, right?'

'Yes. A couple of times.'

'Right. But something interesting's happening. Since we did this, there are new voices on the tape.'

'What?' But I listen anyway.

'OK then.' I hear Jim's voice as he switches on the tape-recorder. 'Let's make a start. The first thing is 1987 and 2005 are connected. Prince Harry went to school for the first time in 1987, and it's like he's being forced back to school in 2005. But it's the school of life.'

'Hang on,' I stop the tape. 'Jim. Play that bit back. I can definitely hear something.'

He smiles and rewinds.

'It's like he's being forced back to school in 2005,' I hear him say again, and then I hear another voice – a man's. It sounds choppy and stilted, but weirdly familiar too.

'Hello, Katie, it's your grandfather here. Henry Pickard.'

'Oh my God.'

'I know.' Jim presses the play button again. 'Keep listening.'

'In 1987 the stockmarket crashed in London. In 2005 it's going to happen again. In 1987 England won the Ashes. In 2005 history will also repeat itself. England's definitely going to beat Australia. I see the lion wrestling the kangaroo and the emu, and the lion wins . . .'

'There,' I wave my hand. 'I can hear something there. Play it back.'

'I see the lion wrestling the kangaroo and the emu, and the lion wins . . .'

'Good luck with the story, Katie. We're very proud of you over here.'

I realize I am hugging myself, because suddenly I feel strangely shivery. 'Jim. This is my grandfather's voice. It's really, truly my grandfather's voice.'

We keep listening.

'In two weeks from now,' I hear Jim saying, 'I see foxes, hare and deer – and a dog turned away. And I see a famous dancer too – she dies in the bath. Then there's a train. It's the queen of the sea. It drowns in the waves – on Boxing Day. There's an English schoolgirl – they should listen to her, but they don't.'

'There.' Jim rewinds the tape again, and we hear my grandfather saying, 'It takes a lot for people to listen to the truth these days. But they will.'

I press play again and hear both our voices. 'And then 2005 starts with a funeral for Nelson Mandela.'

'He's going to die?' I hear myself ask.

'Not him,' Jim replies. 'Someone close. It's a lesson for Africa about AIDS. Then I can see a shark,' he goes on. 'It's a seven-million-pound shark. And then a desk. I see a shark and a desk around Valentine's Day. The shark's eaten the desk. Weird. Al Qaeda want Russell Crowe's head. Bill Gates is knighted. Then after this, the King of Chess is free at last . . .'

Henry interrupts again. 'Have faith, Katie.'

Jim squeezes my hand. I suppose he can see how terrified I must look. 'It's OK,' he reassures me. 'Really, it's OK.' The tape runs on.

'Then I can see mugs, with Prince Charles and Camilla Parker-Bowles on the front. The message is, buy the first mug as well as the second one. And keep them.'

And then I hear it. Andrew's voice. As clear and as normal-sounding as if he was in the room beside us. 'Better buy those mugs then, Katie. You never know!'

I can feel my heart hammering. 'Stop it. That's not my grandfather any more. That was Andrew.'

And then we hear something else. A child, laughing – a little girl.

Jim turns the tape-recorder off.

'Katie. I'm sorry. I swear I never heard that before.'

'And?' I look over at him, feeling slightly sick and scared all at the same time.

'I promise you. Andrew's voice wasn't on there before. Or the little girl's.'

'Let's get out of here,' I stand up, craning my head beneath the low beach-hut roof. 'I don't want to hear any more.'

Then Jim stands up too and squeezes my shoulder. 'I'm sorry.'

Then I sit down again. 'Or maybe I do, Jim. I don't know. Can we just stay here for a bit? Can I have lots of sugar in that tea? Sorry. I think I might be in shock or something.'

'I've got some brandy; I can put in the tea, too, if you want it,' he offers.

So we sit on the floor cushions again while he boils more water, and I mentally replay the sound of Andrew's voice in my head.

I try to work out why I knew it was Andrew, and then I realize it was the jokiness. Not just the flat vowels and the deep, gritty voice, but the tone, I suppose. The bit about buying the mugs was exactly the sort of thing he'd say to me.

'Let's play the rest,' I hear myself saying. 'I've got to know. I mean, if there's more . . .' I press play.

'Then I can see the world's biggest plane taking off, and the French word for seven. And Tony Blair, a victory for him. Australians are taken into Indonesian

161

jails. And New Zealanders celebrate in June. They've captured a tiger . . .'

We listen to the rest of the tape, as I crane to hear Andrew's voice, but that's it. Nothing else.

'I think I'm going to cry,' I tell Jim as he puts his arm around my shoulder. I vaguely register the smell of washing powder and wool in his jumper, and something else? Salt water, maybe.

And then my phone rings in my pocket.

I ignore it at first, until Jim guides it firmly into my hand.

It's Pete. At last, at last.

'Katie? I miss you. I miss you. Miss you, miss you, miss you. Can I see you?'

'Pete. God. Sorry, I'm having such a weird day. And I didn't expect to hear from you. Where are you?'

'At home. At yours. At ours, if I'm still allowed back in.'

Jim opens the door of the hut and steps outside ahead of me, blinking in the sunlight.

'I'll ring you,' I say. 'I don't know what I'm doing, Jim. Sorry. I don't know what's going on. I'll ring you.'

And then I run-walk as fast and as far as I can, until I'm past the top of the stone steps, half a mile down Marine Parade and just ahead of the bus.

I'm panting so hard when I get on that I can barely ask the driver for my ticket, then I run-walk again from the bus stop to my block of flats, while Saturday tourists and locals on shopping trips duck out of the way.

And then I see him, sitting cross-legged on a patch of grass outside the flats, with four plastic carrier bags by his side, a guitar case, a shoebox and a travel bag.

'It might not seem like it,' is the first thing Pete says as we dive for each other, 'but I've decided to turn over a new leaf.' And then he hands me the shoebox and takes out a pair of high-heeled silver sandals; he pulls off my socks and shoes and puts them on my feet. They fit perfectly. They are beautiful. And ... Jim Gabriel and his amazing psychic powers win again.

'You're such a bastard,' I tell Pete when we have stopped kissing and come up for air. And then I realize that the neighbours are probably looking, but I don't care.

'I had to go away,' he stares at the grass. 'I'll tell you inside. I wasn't allowed to use me phone. They took it off me as soon as I got into the place.'

We go inside and I automatically reach for a half-full bottle of red wine on top of the fridge. I've been hanging onto it for the day of his return.

'Not for me,' Pete says, looking in his bag for a bottle of orange juice instead.

I sit down at the kitchen table and pour myself a glass anyway, while he sits on the floor and leans against me.

'Polly's giving me Ben back,' he says at last. 'Every second weekend. It's sorted.'

'Is that where you were?' I ask, though I already know it isn't.

'I went to a nice place in the country when I left here.' He gets up, whispering in my ear, 'And I think I'm better now.'

'What nice place in the country?' I ask him. But he won't answer.

And then he tells me he hasn't had a proper bath or shower since yesterday, so he takes me by the hand and guides me into the bathroom while he drops his clothes along the way. He seems calmer. More solid. More grounded. Less wired.

I think about the day we met, when I interviewed him and we were sitting on the floor in his flat – he seemed to run on pure electricity.

'God that's good,' Pete says through the noise of the shower as he ducks underneath the water.

Then he reaches for my arm.

'Coom on. I'm all clean now. Let's have a shower together. We've never done that.'

'What if I don't want to?' I pull back the other way.

'If you're going to kill me, you might as well kill me under running water and get rid of the evidence,' Pete smiles and happily shuts his eyes as water splashes over his face.

He's gorgeous, I think. Gorgeous, gorgeous, gorgeous.

Andrew pops into my head – we used to shower together all the time, though Pete doesn't know that. Then I realize, with a start, that I am terrified he might be watching, from his vantage point on the other side, and I feel irrationally paranoid.

'What?' Pete insists.

'Nothing.'

'Coom under then,' he tugs at my arm.

And – Andrew or no Andrew – I find myself giving in and peeling my jeans off. God, I'll be glad when spring finally arrives properly. I seem to have been living in my jeans for about 100 years.

Pete pulls me under the warm water before I can even get my bra and pants off, and we stand there for half an hour, maybe more, while he washes my hair and tells me over and over again that he's sorry.

'OK,' I hear myself telling him while he rinses my hair. 'OK, OK. Shut up.'

'So where was this place in the country?' I ask him much later, when we're in the sitting room with a towering pile of toast – Pete's preferred food.

'Oh, it was very private,' Pete makes a serious face as he settles in front of his piano. 'We had to dress up in tree costumes so we wouldn't be seen.'

'And what happened?' I ask.

'Detoxed,' Pete shrugs. 'No more of anything for me ever again. I knew I had to do it when I came home that night. You said you loved me. Well, I'm trying to go one better than that.' He rubs his face with his hands and smiles at me from across the room. 'See? Actions speak louder than words. I'm cleaning up for you. I didn't want to at first – all I wanted to do was get away – but then I did. And now I have.'

He laughs.

'What?'

'I've tried every drug in the United Kingdom except the bloody chav ones,' he says.

It's hard not to laugh.

'Anyway.' He turns back to the piano and plays me a beautiful piece of music, which suddenly makes the room feel warmer and lighter, as if spring really is on the way at last.

'What's that?' I ask when he's finished.

'It's me,' he says proudly. 'It's my number one.'

'Really?'

'It's got no lyrics,' Pete ticks categories off on his fingers. 'No title. No musicians, apart from me. I play everything. There's no video. No record company. And it goes for over eight minutes. And it's going to be number one.'

'Play it again,' I settle back in an armchair and close my eyes. The ridiculous thing is that after all the madness in Jim's beach hut this morning, I have almost reached the point where I can believe anything.

I try to pinpoint what Pete's song reminds me of. It's a little bit Beatlesque, I suppose, but that might be because I associate all his piano playing with the music he played at the tsunami charity concert.

'Like it?' Pete asks when he's finished.

'I do, actually,' I hear myself saying. 'It's funny. It sort of grows on you. Can you play it again?'

'OK,' Pete says, and I realize he's adding things as he goes – twiddly departures at the high end of the keyboard, and then crashing deep chords at the other end.

'See that bit,' he scratches his nose, 'it's where I'm

going to bring the guitar in. I worked it all out at the clinic. They had a piano in the games room. Four part harmonies, drums, three guitars and maybe a bit of keyboard. Nice and simple. It's The Song With No Name. That's what I'm going to call it.'

He sniffs and looks up at the ceiling, as if there's someone floating above his head.

'It's me John Lennon song,' he says. 'Some people at the clinic thought it *was* John Lennon. Mind you, they were crack addicts.'

I wonder if I should tell Pete about my strange experiences with Jim's tape, and hearing my grandfather and Andrew, but I decide against it.

And then my phone rings. It's Guy, in a panic, ringing from his flat. Molloy is dead — he had a massive cardiac arrest this morning at the gym and his wife has just rung from the hospital.

'He died on our deadline,' is the second thing Guy says, 'so we can't run the obit until Tuesday. Katie, you've done loads of those things. Can you put something together?'

'Yes,' I say automatically. There's something wrong with Guy, I think. His boss is dead and all he can think about is our deadline. But then again, that's all Molloy could ever think about either. Maybe that's why he's not here any more. That and the liver damage.

'Is his wife OK?' I ask. I feel sorry for her, despite the fact that I never had any time for her husband.

'Seems to be. The kids are coming back up to see her. I never met them, did you?'

'No,' I say, thinking about the family photos on Molloy's desk, showing a girl in a university graduation gown, and another woman in a wedding dress. I wonder if they knew how much he drank?

'So what do you want me to say in the obit?' I ask stupidly as Pete looks up from the piano.

'We must have his CV on file somewhere, from

when he first started. His wife will know. Maybe you could talk to one of the daughters.'

'All right.' I listen as Pete puts the piano lid down and comes over to massage my shoulders.

'So we're editorless,' Guy says suddenly. 'There's a gap to fill.'

I ignore this. 'When did he die? This morning? I thought he was fit.' Suddenly I feel tears starting in my eyes. 'He was always at the gym. He played golf . . .'

'And just when things were coming good, too,' Guy continues as if he hasn't heard me. 'That's the most gutting thing. We were turning the corner. We're all going to have to keep calm over the next few days. We're going to have to try to keep it together.'

'Yes.'

There's nothing else I can think of to say.

But if Guy has any hopes of keeping things together they're soon dashed the following day, when Courtney doesn't turn up for work and I take a call from the RSPCA, who say they're looking for her – urgently.

I know the woman who calls, because she's been one of the sources for my story on missing cats.

'Beverley,' I remember her name at last. 'Maybe I can help. I know Courtney.'

'We've found two of the cats in her flat,' Beverley gets straight to the point. 'The plumber came in to fix the loo in the flat, and he heard a sound and traced it up to the attic. There was one black and white in there and a ginger tabby. No collars. But both animals were fed and watered. A bit panicked, of course, because no animal likes being trapped in a confined space for long. But otherwise they were OK, except that their fur was cut off. That's why he called us.'

'Thank God,' I say automatically.

'Both cats are perfectly healthy apart from that. But we've been calling the leaseholder of the flat for twenty-four hours – Courtney Creely – and we've had no luck at all. The flatmates aren't answering either,' Beverley sniffs.

'Right.'

'Well, what do you think?' Beverley confides in me.

'It might be what it looks like. The cats slipped their collars. They were roaming around. One of the girls took them in and decided to bung them up in the attic until they could start ringing round the local vets. And the fur—'

'Yes,' Beverley says meaningfully, waiting for my alternative explanation.

I suddenly decide I want to dodge the question. Pandora's Box again. 'Someone out there must have cut their fur off. The same person who did it last time. It's lucky the girls took the cats in. Who knows?'

'But they have clearly failed to call either the RSPCA or the local vet,' Beverley continues. 'And . . . some people here want to inspect the flat. And at the very least we want to talk to Courtney Creely or the other three women. But either our calls aren't being returned or we're having problems getting through to any of them in the first place.'

'Right.'

And then, just as I am wondering what to do next, Courtney appears, dressed for spring, if not summer, in tight white jeans, strappy sandals and a long-sleeved white T-shirt that barely covers her pale, perfectly flat stomach. She even has a white flower tucked behind her ear. She looks positively virginal.

'Where's Guy?' she asks as I make my excuses to Beverley and hang up.

'Sorting things out with management. It's chaos.'

She nods.

'I've been ill,' she says, forcing a cough. 'I've had this thing that's going round. Sorry I'm late in, but Guy knows all about it. I've been at his. Did he tell you I'd be late?'

'I saw him for about a second this morning, before he went racing off,' I tell her.

Then I realize she has a new tattoo – a tiny five-pointed pentagram on her wrist – and lose my train of thought.

'I like your skirt,' she says, looking me up and down. 'Is it new? You've got good legs, Katie. Even Guy said you did once. I got really jealous,' she pulls a ridiculous, pouty face.

'The RSPCA have been trying to find you.' I ignore the pout. 'There were a couple of missing cats at your place, apparently. Your plumber found them in the attic. And they've tried to ring your flatmates as well, but nobody's calling them back.'

Courtney smiles, shrugs and sits down in the nearest chair she can find, drawing annoyed looks from one of the subs, who is territorial about the office furniture.

'Our flat's in a bit of a state,' she says. 'I'm moving out. And the phone bill was in my name, so I had it transferred over to Deb, but they accidentally cut us off. So that's probably why the RSPCA can't find any-one,' she adjusts the white flower clip behind her ear.

'What about the cats?'

'Aww,' Courtney crinkles her nose and aims another smile my way. 'Poor little things. We didn't know what to do about them. So we thought we'd just give them a bit of food and water until we could find out where they belonged. Someone had cut all their fur off.'

'Can you call Beverley at the RSPCA then?' I ask her. 'Let her know what's going on? You probably know – I've been covering the missing cats story for a while now. Beverley's been one of my main contacts.'

'The cats probably had a fight and wandered off.' Courtney smiles. 'That's what happens, isn't it?'

'The RSPCA wants to have a look round your flat,' I tell her, watching her face carefully as she turns the pages of the paper.

'Whatever they want.' She shrugs, not meeting my eyes. 'But like I said, I only moved out yesterday. Guy asked me to, you see,' she looks up at me and smiles radiantly. 'He said he needed me to support him at home now that Molloy's gone.'

Then she returns to the paper, flicking to the sports pages. 'See, they'll probably make him editor now. So you can understand why he asked me to move in with him, can't you? He needs someone to look after him now he's going to have the top job.'

She stinks, I think suddenly. Of what, I'm not sure – it smells like a mixture of leaking gas and cloying, cheap perfume, but she definitely stinks. It can't be anyone else in the office because the smell arrived with her, and now it's leaving with her.

'Is it just me, or did you notice a whiff?' I ask one of the subs, once Courtney has gone.

'Can't smell anything.' The sub shrugs.

But then, that's the problem with Courtney. She gets under everybody's radar.

CHAPTER TEN

The new thrill of commitment has had a predictable effect on Guy. Within days of Courtney moving in – in fact, on the day of Molloy's funeral – he starts flirting with Claudia again.

We're having lunch at the church hall immediately after the funeral when it happens. While Courtney is in the loo I watch Guy steer Claudia into a corridor off to the left, and then emerge with her again about fifteen minutes later with a guilty look I have come to know extremely well during the years I've been working with them. Then they shoot off again into the graveyard.

'Where's Guy?' Courtney asks me when she comes back.

'Sorry.' I shrug. She's dressed in black from head to foot, but has arrived late for the wake. She didn't want to go to the church service, according to Guy, because she doesn't believe in it.

She teeters off again in her spike-heeled black shoes in search of sandwiches, though I know they're all chicken, ham and roast beef, so I wonder if she'll boycott those as well, because Guy's told me that she doesn't believe in meat either.

Predictably, though, I soon see Courtney stuffing them down and knocking back one glass of wine after another. It's the first time I've ever seen her drink so much.

Finally Guy comes back, by himself, and immediately walks straight past Courtney, heading for a small group of marketing people instead.

I expect he wants to make a good impression, now that he's so close to taking Molloy's job.

After this, I watch Mrs Molloy moving around all the guests with her two daughters in tow. I suddenly feel sorry for her. Not only for losing her husband, but for having to put up with him in the first place. Is that the wrong thing to think at a funeral? Probably. But I'm sure everyone else from our paper is thinking it as well.

Since I told Courtney the RSPCA wanted to talk to her, and since the rumours about Guy's new job began, the editorial section of the paper has been in chaos. Courtney has been hopeless in her new role as PA, and I've been working from 7 a.m., and staying as late as 9 p.m., trying to hold things together.

As a result I am constantly knackered, falling asleep on my desk at lunchtime and collapsing in front of the TV almost as soon as Pete hands me a cup of tea and puts the news on. My dinner last night consisted of a lump of cheddar cheese at 2 o'clock in the morning.

I watch Guy charming one of the women from marketing and try to remember if she's married or not. Then I find myself looking for Claudia. Perhaps she's gone back to work.

She has dressed to the hilt for this funeral. She doesn't often make that kind of effort, and I can't blame Guy for wanting to take her off into a dark corner. With her blond hair out of its ponytail, her make-up on and a tight black suit, Claudia looks positively glamorous.

I finally track her down near the photocopier when I get back to work, but see that her hair has been tied back again and the make-up has disappeared.

'I can't pretend I'm sad about Molloy because I'm not really,' I confess to her. Well, I have to tell someone.

'I am,' she says. 'Not that I knew him, but I felt sorry for him. You can't be happy if you drink like that.'

'Actually, Claudia, do you want to nip out for a coffee?'

'Can we?'

'Everything's up the spout today. We may as well. Come on.'

I make her walk as far away from the office as I can, all the way to the border of Kemptown, just in case any of the usual cafés have staff members inside.

'Oh, I like this place,' she says as I steer her into a small shop which is half art gallery, half tea and biscuits. 'I haven't been here for ages. Actually, I haven't been here since Guy took me to the opening.'

'Right.'

I steel myself for what I have to say.

'When I went to interview Courtney at the shop in the Lanes, I found a book of black magic spells.'

Claudia nods.

'She had lots of different spells in there, but the one I saw was really nasty. It was designed to get her money, power, success, love . . .' I think of Jim, but somehow I can't tell her about that bit.

'Weird,' Claudia agrees.

'Think about it. Since then, she's magically been appointed as Guy's PA. She seems to have revived her modelling career. She's won £15,000 on the bingo. And Guy's asked her to move in with him.'

Our tea arrives and I gulp it down, watching the window for birds. Just telling Claudia all this is giving me the creeps.

'In addition to this', I try to speak as carefully as I can to make sure I get it right, 'dozens of cats have gone missing, only to be found with their fur cut off. The RSPCA found two of them in Courtney's attic.'

'And Alison.' Claudia nods, announcing, 'I don't care.'

'Really?'

'I just don't care,' she repeats. 'She can do what she likes.'

'It's not just her. She's got three other women working with her.'

Claudia levels a look at me and changes the subject. 'Guy thinks Courtney is obsessed with Jim Gabriel. What do you think?'

I shrug.

'She says she's over him, but Guy thinks differently,' Claudia continues. 'And . . . I know you think he's a shit, Katie, but Guy and I were really getting somewhere. I just don't think he's meant to be with Courtney, that's all. Whereas Guy and I . . .'

Then she drops her bombshell, which like most of the bombshells I've heard in my life, lands so quietly that it takes me a while to take it in.

'I suppose Courtney is still obsessed with Jim because they had that one-night stand together.'

'Really?'

'Guy said Courtney told him it was just a fling. But still.' She shrugs.

Then she swivels in her chair and stares at the window.

'Stupid birds,' she says, 'what's wrong with them?'

Four blackbirds are trying to get in, beating their wings against the window.

'Dunno,' I look away again. 'Maybe it's global warming. All the birds are going mad.'

Then, once Claudia has gone, I ring Jim.

'Oh hi,' he says when I call. 'I saw your boss died.'

'Yeah, I wrote the obituary.'

'But you're not calling about that,' he says slowly.

'No, I'm not calling about that. You're right.'

'I'm in Brighton,' Jim says. 'I'm here. Watching the sunset by the West Pier. It's amazing. Red, orange, pink. Can you see it from where you are?'

'Come to that bar,' I tell him. 'The one opposite the Electric Railway. I need to talk to you. As in really, really need to talk to you.'

Then I hang up and realize I'm clenching my jaw.

When I arrive, Jim is already at a table in front of the window reading the menu.

'So,' he says, trying to kiss me on the cheek as I sit down and missing. 'What's up?'

'Did you have a one-night stand with Courtney Creely?'

He doesn't hesitate. 'Yes. I was drunk.'

'I don't care.'

'It was the first night I moved to Brighton. I was broke. She said, "If you're so psychic, why don't you put a bet on the football?"' He sighs. 'So I did. And I won £1,000. Never gambled before or since, but I needed the money. And then she made me spend the money on some restaurant, and we drank champagne, tequila shots and, I dunno,' he says, suddenly sounding extremely Australian, 'a six-pack of beer.'

'How could you?'

'Well, yeah.' Jim gestures with his hands. 'But just because you're fortunate enough to have never made a similar mistake, Katie, doesn't mean that I'm some kind of pariah. Does it?'

Then I almost tell him about Courtney's magic book, and the horrible spell designed to bind him to her, but I can't do it.

'Let's go for a walk.' Jim pushes his chair back. 'I don't need a drink. Do you need a drink? I'd rather go for a walk. I dunno, you're making me feel . . . bad about myself. I'm pissed off about it. Do you mind?'

'OK.' I give in.

We head towards the gallopers on the merry-go-round, not speaking, just crunching, as we walk across the pebbles.

'You're right,' I say eventually. 'I'm lucky. I've never had a one-night stand with anyone unsuitable. Maybe I've just never been that drunk.'

'Pete's suitable?'

'He's not a one-night stand. It's a bit more committed than that.'

'Not that I can't see the appeal of loving unsuitable people,' Jim says as we head past the gallopers towards the West Pier. 'King George IV married Maria Fitzherbert in secret. They forced him to divorce her because she was Catholic. So he married his cousin, Caroline of Brunswick, instead. She was suitable. And then he just had one affair after another until the day he died, and they found unsuitable Maria's portrait in a locket around his neck.'

'Absolutely right,' I confirm. 'I'm so glad someone else reads the boring history pages in the back of our paper.'

'King George IV is still around,' Jim says. 'I saw him the other day. He was standing in the gardens of the Royal Pavilion.'

'What? I'm sure he was. Doing anything in particular?'

'He was just checking it all out.' Jim smiles. 'I see Princess Victoria too, sometimes. She's surfing.'

'You mean Queen Victoria?' I pull a suitably Queen Victoria-like pouty face and laugh at the idea of her stuck on top of a surfboard.

'No, Princess Victoria of Hawaii,' Jim says. 'She lived here for a while. And she surfed here, too. I see her out near the power station sometimes, near the pipes.'

'Jim.' I sigh. 'You're being weird again. Too weird.'

'It's a new thing,' Jim says slowly. 'I'm seeing . . .' he

176

sighs. 'Sorry, I know this sounds like The Sixth Sense, but I'm seeing dead people.'

'Really?'

'Not all the time,' Jim reassures me. 'Just now and again.'

'And what do they look like?'

He thinks about it. 'Real. But they're gone in a second.'

I automatically think of Andrew, and then my grandfather, and then Molloy, and then I get the creeps, so I change the subject. If any of them should pop up now, near the gallopers, I think I may start screaming.

'It's just energy,' Jim tries to return to the subject of dead people.

'Not interested. It's too much, Jim. There's too much going on and I can't handle it, all right?'

'So what are you trying to tell me about suitable and unsuitable love then?' I ask as we trudge towards Hove.

'Nothing. It's just that I can understand the Pete thing. OK?'

Then I make him stop because my eyes are watering in the wind.

'And because you've got these' – I wave my hands around – 'powers, you just know that he's unsuitable. Is that right?'

No answer.

We walk past the netball and basketball courts – they'll be packed with people in a few months, once summer is here – and make our way towards Hove, because one of Jim's favourite vegetarian cafés is there.

'Your grandfather gave me a message last night,' Jim said.

'What?'

'It's all right. He wants to help us with the book. I think he wants you off the paper. Anyway, he said

177

I had to go to an art gallery exhibition about fishermen, in Hove, and look for the BBC.'

'*What?* So nothing too specific then.'

'Please don't laugh,' Jim says, suddenly looking serious. 'I can't tell anybody else about what is happening to me, you know?'

'OK.' I nod. 'I understand.'

We find a bench and sit down.

'I've read tarot cards from the age of eighteen,' Jim explains. 'That's all. Very tame stuff. I mean, things came true and all that, but what's happening now is *different.*'

'You can say that again.'

'But you're OK with it? Andrew and your grandfather?'

Unwanted and uncalled for, tears begin to sting my eyes.

'Let me think about it,' I croak back as he squeezes my hand.

'Yup,' I manage to say. 'It's great. Really, Jim. I'm not complaining. It's great.'

'Good,' he nods, and we get up again and continue walking.

'One thing I keep thinking, though, what's all this about? Why now?'

'They're not telling me.'

'And when you say *they*, you mean spirit people?'

Jim nods.

'Can't you tell them to go away then?'

'They know what they're doing.' He shrugs. 'Even if I don't.'

'But why trust them?'

'Experience has always proven them right.' He shrugs again. 'So I have to let them put the jigsaw together. They throw me the occasional piece and I take it. That's it. We work together, I suppose. Though I don't necessarily know what they're doing, it's always the right picture in the end.'

'Too waffley.' I give up trying to understand him.

'Sorry.'

'If we ever do manage to do this book, you'll have to be clearer than that.'

'All right.' He gives in with a lopsided smile.

'OK. So where are these spirit people, then?' I point upwards hopefully. 'Where is Andrew? Where is my grandfather? Where are all the people you talk to?'

'My team?'

'Oh, it's a team, is it?'

'Like a work team,' Jim takes my hand as I jump over some railings.

'OK. Your spooky work team. Where are they?'

'Not up. Not down. It's ... a different world. A different sort of time and space bandwidth. A different consciousness, if you like. Like the place you go to when you dream.'

'Too vague.'

'You're taking this asking-questions thing seriously, aren't you?' Jim pulls a face at me.

'Well, come on. If I'm going to write a book with you ...'

'OK. Think of your most vivid dream.' Jim sighs as we keep walking. 'One with colour, sound, depth, height and temperature. One with detail.'

'Yes,' I think of my Pete dream from a few weeks ago.

'Did it have a definite sense of time and space?'

'Not time. It just seemed to be ... now. But space? Yes.'

'Did it feel any less vivid, or real, or natural than the time and space we're in now?' he asks as I look down at our feet, trudging along the beach.

'No,' I admit.

'So, that's what it's like for people who've died. The bodies go' – Jim waves a hand – 'but the consciousness

179

remains. When you pass over, the part of you that dreams survives. And spirit,' he emphasizes, 'is just a word for a big, complex chain of souls. It's an energy grid of consciousness. Lots of souls linked together, like the internet.' He sighs heavily. 'I don't know how else to explain it. I mean, Katie, I'm still learning.'

'Aha. A worldwide web of dead.'

Jim smiles.

'Or is it like a beehive? Or the Borg?' I think of *Star Trek*.

'A bit.' He shrugs.

'And you didn't know about any of this before?' I push him.

'Didn't have a clue.' He shrugs again. 'I thought I was just seeing the future in the bucket and the tarot cards. In the fish tank. In the washing-up water. I thought I was just a bum Aussie psychic making some cash to go surfing.'

'And?'

'And I am a bum psychic, but the pictures had to come from somewhere,' he emphasizes. 'And now I know. *They've* been sending them to me.'

'Like a TV transmission?'

'Yes,' Jim grabs my arm, 'like TV. That's perfect. They send the images, I'm like the set that picks them up.'

'But in water, not on a TV set,' I smile up at him. 'Now we're getting somewhere. Though I still can't forgive you for sleeping with Courtney.'

Then, a few days after this, Pete writes his number-one hit.

I know it as soon as I hear it, even though I'm not psychic. And why do I know? Because I am one of those people who only buy albums about once every two years. I am not a music person. Consequently, when I like something, I am usually a small statistic in a very large worldwide audience for what is going to be a very, very big hit song. I bought the New Order album with 'Blue Monday' on it when I was a teenager. I bought the album with 'Macarena' on it. I think I may even have bought 'The Ketchup Song', by Las Ketchup. I like Abba, I like Kylie, I like hits. Call me a pop prole (Andrew always did), but that's me.

'It was going to be that song I had in me head, when I was writing about you,' Pete says sheepishly as he sets up his computer and speakers in my sitting room one evening. 'Then it got all tacky and commercial. Sorry about that.'

'That's all right.' I lie sideways on the sofa. We still don't have a replacement for Molloy, and now almost every evening is spent like this, because I'm working so hard I'm incapable of remaining vertical any more.

'It's called "Beach Boy, Beach Girl".' Pete shrugs, but I can tell he's dying to see what I think of it.

'Stop right there,' I hold up my hand like a policeman stopping traffic as soon as it begins.

'Why?'

'Because it sounds exactly like the Beach Boys.'

'Everything sounds like the Beach Boys.' Pete shrugs. 'It's like, write a summer song and it sounds like them. Write a winter song and it sounds like the Beatles. What am I gonna do? There's only ten notes in the whole of the pop pack.'

'OK then,' I relent.

And I listen to the rest of the song with my eyes closed – and then I realize something awful: my foot is waggling up and down in time to the music.

'See,' Pete explains once it's over, 'you can sing along with it.'

'Yeah,' I experiment. ' "Beach boy, beach girl, lying by the pool. Beach boy, beach boy, why you with that fool?" God, Pete. I am singing along with it.'

'Bit of Spanish guitar, a few castanets,' he continues,

'a bit of foreign phrasebook, a dance routine, a girl with huge norks in a gold bikini . . .'

'Where's all this going to come from?' I say.

'Me internet guy's going to line it up.' Pete rolls his eyes. 'He wants fifty per cent. Then I can get on with other things. Let's hope we're going to have shit weather here this summer, he says that's the clincher. Oh, and he knows every holiday rep and DJ in Ibiza, apparently. So I'm sorted.'

'Who is this internet guy?' I ask.

'He's called Magic Marky. He's a sort of . . .' Pete waves his hand in the air, as if this will help me understand who or what Magic Marky is. 'He's worked with everyone. He was a producer in London and now he's onto the whole download thing.'

Then he plays the beach boy, beach girl song back, turning down all the tracks so that all I can hear in the background is him chanting my name. 'It's still sort of your song in a way. I mean, I got you in there, in the end. Though nobody will pick it up' – he smiles – 'except me and you.'

'Wow.'

He comes over to kiss me on the sofa. 'Love you, nineteen fifties girl. Love you to bits.'

And then Polly calls – Ben is missing Pete badly.

He arrives, with a new haircut and a wobbly tooth, the following weekend.

Pete collects him when Polly drops him off in her car because I am at work on Saturday afternoon, filling in the gaps on the pages Molloy has left vacant.

'Hello,' I greet Ben, suddenly realizing that I do not actually know much about five-year-old boys.

But Pete's son (he looks even more like him than he did in the photo) is too shy to say anything, and so he turns a sharp left into Pete's leg, holding tightly onto the straps of a very old, very dirty, Bob the Builder rucksack while he chants one word over and over.

'No! No! No!'

Pete has the rest of Ben's things in what looks like one of Polly's bags. It's a large, flowery travel bag with a gonk on a keychain and big pink plastic tags on the zip. It looks all wrong in my flat – like her son, I think. There, I can only think of him as her son. Not Pete's. And . . . I'm not proud of it, but there it is.

'Do you like cars?' I ask Ben once we're settled inside at the kitchen table and Pete has produced some freshly squeezed orange and lemon juice for us – it's his new obsession.

'Don't know,' Ben replies, shaking his head from side to side and playing with himself.

'He's feeling a bit tired.' Pete ruffles his son's hair.

'Jim and I are going to the Jaguar Promenade on the seafront tomorrow,' I tell Pete, realizing I haven't told him anything about it yet. It was one of Jim's suggestions on the night we walked along the seafront to Hove. 'It's sort of a birthday thing. I've always had this stupid thing about Jaguars.'

'I didn't know you'd always had a stupid thing about Jaguars.' Pete catches my eye.

'Well, it doesn't matter.'

'But Jim seems to know all about it, doesn't he?'

'Anyway,' I hear myself rattling on, 'I was thinking, if Ben likes cars, maybe we could meet you there afterwards.'

'Your birthday,' Pete gives me a long look. 'That's on Tuesday, isn't it?'

'Monday,' I correct him.

'I knew that,' Pete tries to joke, and then he pulls Ben's hand away from his face because he's picking his nose. 'And anyway, love, I'm getting you a Jaguar. All right?'

But . . . it's not funny.

In the meantime, apart from picking his nose (which he does often) here are some other things that Ben

Oram does to thrill and delight me over the next eight hours.

He switches the television on and off, repeatedly, pushing the volume button up as far as it will go, despite being told by Pete to cease and desist. He screams a lot about nothing. He whines that he wants Polly. He refuses to look at a Thomas the Tank Engine book I bought him yesterday in my precious lunch-break. He kicks Pete in the leg because he's angry with him. And above all other things Ben will neither talk to me nor look at me. It's as if I am some kind of monster woman who's forcing him to stay in her dungeon.

And most of all he clings to a one-word mantra, emitted at ear-splitting volume, even after I have forgotten myself and shouted at him.

'No! No! No! No! No!'

In the end, Pete pulls the television out of the wall, drags it into my office, which we have temporarily converted into a spare room for Ben, and plugs it in, so he can pass out watching television in bed.

'Is that really good for him?' I ask as Pete leaves him to it.

'Do you really care that much?' he says, and I can see that the news about my day out with Jim at the Jaguar Promenade has hurt him.

Then he sits down at the piano, plays like a madman and ignores me for the rest of the night.

The following day we shout at each other about Ben, which I know is the wrong thing to do but I can't resist. In the end, Pete is close to tears about it all and I have to ring up Jim and cancel our day out.

'And admit it,' is the last thing I say to Pete in the horrible argument that follows. 'You forgot my birth-day. We live together, Pete, and you still bloody forgot.'

In reply, Pete slams the bedroom door again, but this

time it's behind him, and this time he is on the way out of the flat, dragging Ben with him.

'And you never told me you were a weirdo posh-car freak,' he shouts back.

But there is a reason I have never told Pete about the Jaguar thing. It's because Andrew had one – a second-hand one – and it's also the car he died in.

Jim picked up on it straight away when he was wondering aloud what to get me for my birthday.

'But how do you know?' I said.

'You've loved Jaguars since you were little,' he told me. 'That's why Andrew bought one. And you had fun in it. And then he died in it.'

'Oh my God.'

'That's no reason to stop liking them, though,' he said. 'There's a Jaguar Promenade on this weekend. Let's go. That can be your birthday treat.'

When I go back to work on Monday we are gathered together in Molloy's old office by one of the men from our London parent company and told that, from Monday, we will have a new editor.

'Her name is Jennifer George,' he tells us, reading from a piece of paper as jaws drop around the room. 'Jennifer has wide experience with both regional and national newspapers, and – something new for us – a background in internet and website development.'

I steel myself not to look at Guy, but then everyone else does, so I join in. Courtney is standing by his side like a mannequin, in strappy sandals and a tight blue skirt, with an expressionless face, just like Guy's.

'Jennifer is enthusiastic about the move to Brighton,' he goes on, 'and we feel that with her strong cross-media background and her reputation in the industry, she will be a sound choice for our newspaper in years to come.'

Across the room, Claudia rolls her eyes at me, then

at Guy, who winks over-confidently, as if he has known about Jennifer George all along, though I suspect he hasn't.

'So what do you think of the news?' Guy approaches me as we all walk back to our desks.

I shake my head.

'Interesting management decision,' he concludes, but I can see that he's rattled. I wonder if he's ever worked for a woman before and decide he probably hasn't.

Then Courtney takes his arm and steers him away, whispering something as she goes.

I think of Jim going to bed with her and feel sick.

CHAPTER ELEVEN

Our new editor makes some quick decisions on her first day at work.

Firstly, she sacks our astrologer, a strange little woman called Ceres, from Newhaven, who nobody has ever met and who apparently hasn't been paid since 1997 anyway. The column space is filled with something new – a feature called 'Letter From France' – which Jennifer has hired a good-looking journalist called Simon White to write. A rumour immediately begins that he is her boyfriend, or her husband, or her ex-husband, or at the very least someone she wants to shag. Because we've never ever had a 'Letter From France' in the paper before.

'We're virtually as close to France here as we are to London,' Jennifer explains to everyone in editorial, as we stand around in Molloy's old office for our first meeting. 'Market research reveals a high percentage of the readers we want in Brighton are regular travellers. Pro Euro and cosmopolitan in their tastes. I think it's time the *Courier* reflected that.'

To which the general reply from everyone appears to be 'Ooo-er', except for one dissenting voice – Guy's.

'You say the readers we want,' he emphasizes in his ponciest voice; it's amazing how his public school

187

vowels return to him when he needs them most. 'But can we clarify that?'

'Sure,' Jennifer picks up a sheaf of papers from her desk and puts her glasses on. Then she puts the paperwork down again and takes her glasses off. 'Actually, I was going to read you some stats.' She smiles. 'But I think it's easier to talk common sense. We need to increase our advertising revenue. And we're missing the top end of our market. In the light of that, we want a little more Paris in the paper and rather less bingo.'

I cannot bear to look at Guy, so I stare out of the window instead.

'And then there's the pink pound,' Jennifer adds.

'Pink pounds is gay, isn't it?' our sports editor asks. Jennifer nods slowly in reply, as if she's dealing with a congenital idiot who needs a lot of time to process new information. Which, in fact, she is. He was hit in the back of the head with a Crazy Golf ball a few years ago and he's never been the same since.

'We also need to be a little more sympathetic to our female readers,' Jennifer goes on, giving Courtney – who has squeezed into the office next to Guy – the slightest of glances. 'So as a general change in direction for the paper, I'd like to see us all thinking as the women of Brighton think.'

Guy gives me a meaningful look, as if any deficiency in this area of the paper is all my fault.

'Less glamour-girl photography is a good place to begin.' Jennifer nods while Courtney stares out of the window. 'I like some of what we've seen in the paper this year,' Jennifer goes on. 'But I've also been given a firm directive by management, and I'm sure you all know we have circulation and advertising targets to meet.'

'So what do you actually like about the paper then?' Guy asks sulkily.

'Just as an example, I rather like the way we're going

with this stolen cats piece,' Jennifer says. 'And it's not a story I would normally take much interest in. But I guess my antennae are twitching. I'd like Katie to keep going with it.'

I realize I am the first staff member that she has actually mentioned by name in the meeting, and I feel a wild, schoolgirlish thrill, as if the headmistress has singled me out for praise. It goes instantly, though, when Jennifer attacks my feature on Pete.

'I understand there's a saying in the office – "local heroes or local zeroes".' Jennifer nods. 'In theory, that's not bad, but we seem to be dredging up almost anyone we can find to play those roles, particularly the heroes. There are an awful lot of musicians in Brighton and Hove, and I'm afraid unless their first name is Fatboy and their second name is Slim, I don't really think people care. Do you?'

There is a grinding noise after this, and I realize that out of habit Guy is trying to wheel himself around in his swivel chair, but thinks better of it and stalls himself on Jennifer's floorboards.

That's another change. Molloy's office has had green, swirly carpet for ever, but no more. In the course of a weekend the carpet has been ripped up and the underlying floorboards have been polished.

I look at Jennifer's shoes and then at her shirt.

I tried the black and white clothes thing ages ago, when I wanted a new start after Andrew and was trying to be chic. In the end I just looked like a penguin. But Jennifer – all fortysomething years of her – looks good.

'She's actually fifty-one,' Claudia lets me know, once we have been released for our morning tea break and are hanging around near the chocolate machine.

'How do you know?'

'Courtney told me. And Guy told her. And he's seen her CV. Fell off the back of a lorry.'

'So,' I give her a long look. 'You and Courtney. Talking to each other. That's new.'

'It's easier to be friends.' Claudia shrugs.

'What? She pinched your cat!'

Claudia shrugs again.

'What about Guy?'

'Guy's fine.' She smiles happily. 'We all had dinner together – last night.'

'What? You, Guy and Courtney, and the harem?'

'I suppose it is a bit of a harem.' She smiles again.

I give up. I will never understand other people's love lives – any more than other people will understand mine probably.

And sure enough, after Ben goes back to Polly, life with Pete becomes even more difficult.

I am accused of talking too much about work, in bed, in the early hours of Tuesday morning, after he has discovered he can't get it up.

'You're tired,' I say. 'I don't mind.'

'You've worn me out.' He sighs, turning his back on me. 'All that talk about Jennifer Cobbles.'

'Jennifer George.'

'Whatever,' he offers, yawning as he leans on his elbow, then a few minutes later he's snoring.

Then, the following day, he gives me a late, late birthday present.

I have deliberately not mentioned my birthday again, since the conversation about Jim and the Jaguar Promenade. Consequently Pete and I have been playing a silly game with each other. Birthday cards and presents have landed on the front doormat; he has overheard me laughing at some of the e-cards which have arrived on my computer, and all the time he has avoided my eye as much as I have avoided his.

The late, late birthday present is a ring. It is beautiful, modern and gold, and studded with a single line of small, white diamonds.

'It's not that sort of ring,' Pete tells me when I find it hidden under a flower in my cereal bowl at breakfast. 'But then you know that.'

'What sort of ring is it, then?'

I turn it over and over in my hand – I can't quite believe that he's done it.

'A sort of maybe-one-day-we-could kind of ring. A kind of first course.' He shrugs. 'A beginning ring.'

'Really?'

And before I know it I'm crying.

'Oi,' Pete pulls me towards him.

'Don't ask how I paid for the ring.' He sighs as I snuffle into his shoulder. 'A load of Japanese tourists turned up at the casino and gave me a tip. In chips. I played all these bloody horrible songs – real karaoke stuff – and they were mad for it.'

'Chips?' I say stupidly.

'Gambling chips. Not salt and vinegar. They piled them up on top of me piano. So . . . I had a bit of a punt, and I won some dosh and I found your birthday present,' Pete whispers into my neck.

Then he adds, 'Ben's frightened of you,' he shakes his head once we've broken away from each other, and I have found a tissue. 'It's not that he doesn't like you, it's that he's scared of you, and he's hardly ever been away from Polly before. And he thinks I'm a bad man, probably, because I'm not there any more. So try to understand.'

'I do,' I say helplessly. 'That's not it.'

'Well what was it then?' Pete watches me as I take another tissue from the box. 'What was it, the other weekend? It was like a storm coming up.'

'I know.' I blow my nose.

'Anyway,' Pete moves the conversation along, 'the ring fits, that's the main thing.'

We drag each other to bed and Pete sheds his clothes along the way, pulling mine off in turn, driving me mad.

'I was once told my taste in sex was impossibly vanilla, my dear,' Pete whispers in my ear, putting on a silly voice. 'Could it be true?'

'But I like vanilla.'

'Well that's all right then.' Pete takes me by the hand.

Then he fishes around on his side of the bed and presents me with a Japanese porn magazine. 'The businessmen at the casino gave it to me.' He flicks through it. 'It's from Tokyo. What do you think?'

'I don't know what I think,' I say, and then I realize he's trying not to laugh.

'Sorry.' He throws the magazine down again. 'I couldn't resist.'

'It looks a bit like a kung fu film,' I try to say before his hand goes gently over my mouth.

'Shut up while I give you your birthday present,' Pete says. 'And kung fu's Chinese, not Japanese.'

I stop talking and give in.

'Pants off ankles,' Pete continues, pulling off the last of my clothes. 'And now put your mobile on vibrate.'

'Very funny.'

'Here,' Pete reaches under the bed and throws me a box that's gift-wrapped in pink tissue paper and silver ribbon. 'I'm serious.'

'Is it really a vibrator?' I look down at him.

'Do you want it?'

'No. Yes. All right then. What does it look like?'

'Like this,' Pete unwraps it and turns it on, buzzing it against the side of his finger. 'White. Smooth. I told you my taste in sex was vanilla.'

I can't think of anything to say now, so I lie back, close my eyes, try not to think about Japanese porn and give in.

'And by the way,' Pete says, trying to sound casual once he's finished with me and I've got my breath back, 'they want some ringtones off me.'

'Who wants ringtones?' I manage to say.

'The Japanese at the casino. They work for a big phone company in Tokyo. They want me to give them some animal noises.' Pete moos, baas and then barks.

'What? Japanese animals? Hey, are you getting on top of me now?'

'Oh yes.' Pete chucks the vibrator aside. 'I'm definitely getting on top of you, Miss nineteen fifties girl. In fact, you might say,' he whispers, 'I'm getting on top of everything.'

Then, later – much later – Pete talks to me about Polly.

We are showered and in our dressing-gowns when it happens. Or at least I'm in my dressing-gown and he's in an ancient Doors T-shirt and a pair of boxer shorts.

'See, with the central heating turned up all the way it's like being on holiday,' Pete nods.

'Summer's not far off,' I say, pouring us both a cup of coffee now that Pete has finished plunging it up and down a few hundred times. As is always the case with him, after a long time in bed, almost everything he does or says, makes me think of sex.

'Polly and I had a bit of a summer relationship,' Pete sighs. 'It went in cycles. She was all down in the dumps during the winter and we hardly ever did it.'

'Too much information.'

'All right then.' Pete shakes his head. 'Sorry. But anyway, she was always good in the summer, and that was what kept us going.'

'Drugs?'

'Oh yeah.' Pete shrugs. 'We had all the summer drugs. Ibiza was brilliant. Happiest days of our lives.'

'Happier than with me?' I tempt fate.

'It was about having an unnatural high, you know?' Pete shrugs again. 'And it's not a fair question, really. We're not having the benefit of chemical enhancement in this relationship. With Poll, it was tons of e and

193

lots of lying around on the beach. Totally different vibe.'

'I had to write an article on ecstasy for the paper a few years ago. You know it was prescribed by American marriage guidance counsellors to keep couples together?'

'Thank you for the lecture.' Pete puts on a prim face. 'Yes, I know.' He smiles. 'Worked a treat for me and Polly.'

'How is she?' I ask dutifully.

'Fine. But it's hard having Ben on her own.'

'So the bloke with the flat in Spain never happened in the end?'

'It's gone nowhere,' Pete replies. 'So she's got Ben on her own, no money for childcare and . . . that's why we've agreed I should have him now and again. She needs time to herself.'

'Oh.'

'I gave her a ring once.' Pete inspects the new ring on my finger. 'It wasn't as nice as yours.'

'What sort of ring?'

'Proper one. Engagement. But she chucked it off the pier when we had a fight about me career, so that was that.'

I nod and I realize I suddenly feel so tired I really should go back to bed. The coffee is unbelievably strong, as it always is when Pete makes it, but even the caffeine isn't enough to keep my eyes open.

I try not to feel upset about Polly's engagement ring and fail.

Every time I think I know where I'm headed with Pete, a wave comes up and hits me in the face. It's like watching Jim go surfing off the pier.

Then a few days later I read the first 'Letter From France' by our handsome new Parisian correspondent Simon White. It's all about a new 555-seat plane, the largest passenger aeroplane ever built, on which he seems to have conveniently wangled himself a free seat and a few glasses of champagne.

The new plane is seven stories tall. Then something clicks. I ring Jim.

'You saw the world's biggest plane taking off,' I tell him. 'And it has. And you saw the French word for seven. It's seven stories high.'

Jim laughs. 'Great.'

'Anyway. How's Hastings?'

'Hastings is great too.'

'Did that girl who liked you ever turn up again?' I ask.

'The one who took one look at me and got hospitalized for meningitis? Nuh.'

'And how's life otherwise?' I ask.

'Courtney's been calling.'

'Oh.'

'About a hundred times.'

'Why?'

'It varies.' He smiles.

Then, at last, something makes me tell him.

'Courtney cast a love spell on you. Or at least a love spell about you. I suppose I should have told you ages ago, but anyway.'

'Ah.'

'I saw it in her book when I came round to the shop to interview her that day. It seemed to involve shit of some kind.'

'Oh.'

'The spell was in a pentacle shape, or a pentagram – I can never tell the difference. Any woman who comes near you gets it in the neck, basically. Oh, and she cast a spell for a few other things: money, success, fame, power, riches, you know.'

'I know about the spell,' Jim says at last. 'Actually, there are a few of them.'

'Really? Yuck.'

'She hasn't told me, but I know.'

'Bucket?'

'Bucket,' Jim confirms.

'This girl at the bakery who you nearly started dating just ended up in hospital. Her spells are working.'

'Oh, I know they're working,' Jim agrees.

'Well can't you do something?'

'No.' He sighs. 'And before you say anything, I've already tried. She wouldn't listen. Do you think I can stop black magic? Even a psychic has trouble stopping a psychic attack.'

'Great.' I think of poor Alison and the pigeons. 'Meanwhile Guy's PA got forced out of her job.'

'But it eats itself, Katie,' he tries to reassure me. 'Trust me. The energy eats itself in the end. It self-destructs.'

'So what's going to happen to Courtney when that happens?'

'It's not just Courtney. It's all of them. Courtney, Jan, Lou, Deb and Claudia.'

'Claudia?'

'She's joined them.'

'What?'

'I can feel it.' Jim sighs.

After he hangs up I make my way down to the pool for an end-of-day swim. The fact that Jim Gabriel once made the hideous mistake of sleeping with Courtney Creely is only slightly my business and that's all. It's not something I should have any feelings about.

It's not as if he's going to sleep with her again, I comfort myself as I hit the wall with my hands – old-school-swimming-carnival habits die hard – and stand gasping for breath in the shallow end.

I think of Pete with Polly and let myself feel painfully jealous for a few moments. Then I imagine Courtney on top of Jim – of course she'd be on top,

196

wouldn't she, with her hair flying about all over the place? – and see what that feels like.

And it feels . . . nowhere near as bad. Which is a relief, I suppose. Because every time one of Jim's bucket predictions comes true, like Russell Crowe or the French plane, there's a part of me that still can't help thinking about my middle name on a marriage certificate alongside his.

I switch to breaststroke for another length, deciding to get out of the pool at the other end as soon as I see dozens of schoolgirls come screaming in.

I can't believe Claudia has got involved with Courtney's weird coven. But Jim and his bucket are seldom wrong. What the hell is she thinking?

Then I go back to work and see her thin, very English blond hair has become thick and wild and LA sunshine yellow.

'Hiya.' She waves me over to her desk.

'Wow. Your hair.'

'Do you like it? The girls did it at the salon.'

'Is it hair extensions?'

'Yeah. And they did my nails, too,' Claudia holds out her hands, showing me a set of new, perfectly painted fingernails.

Then she remembers something. She's selling pin-on flowers in aid of one of the local childrens' hospitals.

'Want one?' She attaches it to my shirt before I can reply.

'Sure.'

'Five hundred pounds.' Claudia pats the rucksack under the desk. 'Can you believe I've sold five hundred quid's worth in a week?'

'Really?'

'I just went down to the Churchill Centre and they went like hot cakes. I sold two hundred in one hit, to a woman with a jewellery shop in Lewes. The hospital absolutely loves me.'

197

'You've just sold *five hundred pounds'* worth of flowers?'

'It's magic.' She smiles, taking my money and putting it in her sack.

Then Jennifer calls me away for a meeting.

'Do you mind if we go out somewhere?' she says. 'We won't be long. Maybe half an hour. I've become quite fond of a place near my flat. It's Italian, so proper cappuccinos for a change.'

Jennifer drives a BMW, like Guy – which must annoy him – but hers has dog hair on a blanket on the front seat, and dusty white marks all over the back seat, so apparently she owns hers.

'That's my baby,' she says, noticing me looking at the photo of a Heinz 57 variety dog she has stuck on the front of her glovebox. 'His name's Oliver.'

Aha. A human side to my new boss. Well – maybe.

She presses play on her CD and we listen to one of those Frank Sinatra/old crooner compilations which everyone in Brighton seems to own these days.

' "Blue Moon",' she recognizes the song as it comes on. 'Oliver loves that song.'

Apart from the smell of the music-loving dog, I can also smell chlorine inside the car, which I am embarrassed to think might be me because I haven't washed my hair properly after my swim. Then I see a damp plastic bag at my feet, with a black swimming costume falling out of it.

'Sorry,' Jennifer kicks it out of the way.

And she smokes as well – lots and lots of cigarettes, which shed ash everywhere as she navigates her way from the office to Hove.

'Here we are.' She pulls up and we go inside the café where, it seems, she is already known to the waitress, who smiles and nods a lot. I suppose Jennifer gives good tips.

We sit down and order.

'I want to know what really happened with your Australian psychic friend,' Jennifer levels with me.

'Right.'

'Guy mentioned an interview tape had gone missing. Can we have that back please? It's the property of the newspaper after all, as you know.'

Jennifer licks her lips and the creamy cappuccino moustache disappears. Amazingly, though, her lipstick stays on throughout.

'I lost the tape.' I feel myself blushing. 'And I don't have the transcript any more.'

'That's a shame.' She stares into space. 'And it's been deleted from the system too, though we still have the photos of Jim, of course. But . . . would he speak to us again, do you think?'

'I don't know.'

'I keep hearing about him.' Jennifer smiles. 'He's got quite a reputation, hasn't he? Doesn't he live in Hastings now?'

'He had to move,' I tell her, 'because of us.'

'Mmmm. We definitely owe him an apology for that dreadful shark story,' Jennifer stops smiling. 'Can you speak to Jim sooner rather than later? I was talking to one of the sub-editors about the original interview he gave you. I'm fascinated. If the shark and desk thing really was about the Damien Hirst piece and the Kennedy auction, then I know our readers would be intrigued. I'm a sceptic, obviously, but I'm genuinely intrigued by this. There's more to this story than I think Guy has seen.'

Then she pauses to light a cigarette and leans back in her chair.

'And I'm thinking of moving Guy across,' she goes on, 'into a different role on the paper – as our sports editor. We've just had a resignation.'

Aha. Mr Crazy Golf. The man who didn't know what

a pink pound was. I wondered when that would happen.

'Sport? Guy?'

'I've been told that's his true area of speciality by other people on the paper. And he seems to agree.'

'What? I think they were joking. Or he was. He can't even . . .' I try to think of something Guy can't do connected with sport, and realize this means everything in the entire sporting world. 'Jennifer, he can't even play darts. He didn't even do sport at school, I don't think. He just used to skive off.'

'But he must know about cricket,' she says, as if all men are born with a knowledge of cricket.

'Nope. He knows less than me, and that's nothing.'

'Football?'

'He buys the same sunglasses as David Beckham. And he knows his name. That's it.'

'Really?'

She gives up. 'Oh well.' She waves a hand. 'Some sort of other role. What do you think?'

'I'm not sure what I think,' I tell her.

'We'll get there.' She nods. 'Would you like something to eat as well? I'm suddenly feeling hungry.'

Later on I ring Jim to tell him what Jennifer has said about running another feature on him in the paper.

'OK,' he says, 'whatever. Can we talk about it another time?'

'I can hear the sea. Where are you?'

'In the hut. I was meditating.'

'Oh. Sorry.'

'And I've decided', Jim tells me, 'I'm going to give you a spare set of keys.'

'Keys?' I say stupidly.

'So you can use the hut, too,' Jim says patiently. 'Whenever you want.'

'Wow. Are you sure?'

'I can't give you the cottage by the sea,' he finishes, 'but I can give you something. I'll put the keys through the letterbox tomorrow.'

Then, when he hangs up, I realize there's something weird about our conversation, and it rests on the fact that a cottage by the sea is my oldest, favourite daydream and, apart from Andrew, I've never told anyone else about it. Ever.

I buy a new journal the following day – the Edwardian lady book is now completely full.

I'm fed up with dating everything; the gaps between the entries are so long it makes me look like a slacker. Instead I find myself writing about a cottage I've seen in the property section of the paper.

I could never afford it in a million years, but I don't care.

Sometimes you have to hang onto your dreams. And it's a cottage with a garden at the front, the South Downs at the back, blue skies overhead (the photographer picked the right day) and ... it's the kind of place where I can imagine being happy.

'HAPPY', I write in block capitals and underline it, just in case I've forgotten what that might actually feel like.

CHAPTER TWELVE

Jim wakes me up in the early hours of Sunday morning to tell me that he's getting messages for hundreds
of people from their dead relatives and he hasn't slept
for almost twenty-four hours.

'What do you mean, hundreds of people?'

'I don't know who they are. But I'm getting the
name, then the street name and then the message. I've
been looking them all up in the phone book. They're
all local. I guess I'm going to have to ring them all up
and pass on the messages.'

'What?'

Pete's asleep, so I take my mobile into the sitting
room and wrap a blanket round me, like a shawl.

'All right. Read me some of these messages.'

'OK.' Jim sounds relieved. 'Name, Appleton, street,
Somerset, message, uncle says you'll pass your exams.
Name, Pearson, street, Silverton Rd, message, ex-
husband says sorry and hopes you're happy. Name,
Clifford, street, Crabtree Avenue, message, daughter
says hello mummy and thanks for putting my teddy in
the coffin.'

'Oh my God. How many?'

'I counted just now. In total, four hundred and
seventeen.'

I pad into the kitchen in my bare feet with my heart

hammering – the floor is freezing – and put the kettle on. I am wide awake now, so I may as well make myself a cup of tea.

'Jim?'

'Yes.'

'Go back to bed. And don't call anyone. You'll just upset them.'

'I have to. They want to hear from these people. They've been praying for it, whether they call it a prayer or not.'

'You know that, do you? Was that in your bucket?'

Tiredness is making me irritable.

'I can't lie down, Katie. I can't sit still. I can't sleep. I can't eat. The only peace I get is when I put the pen in my hand.'

I realize I have no idea what to say to this. But then Pete's phone rings too, and soon he's out of bed as well, shouting at Polly in the bedroom while I listen to Jim rambling on in the kitchen. There must be a full moon – everybody's gone mad. Then I look out of the window and see that I'm right.

'I've got to go, Jim,' I tell him. 'Maybe talking to me will make the messages stop, but trust me, you can't just ring people up and say you've got their dead ex-husband on the line. Or their little girl, or whatever. I mean,' I try to explain it to him, 'I was so happy to hear Andrew was there, and my grandfather. I'm grateful that you did that. But I know you, Jim, and even for me it was a shock.'

A pause.

'Well, you're not getting messages now, then,' I encourage him.

'Wow,' he concludes. 'Yes, I think it's stopped. What a night.' He sounds exhausted.

'So go back to bed.'

And then I take my tea back into the bedroom to find that Pete has stopped shouting at Polly and is now

203

telling her that he loves her. Or, to be specific, that he'll always love her.

It's not the words that upset me, though: it's the sound of his voice, and the way he's hunched over the phone, as if it's pulling him closer to her.

Then he notices me and hangs up.

'Polly's not in a good way.'

'Yeah, well.'

'Don't be like that.'

'You were with her for years. She's Ben's mother. They're your family. How can I be annoyed if she calls you in the middle of the night? How can I have a problem if she needs you? Especially if I'm being rung up in the middle of the night by people, too.' I hold a logical debate with myself.

Then I realize I feel like crying. He'll always love her. So much for logical debate.

'I might have to go up to York for a bit.' Pete sighs.

'Do you think life's more boring with me?' I hear myself ask.

'Eh?'

'I mean, I know it's more peaceful and you're less likely to be arrested for possession of Class-A drugs and all that, but is it more boring than it was with Polly?'

Pete shakes his head and stares at his feet.

'And we should talk about Ben,' I hear myself saying. 'Because if you're going to have him here every two weeks, and if we're consequently going to have Polly in our lives every two weeks, well . . . can I be honest? It's not really my dream life. Because, Pete, I got into a relationship with you – just you, by yourself – and I didn't realize they were coming along, too.'

'But of course they were coming,' Pete fires back. 'What did you think? I can't leave my family.'

'But they left you. Or Polly did.'

'You know what I mean. They're still my family.'

204

And then before I can say any more, Pete is out of the room. The door slams a few minutes later, and I realize he's out of the flat, too. In his pyjamas. Probably accessorized by filthy old trainers and a black leather coat he keeps on a hook by the front door.

I plump up Pete's pillow, doubling it up with mine, and lean back against the wall with my tea. For some reason my grandfather suddenly pops into my head, along with his rules for journalism, which he first taught me when I told him I wanted to be a reporter.

Have I been fair, in my conversation with Pete just now? Have I been reasonable? Have I given all parties concerned equal opportunity to state their case? Is what I said in everybody's interest?

The answer is no, of course, all I've done is made myself sound like a jealous harpie, but suddenly I seem to have stopped caring.

I realize how exhausted I am. I feel as if I've been doing half of Guy's job and half of Courtney's, too, since Molloy died.

For no reason at all I think about a mad conversation Andrew and I had at the beginning of our relationship, after we'd gone out one Sunday afternoon in his brand-new second-hand Jaguar, and I had worked my way through a bottle of white wine in a country pub.

It was the beginning of Spring and all the flowers were out, which made us fall in love with every village we drove through. Just when we thought we'd found our dream cottage, or our dream garden, or our dream local pub, another one would fly past.

We were so sure of each other, back then, that we found ourselves talking about exactly what we wanted from life. He wanted to retire from work early and wave goodbye to working with other people's money in the city, and go travelling with me through Egypt, and then after that, through Australia and Asia.

I wanted a thatched Sussex cottage with roses around the door, just like the one I was daydreaming about in my journal, and a baby to call our own. But mostly, as I told him, I just wanted to be with him, as often as possible for as long as possible. I wanted to hear the sea through the window, and I wanted him, and his sons and daughters, holding both my hands on the beach.

Just because all the dreams you have are other people's dreams too doesn't make them corny. Just because they're clichéd, or popular, or appear in advertisements for banks doesn't make them wrong. Andrew explained that to me. So after that we confessed all our bits to each other, even the stuff about growing old together, and then we went for a long walk on the South Downs to see an electric-pink sunset I can still remember.

I try to remember if I knew about Andrew's depression back then, and I realize I must have done. It was one of the first things he told me about himself. It didn't worry me at the time because he played it down so well. He told me that it ran in his family and that it turned up every other year, as cold sores do for other people. His doctor understood, and the people at work understood, too, he said, so it was only right that he should explain it all to me.

I listen for Pete coming back now in the stillness, and am let down to realize how completely unmoved I feel when I realize he's gone.

I know he won't have gone far – even Pete Oram isn't capable of transporting himself to York in the middle of the night in pyjamas and a leather coat – but still.

Ben is due for a visit soon. It's written on our calendar, stuck to the fridge door. And it's not that I don't feel guilty, but honestly, nose-picking, book-chucking, TV-addicted Ben was never in my seaside-cottage fantasy.

Ben will always be Polly's son, and that's the whole problem really. With every tantrum he threw the other weekend, I blamed her.

The next morning I wake up to an empty bed, and for a moment I remember what it's like to be single on a Sunday. When I pick up the papers from the front doormat, they're full of Tony Blair's election win. It's another triumph for Jim and his bucket, though anyone, even good old non-psychic me, could have seen that one coming.

I realize I don't know how Pete voted, or even if he voted at all. He probably didn't. Or am I being too judgemental? I worry about it all the way through my muesli – how can we call ourselves a couple if I don't even know what his politics are? Or if he bothered to vote? Then I give up and call Linda.

'Stop worrying so much. Get out of the flat,' she says through a mouthful of toast. 'And stop thinking so much, as well. God, my hangover's bad. Can they not make vodka with less evils in it?'

'Sorry,' I apologize.

'Nah, it's OK. But you should get out of the flat. The sun's shining. The war's still on, but the sun's shining. Get down to the beach or something.'

And then I remember I have the keys to Jim's beach hut. Oh the joy. Except that when I look for them, in my purse and then in my coat pocket and then in every item of clothing I own, I realize they're missing.

I turn the flat upside down. Never in my life have I wanted to be somewhere as much as I want to be in the little hut with the turquoise blue roof. But in every place I look all I find are bits of Pete's mess.

And I realize, as I pull out all the clothes from our wardrobe, that I still have this lingering paranoia about finding drugs. Why can't I trust him? Why don't I believe him when he says he's put all that behind him? And why didn't I believe him about the Japanese businessmen and the casino chips? There's still a part of me that thinks the diamond ring was paid for with little plastic bags of ecstasy.

I look at my beautiful ring now and twist it off my finger. Pete's favourite thing in the world is talking about the beginning of the beginning of the beginning. And that's all my new diamond ring represents. So why am I wearing it? Why have I let him con me? At least Polly had some sort of ending thrown in when she got hers.

I put the ring with my other jewellery and decide to walk down to the beach hut, keys or no keys. Maybe Jim will be surfing out there – he might have caught an early train from Hastings in pursuit of this morning's north-easterly gales. Then I think, Linda's right. I just need to get out of the flat.

I take the road less travelled and walk past the Royal Pavilion, or Prinny's Palace, as my grandfather used to call it. As always, it reminds me of pickled onions.

Backpackers and daytrippers blunder past, running into me because they are too busy gaping at the pickled-onion Pavilion domes to see other people. I'm in such a bad mood now that I shove one of them with my elbow – I'm fed up with the way my town becomes a tourist trap as soon as the temperature goes up five degrees. Usually I don't notice them. But right now I feel like machine-gunning the lot of them.

I look in vain for Pete's face among the crowd, or even his back. I miss him almost as much as I can't stand him at the moment.

I spend the best part of an hour walking along the seafront to Jim's beach hut, until I suddenly see Pete inside it, with the door open and his head sticking out, as if he's part of a conjuring trick and someone has just sawn him in half. He has his rock-star sunglasses on and one of Jim's New Age books covering the rest of his face.

'Hello darlin',' he says in a stupid cockney accent. Then he switches to Liverpudlian. 'I fooked up. Sorry.'

'You took my keys,' I say.

But Pete doesn't reply. Instead he gets up, throws the sunglasses and book inside the hut, takes my hand, shuts the door and kisses me hard, up against the wall in the dark.

'No,' I protest pointlessly. Because the rest of me, as usual, is saying yes.

He takes my bra off.

'So did you spend the night in here?' I ask – or try to, before I give in and let him guide me gently onto a pile of old blankets on the floor.

And that's how Jim finds us, of course, about ten minutes later, when the door suddenly swings open and Pete and I find ourselves blinking in the light, me without my bra and him without anything at all, as the sun streams into the hut.

'Hi,' Jim says. 'Sorry.' And then he shuts the door again, leaving us in the dark.

'Christ,' Pete says. 'I don't think his psychic ability's working this morning. I think he might have switched himself off.'

'Pete. Shut up.'

I expect Jim has bolted all the way back to Hastings now, or at least as far out into the English Channel as he can swim. He probably came here to get his surfboard. I can't let him go without it, not if he's taken a train all the way here.

I push Pete away as he tries to wrap his arms around me, and do my best to get dressed, squinting in the thin band of light under the door, as I try to see what I'm doing.

'I've got to find Jim. I've really got to find him. Shall I see you back at the flat?'

'Maybe.' Pete sighs.

'Look. Just go back to the flat. Is that all right?'

'Yeah, yeah.' Pete sighs again.

So I leave him to it and close the door behind me, stepping out, like Doctor Who emerging from his Tardis, onto the foreshore. It's the first proper sunny Sunday we've had, so people are using every available inch of sky, sea and land while the weather holds.

I look above me, and see a hang-glider, then I look ahead of me and see children bobbing around in the water wearing armbands, as a jogger in shorts puffs past. Then Jim calls my name, and I see him, running to catch me, soaking wet and smiling. His hair is shorter these days – the shaggy lion of winter in the billowing white cricket trousers has gone.

'I'm really sorry.' He shakes his head.

He's seen my breasts, I think, like an idiot. He's seen my breasts.

'Oh God. It's not your fault. Pete nicked the keys. He stayed the night there because we had a row.'

'And you made it up. That's good.'

I feel myself going red and turn away.

'No really,' Jim goes on, pulling his towel around him. 'That's good. Make love, not war. You know.'

'Shall we sit over here?' I point to the sea wall.

'I've written down five hundred and seventy-three messages now.' Jim rubs his face. 'It only stopped when the sun came up.'

'And is it over now?'

'I think so.' Jim wipes his nose with the back of his hand, then catches me noticing and stops.

'So what are you going to do next?' I ask.

'Take them to the art exhibition that's coming up in Hastings,' he says. 'That's where the BBC are going to be. It says so on the poster. And that's where I have to be.'

'Because some of the people will be there? The ones you have messages for?'

'I don't know.'

'Isn't your bucket telling you?'

'I just have to trust. Your granddad told me to go there, and I have to go.'

'Well,' I think of my grandfather for a moment, all white hair and old Barbour jacket, 'I wish he hadn't.'

Jim laughs.

'You're the only person I'm telling about this.' He blinks in the sunlight.

'OK.'

'It's weirding you out, though,' he shakes his head and stares at the sea. 'I can tell it's weirding you out.'

'No,' I lie. 'People might think you just hired a private detective, though, to get the messages. Or they might think you've got their information from a credit-card company or any of those direct-marketing places. Sorry.' I catch his look. 'I'm just being journalistic. Playing devil's advocate.'

'The messages are personal.' Jim shakes his head. 'And there's one for you,' he says. 'From your maths teacher.'

'Mrs Durrant?' I name her automatically. She died young, of breast cancer.

'The message is, thanks for the free gherkin.'

'Yes,' I give in. 'That was a huge joke. I did my maths homework while I was eating lunch because I was in a rush. A bit of gherkin came out of the sandwich and it got stuck between the pages. She held it up in front of the whole class.'

I stare at him.

'Was that it?'

He smiles. 'Yeah. Just thanks for the free gherkin.'

Then he looks down at his feet and picks up a sports bag, fumbling for something in the bottom. It's a folded-up piece of paper, wrapped carefully inside a sheet of newspaper.

'For you,' he says.

And that's when I cry, and cry, because he has drawn Andrew – to the life – and signed his name, with love, at the bottom.

Jim rubs his hand on my back, round and round to try and comfort me, and then, when I cannot stop crying, he pulls my head gently into his chest. His skin is cold and wet, but he feels incredibly warm at the same time.

'I hesitated,' I hear him say. 'I thought about it. I nearly threw it out in case it upset you. But then I realized he wants you to have it.'

'It's him,' I look at the drawing again. 'It's exactly him. And that's his handwriting. God, why am I crying all the time at the moment? I'm just so tired, Jim.' I flop into him. 'Sorry, but I'm really, really tired.'

I stare at the drawing for a while. There is no drawing of Andrew that looks like this. In fact, I'm fairly sure nobody ever did a portrait of him in his life. And there is certainly no photograph of Andrew that resembles this sketch. It's as if Jim has caught him unawares in the street, as if he were still alive somewhere.

'How could you know what Andrew looks like?'

He shrugs.

'Just don't be weirded out by it, Katie. That's all. Please.' He sighs.

'All right,' I hear myself telling him.

'Hang in there with me.'

'OK.'

'Because', he sighs as we watch the waves rolling in from France, 'it's going to get weirder. OK?'

I nod.

And then I decide what I'm going to do with the rest of my Sunday. I'm going to visit Claudia and find out exactly what she's up to with Courtney.

It's all very well for Jim to say there's nothing he can do, but I refuse to let her become one of them.

* * *

When I arrive she's watching an old black-and-white film on the television wearing full make-up. She looks tanned, until she takes her slippers off and I see that she has white feet, where the tan stops at her ankles.

'They gave me a free sample at the salon,' she says, following my gaze. 'So I could see what I'd look like if I get it done all the time. What do you think?'

'Not sure,' I lie. She looks like one of those unnaturally golden morning-TV presenters who dance around in strappy tops in the middle of January.

'And you've got more hair extensions,' I notice.

'Jan said I suited really long hair,' she says. 'And they didn't charge me. It was all free. Courtney said it was my reward for selling all those flowers for the hospital.'

'That's good,' I say automatically.

'I've got more now,' she pats a stack of cardboard boxes next to the sofa. 'I'm doing it on e-Bay. The hospital said there's a company which does all the charities, so they're putting me on commission.'

'Wow.'

'I might even be able to leave work.' She laughs and then looks serious. 'I've been wanting to. For ages. I only stuck it out for Guy, really.'

I look through the TV guide while Claudia puts the kettle on. It seems like a hundred years since I watched television properly. I remember when I used to go through all the programmes with a biro, circling what I wanted to watch. Not any more.

I try to remember what my life was like before Pete – and Jim, and the crisis at the paper, for that matter – and realize it's all gone soft and blurry, like an out-of-focus film.

When Claudia comes back with some coffee on a tray, I notice her new, long, painted fingernails again.

213

And then I see she's wearing a pentacle ring. Just like the pentacle in Courtney's book.

'They gave me falsies,' she says happily. 'And I got a pedicure as well.' She takes off her socks and displays her toenails, which are also pearly pink and polished. 'Jan spent ages on me. Guy loves it.'

'Guy?'

'We all went out again last night and he made me take my shoes off to show him.'

Claudia gives a little hum. 'I feel like a new woman, know what I mean? And Courtney is going to take me shopping, too. She gets a discount at this place where she does modelling.'

'So are Guy and Courtney still on then?' I try not to sound too interested.

'Oh, they get on really well,' she says. 'And Courtney says they've stopped arguing so much now he's free to be with who he wants to be with.'

'So they've split up?'

'No,' Claudia looks amazed at this suggestion. 'They're just having an open relationship. So if Guy wants to be with me, he can be with me, and if he wants to be with Jan, he can be with her. Or any of us.'

I try to let this sink in.

'So, all good friends then?' I check.

'Guy loves it.' She proclaims. 'But then most men would, wouldn't they?'

'Right.'

'I feel great.' She gives a little jiggle on the sofa.

The talk about witchcraft and her exciting new friends can wait for another time. I can't get through to her now.

'You should come out with us some time,' is the last thing I hear before I close the door of her flat behind me.

The next day I see Guy with Jan. At first I think it's

Courtney, because the long, fox-red hair and tight, white trousers are the same, but it's not.

They're having lunch outside in the sunshine near the Pavilion when I notice them, although they don't notice me. Guy is wearing his sunglasses and looks as if he's been thoroughly spray-tanned by someone at the salon. Jan is laughing at his jokes and leaning in close, as if she can't afford to miss a word he says.

I disappear into a shop – I need to get at least one new shirt to wear to work now that the weather is warmer – and forget all about them, until I walk outside and realize they are still at the café, only this time Guy is kissing Jan goodbye.

It is a long kiss, as if she doesn't want it to end, although Guy – being Guy – remembers that they're in public and pulls away.

Automatically I worry that if I've seen them, then half of Brighton will have too; consequently a shouting match with Courtney or a showdown with Claudia cannot be too far away. Then I remember, Guy Booth is king of open relationships now and everybody's friends.

I walk back to the office, picking up a sandwich on the way. Guy's BMW is hired, and his flat is mortgaged on his father's money. Surely his new harem must have found all that out by now? So it can't be the lure of his lifestyle that's tempting them to share him.

I try to imagine what sex with Guy Booth must be like, and fail. I expect he's one of those men who want you to admire him a lot before he can get going.

I wonder if the women split into pairs for him, or even threesomes – or fivesomes? – and then I think about the porn mag I found in his desk when I was taking Jim's tape. Guy must think he's landed in paradise.

Then, inevitably, I think about sex with Pete. And then I think about Polly having sex with Pete, and then

I have to go into another shop to look at another shirt just to distract myself.

Pete texts me just as I decide it's time to go back to work.

MICE SING LOVE SONGS is his message, followed by – typical Pete, all his messages end like this – a row of question marks and exclamation marks.

I text him back a question mark, in reply. And then, a few seconds later, I am rewarded with a second message. MALE MICE SING SQUEAKY ULTRASONIC LOVE BALLADS XXX

In the end I call him, only to receive a series of high-pitched squeals in my ear.

'I'm wooing you like a male mouse, Katie,' he says. 'To make up for my total crapness of late.'

'What are you on about?'

'To make up for my' – he tries to think of the right word – 'unacceptable behaviour, I've decided to sing you a mouse love song.'

'What?'

'You know I'm doing these ringtones for the Japanese,' he goes on as I cross the road and am nearly wiped out by a bus, 'well, I'm doing them mating mice.'

'I thought only frogs sang mating calls.'

'They all do it,' Pete's voice breaks up for a minute as my phone reception wobbles in front of another bus. Then his voice comes back to me again. 'And rats laugh, too, I found out. Sort of a chirpy little laugh. Did you know that?'

'No. And please don't do one.'

'Anyway,' Pete goes on, 'I love you and I'm going to cook you dinner tonight. All right? I've been playing mouse squeaks back at one-sixteenth of the normal speed and dropping the pitch. Sounds beautiful, man. Sounds like a hit ringtone. Or even just a hit.'

'Don't call me man. Honestly, Pete, you're breaking up again. I can't hear you!'

'And did you know that the men mice are driven to sing by the scent of female mouse urine?' he asks. 'Get that.'

And then the phone beeps, and I lose him. I suppose he'll tell me about it later.

When I get back to my desk I spend the first half an hour sighing a lot and not concentrating. I realize it's the Pete Oram effect again – and all it took was a mad call about rodent love squeaks.

Maybe that's what he's doing to me, too – emitting ultrasonic sounds through the atmosphere, which nobody else can hear. There's got to be some explanation for the way I keep going back for more.

Later I get another text: SEE YOU TONIGHT, 1950s GIRL ???!!! XXX.

Then Jennifer appears at my desk and pulls up a chair.

'Have you had a chance to speak to Jim Gabriel yet?'

'He said he'd do the story,' I reply automatically. 'Or at least he said he was still interested.'

'One of the sub-editors who worked on the original piece – the shark story– said he remembers Jim predicting something about Madonna. I'd quite like to run a piece on that. Perhaps he can tell us more now that it's a little later in the year.'

'OK,' I say as I register the fact that Jennifer is doing three things to me simultaneously. She is terrifying me, charming me and hypnotizing me with her astonishing black and white clothes.

Jennifer is wearing beautiful black strappy sandals tied around her thin black ankles and a white skirt, black and white spotty shirt, white jacket, black jet necklace and long dangly white earrings. She has white teeth, smooth black hair in a ponytail and browny-black lipstick. It's like looking at a monochrome work of art.

I wonder absent-mindedly if she spends ages getting

ready for work, and then decide she doesn't. She probably has a printout from her computer every morning which tells her how to dress for maximum impact.

'Madonna's of perennial interest.' Jennifer fiddles with a box of matches on my desk. 'Can I have these?' she asks suddenly, getting up from her chair.

'Sure.'

'I'm smoking so much since I moved here, I'm always running out of them.' She smiles. 'Let me know about Jim anyway. A little bird told me you were working on a book together.'

'Not any more,' I say quickly, in case I'm about to be bawled out for it. 'The publishers changed their mind.'

'Oh.' Jennifer pulls a mock-upset face. 'That's a shame. Anyway. You're a good reporter, Katie. I'm sure you could tell his story well, if the chance comes up again.'

'Well, if it happens,' I say uselessly. What does she mean, I'm a good reporter? I'm one of the worst reporters in the world.

'And ask Jim about the stockmarket crash he saw, when you talk to him,' she adds.

Then she lets me know that her ex-girlfriend works in the City, and that if Jim is still available for private readings, there are plenty of people at the company who would like an appointment with him.

Jennifer's smooth phrase 'ex-girlfriend' is still in my head hours later when I'm trying to rehash the piece about the stolen cats.

So much for all the theories about our good-looking French correspondent and the private life of Jennifer George. I wonder if I'm the only person on the newspaper that Jennifer has told about her sexual preferences and decide I must be. I suppose the idea now is that I act as a kind of unofficial one-woman news agency, spreading the facts discreetly on her

218

behalf, so the other staff don't embarrass her by getting it wrong.

When I tell Guy about Jennifer a few days later, though, he already knows.

'Oh God, yeah.' He tuts and waves this aside.

'So she told you she was gay?'

'Honestly, Katie, after living in Brighton all your life you think you'd have the official parlance right. Lesbian, not gay. Gay is . . .' he looks up at the ceiling vaguely for inspiration. 'Gay is moustaches. That's not her.'

'Well, no. Except when she drinks a cappuccino. Then she's got one.'

'By the way,' he smirks, 'circulation's dropped another fifteen per cent since she took over. Did you hear?'

'Oh no.'

'Oh yeah,' he wheels himself around in his chair, skidding from his desk to the air-conditioner and back again. 'If I were you I'd start looking at the job classifieds up in London.'

'We'll be OK,' I try to convince myself.

'No we won't.' Guy smirks.

'Just because she got the job you wanted—' I start to lecture him.

'No, no,' Guy shakes his head, pushing up the sleeves of his shirt. 'Nothing like that. I like Jennifer. In fact,' he leers at me, 'despite the lesbian stuff, I happen to think Jennifer is a total babe.'

'Oh for God's sake.'

'Oprah Winfrey, Condaleeza Rice, bring it on.' Guy clicks his fingers.

'You know you're being stupid now,' I say. 'So stop it. Stop being deliberately stupid and lad-maggy.'

And then Guy laughs at me, because it seems I've hit the nail on the head.

'A mate of mine is starting up a new magazine called

His Stuff.' He waggles his eyebrows at me. 'Funny you should mention lad mags.'

'So is that where you think you might go?' I ask.

'Oh yeah.' He wheels himself away again, pedalling his Hush Puppies on the floor. 'Men's consumer titles, they're still the next big thing. And ... I know what they want and they know what I want. We'll meet in the middle,' he locks his fingers together, 'just like that.'

CHAPTER THIRTEEN

Here's another person I don't have to tell about Jennifer's sexual preferences – Courtney Creely.

'I love the way black women look,' she says one evening, as I'm trying to clear my desk and go home. 'It's so exotic.'

God she's thick. Powerful and thick. The worst of all combinations.

And ... I just wish she'd go away. Can't she marry Guy and move to London or something? Or go back to Cornucopia?

Now that summer is in sight Courtney is interpreting the occasional hot day as an excuse to come to work in dresses so sheer they look as if someone has woven them out of tights. She is wearing too much perfume and long, dangly earrings that swing when she walks and ... I've had enough.

'Don't you love the way Jennifer dresses?' she tries again, watching me shut down my computer.

'I'm just on my way out.'

'I bet she's a wonderful lover,' Courtney interrupts me.

'Yep.'

'She's not young any more, but her body's really young,' Courtney rambles on as I search around the room for someone else to talk to and realize we are the last two people left on this floor. 'Apparently she goes to the gym every day. And she only eats organic food. I mean, she smokes, but she's really fit.' She smiles sweetly. 'You get on with her, don't you?'

I make my way to the lift while Courtney follows. It's stuck on the ground floor. Typical. I push the button and then push it again, as if it will make any difference.

'Do you like Jennifer?' Courtney persists.

'I'm living with a man.'

'So am I,' Courtney says, playing with her long, dangly earrings. 'But that's not really an issue. Guy and I have an open relationship now.'

She drones on telling me how patient Jennifer is with her because she still makes mistakes on the paper sometimes, even though Guy has taught her everything she knows.

'I bet Jennifer would take it really slowly in bed, too,' Courtney says. 'I bet she'd be really patient with me if it ever happened.'

I feel like covering my ears, like Ben, and singing, 'La, la, la, la,' at the top of my voice.

'Jennifer said she doesn't know any good hairdressers in Brighton yet. I told her to go and see the girls. Jennifer says she loves what they did for Claudia.'

'Yeah.' It's all I can do to remain polite.

Then finally, finally, the lift arrives.

'If you ever want to go out for a drink after work,' Courtney calls after me at the top of her voice, 'tell Jennifer to come along.'

And then Courtney is gone. I suppose she's just magicked herself away, or found her cloak of invisibility or whatever it is she uses.

I looked up witchcraft on the internet last night and it was terrifying. There are thousands of them. No, hundreds of thousands of them. All like Courtney, Jan,

Deb, Lou and Claudia. All sewing herbs into velvet pouches, chanting for money, lighting candles to make men fall in love with them and . . .

It probably wouldn't bother me so much, I realize, if I didn't think it worked.

I suppose Courtney wants to be Jennifer's new PA if Guy's leaving, and she's so phenomenally crass that she believes the way to the job is via Jennifer George's pants. And I'm supposed to pass on her interest, apparently, because Courtney thinks I have Jennifer's ear.

I walk faster and faster along Marine Parade as I make my way back home to sweat all the work politics out of my system, but then, just when I feel ready for a book in the bath, I discover my flat has been turned into a recording studio.

Pete is lying on the floor, bare-chested, with a pony-tailed person who can only be his internet guru Magic Marky, judging by the way he's wired up to two laptop computers. One earpiece is in his left ear, trailing back to a large, orange Mac, while the other is connected to Pete's ancient PC.

'Hey, we're writing a new song. What rhymes with bird call?' Pete looks up from the floor and blows me a kiss.

'I dunno. Bronwyn Birdsall. She works in our advertising department.'

'Nah.' Pete waves me away, while Magic Marky suddenly sits bolt upright and says, 'Wow. I think I'm channelling "The Birdie Song".'

'Are you?' Pete looks impressed.

'Yeah,' Magic Marky fiddles with his ponytail. 'It was the most irritating song of the year 2000 and I'm channelling it. Hey!'

'Great, man,' Pete enthuses.

I sit on the sofa and take my tights and shoes off. I could care less about what Magic Marky thinks, although I suspect he doesn't think about anything much except hydroponic dope.

'So is this your number-one hit, then?'

'What it is,' Pete taps the side of his nose, 'is the mating calls of every species in the world, or at least anything the Japanese have heard of. Bird calls, frog calls, dog calls, cat calls, the lot.'

'We're basically giving preference to the sexy animals, though,' Magic Marky adds.

'So what's a sexy animal?' I am starting to worry about Marky's personal life now.

'Well, stallions, obviously,' he offers. 'And virile pets . . . labradors, things like that.'

'Labradors?'

'Then we're putting it all on me website,' Pete interrupts, 'and telling the Japanese that if they want it they have to license it from me. Simple,' Pete slaps Magic Marky on the back, which nearly sends him face down on the floor. It's been a long time since I have seen such a spindly-looking man.

'Pod-tastic!' Marky agrees.

I lie on the sofa and read one of Pete's music magazines. Then I remember something.

'What about that "Beach Girl, Beach Boy" song?' I ask him.

'Nah.' Pete waves me away. 'I sent it to Parrot last week. They hated it.'

'Oh,' I try to keep up. 'That's a shame. I like that one. So you're still friends with Parrot?'

'They've bought it,' Pete shrugs, fiddling with his keyboards. 'But they don't like it. They want to put one of their producers onto it to change everything. I'm past caring.'

'The Japanese,' Magic Marky nods knowingly at me. 'Ringtones and all that – that's where the money is.'

'Man,' Pete adds, winking at me.

Strange noises begin to fill my flat. Magic Marky and

Pete keep the volume down, so I can't complain that the neighbours will call the police, but I don't feel I can throw them out either.

'Mind if I do?' Marky lights a spliff and gives me the faintest of glances. I suppose Pete has told him I'm the neo-conservative devil woman who has forced him to give up everything except his evening cocoa.

Then, just when I consider escaping altogether and going to visit Linda, there's a rap on the door, and Pete jumps ahead of me to let a woman called Tania in.

Tania is short and pretty, and she hugs Pete and holds him – and holds him – with her breasts squashed into his chest until he breaks away first.

And she hugs Magic Marky too, of course, but without the breast-squashing.

'Tania. Right. What we need', Pete gives her his full attention, 'is a human version of some animal sounds.'

She giggles.

'Can you make a sort of squeaky sound like a bunny rabbit who wants to have sex with another bunny rabbit?' Magic Marky leers her way.

'I bet you can,' adds Pete as if I'm not there.

Finally he introduces us, and she gives me a little nod. 'Tania and I worked together on my first album,' he explains.

And shagged each other, too, I deduce from the way she's looking at him, or maybe they just wanted to and never did anything about it. I wonder what Polly thought of her?

Tania produces a bottle of Scotch from her handbag. The handbag is plastic, grubby and shaped like a giant daisy, and she pulls an endless amount of rubbish out of it – tampons, foundation, cassette tapes, cigarettes – to get to the Scotch.

'It's for her throat,' Pete deadpans in his best Manc accent, and Magic Marky laughs.

I calculate the pros and cons. If I leave now the three

225

of them might finish whatever music they're making, which means they'll never be here in my flat ever again, which can only be a good thing. Alternatively, if I leave now I may also return at 3 a.m. to find Magic Marky stoned on the floor, Tania drunk in my bed and Pete on the road to nowhere – possibly with Tania if she gets her way. I'm not even sure Pete has properly explained to her who I am, and whose flat this is.

Then Jim rings and asks me to meet him for a drink.

'The Prince Regent?' he suggests.

Half an hour later I am away from Magic Marky, Tania and the animal sound effects, and nursing a glass of red wine.

'Can I have a moan?' I ask Jim.

He nods.

'OK then. Some horrible woman called Tania is in my flat, drinking Scotch and ashing in my cups. And so is a man called Magic Marky, who's basically just smoking everything he can find. I left them to it, but I just can't trust Pete not to join in.'

Jim nods.

The pub we are in is so local that every sign on the wall and every photograph stuck to the post near the bar makes me feel as if we're foreigners. But I used to come here, too, a long time ago. In fact, I think I may even have seen Pete play here once.

'So how's Hastings?' I ask, mainly from politeness because I realize I've been droning on about Pete.

'I found out about the girl who had meningitis.' Jim stares at me. 'She nearly died.'

'What?'

'Not from the meningitis,' Jim adds. 'From a bug she picked up while she was in the hospital. She's OK now. She got better when her old boyfriend came back to see her and she forgot all about me.'

'Oh. But either way,' I say pointedly, 'Courtney's spell worked.'

Suddenly Jim stares into his glass of water and gets a look in his eyes I know well.

'She's tapping in,' he tells me above the sound of Abba on the pub jukebox. 'She's tapping into something bigger than she knows. They all are; they're just not smart enough to realize what they're doing.'

'I believe you. Do you know Claudia's made over a thousand pounds now from selling flowers for charity on the internet? I remember when she had trouble getting rid of a dozen of them.'

Jim nods.

'Is she taking commission?'

'Yeah. Forty per cent now, apparently. She never used to. In fact, I remember her once saying how wrong it was to take money from a charity. She's doing it all on e-Bay. And her hair's changed and she's got this fake tan and long fingernails, and she's sleeping with Guy – they're all sleeping with Guy – and . . . I went round there to try and talk sense into her, Jim, and I couldn't do it. I just couldn't physically do it. What's going on?'

Then Jim stops staring at the water in the glass and stares at me instead.

'I want to kiss you.'

'Well, don't then.' I try to turn it into a joke.

But then he suddenly leans forward and kisses me.

I hear a voice in my head saying, 'Yes, yes, yes.' He tastes of mint and the sea.

'And there,' he says when he's kissed me again. 'If that's the last chance I ever get, I want to use it.'

'I have to go the loo,' I say stupidly.

Then I realize I have no idea where it is, so I have to cross back across the bar, with Jim watching me, then re-cross it again when I realize all I've found is a storeroom.

Eventually I find it downstairs and lock myself in.

I need to listen to that voice in my head again. The one that was just saying, 'Yes, yes, yes.'

'Andrew?' I ask the empty air. 'Is it him?'

Silence.

Then I go outside, splash my face with water, pull up my T-shirt to dry myself, and go back to the table.

'OK. So you think we're going to be together,' I get straight to the point. 'Obviously.'

'I have no idea.' Jim smiles.

'Oh come on. You knew my maths teacher found a gherkin in my homework. How come you can't see us? I mean, are we getting married or not?'

'When I first started seeing things', Jim leans back in his chair and gazes at me, 'it was in the bath water at home. And I saw the future, but only the parts of the future I was meant to see.'

Then I realize something. For the first time in ages he's wearing normal clothes. Jeans. A blue T-shirt to match his blue eyes and black boots I've never seen before.

The stubble and the wild hair of last winter has gone, even though the thin leather cord with the turquoise stone is still around his neck. I wonder if he wears it to bed?

Concentrate, Katie, *concentrate*.

'What do you mean, you were only allowed to see the bits of the future you were "meant" to see?'

'I saw some exam results.' Jim smiles at me with his blue, blue eyes. 'But not others. That was to encourage me – to help me think I could make it. Then there was some stuff about this girl I was seeing, but only the things I needed to know, like the fact that she had asthma. They didn't tell me she was going to leave me too or I wouldn't have got involved in the first place.' He shoots a look at me. '*Comprendi?*'

'Yes, all right.'

The kiss is making me irritated now, I realize,

because it didn't go any further. Or am I just irritated with myself for wanting more?

'Anyway,' I pick up the thread as more people come into the pub, 'I need to sort this out for the book, if we ever do it. Why do you think the spirit people give you some bits of the future and not others?'

'Seeing it in chunks has its own purpose in the present. What I worked out when I was first seeing visions was that it's all woven in. The predictions are part of the stitching of the tapestry. The spirit world has its own agenda.'

'So it's all like a big loom. They spin it, you see it. Or you see the threads they want you to notice. You just play your part. It's like websites on the internet; they co-exist and together make up the whole.'

'Right.'

'Tapestry, internet, beehives. It's all patterns.' I look at Jim's extremely kissable mouth without meaning to. 'I'll get a headache if I keep thinking about it.'

'I see the future. I see the past. I know things I can't possibly know. And I hear from people who are supposed to be dead.' Jim turns the glass around on the table and stares into it.

'Yes.'

'I have my place in the scheme of things, but I'm also kept in my place. Bakers make cakes, doctors cure patients, psychics plant the future ahead of time, so that when the future finally does come towards us it ends up panning out, just the way *they* want it. It's down to *them*.'

'And you trust them?'

'Always.'

I try, unsuccessfully, to ignore the fact that he's moved his chair closer to mine, close enough to touch again.

'OK, Jim. This spirit world – is it lots of them acting

as one? Are they God? Or are they just working for God? Is that what it's all about?'

'God.' Jim rubs his face with his hands. 'Now there's a concept.'

'All right then. But if not God, what?'

'Get back to the internet-of-souls idea. That was good.'

'I'll use it in the book.' I decide to get another drink. 'If we ever do it.'

'We will.' Jim calls after me.

Then when I come back it's my turn to kiss him.

It feels incredible, like coming home.

'I'm seeing things in my beer,' Jim says when we have finally let go of each other.

'Oh no. Not now.'

'It's the same picture, the same one again. A marriage certificate. Both our names. And the calendar is turning – it's in four weeks' time.'

'Four weeks?'

Then he folds his arms, shutting me out again.

'I'm sorry. You belong to Pete. You're not mine.'

Then I laugh. Really, I can't help it. I feel as if I've run away and joined the circus. Pete and mad Magic Marky and their animal mating calls, and crazy Courtney and her spells, and now this.

'Well OK,' Jim says, finishing his water. 'Let's laugh about it. What else can we do?'

Then he squeezes my hand.

'You're not sure about me,' he says, 'and I'm not sure about you.'

'It's too much. I need more time. We need more time.'

'Right.'

'You said ages ago to forget about all the predictions. You said it was getting in the way of us being friends. Can I tell you what I think?'

'You think it's now getting in the way of us ever being together. Yes?'

'Absolutely, yes.'

'More time then.' Jim nods.

'I've got this heart with lots of rooms in it at the moment. All different sizes. It's like a doll's house. Andrew's in one, Pete's in one, you're in one.'

'It's all right.' Jim rubs the scar on his thumb. 'I know all about those kinds of hearts, with all those chambers. The poets would tell you they're the only kind to have.'

He leans back in his chair again, so far that I'm worried he'll fall over.

'You taste as sweet as you are, Katie,' Jim gets up and goes to the loo, leaving me to sit and think. Or rather, sit and not think. Because that might lead to a decision, and at the moment I don't think I can take any more changes in my life.

When Jim comes back he asks me to go to the art exhibition in Hastings with him the following morning, where the BBC will be.

'OK, if we can make a deal.'

'What deal?'

'I need you to do the story for Jennifer, in the paper.'

'Right.' Jim nods. Then abruptly he shakes his head. 'No.'

He pushes a beermat around the table as if it's a token on a Monopoly board, taking it left, then right, then round in circles.

'But why not?'

'Nope. There's a voice in my head saying the message is too important to be carried by her, or your paper. Hey, does she want me to read for a friend of hers too?' Jim looks up at me.

'Her ex-girlfriend. She works in the City. She was curious about your stockmarket prediction for London.'

'Absolutely not.' Jim frowns and shakes his head.

'All right then.'

231

'Jennifer is black and white, she's black and white,' Jim says softly, staring into his empty glass. 'She sees everything in black and white too. Bad and good. Nothing in between. Her father was like that too. And his father before him. It's the way her family trained her.'

'You're right,' I tell him, hoping for more. 'She dresses in black and white. And her office is like that. It's absolutely true.'

But if there is any more that Jim's spirit people want to transmit about Jennifer George, it comes to an abrupt halt as he pushes the glass to one side and gets up from his chair.

'Will you come to the art exhibition?' he asks.

I nod.

'OK then,' Jim holds up his hands as if I've just arrested him. 'Still friends? Shall we just rewind? Shall we walk back together?'

'It's OK,' I hear myself saying. I want to be alone, I suppose. It seems like a long time since I've just had half an hour to go anywhere by myself and have some peace and quiet.

Most of all, perhaps, I need a big blank space in my head. It is filled up with Jim at the moment, with Pete not far behind, and even one of them is more than enough for me to think about.

As I watch Jim trudging up the road to the station though, a text from Claudia arrives, and any ideas I had about being left in peace vanish.

CALL ME URGENTLY, it says.

A phrase of my grandfather's, which my father also sometimes uses, floats into my head. 'Hold your friends close and your enemies closer.'

What if Claudia is holding her enemies too close? Letting them change her hair and paint her nails and dress her up in their clothes? Letting Courtney allow her into Guy's harem?

I'm scared for her. What if they've turned against her? I remember the night in the pub with them when I saw pimples on my skin that hadn't been there since school, and the gulls that came from nowhere, and my phone disappearing.

I ring Claudia back repeatedly until she answers.

'Hey!' is the first thing I hear when she finally picks up the phone. And I realize that she's drunk and she sounds happy enough. She's also somewhere loud, with raucous laughter in the background.

'What's up?'

'Your presence is urgently required, Katie,' she slurs.

'Oh.'

'Come on,' she insists. 'Come out with us girls for the night. And Guy's here, too. Say hello, Guy!'

But he doesn't, so she's left to rant on alone.

'My birthday and Deb's birthday are the same,' she tells me. 'Can you believe that? Isn't it spooky?'

'Mmm.'

'You should come out with us, we're at the . . .' Claudia checks with someone because she clearly has no idea. 'We're at the Three Jolly Pigs. Except we're not really,' she goes on, 'because we're four happy witches. No, five happy witches. Guy, are you happy to be with your five happy witches?'

Once again, though, there's no reply from Guy. I suppose he's busy with Courtney. Or Jan. Or both of them.

I make my excuses, hang up and keep walking in the direction of my flat.

Courtney's surname pops into my head. Creely. It's like creepy, but it's also like greedy. I suddenly realize I am furious with Claudia.

She's never been my friend – not really – certainly not the way Linda is. But Claudia was always the one person at work you could count on to do the right thing. Even though we worked in different departments, I could always trust her. And now look.

When I finally make it home, Pete is still up with Magic Marky, experimenting with strange electronic bird noises. My sitting room smells of dope, but Pete doesn't appear to have touched any of it – at least when I kiss him, he tastes the same as he always does.

'Magic Marky might stay on the sofa,' he says. 'He's a bit tired. Is that all right?'

'If he's creating a work of musical genius that will make you a global superstar, I don't care,' I say. 'He can sleep on the sofa, he can sleep in the bath, he can sleep anywhere he likes. Did you get the fluffy bunny sounds right with' – I nearly forget her name – 'Tania in the end?'

And then I switch off my mobile, just in case Claudia tries again, and make my way to bed.

The next day I take the train to Hastings and find Jim outside a small art gallery in the Old Town.

He is holding a telephone book in his hands, hanging around near the BBC van, looking shy.

'Well, there it is,' I point the van out to him while some teenagers hover. I suppose they want to make rabbit ears behind somebody's head.

'Yep.'

'Why the telephone book?' I ask.

'It's not just that. I've got the messages as well.' Jim shows me a sheaf of paper.

'I'm just going to knock on the door and show them.' Jim takes a deep breath.

Then he bottles out and has to go to the loo, so I spend ten minutes wandering around the exhibition. It features photographs and paintings of Sussex fishermen and their families, going back to the founding of Hastings Old Town.

It's a nice idea, I suppose, but pretty boring unless you happen to be one of the fishermen.

Jim comes back, still with his telephone book under his arm.

Then suddenly, 'Oh, it's you,' says a loud female voice behind me which I recognize as Sue's.

She looks both embarrassed and pleased to see us.

'Are you here for the exhibition?' she asks.

I decide to tell the truth.

'Jim got a message from the spirit world to be here,' I say. 'We don't know why, but he's been getting messages for people – hundreds of strangers – with their names and addresses. So he's been finding them all in the phone book.'

'My husband works for the BBC,' Sue says. 'He's here. Do you think the spirits want Jim to talk to him?'

'Maybe,' Jim says carefully.

'He's the world's biggest sceptic, though,' Sue nudges me.

She flicks through the phone book. 'Here's my name,' she says. And then she looks excited: 'Oh, it's ticked off. There we are. Johnson, Blakes Way.'

'So you're on there. Let me match it up.' Jim looks at his sheaf of papers. 'OK, here's the message. Your grandmother says, don't buy the house.'

'What? But we are buying the house,' Sue looks horrified. 'It's lovely. It's in Eastbourne.'

'Wait,' Jim holds his finger up in the air as crowds begin to mill around outside the gallery. 'I'm getting the rest of the message now. You've offered on a house with a cartwheel in the garden.'

'Yes!' Sue interrupts.

'Your grandmother says, buy the house with the cartwheel in the garden and you'll be doing cartwheels over the repairs. She says, don't be daft.'

'Oh. My. God.' Sue shakes her head.

'That's amazing,' I tell Jim, suddenly feeling proud of him.

Sue races off to find her husband.

'Interesting,' John says when he's finally dragged out of the BBC van and shown the phone book.

'But it's just unbelievable!' She looks at him, then Jim, in turn. 'How could Jim possibly know about the house we've been looking at? And that was my grandmother. When Jim said, "Don't be daft," that's her.'

'Bit busy at the moment,' Sue's husband says non-committally.

But then Jim interrupts him.

'Match the names of the people in the exhibition against the names in the phone book.'

'Could we talk later?' John turns his back.

'Is there a fishing family called Sole?' Jim persists. 'I had lots of messages for a family called Sole.'

'Yes, there is,' John snaps. 'Probably a family called Cod too, and Plaice. All right?'

Then he disappears into his van.

Sue takes the phone book, and I see she has tears in her eyes as the connection with her grandmother starts to sink in.

'Sole, Burgess Hill; Sole, Brighton; Sole, Hassocks; Sole, Hove,' she reads from Jim's notes.

Then one of the lurking teenage boys overhears us and interrupts.

He is wearing a baseball cap like the rest of his friends, and jeans with pockets somewhere around his knees.

'Are you looking for us?' he asks.

'Yes,' Jim says immediately.

'We're from Hove. We're the only Soles in Hove.'

'Message from your old goalkeeper,' Sue reads from Jim's sheet. 'Get rid of the coach, he's useless.'

'Ha, that's funny, because that's my dad,' the boy says. Then he swears. 'Is that Robin you're talking to?' he asks. 'Because Robin's dead.'

'Not dead,' Jim says. 'Just somewhere else.'

* * *

236

For the next three hours, the BBC live broadcast of the Hastings Old Town Gallery 'Fishing Lives' exhibition is overtaken by all the Soles (not just the Hove branch), and in addition the Knights, the Murphys, the Muirs, the Sextons, the Tingleys and hundreds more. Everyone, in short, who is circled in Jim's phone book.

Generations of Sussex fishing families and their friends are connected across the spiritual internet through a long list of messages which seem ever more bizarre, or even meaningless, to Sue and I, but which produce oohs, aahs and even tears.

Jim is so frantic at the centre of a crowd that he barely notices when John finally gives in and turns the camera on him.

'Tinker, Maurice Road. Grandmother says you left your ring on the plane – call the airline,' Jim reads from his sheet of paper above the noise of the small crowd. 'Oxley, Bedford Street. Sister says cat's not happy, get him a friend. Southwell, Cromwell Court. Mum says she's fine now, and thanks for putting the Man United scarf with the flowers.'

It's hard to tell if John is horrified or pleased that he appears to have accidentally stumbled on some live reality TV in the middle of his news feature.

'Was there a message for everybody at this exhibition?' he asks once the camera has been switched off.

'Them, or their friends, or their families.' Jim sighs. 'Sorry.'

'He was told to come here by the spirit world.' Sue is almost jumping up and down on the spot. 'They knew about this, John. You've got to show this.'

'Maybe.' John frowns. 'We'll see how it comes up in the edit.' Then he laughs nervously. 'See what the exec producer thinks.'

'Is his name Milburn?' Jim asks suddenly. 'That's the

only name in the phone book that nobody knew. Does he live in Ringwood Road?'

'Yes,' John gives in.

Sue grabs Jim's paper and reads from it. 'M for Milburn, Ringwood Road. The message is your ex-wife says "rhubarb".'

The cameraman grins and switches his camera back on.

'All right then.' John finally sees a joke in the middle of his day as Sue begins to laugh. 'Got that? The message is "rhubarb". Cut.'

Later, after John has gone home, Sue, Jim and I go for a coffee.

'Jim knew this was the right place to come,' I say, still trying to take in the strange way everything has worked out. 'He's known for weeks.'

'Serendipity and synchronicity,' says Sue. 'I'm into all that. You're not, though, are you?'

I have to think about this. I'm not sure what I believe any more.

'I see psychics all the time,' Sue goes on. 'My friends think it's a joke, but I can tell you, there is more on heaven and on earth, Horatio, and all that. We think we know what's going on, and we think we know what we're doing, but we don't really. We'd probably be better off' – she smiles at me – 'if we co-operated with that side of it a little more.'

'Sometimes, with Jim, I trace the events back, in a line, to try and work out where the joins are in the puzzle,' I tell her.

'Well it's up to John now.'

Then she changes the subject.

'So what's your new boss like?' she asks. 'Is it more of the same, or have they dropped the tabloid thing? That piece on the shark was awful for Jim, you know. It's the main reason we decided not to go ahead with a book. Marketing took one look at the photo and got the fear.'

'Jennifer's good,' I say, explaining about my new boss. And then I realize I might need to rethink the good part, because I'm not entirely sure if it's true. 'She's just really different.' I try to describe her to Sue. 'She's a woman and she's black – first black person on the paper ever. And she's a workaholic. She's even there on weekends. Molloy never was.'

Sue takes a call from John and laughs.

'His boss has seen the footage of the message from his ex. He got the rhubarb thing at once. He said he doesn't want to explain, but he knew it was her instantly as soon as he heard, and he understood the message. He said don't call him now, Jim, because they're up to their necks in it – call him Monday.'

She writes down the number.

'Anyway, Sue,' I give her my card. 'If you're ever near our office, give me a call. Maybe you could meet Jennifer George yourself. She said she wants to put more books in the paper.'

When I go back to work the following day, though, it turns out Jennifer isn't there.

'She's been asked to go up to London,' Guy shrugs when he calls us all in for a quick meeting. 'Urgent business. She rang in to say she won't be back until next Monday. No problem though. I'll be looking after things here for the next few days. OK?'

CHAPTER FOURTEEN

Because it is now June, I watch the news feeds daily in the office in case a story about New Zealanders capturing a tiger comes in, as Jim predicted. I want to be the first to let him know when it happens, and the next person I'll call will be Sue. After everything she saw at the art gallery in Hastings, I'm sure we must be closer than ever to a book deal.

'Do you think Sue's still keen to do something on Jim?' I ask Linda over a drink.

'Yes.' She looks at me thoughtfully. 'I'd give it a go. Any word on Jim being on telly?'

'They're not going to use it. Too weird. But John said he's been moved to a daytime chat thing, and they'll think about Jim then.'

'Wow.'

'It would be amazing if it all came together with the book and the TV at the same time.'

'Life's moved fast,' Linda clinks my glass. 'Good. You needed it to.'

'Still weird, though,' I interrupt her. 'But Jim says he wants publicity now. He didn't at first because Guy and Molloy did all that crap about him on the front page, but he feels as if he's on a mission now. And he can trust Sue, and her husband.'

'I thought *you* might have been the mission for Jim,'

Linda says, 'never mind convincing the country that the dead can talk.'

'God no.'

'Are you all right with Pete then?'

'Fine,' I nod a bit too often, and a bit too long.

The following day, I have all the excuses I need to ring Sue. On 19 June a New Zealand golfer called Michael Campbell beats Tiger Woods in the U.S. Open. The celebrations in Auckland go well into the night.

'That's good,' Jim says, when I ring him to let him know. 'They captured the tiger.'

'You sound strange,' I tell him. 'Are you OK?'

'I'm just going into the TV studio,' he replies. 'I don't think we're supposed to have our phones on.'

'What?'

'John rang me. He was desperate. They had to cancel the show they had planned because two of the guests couldn't make it. I'm on in . . . I don't know. Soon! Switch it on. It's on BBC2 – it's called *Lunchtime Forum*. They're going to talk about life after death.'

'Deep breaths,' I counsel him. 'Just slow, deep breaths.'

I run straight into Jennifer's empty office – I am sure Guy won't mind – and turn on the TV.

The news is on first. And I am seeing . . . Michael Campbell celebrating his victory over Tiger Woods, and footage of crowds celebrating at a street party in New Zealand. Another stitch in Jim's tapestry.

I sit on Jennifer's new polished floorboards close to the screen. It's been ages since I've watched daytime TV, but I remember the programme now. It's a panel show – one host, matched with one person speaking for the topic, and one person against it.

I don't know the host, whose name is Paul Saxon, or the person sitting on the left side of the desk, pitted against Jim, but I recognize part of the graphic on the wall behind them. It's Guy's shark headline, cut out of our paper. Despite myself I squeak.

Then Guy comes in and swears as he sees the TV.

'Him,' he says. 'Him. Jim. Shit. Him.'

'Shhh.'

I move even closer to the screen as my heart thumps nervously on Jim's behalf. He looks incredibly tanned next to the pale faces of the female guest and Paul Saxon. And his hair is sticking up. Why didn't they fix that? Why did they let him go on without stopping his hair from sticking up?

Blah, blah, blah goes Paul Saxon. I suppose the fierce woman sitting opposite Jim has been dragged in from some lofty hall of academia to expose him as a fake.

Paul begins with an introduction about the overwhelming rise in the popularity of psychics and mediums, and the explosion of interest in the supernatural, the decline in church attendance, the rise in alternative spirituality and . . . it's nothing I haven't heard before.

And then Jim starts writing. He fishes what appear to be old BBC call sheets from somewhere inside his denim jacket and starts scribbling furiously, using his knee as a desk while the camera pans from his face to the presenter's face to the irritated face of the woman in the opposite chair.

'Sorry.' He nods up at the camera, which has now moved back to him. 'I'm getting messages. I can't stop. Sorry.'

Possibly because the director doesn't know what else to do, the camera remains parked on Jim's face, and then focuses on his right hand, which is flying across the page as if someone else is moving it.

'Well, we seem to be cutting straight to the chase here,' Paul Saxon says. 'We're with Jim Gabriel, Brighton-based, Australian-born psychic and medium, as the subject of our lunchtime forum today is life after death. And I suppose we can say, Jim – am I right in thinking you're getting messages from the spirit world here?'

'Sudbury, Shirley Road,' Jim counters.

'Which is my partner's name and address,' Paul interrupts, looking stunned.

'Message is,' Jim says, still scribbling, 'aunt says she's got the dog and it's come with the golf tee.'

Paul Saxon, on professional autopilot, though still looking stunned, addresses us, the audience, through the camera.

'That's rather interesting,' he says, 'because my partner's dog did indeed swallow a golf tee. Although,' he suddenly remembers, 'both the dog and my partner's aunt are dead.'

He looks at Jim.

'Though you'd say that wasn't the case, Jim Gabriel?'

The woman in the blue suit snorts with laughter, and the camera crosses to her face while Jim reels on:

'Donaghy, Cherry Close. Uncle says glad you got his shoes and wear them to the job interview. Bradley, Hacketts End. Boyfriend says look in your filing cabinet. Arlidge, Meads Road. Sell the piano on and don't worry.'

It must be the first time the academic woman has ever been hauled out of her university to appear on television, though, because now the camera is on her she can think of nothing to say.

It's awful. I can't watch. It's the worst television I've seen for ages. Embarrassing, out of control and wrong, all wrong. My heart is breaking for Jim, who's reeling off names like the speaking clock. Any minute now they'll pull the programme. Any minute now we'll be watching an unscheduled wildlife documentary.

'King, Hindover Road. Message is you're forgiven by your mother about the wedding,' he goes on, 'Garner, Freshfield Street. Message for someone called Ray. Mother says you'd never have believed in this until you switched on the TV and saw it for yourself, would you?'

Paul Saxon hears something in his earpiece.

'Apparently we're having calls through from some of these people on your list, Jim,' he says. 'Mr Emlyn Donaghy of Cherry Close says he has just switched the programme on and is actually wearing his uncle's shoes – rather nice new brogues apparently – left to him in the will. And he has in fact worn them to the job interview you mention, this morning.'

Cut to the woman in the blue suit, looking blank, and cut back to Jim, looking sweaty as he keeps scribbling on page after page. He'll need more paper soon. Don't they give them powder to wear on these shows? My heart is going out to him.

'Another call to our switchboard here,' Paul Saxon says as the number goes up on the screen, 'Mrs Petrea King from Hindover Road, also watching, says that she must be the King you mention, for personal reasons, but she's very glad for the message and knows what it means.

'And if you've just joined us,' Paul Saxon's face reappears again in close-up, 'we are in the company of Annie Prideaux, academic and author of *A Sceptic's Guide to the 21st Century*, a critical look at modern mumbo-jumbo, as she describes it, and Brighton psychic Jim Gabriel, who claims to be able to receive messages from those who've passed over, as well as see into the future.'

The camera switches to Annie's face, which is not happy at all, and then to Jim's, which is beginning to look even shinier under the studio lights. When he gets hot, I remember, he gets sweat patches under his arms too. Please don't let him get sweat patches under his arms on live television.

'Any more messages for me about the dog?' the presenter forces a laugh. Then he realizes he has no idea what to say. 'Really delightful, that, about the golf tee, Jim.'

Suddenly someone has the bright idea of simply taking Jim's sheets of paper and putting them up on camera.

'Feck,' Guy swears as we see line after line of scrawl. 'How could he have written all that down?' There are dozens of names in tiny capital letters on each sheet.

'It's a joke,' we hear Annie Prideaux say, although she doesn't sound as if she finds it very funny.

'Back to you Annie,' the host remembers she is there. 'What do you make of this? I mean, this certainly is extraordinary. We've had people ringing in saying they recognize the messages, and unless this is one of the largest hoaxes we've seen here on the programme, it would appear that Jim Gabriel is doing what he says he's doing: communicating with the dead.'

But before the extremely annoyed Annie Prideaux can say a word, every light in the television studio goes off, as if the whole of the local power station has suddenly gone down. Seconds later a BBC2 commercial is quickly put up.

Guy nudges me without saying a thing. And then he nudges me again.

'Christ,' he says. 'Aargh. Ring him.'

'His phone is switched off. I can't.'

'Where's the tape?' Guy stands up and stares down at me. 'Where's Jim's tape, Katie?'

But before I can put him off my phone rings. It's Jennifer.

'A friend of mine at the BBC says that Jim Gabriel is on *Lunchtime Forum*, and the switchboard has jammed,' she says. 'She says they've received so many emails that they've had to close down their website.'

'Yes. We're watching it here.'

'Apparently there has also been a power failure

across West London. I want Jim on the front page of the paper tomorrow. If he's not accessible today, I want you to write a first-person piece about your experiences with him, your friendship with him.'

'No,' I hear myself saying. 'He doesn't want to be in the paper. He said no.'

'Before Christmas he said yes, and now he's saying no?' Jennifer replies. 'First there was a tape and now there isn't? You're employed by this paper, aren't you, Katie, to do a job here?'

I say nothing.

'If he's not accessible to us, then at least you are,' she says firmly. 'And I am going to take it very seriously if you do not have a detailed feature on your friendship with Jim Gabriel by 3 p.m. this afternoon. Is Guy there?'

'Yes.'

I put him on and a long conversation follows. I guess it's probably about me.

Pete rings. I take the phone out of Jennifer's office and into the quietness of the corridor.

'Jim's just been on the phone,' he says.

'What?'

'He said he was at the BBC. He said he was hiding – he's doing a runner.'

'Oh my God.'

'Anyway, he made me put the phone on speaker and then record it.'

'Record what?'

'Then he asked me to ring you,' Pete says. 'He didn't want to ring you himself in case there was any chance of other people tracing your number. He said it's going to go nuts out there – worse than he thought. But he said stay calm. And don't write a single word about him, or talk about him, to anybody. He said be strong and don't betray him. There,' Pete sounds satisfied.

I think of Jennifer's voice, cold and hard, on the

phone – and I panic. Then I take the phone into the loo so Guy can't find me.

'What do you mean, Jim made you put the phone on speaker?' I ask.

'Well,' Pete says, 'he was singing into it.'

'Singing what?'

'Tunes. It's for me song,' Pete scrambles for the right explanation. 'I was having trouble with the middle section, right, for that instrumental thing I wanted to do. The one –' he takes a deep breath '– the one I'm doing for love, not for money.'

'Jim can't sing. What do you mean he was singing through the speaker phone?'

'It wasn't him.' Pete sighs. 'Listen to me, Katie. It wasn't his voice. I'll play it to you when you get back. Then you'll hear it for yourself. It's all la, la, la, la, all right? But it's musical la, la, la. A beautiful tune. A beautiful hook. By a proper musician.'

'Who?'

'John Lennon.' Pete laughs. 'And it is!' he whoops. 'One hundred per cent, no messing. I swear to God, Katie, it's the most unbelievable thing that's ever bloody happened to me. Lennon! Me, getting a middle eight from John Lennon!'

Trust Pete's luck, I think. Everyone else is getting messages about dogs swallowing golf tees and their uncle's shoes, but Pete gets one of the Beatles to give him song ideas.

Then I hear someone else coming into the loo and hang up. I call Jim, but as I expected his mobile is switched off again.

When I come out I see Courtney, with her back to me, fixing her make-up in the mirror.

'Just so you know,' she fiddles with her hair, 'Jennifer wants you to bring in any personal photos you have of Jim, as well. Guy just told me to come in here and tell you.'

'I don't have any,' I talk to her back. 'Though I suppose you might.'

'No.' She shakes her head.

Then she turns round and offers me some of her patchouli oil.

She stinks, though, not of patchouli but the worst kind of smell. It could be the loo, but it isn't. It's her.

'Try,' she coaxes me. 'And by the way, I'm switching jobs. Jennifer's asked me to be her PA.'

'What about Guy?'

She shrugs.

'And what happened to the new PA Jennifer just hired?'

'She got a better offer.' Courtney shrugs again.

I leave her to her make-up bag. I suppose at some point today I'll discover that the fiftysomething woman who just took the desk outside Jennifer's office has been infected with ringworm, struck down by meningitis or plagued by pigeons.

Then I think about Jim again and what has just happened. I have to find him. Jennifer can stuff her front page.

All of which means, of course, that I will probably be sacked this afternoon. But maybe Pete can support me for a while. Even if we have to live on baked beans and casino chips from Japanese businessmen.

There. I've made the decision. Or rather I've just made two decisions. Out of my job for ever, perhaps, and also firmly back in the land of Pete.

I take a deep breath, hover in the corridor for a minute until I'm sure I am alone, and then I make my way out of the office and out of the building for the last time?

I call a taxi to take me to the station. There's a long discussion about Jim on the radio when I climb in.

'Have you ever had a psychic reading in Brighton with Jim Gabriel?' the announcer is asking. 'Were you listed today on the BBC programme *Lunchtime Forum*? Did Jim have a message for you?'

Then he plays John Lennon singing 'Imagine'. Very funny. Another stitch in the cosmic tapestry. I hope Pete is listening.

I arrive at Brighton station to find queues behind all four ticket machines – one of which isn't working – and an even longer queue at the ticket office. The next train to Victoria leaves in four minutes.

I stand behind one of the queues and watch a man staring at the computer screen as if it's an intelligence test of impossible proportions, which for him, I guess, it probably is. It's taken him two minutes just to work out if he's going to use cash or a credit card.

I stamp my feet. There is no other London train lit up on the board.

Then my phone rings. Jim.

'Don't talk,' he says. 'I'll see you at the doughnut shop at Victoria Station at a quarter past three.'

'The doughnut shop?'

'It doesn't matter. Anywhere. But let's meet there.'

I try to tell him I can't possibly make it by then because of the stupid ticket machines, but I'm not allowed to.

'I need you,' he says. 'Katie. It's beyond me. It's too much. Too fast.'

'I know.'

'Shit, you know?'

'It's OK.'

The man who cannot understand the computer screen is still stuck at the front of the queue. Like everyone else who is waiting for the train to Victoria, I look longingly across at Platform Four where it's waiting for us.

And then I notice something. The barricade fencing that normally runs along the left side of the platform is no longer there, and there are no guards either.

I walk towards it, and then I walk faster, and eventually I give in and start running. Still no guards.

And then I see one, but all he does is look bored and wave me on.

The doors close on the train to Victoria a few seconds later, and I find myself alone in a long, empty carriage of seats, full of abandoned newspaper sports sections, all carrying the news about Tiger Woods' defeat at the hands of a New Zealander in the U.S. Open.

I call Jim again as we go through East Croydon, but he's turned his phone off. Then I turn mine off, too, in case anyone at work calls.

Finally, at ten minutes past three, I turn up at the doughnut shop at Victoria Station to find Jim standing on the other side eating a bag full of them.

'Blood sugar hit,' he says, waving the bag apologetically.

I try not to want him too much. I have already made up my mind about Pete.

'They were talking about you on the radio in Brighton,' I say, as he fast-walks me in the direction of a hotel entrance at the front of the terminal.

'In here,' he advises, guiding me up the steps.

Then he guides me into the lift and along a series of corridors, where he produces a hotel room key.

'Really?' I check with him as he nods and holds the door open for me.

Then he sits on the bed and tells me that all he can think about is me, all he wants is me, and he is wondering if we can do something about it right now in this room.

I look at him. His hair is still sticking up, as it was on television, and his eyes look clear and blue in the light streaming through the hotel windows.

'I wouldn't ask unless I was sure,' he says.

'What? Psychic sure, or normal sure?'

'A bit of both.'

'But it's not fair. I'm with Pete.'

'I have to know where I stand.'

'But I can't.'

'Do you want to?' he interrupts me. 'Because if you do, it's OK. We're alone. Nobody knows we're here.'

'Except for the fact that it's wrong,' I point out.

'Unsuitable.' Jim smiles. 'We've talked about suitable and unsuitable before, haven't we? Didn't we even talk about the Prince Regent once, and Mrs Fitzherbert?'

'What have they got to do with it?'

Stress has made me scratchy and sulky.

'Katie. You know that in the space of five minutes suitable can become unsuitable and unsuitable can become suitable.'

And again, despite myself, the small voice in my head says yes, yes, yes.

Jim gets up from the bed and searches the fridge for two bottles of water. Then he switches the air-conditioner on.

'What if Pete wasn't around?' he asks.

'I can't believe you want to talk about it.'

I stare blankly at the framed print of a leopard above the bed. It's always a leopard or a Chinese junk in these hotel rooms.

Then he stands behind me and pulls me gently back into him, as if I'm falling and he's catching me.

'I'm not sleeping with you. It's not fair on Pete. I can't even believe you've got this hotel room.'

Jim holds me close.

'Jim, is this going to be one of those crappy you-know-you-want-to things?'

'Nope.'

'Well I don't want to sleep with you,' I pull away, 'and I'm not going to.'

'Let me ask you something else, then. If I'd never

made the prediction about us getting married, would it be different?'

'No,' I shake my head. 'And anyway, your predictions get jumbled up. You said that yourself. A tiger wasn't captured in New Zealand. A shark didn't eat a desk. Your pictures are all back to front. I bet our marriage is too – if it ever happens, which it's not going to.'

'What if I wasn't psychic?' he confronts me. 'What if I wasn't weird? What if all that hadn't happened just now on the BBC?'

'OK then,' I think about it. 'Maybe. Now you're talking. I do fancy you – there. And I do like you. And Pete worries me, if you must know, and he's got a son and all of that . . .'

Jim nods.

'So,' I think about it again, 'if you weren't psychic? Great. Because I can do the human-being bit with you, Jim. It's just the bucket, and the messages from people's uncles, and the responsibility of being a partner to a man who can see the future of the world and all that. And' – I think of the really important thing – 'the responsibility to *Pete*.'

And then I pick up my handbag, kiss him goodbye and walk out of the room. I owe Pete that much.

About an hour later, after another long queue at the ticket machine, I arrive back at my flat in Brighton to find Pete having sex with Tania in the shower. I follow the trail of her clothes around the house – it's astonishing that he randomly disrobes her in exactly the same way he always undresses me – and I find them under the hot water, stoned, laughing and fumbling at each other through the shower curtain like teenagers.

The joint is stubbed out in a yoghurt lid on a corner

of the bath. That was my breakfast yoghurt, I remember. Breakfast seems like days ago now.

'Pete,' I announce myself from the doorway as I go into numb shock.

He doesn't hear me.

'Oi, Pete.'

Is that me, saying oi? It doesn't sound like me at all. But here I am saying it.

Tania looks around first.

'Oh shit.'

All I can do is nod, as if, in some weird way, I'm agreeing with her.

Then Pete looks up with the water in his eyes.

I still can't talk.

So I nod instead, like a nodding dog in the back seat of a car, until I realize this is not the thing to do and walk away instead.

I go to the kitchen to pour myself a glass of water – I am dying of thirst suddenly – and promise myself that I will finish that, and another one, and then – only then – check to see if she has gone.

I can't go back in there. It's awful. Maybe, maybe, if I just stay here long enough with my glass of water, they'll disappear.

It is half-past four. I wonder how many other afternoons Pete has spent with Tania when he thinks I've been at work?

I stop myself right there. The adrenaline is still booming through my chest and throat, and I realize I've been biting my lip in the same place for so many minutes that I've left a dent there.

There is a plastic bag full of red and white spotted mushrooms on the kitchen table. I recognize them instantly – the mushrooms are fly agaric. I wrote a story on them last year. Unlike other magic mushrooms they're still legal.

I wonder where else in the flat Pete and Tania might

have been at each other, apart from the shower, and guess the bedroom floor. Then I wonder if Pete has used my birthday vibrator on her too and feel sick.

Go, go, go, I pray, in my head.

Then a stray thought pops in – why didn't my grandfather warn me? Why didn't Andrew warn me on the tape? Why didn't Jim see it coming?

'Sorry,' Pete staggers to the kitchen doorway in a towel while I finish one glass of water and start on the next. 'She's just gone,' he says helplessly, holding up his hands as if he is begging.

I nod. That's all I can do – nod.

'What now?' Pete sighs.

'You tell me.' I feel surprisingly calm and the three words roll out of me smoothly, as if I'm reading an autocue, like Paul Saxon on the television.

'Shall I move out for a while?' he offers.

'Yeah.' I think about this. 'Actually, that's a good idea. Would you mind? Take a case or something tonight, go and stay with Polly and Ben. No, hang on.' A clever idea struggles into my head. 'Why don't you move back in with them? That would work.'

'Yeah,' he agrees.

And then I realize he's crying. In all the time we've been together, I have never seen Pete Oram cry.

'Fook,' he says in his Manc accent. 'They're Tania's mushrooms,' he says, pointing to the bag.

Another clever idea comes into my head.

'You just need to go,' I say slowly. 'That's all. Can you go now?'

He doesn't move.

'Well then, I'll go. But can you wait outside? Because I need you to just . . . be away from me.'

'I thought you were at work,' he says stupidly.

'Am I going, or are you going?' I feel suffocated by his nearness now. And then I worry about something else. There's a drawer full of large kitchen knives not far away from my hand. And I honestly, honestly, feel as if I'll pull it open, take the big, serrated one and stick it into him.

Instead, more calm words roll out of me.

'I suppose you did think I was at work, otherwise you wouldn't have taken her clothes off.' I pour myself another glass of water, as if it will wash everything away. 'You took her clothes off – not the other way round. You started in the sitting room, and you went to the kitchen, and you came out of there and pushed her up the corridor, and every time you took another thing off. Just like you do with me. Did you do it that way with Polly as well?'

'Sorry.' Pete sits down cross-legged on the floor and bends his head forward, as if he'll never get up again.

'I'm going to work. I've got to get my stuff. Clear out my desk. I had thought, now that they're sacking me, I could have lived off your money for a while. But I should have known better.'

'Beatles song,' Pete says uselessly.

' "I Should Have Known Better" – yeah, I do realize. You put it on my iPod. I don't like it. In fact,' I happily think of something that will really hurt him now, 'I don't like anything you put on my iPod. And I don't like The Beatles much either. They're over-rated. Just like John bloody Lennon.'

'Go on, say it,' Pete sighs up at me from the floor. 'Like me.'

And then I throw the glass at him. It still has water in it, so the water goes everywhere, and I miss, so he doesn't end up covered in blood, but it breaks apart on the floor, close enough to his foot to make him finally get up and go.

But . . . even as Pete is still fumbling around, stoned, I am out of the flat and down the street, with my bag under my arm.

I walk back to work, realizing I'm in shock, not

caring, just curious about the sensation of being on autopilot, and willing myself up the hill, looking at the billboards for the paper, wondering if Jim's name will be on there tomorrow.

I know Guy well enough to realize that with or without me a story about Jim will appear. And they'll probably use the shots the snapper took of Jim and I holding hands on the undercliff during the storm, and then Pete will see them and say it must be all right about Tania after all, and then Courtney will see them and curse me for all time because I've taken the only man she ever wanted from her.

When I get back to my desk, I discover that I have turned into a non-person. Oh my stuff is still there, but nobody is acknowledging me.

'Have I just been sacked?' I ask one of the subs, but he doesn't reply.

'Storm coming.' He points out through the window, in the direction of some grey-black clouds that are rumbling over the top of the English Channel.

I wonder if Pete has been caught up in it and then remind myself that Pete is no more.

Then—

'Just get your stuff,' Guy says when he walks into the room and sees me a few minutes later.

'Can we talk outside?'

'Might as well talk here.' He shrugs. 'Get your stuff. Don't talk to anyone, unless you want legals. Don't even think of selling any tapes you recorded while you were on our time or on our property.'

'Says who?' I challenge him.

'Says me,' Guy counters.

'But you're not the editor. Jennifer George is the editor. Are you acting on her instructions?'

'Katie, for God's sake, will you just handle this with some dignity,' Guy says irritably, 'and just go?'

Before he can say anything else, though, he is inter-rupted by Courtney.

'I've got a message from Jennifer.' She stares at me with her big, black-rimmed eyes. 'She says she wants a meeting with you, Katie, as soon as she gets back from London on Monday. She says, 9 a.m. in her office.'

'But she's sacked, right?' Guy stares at Courtney. 'I mean, she's not doing the Jim story. So . . .'

'Jennifer didn't say anything about that.' Courtney cocks her head on one side.

Guy looks at Courtney as if he suddenly wants to kill her.

'First she was working for me,' Guy turns to me, jerking a thumb at Courtney, 'now she's working for Jennifer. You have to keep up around here, Katie. If you don't, you can go out for lunch, come back and find the whole office has changed while you've been having your first course.'

Courtney smiles. Courtney Creepy. Courtney Greedy. I wonder if she and her friends – and Claudia – are still all sleeping with Guy? Right now he's look-ing at her as if he wishes she would die.

'You won't do what you're told,' Guy points his signet-ring finger at me. 'If Molloy were still alive, he'd sack you on the spot.'

Courtney ignores this.

'Jennifer says as soon as you've finished the feature on Jim tonight, email it across to her at this address.' She hands me a scrap of paper.

'I'm not sure about that.' I shake my head. 'Not sure I'm doing a feature on Jim for the paper.'

'See?' Guy stares furiously at Courtney. 'How many syllables in "not doing it" do you not understand? The journalist is continuing to be difficult. The source is still saying no. Now why don't you ring up Jennifer, seeing as you're her PA now, and tell her the good news?'

Courtney turns on her high heels and walks out. She smells, as always, of gastric problems and bad drains.

I wake up the next morning at about 6 a.m. – my last memory is of crashing onto my bed after microwaving something frozen and very old – and suddenly remember everything at once. Jim and the TV show. Jim and the hotel room. Pete and Tania. Me and Guy. Me and Jennifer. Guy and Courtney.

Then I steel myself to go and get the paper, throwing on an old mac over my tracksuit and trainers.

I have no idea what Guy will have cobbled together overnight about Jim, but I'm expecting the worst.

Most of all I'm expecting a grainy shot of me and Jim holding hands on the beach, with a beat-up story about our relationship, sorry, friendship. TV psychic and the *Courier*'s own Katie Pickard – did he see their secret love affair in his plastic bucket?

What was it that Pete said in the days when I used to be properly in love with him? More people in Brighton buy fish and chips than buy the *Brighton & Hove Courier* they are wrapped in.

And he's right. Old ladies ask the newsagents for all the unsold copies so they can shred it for cat litter. I've seen them.

Nevertheless, I do not want to see Jim plastered all over the front page again. Or me. I don't care about his mission. I wish he'd never gone to the BBC, or the Hastings Art Gallery.

When I grab the *Courier* from the pile on top of the newsagent's counter, though, there is nothing about Jim Gabriel at all – or, for that matter, me. I flick from front to back, and then from back to front. Council tax outrage, sex pests in the park, lose weight for summer, blah, blah, blah, but no Jim.

What Guy has produced, though, is a full-colour

double-page spread on the latest social trend everyone is talking about – at least in his mind.

LONDON LIPSTICK LESBIANS TAKE OVER LANES is the headline.

It's about a new women-only day spa opening in The Lanes, which I didn't know about. And yes, the owners are a lesbian couple, and I suppose one of them looks as if she's wearing lipstick, and they have just moved down here from London, so full points to Guy for that one. Although they're not really taking over the Lanes, are they? They just appear to have moved into one of the vacant gift shops to the north of Cornucopia, which have been empty forever.

But it's the rest of the story that Jennifer will really hate.

It's hard to believe that Guy has done it. But there, buried among the advertorial waffle for the new women-only day spa and the interviews with the glamorous London lesbians, is a tiny photograph of Jennifer's head bobbing around next to Ellen de Generes' head, who apparently has also been *seen* (oh, sure) in Brighton lately. The caption reads, 'New *Courier* Editor Jennifer George – Brighton lesbians say, "Our verdict is, she's gorgeous."' And over the page there are more shots of Jennifer taken with a mobile phone – probably Guy's – and we are treated to Jennifer (fuzzy) at her desk, and then Jennifer (slightly less fuzzy) waiting in a corridor. Probably for the ladies' loo – there's always a bloody queue.

Later, much later, I ring Linda.

'Come round here. I've got brandy and a fold-out bed,' she says when I tell her everything that's happened. 'You're still in shock. I can hear it in your voice.'

'Bit wobbly,' I hear myself saying.

'No. You stay there. I'll come in a taxi. Don't move.

Well, move a bit. Just walk down to the fish and chip shop and stand on the corner.'

She has brought dark glasses for both of us in case any idiot media are onto me because of Jim, and we both put them on, like spies.

'Christ these are bad glasses.' She laughs, looking at herself in the mirror. 'We look like sad old dads. These are bloody dad glasses from the Eighties.'

I cannot laugh, though. All I can think is that I look ugly and stupid and awful.

I look ugly and stupid and awful, and I am a sad old woman, never mind a sad old dad, and I have never, ever got it right in my love life. Not ever.

CHAPTER FIFTEEN

I cannot write anything in my new journal. I am worried that the bits about Tania will make the pages burst into flame.

I go into work instead, earlier than usual because I cannot stand being in the house, and I hear that Jennifer has already sacked Guy. She did it on Sunday night over the phone.

It had nothing to do with his choice of stories, she tells me later, without referring to the Lanes Lesbians feature directly, it's a cost-cutting measure. It turns out that Jennifer's urgent business in London last week was a prolonged war cabinet meeting with senior management. Unless twenty people are made redundant immediately from all sections of the paper, we will close by 1 July.

'Why Guy?' I ask when she shuts her office door and calls me in. 'Why not me?'

She's wearing a white sleeveless shirt today, and long black shorts and black sandals. White plastic bangles, white plastic earrings. I've got to hand it to her, considering the paper is in crisis she looks immaculate.

'We have clear evidence that winning over the female demographic in this part of the UK is the best way to increase circulation and advertising revenue. I believe you have your finger on the pulse, Katie. You're our best female journalist.'

I try to ignore the compliment. Why does she always make me feel like I'm at school and that she's giving me a gold star? And I'm a rubbish female journalist. With or without Linda's dad sunglasses, I'm a joke.

'I wouldn't help you with the piece on Jim.' I face her. 'And this morning he's all over the London papers. He's on page two in one of them. If I'd given you the scoop on Jim you could have syndicated that everywhere. You might even have sold out. Everyone's talking about him.'

'I know.' Jennifer smiles.

'Guy wanted to sack me.'

'I know that too.' Then she tells me she needs to see the next person who is waiting.

'So,' I persist, 'I just think you should sack me. That's all. Or . . . I'm wondering why you're not.'

'Later.' Jennifer smiles. 'We have plans.'

I close the door behind me and see worried faces in front of me. It's like coming out of the headmistress's office at school after you've been bollocked.

'Can't talk,' I say. I can't bear to tell the assorted subs and production staff in front of me that I'm still going to be here next Monday.

Some of them are on whopper salaries compared with me, and they have whopper mortgages too, I know. Losing a job like this in Brighton is like losing a chunk of your life.

And then it occurs to me. I'm cheap. I'm the cheapest, cheapest writer they've got on the paper. I always was.

No wonder Jennifer's got plans for me. They probably involve doing three more people's jobs and unpaid overtime.

Guy has already gone. The mess on his desk has disappeared, and the only sign that he was ever there at all is a real-estate magazine advertisement showing some East Sussex pile worth £2.5 million which he has had taped to the corner of his computer for ever.

Oh, and there's a toothpick with a Union Jack on the end, stuck in a piece of old chewing gum on the corner of his desk.

'Guy said if you want to contact him he's on his mobile,' Courtney says, appearing in the doorway.

I nod. I can't even be bothered speaking to her – stinking Courtney.

'Or if you like, he's at the Merchant Arms. He was there having a few drinks the last time I heard.'

I watch her wiggle her way out of the room and wonder if she and Tania went to the same kindergarten. They both seem to have been taught to walk in exactly the same way. Bottom out, ankles together, breasts jutting out like the masthead of The Cutty Sark approaching dry land.

A work-experience boy hands me a press release. It's a statement from the Canadian Embassy about a new law which has been passed legalizing marriage between gay men.

Jim Gabriel's bucket triumphs again. And full marks to Guy, too, for sniffing the zeitgeist – even though he got it wrong and his London Lesbians in the Lanes story has done nothing but bring in complaints from annoyed lesbian readers this morning. There's a pile of angry faxes on his desk.

I think about going down to the pub to buy Guy a farewell drink, and then I read the faxes and find myself sympathizing with them so much that I remember all the reasons why he annoys me, and decide it's better if I don't go.

At lunchtime I go shopping. It's almost July, and I'm still wearing my winter jeans and clothes from last summer, which seem all wrong now. I've been wearing the same horrible white peasant top for weeks.

I wander from one clothes shop to another in Churchill Square, seeing exactly the same clothes on sale in each one, and listening to exactly the same music.

The shop assistants, the summer songs, and the hot-weather cotton skirts all seem to be produced from the same laboratory. Even the girls going up the escalators look like they've come from the same Mattel factory.

And then I realize that I'm listening to Pete's song in every shop I walk into – the 'Beach Boy, Beach Girl' song. The one I couldn't get out of my head.

I stand under one of the ceiling speakers in one shop, and tilt my head up so I can hear it properly. It's definitely the song Pete wrote.

'Beach boy, beach girl, lying by the pool. Beach boy, beach boy, why you with that fool?' Boom, boom, boom goes the bass.

It's a thudding, thumping, irritating monster of a song. The Spanish guitar has gone, and so have the castanets. Instead, the producer at Parrot seems to have added a gigantic doof, doof sound in the chorus, behind the booming of the bass, and a lot of wailing keyboards.

I look at the counter and realize one of the salesgirls is pouting in time to the doof, doof, pushing her lips out like a beak, and pecking her head, like a chicken.

Then I look above her head and see there's a video to go with the song. An exotic model with long blonde hair and a gold bikini is spilling coconut milk down her front and laughing – and Pete's name is subtitled at the bottom of the screen. 'Beach Boy, Beach Girl', Pete Oram.

'Oh my God,' I say to nobody in particular. The sales assistant looks at me for a moment, as if I'm mad, then makes the beak face again, jutting her head in time to the music.

I ring Pete.

'You called,' he says.

'Your song's on the television. I'm in a shop in Brighton. There's a video.'

'Yeah. I'm number one.'

'It's that song,' I say stupidly. 'That song you wrote with my name hidden in it.'

'Yeah,' his Manc accent drifts back. 'They took that bit out. But yeah, it's number one in Italy. Number eight in Germany. Number thirty here, with a bullet. It went ballistic as soon as they put it out apparently. Bastards. I hate it.'

I hear him taking a deep breath and continue, 'Can I see you? I'm only in Kemptown. What about outside the Honey Club in ten minutes?'

'No.' I realize he has caught me unawares, or I have caught myself unawares with this phone call. It was the shock of hearing his song, really, the song that Jim was right about after all this time.

'No, Pete,' I repeat myself. 'I mean, I sort of hate you. Vaguely. Does that make sense?'

'Always the emotional one, Katie.'

'Fuck off.'

A pause. A very, very long pause. The other day I saw Pete cry for the first time. And now he's heard me telling him to fuck off for the first time.

'I know you vaguely hate me,' he shoots back. 'Or even just hate me. But this is the last goodbye, all right? No more me after this. I'd just like to say good-bye properly to you. And I think you'd like to say goodbye properly to me. Yeah?'

I think about it.

'OK,' I give in. 'Last time. Honey Club.'

I never said goodbye to Andrew, I think, as I start walking. At least I can say goodbye to Pete.

As I make my way down to the seafront, I realize that the difference between being in love and not being in love any more comes down to mirrors. If this was

265

November, or December last year, then I would be panicking at the thought of being on the beach in ten minutes to see Pete.

I would be in the changing room like a shot, with my make-up bag out and my hairbrush already in my hand. I would be jumping around in front of the mirror thinking, too fat, too thin, too much, too little. My heart would be racing, the state of my skin would be causing extreme anxiety, and I would be torn between looking halfway decent and being late.

And now look. I could take my time getting there, if I wanted – even pop into a loo to get my foundation on in time – but I just can't be bothered. Pete Oram can take me as he finds me. Even if he is number one in Italy.

I text Jim as I wander down to the Honey Club.

PETE NUMBER ONE IN ITALY – ALMOST RIGHT – CONGRATULATIONS.

Then I take out the bit about being almost right and send it. How can anyone complain about that? Jim told Pete he would be number one at the end of last year, and now he is. He could be top of the charts in Botswana for all the difference it makes. It's still an astounding prediction.

When I walk down to the beachfront to find Pete, I see him before he sees me, and I notice he's girl-watching. He probably did it the whole time I was with him, but I never noticed. Now it's all I can see.

'Hello.' He jumps up from the table to kiss me, aiming for my mouth, and then my cheek, as a last-minute idea.

'You did it,' I congratulate him, despite myself, as I sit down. How can I hate him in his finest hour? With a song that had my name hidden in it somewhere? With a song that will change his life? He is wearing a floppy terry-towelling hat and dark sunglasses, and a T-shirt that shows off the muscles in his arms. He still looks thin, though. Probably too thin. Another thing I never really noticed until now. It's amazing what happens when your six-month love goggles come off.

'Parrot did it. Their producer did it.' He shrugs. 'I had fook all to do with any of it.'

'You don't seem very happy.'

'Me relationship's gone down the tubes.' He gives me a long, almost-teary look. 'How can I be happy?'

I can't think of anything to say to this and wave at the waitress instead, flapping my hand steadily until she stops pretending she hasn't seen me and finally wanders over. She takes my drinks order after I've repeated it three times – like all the waitresses here she's a Spanish tourist – and then traipses off again.

'Are you in a bad mood with her,' Pete indicates the waitress, 'or in a bad mood with me?'

'I don't know.'

'Jim Gabriel's a cunning bastard,' Pete says after my drink arrives. Predictably, the waitress has got it wrong, but I can't be bothered making a fuss.

'Why is he a cunning bastard?' I stir the ice-cubes around with a straw.

'He got me number-one hit right, but he never said anything about what would happen to me and you.'

'Jim only sees what the spirits want to show him.'

'Well they could have shown you throwing me out and chucking a glass at me head. That would have been handy, wouldn't it.'

'It wasn't at your head.'

'Bit of a patchy psychic, though, eh?' Pete interrupts me.

'The tapestry has to be woven. The threads have to fit. If Jim had seen that, maybe the tapestry would have come unstuck.'

'You sound like his' – Pete looks for the word – 'his disciple or something. Or his groupie.'

'Shut up.'

He grins and stretches back in his chair. The beach is packed this afternoon, and the more enterprising locals are tramping down to the water in their work clothes, stripping off in front of us and leaping into the sea ten minutes later, leaving their work shoes and bags on the pebbles.

'I rang Parrot.' Pete sighs. 'Then I rang me old manager. Then I rang a mate who works for another record company. I'm looking at two hundred and fifty thousand sales across Europe in the last two weeks. They're putting out another fifty thousand copies next week. The word is I'm instantly rich.'

'Fantastic,' I say, and I mean it.

'Doesn't make me more desirable in your eyes, though, does it?' Pete takes his sunglasses off and squints at me.

'No,' I give him an honest reply.

'Well, it's not worth it then.' He sighs.

'Come on, Pete, you've made it. I know it was their remix, but it's your idea, your words, your music, your name on the television . . .'

'Was it just Tania that put you off me?'

'No. Maybe. I just . . .' I try to think of a way to describe what happened to me when I found them together, and I can't do it. Instead, to show him, I bring my hands quickly into the pit of my stomach, as if a football has just hit me. 'I just felt – ooff! when I saw you with her. Sorry. I can't explain it. I just lost the feeling, I suppose. Whatever it was that happened to me when I met you suddenly went away.'

'Shit. I knew it.'

'It's just gone, Pete.'

'Look at that,' he points to his eyes and then mine. 'Both of us getting all teary at the same time.'

I cannot speak.

'I've cried more tears in bloody two thousand and

five', I hear myself telling him, 'than any other year of my life. Even including the Andrew year.'

'So it's over for us then?'

'Please don't make me talk about everything with all these people watching.'

'Jim?'

'Nothing to do with him.'

'Is he not interested in you, or are you not interested in him?'

'Oh God.'

And that's another sure sign of the end in sight, I realize, after we've made our farewells and I'm wandering up Ship Street, back to work. It's the irritation factor. At the beginning, all-forgiving lust and mad obsession, at the end, exhaustion and sheer bloody irritability.

He would be insulted if he knew, I think. Despite everything he's done to me, everything we had together and everything he's just lost for us, it's just ended in me feeling . . . .mildly pissed off.

Then Claudia rings and asks me to meet her in Starbucks, because Jennifer has just added her to the list of redundancies.

She tries to tell me about something that sounds like Guy's blood, although it can't be.

'What, Claudia? You're breaking up.'

'Starbucks,' she repeats through a mad rap of broken-up words. 'Blood.'

Her mobile phone is making her sound like a dalek.

When I arrive I find Claudia squashed into a corner, wedged into an armchair, with her handbag on the opposite seat. Her awful tan looks more fake than ever, along with her plastic nails.

'Katie!' she says, standing up and then sitting down again.

I pass over her handbag and sit down.

'Courtney, Jan, Deb and Lou have been taking

Guy's blood. They've got my hair and my nails and his blood. And Courtney killed a cat.'

I nod. Long experience as a journalist has taught me that sometimes it's better to just let people talk.

'I've got lots of time,' I hint. 'So you can start from the beginning if you like.'

'I've lost my job.' Claudia gulps for breath. 'Jennifer just got rid of me. But Courtney said if I did magic with them I'd get everything I wanted. She said if I got Guy's blood on a tissue and gave it to her, I'd get love, success and money. Well, I haven't. It hasn't worked, Katie.'

'OK. Guy's blood on a tissue?'

'Every time one of us slept with him, we pricked his finger and squeezed it while he was asleep and put the blood on a tissue. Then we gave it to Courtney. She was collecting all the tissues in this little velvet bag she had. I know it sounds stupid, Katie, but it was what she told us all to do.'

I nod. I'm waiting for her to get to the dead cat.

'And she wanted Guy's things. His used condoms.' Claudia pulls a face.

'Really?'

'I said I wouldn't. But Jan gave her one. And I think Lou and Deb did as well.'

'Bleurgh,' I forget to be a good listener and make a face.

'Courtney is mad, Katie. She's just mad. She said she needed female blood and male seed. She told me it would make the spells more powerful, and the more times any of us had sex with Guy, the more the power would build up for all of us. Like a proper coven, she said. And that knife she's got is a Hitler Youth knife. It's got a swastika on the case. I saw it.'

'No. What else?'

'Courtney said if I joined the coven magic would happen. She said it would be good for charity. And it was. Katie, you know how much money I normally make selling pens and things. I've made £5,000 on eBay selling those flowers.'

'But you took a commission. I always thought you were against that.'

'Courtney said it wouldn't hurt.'

I think of something.

'Claudia, do you think you've been got at? I mean, you don't look like you, you haven't been acting like you. Sharing Guy around, having your hair done like this . . .'

'Do you mean, have they put a spell on me?' she asks.

'Are you aware of anything?'

'My cat,' she says, and she looks as if she's close to tears. 'That's it. That's how they got to me probably. And I knew they were the people who took him.'

'Tell me more about the cat thing.'

'They were just cutting their fur off for a while because Lou didn't like killing them. And then Courtney said no, we had to sacrifice one. To the Egyptian cat god.'

'Did you see it?'

Claudia stares long and hard through the window. 'Yes. She did it on the South Downs one night, on the new moon. She cut its throat with her knife.'

'The Hitler Youth one?'

Claudia nods.

I breathe in the air-conditioning long and deep, then join the queue to get us both an orange juice, behind a long line of people in shorts, flip-flops and summer hats. Children are giggling and teenage girls are gossiping. It's a beautiful day outside and some people in the queue are already brown, while others are just starting to go red and peel after a weekend of Brighton sunshine.

Blood, used condoms, Nazi memorabilia and dead cats. Courtney, Guy, Claudia, Jan, Deb and Lou.

Pigeons that invade a woman's house and give her ringworm, a bakery assistant with meningitis and a flock of seagulls outside a phone box which will not go away. £15,000 at the bingo and £5,000 from a lot of plastic flowers – it seems like another world. But it's this world, right here.

I suddenly realize how the coven got Claudia's hair, and the nail clippings must have come from the day Jan, Lou and Deb so generously gave her a manicure.

'Do they still think you're one of them?' I ask Claudia when I return with two bottles of orange juice.

'Yes. I suppose so.'

'How did you find out they had your hair and nails?'

'Jan and Lou told me. Did you know they're sisters?'

'But they were still both sleeping with Guy.'

'We all did.'

'I gathered.'

'I still love him. And I think he still loves me. I think he liked me best all the time. He just didn't want to let on in case Courtney got angry with him.'

I nod. What in the end can anyone say to that?

'Claudia.'

'Yes?'

'When are you meeting again?'

'This weekend. It's a full moon.'

'What would you do if I told Guy about all this? Killing the cat and getting his blood on a tissue and his condoms?'

'Should you?' she looks terrified.

'He could help us. He could help you specifically.' I think fast. 'You need to separate yourself from them now. That's the only way to get back to him.'

'Are you afraid of them?' she asks, finishing her orange juice.

'Not sure.'

'I'm not,' she leans forward in her chair. 'They can

do what they like to me,' she says, getting something out of her handbag. And then she shows me: it's a crucifix. 'If I don't believe in them any more, they can't hurt me,' she says.

I take a deep breath. Starbucks is rammed with people, it's noisy and nobody is clearing the cups and glasses away. And there, just out of the corner of my eye, I can see pigeons flocking.

'Pigeons,' I point outside.

'I know.'

'They never do that. They're moving in, look at them.'

'Courtney used to make us invoke the four elements,' Claudia remembers. 'Fire, earth, water, air. The birds are air. We worked skyclad – naked – and she just used to hold her hands up and they'd come. She said it was commanding air.'

'Commanding air,' I repeat.

Then I realize what I want to do, quite apart from escaping this noisy, crowded coffee shop.

'I'm going to talk to Guy about getting the RSPCA involved, because of the cats. They've been on this for ages. And you never know, there used to be a Witchcraft Act once. But you'd have to be a witness, Claudia. Especially for the cat they killed.'

She stares out of the window.

'Are you ready?'

'Not really,' she says. 'But I'm not afraid any more. And that's half their power gone isn't it? When you stop being scared, you start taking it away from them.'

I get up and she follows me, with her long, blond hair, and floaty purple skirt still sticking to her legs.

'Text me when you know when and where they're going to be.'

Claudia nods as we go out into the street.

'Scram!' Children are shouting at the pigeons, but they're not moving.

'Shoo!' Claudia tries to scatter them with her feet, as she kicks her way along the pavement ahead of me.

Eventually, with enough screaming and clapping from the children, and enough hard kicking from us, they go. But the dozens of milling birds have managed to give both of us the creeps, despite everything we've just said to each other.

As the full moon approaches, Claudia texts me. She has agreed to meet Courtney, Deb, Lou and Jan at midnight on Sunday night, near the site of an old stone circle on the South Downs, at the place where a bridle path divides the road. I used to go for walks there sometimes with friends from school.

'It's covered by trees on both sides,' she says when I call her back.

'Yes, I know. My friends used to take their dogs down there.'

Then she takes a deep breath. 'Have you spoken to Guy?'

'I'm going to break it to him gently, but I'll make sure he comes with me, on Sunday night. He has to see this.'

That evening I find Guy at home, watching a bad American film, slurping instant noodles from a plastic cup. His flat still looks amazing. The rented white leather furniture remains spotless, the family heirloom paintings are still hanging on the walls and the expensive woven rug still looks expensive and woven. Guy, however, looks like he's given up.

'Sit down,' he offers me a seat. 'And help yourself to a gin and tonic.' He waves at a row of cans on the mantelpiece.

'Thanks.'

'And I'm sorry' – he sighs heavily – 'about all that. Wanting to sack you. I was . . . I don't know.' He sighs again.

274

'It's all right.'

'Rubbish. It's not all right at all.'

'But thank you for apologizing.'

'I still know people in London,' he says. 'I've got some numbers. If and when you want to get out of there.'

Then we sit and watch the bad American film for a while.

'Were the letters about the lesbian thing very angry?' he asks.

'Furious.'

'Shit.'

We watch the film mindlessly.

'How much do you know about Courtney?' I ask eventually.

'I know she's a completely disloyal bitch with no allegiance to anyone or anything except her career as PA of the bloody year,' he says as he channel surfs.

'Did she ever tell you about her Hitler Youth knife, her magic spells or the cats?'

He sighs. 'Oh, maybe. A bit about the spells. She didn't have any normal books. Just all this witchcraft crap.'

'What if I told you she'd been using you for black magic rituals on the Downs?'

Guy pulls his favourite 'Are you mad?' face at me.

'Every time you slept with her, or Deb, or Jan, or Lou, or Claudia, she told them to prick your finger with a pin when you were asleep and collect a bit of your blood on a tissue.'

Guy stares and continues to stare.

'Courtney asked them to keep all your condoms too. I'm sorry, Guy, but she wanted what was in them.'

'What?'

'They just took the cats for their fur in the beginning. But Courtney killed one, too. With her knife. She cut its throat, Claudia saw it happen. And they cut Claudia's hair, too, so they could use that, and they gave her a manicure, so they could get her nail clippings.'

Guy puts down his noodles.

'Can't finish this,' he says. 'Shall I find some real gin?' Then he shakes his head. 'Sorry. I don't believe it.'

'Claudia wouldn't lie.'

He thinks about this. 'No,' he agrees.

'Come to the South Downs with me at midnight on Sunday. Claudia's going to be with them. They're going to cast a full moon spell. They still think she's involved.'

Guy Booth is nothing if not an old hack. Once he's come to terms with the awful news about the blood and the condoms, he sits bolt upright on his white leather armchair and starts making headlines with his fingers.

'Got a story for you, Katie. Brighton's Bitch Witches. Callous cat killers revealed after six-month search.'

I think about it.

'Not for us,' Guy jerks a thumb in the direction of the *Courier* office. 'Not for her. Not for Jennifer. For one of the London papers. The big boys.'

'But then you'd have to be in the story, too, and Claudia.'

He hesitates, then half laughs at himself. 'Oh. Claudia. Couldn't do that to her. Nope, not thinking.' He taps the side of his head.

Then he goes quiet for a while as we both stare out of the window at the sea below.

'The Nazi knife . . .' Guy broaches the subject at last. 'When I found out Courtney had it I told her to chuck it in the sea. My grandfather fought in the Second World War,' he says proudly. 'He got medals. I said to Courtney, I'm not having that piece of crap in my flat.'

'But she kept it. Claudia said she uses it all the time.'

I look around the room. There's no trace of Courtney

left, except – I swear I'm not imagining it, not any more – the smell of badly cleaned lavatories.

'Courtney's gone to stay with Jennifer.' Guy lights a cigarette. 'She's her new best friend. She's got some vast pad up near Seven Dials, apparently. Plenty of room to go round.'

'And it's really over?'

'I used to have a normal love life once, Katie, believe it or not,' Guy blows out his cigarette smoke, catching the dust in the sun. 'I had a beautiful blonde in my life. She was called Sophie.'

'I met her.'

'She had a decent upbringing, decent family, wanted kids, the lot.'

'Yes, I remember her.'

Then he stubs his cigarette out. 'Bloody hell, did they really take all my condoms? I always thought Courtney cast a spell on me.'

About an hour after this Jim Gabriel asks me to marry him.

'What?' I can hardly hear him over the traffic. I'm standing near the Steine in the middle of Brighton when he calls, trying to find a taxi home.

'Can you come to the register office at five p.m.?'

'No!' I yell into my phone as two buses roar past.

'Courtney rang up the police. Then she rang immigration. They're going to deport me.'

I give up and take the phone into the nearest doorway, up an alleyway which is normally used as a gay pick-up place.

'Start again.'

'If you marry me today, there's a chance I can become a resident of the UK. And then there's a chance I can stay. I just rang an immigration lawyer.'

I think about it. It's July next week. He saw our summer wedding in his plastic bucket and now it's here.

'I don't want to,' I hear myself telling him. 'I can't.'

'Katie. Please. Can you think about it for a sec?'

'I'm in the middle of the road!' I yell back. 'I can't talk now!'

'Think about it,' he repeats. 'Courtney told Jennifer about my visa. They're going to do a hatchet job on me in the paper tomorrow. Jennifer just rang up and asked all these bullshit questions. She said it's ready to go to the printer.'

'Aussie TV psychic freeloader scandal,' I recite, automatically thinking in headlines like Guy. 'They hate illegal immigrants at the *Courier*. Actually, they hate immigrants full stop. It's like their love for psychics, it's practically equal.'

I walk towards a quiet alleyway up near the Pavilion to get away from the noise of the traffic.

'I could be sent home in a week unless I do something. Maybe two weeks. I had a six-month working holiday visa and it expired in 2003. When Courtney and I first got together I had my passport in my bag. She looked at it, said she wanted to see my photo. I didn't think she'd noticed my visa.'

'She can't have you,' I say, 'so she's trying to get rid of you instead. Not just get rid of you, either – remove you. I suppose she thinks we're together.'

'She rang one night,' Jim says. 'She asked me if I could ever be with her.'

'What did you say?'

'I told her the truth.' He sighs. 'It was a one-night stand.'

I think of the shit and broken glass spell in her book.

'Don't give her power, don't give them any power at all, with your fear,' Jim says, and I think of Claudia saying the same thing earlier in Starbucks.

I shrink into the doorway as a speeding cyclist takes a short cut in front of me, then I look up.

'Pigeons, Jim.'

'What?'

'There are pigeons everywhere. There are about fifty of them. They just appeared. They flew into the alleyway.'

'OK. Look. Don't worry. Katie? Seriously, don't worry. Just walk slowly and steadily. Walk right through them and around them if you have to.'

'Yes.' I steel myself.

Then I flinch as a bird flickers past me, and press myself into the doorway again.

'Keep going,' Jim instructs me. 'Walk and talk, OK?'

'Jim,' I pick my way forward along the side of the alleyway. 'I know that marrying you probably won't get you off. I did a story on it last year. Illegal immigrants and sham marriages – the government's cracked right down on it.'

'But there's a chance.'

'Yeah, I suppose there's a chance.' I keep walking.

'My own prediction . . .' Jim cannot finish the sentence.

I try not to flinch as another pigeon flaps past me while I walk carefully ahead. And then I think of what life would be like without Jim, if he is exiled to Australia.

If I go to the register office with him now, he can do a radio interview as soon as the paper comes out and tell them that he's just married me, his best friend, the local girl who's made him want to stay.

I can spin a story as well as Jennifer George if I bloody well have to. If nothing else, my years on the paper with Guy and Molloy have taught me that.

Guy used to sing a little song about all our rival newspapers, 'Anything they can make up, I can make up better,' and it comes back to me now, instantly cheering me.

'They won't let me back in again if they send me home,' Jim says.

'I know.'

'Unless you come to Australia, I might not see you again, Katie. And even then, if we wanted to be together you'd have to stay. Because I could never come back. You see?'

'Yes. I see. I'd have to move to Australia. Right.'

'Do you think you can marry me? I don't mind if you pull out of it when you meet someone else,' he tries to force a joke.

'First a quickie marriage, Jim Gabriel, then a quickie divorce?'

'Please.'

I hear the panic in his voice and my heart goes out to him. Was there ever a time when it didn't? Even when I first interviewed him for the paper and then when he was begging me to get his tape back for him?

'All right then.'

'All right?'

'Yup. I'll marry you. Whatever. It's fine.'

I realize that my future – on hold for a few minutes – has now come rushing towards me again from a plastic bucket of sea water. Then I realize that pigeons are landing in their hundreds, blocking me at both ends of the alleyway.

The sun is shining overhead, but it's suddenly dark in the doorway where I'm standing.

For no reason I suddenly remember Claudia's crucifix in Starbucks. Then I pray to my grandfather for help, and Andrew too, and run as fast and as far as I can, with the birds flapping up around my legs, until I make it to Marine Parade and the daylight and the sea.

Moments later, the birds are behind me and the sun is breaking through the clouds.

Then there's a text message on my phone.

FORGOT TO TELL YOU. BOUGHT YOU A WEDDING RING, JIM XX

I take a deep breath. Mrs Katie Gabriel. Jim and Katie Gabriel. Or will I keep my own name? No, I'd better not. Then it really will look like a sham marriage.

I walk to the edge of the water and find myself doing what Polly did a long time before me: I pull Pete's diamond ring off my finger, stand below the pier and chuck it into the waves. I suppose some child will find it.

Sometimes it's best to do these things before you have a chance to think about it too hard. I should have given it to one of Claudia's charity shops on the same day I caught him with Tania.

I sit on a bench and stare at the sea, grateful to be away from the birds and to have some time and space to think. My life has been like a video on fast-forward.

Time passes, while I sit in the sun and try to take it all in. Even if Jim doesn't get his visa, I realize, we'll still be married.

Then Jim texts me again to say he'll pick me up in a taxi at half-past four on the Western Road, and we can go from there to the register office.

THANKS, I text back, adding, PIGEONS GONE XX at the end of the message.

He must be nervous. He's sent me more text messages in an hour than he usually does in a week.

I walk up the road and into the bridal department of BHS – well it's cheap, anyway – as a kind of mad experiment.

I suppose I never fancied myself as a blushing white nylon bride, so in the end I buy a floaty white cotton skirt – on special – a pale blue T-shirt and some cheap white ballet shoes.

I change into my bridal outfit in the women's loo on the top floor of the shopping centre, near the escalators, and do my make-up in a cracked mirror above the sink for good measure.

I wonder what Jim will wear. What a wedding. I

don't suppose we've got time to invite any guests, before Jennifer sends the paper to print.

I buy a slice of pizza and lick my fingers.

Do I think Jim will still be in the country in two weeks' time? I doubt it. Do I think the fact that we'll be man and wife soon will really make much difference to the bollocking Jennifer's about to give him, with Courtney's assistance, or the media madness that's bound to follow? Not really.

Nevertheless. The glory is in the attempt, or whatever it was that my grandfather used to say. I have to try. Or trust. Maybe both at the same time.

I stand next to the traffic lights on the Western Road, as instructed, at half-past four, and look for the taxi. Intead I see a white Jaguar. Jim is waving like an idiot from the front seat.

'No,' I say stupidly as the car pulls up and shoppers gawp. 'Not. No. How could you get a car like this?'

'Come on,' Jim gets out and holds the door open for me.

'It's a Jaguar.'

'You like them.'

I think of Andrew. 'No.'

'Get in,' Jim guides me in with his hand on my back. He's wearing a black suit, white tie and white shirt. His hair looks golden in the sun and shaggy. A clipped lion.

Even the driver of the car is staring at me now as I hover on the pavement, and then, because I can't stand the embarrassment any longer, I climb in while Jim ducks his head and follows me onto the back seat.

He kisses me, offers me champagne from a small bottle wedged into a cup-holder in the car door, and then he tips a ring out of his pocket and shows me. It's a simple silver band. I suppose once I really do meet the love of my life – or he does anyway – it will be easier for both of us to forget it.

I have no illusions about Jim Gabriel, I think, watching other people watching me through the window of the Jaguar. Despite the yes, yes, yes voice in my head, he's not the man in the seaside cottage.

'I threw Pete's ring away,' I tell him.

Jim squeezes my hand.

'It wasn't a proper ring. It was just about the beginning of the beginning of the beginning,' I quote Pete. It's astonishing to think that he has only been out of my life for a few days. It feels like years.

I take a mouthful of champagne.

'Jim, when you were in the hotel room at Victoria,' I make sure the driver's intercom button is switched off, 'did you know that Pete was with someone else? Did you actually know he was at it with somebody else there and then?'

'They poured me a glass of water at the BBC.' Jim sighs. 'Just before we went on air, I looked into the glass, and saw his face and hers. I thought' – he struggles for the right words – 'it might make you feel better about Pete if you were even with him. If you'd had your chance to be with someone else too. Even if it was me.' He shrugs.

'Did he sleep with Tania more than once?'

'I don't know. Honestly.'

'Did he ever see Polly behind my back when I was at work?'

'Would it help you now to know that he did?' Jim asks.

I think about it. 'Not really.'

We drive past the summer crowds and I finish the champagne by myself. Never in a million years did I imagine my wedding day would be like this.

'I told Andrew once that when we finally got round to getting married I didn't want a register office wedding. He did because he didn't go to church, but I thought it sounded boring.'

Jim strokes my hand with his scarred thumb.

'Your bucket didn't tell you that Courtney was going to do this to you,' I turn to face him on the back seat.

'No.'

'But this is a mess. You're about to be sent home. The paper's going to stitch you up, and this time you'll really be finished. How could all these people of yours in the spirit world let that happen?'

Jim stares at his feet.

'You can see Tiger Woods in a bucket, losing a golf game, but you can't see your own deportation? Jim, are you listening?'

But my new husband-to-be is miles away, staring at the champagne bottle as it rests in my hand with a look in his eyes which I've seen before.

'Lessons,' he says, gazing through the green glass. 'I wasn't warned. It had to happen. I had to learn. I'm seeing a pile of school books.'

He stares out of the window as people stare back at the car. I suppose the tinted windows make them think someone famous is inside. And maybe, I suppose, Jim is.

Jim pulls my head onto his shoulder. 'I saw your name on our marriage certificate last November. If Courtney hadn't rung up immigration just now, I wouldn't be asking you to marry me and you wouldn't be saying yes. If I'd seen all that coming, we wouldn't be doing this now. So you see?'

'It's all too hard,' I tap the side of my head. 'It's my wedding day, and it may be the only wedding day I get. For God's sake, Jim, can I just drink the champagne and not think about destiny for a change?'

We are husband and wife by Friday night, and Linda joins us at a bar on the seafront to celebrate, giving us an entire second-hand cocktail cabinet, plus glasses, as our wedding present. It's all delivered in a white van, shown to us on the pavement, then transported back to her house again for safekeeping.

'For your new flat in Brighton,' she says firmly, 'when you get it. They're not going to deport you, Jim.' She kisses him hard on the cheek. 'They wouldn't bloody dare.'

'She sort of fancied you once,' I tell Jim on the way home, but he's already asleep, his head resting on the seat belt and his chin on his chest.

When we get back to the flat I shake myself into being practical, despite the after-effects of all the champagne.

First I put Jim to bed – on the sofa. I can't even think about sharing a bed with him yet, even if we are man and wife.

Next, I answer all the phone messages and texts that have been pouring in since we left the register office and Jim forced me to text my entire address book. My mother has sent about 143 replies all by herself.

The following day we both wake up feeling slightly hungover, only to find the following screaming headline in the paper, accompanied by an ugly, fuzzy, long-lens photograph of Jim, taken in the street. The headline reads, TV PSYCHIC A FRAUD, SAYS EX-GIRLFRIEND. A shot of Courtney looking beautiful has been blown up next to it.

This is then followed, on page four, by another headline which declares TV AUSSIE FREELOADER OVERSTAYED VISA and a smaller headline, stating YOU PAY – HE STAYS.

I hold Jim's hand.

'Do you think if we finally go to bed together now', I suggest, 'the impact of that will take away the impact of this?'

He smiles and kisses me, long and hard.

'I'm going for a surf,' is all he will say.

'We can hit the radio first thing on Monday morning, and have right of reply in the paper by Tuesday morning,' I suggest while he looks for his socks and shoes.

He laughs at me. 'Katie. You work there. You know what it's like. Since when did any of their local zeroes have a proper right of reply?'

Linda is furious when she calls, and says she has gone through the paper with a pen, drawing a Hitler moustache – appropriately enough – on Courtney's face. She's been counting all the lies and has reached seventeen already.

'Twenty-one over here,' I check them on my fingers as she effs and blinds down the phone. 'They even got my age wrong, and they've had my CV on file there for about a hundred years.'

'Jim Gabriel takes advantage of grieving mourners,' Linda recites into the phone. 'He is a fraud and a fake who deserves to be exposed, and sent back down under, where he belongs.' She gives a loud sniff. 'That expert commentary is provided by local astrologer and clairvoyant Ceres, 51, of Sussex, it says here. Wasn't she your horoscope woman?'

'Jennifer sacked her. She's probably just promised to re-hire her if she sticks her name on the end of the quote. I expect Jennifer wrote it for her. Ceres could barely string two words together. The subs used to have to rewrite everything she did.'

I go through the paper again, and try not to be depressed at the way Jennifer has blown up Jim's face on page four, distorting the picture to make him look ugly.

'They've rung up people in Australia who went to school with him,' Linda sniffs. 'It says here, a former schoolfriend agrees that charlatan Gabriel has always been a callous and uncaring con man.'

'But of course, they don't name the former schoolfriend.'

'No, you're right. Oh, there's that stupid picture of the shark eating the desk again. Oh hang on, they've used the photo with you in it, too. But you're not mentioned. It just says, "Charlatan Aussie Jim finds it all too easy to win friends and influence people in Brighton." '

'Yeah, great.'

'Courtney says Jim's a hopelessly addicted gambler who cannot leave the betting shop alone with his psychic bets. Is that true?'

I laugh. 'The best thing, Linda, is the way the whole story is written in *Courier*-speak. It sounds as if Courtney's suddenly found a dictionary or something.'

'Gabriel is guilty of the worst kind of deceit,' Linda reads, 'and clever manipulation of the public imagination, says well-known academic and author Annie Prideaux, who recently penned *A Sceptic's Guide to the 21st Century*, a critical look at modern mumbo-jumbo. Prideaux, who appeared alongside Gabriel on the BBC2 programme *Lunchtime Forum* demands that the immigration authorities send him HOME.' Linda emphasizes the capitals.

'And what's on the next page?' I ask.

'A story about the Newhaven Women's Institute tombola.'

'Oh well.'

'I'm ringing them,' Linda finishes. But then, before she can do anything else, Sue rings her.

She calls me back afterwards.

'Sue's writing a letter to your editor,' she says. 'She feels the same as me.'

'Jennifer won't print it. They never do. You wait, Linda. Tomorrow, there'll be a whole load of made-up letters put together by the work-experience kids. "Deport that Aussie fake now," signed Angry of Wivelsfield. Or, "Even my budgie would know he's not psychic," signed Loony of Lancing.'

'What are we going to do?'

'Not sure yet. Let me think about it.'

'He should sue Courtney.'

'Yes. She lied.'

'He should sue your paper, then sue Courtney.'

'It's all he can do, yes. That's the way it works.'

'But he's not going to,' Linda gives me a hopeless look, 'is he?'

'No,' I shake my head. 'You know that thing that people always make up and never mean, about life being too short? Jim actually believes it. He lives by it. They could have said his mother was a mountain goat and his father was a lump of brie and he'd still never sue them.'

For what it's worth I left a message for Jennifer on the switchboard after I got home, via Marine Parade, and gulped in some sea air.

She won't be there today – she probably feels as if her job is done, because I'm sure the feature she has been secretly preparing on Jim must have been keeping her at her desk every night this week. No wonder she kept my job on; she was probably hoping she'd be able to squeeze a quote out of me at the last minute. That would have been a great return on the crap money they pay me.

'Oh, it's you,' says our receptionist when I ring.

'Yeah, it's me. Tell Jennifer I quit. I mean, I know it's over the phone and everything, but I resign. Is that all right? Thanks.'

'Oh, Katie.' She sighs.

'I know. But I've got to go. By the way, did we sell out?'

'Yes,' she says sadly. 'From Preston Park to Lancing. Sold out by lunchtime.'

Jim, my new husband, vanishes for the weekend. I make a half-hearted attempt to text him, and then leave a message on his phone, but I know he will be hiding in Hastings, in his sanctuary on top of the twittens.

I run a long bath, using some lavender aromatherapy stuff that Pete bought me once. He has left so many bits and pieces behind in my flat that it still feels as if he's here, except for one thing: my flat is silent. No electronic animal sounds, no blaring television, no digital radio, no podcasts, no sound effects.

I think about the front-page story on Jim again.

In all the time I've worked at the paper nobody has ever sued us for libel, except the very rich. Half the time they lose, because we pay a legal firm in Hove a fortune to be sneakier than everybody else. Ordinary people, like Jim, almost never see us in court. They can't afford the money, the time and the hassle. More to the point, they know that even if they win all they'll ever gain is a lousy five-line apology, jammed underneath the tides report, where nobody can see it.

There are newspapers in London that deliberately print lies about celebrities, wearing the cost of a £50,000 lawsuit because they know they'll sell so many copies the £50,000 can be written off as a necessary expense.

I get into the bath, trying to forget about the real world – increasingly it seems more like the unreal world – and breathe in the lavender. It's heavenly. I wish I'd run a proper bath before the register office ceremony on Friday. The whole time the marriage celebrant was speaking, all I could think about was the fact that my deodorant was wearing off.

I twist Jim's silver ring around on my finger and examine my legs under the water. I look as white as a ghost. I haven't even been in the sun yet and summer's practically here.

Oh well. Now that I'm unemployed I'll have plenty of time to work on a tan.

*   *   *

Claudia rings me at 11 p.m. on Sunday night, when I'm at Guy's flat, having a gin and tonic – it seems to be his new drink of choice. He's checking the batteries in his torch when she calls, ready for our moonlit adventure.

'I've changed my mind about you and Guy coming,' she says. She sounds terrible.

'OK,' I begin, but before I can say anything else Guy snatches the phone away.

'Are you wibbling?' he asks sternly. 'Are you wobbling, Claudia?'

A pause.

'Don't be so bloody pathetic, woman,' he tells her off, but he's flirting with her at the same time.

Another pause.

'All right,' he switches to extreme public-school-charm mode. 'All right, sweet. OK. I promise you. Yes.'

'Is she OK?' I ask.

'Needs taking in hand,' he shrugs. 'That's the trouble with Claudia. She needs to toughen up.'

'Right.'

But he's saying it fondly, so he must have managed to forgive her about the blood and condoms, or at least blamed it on the others.

Guy shows me a new camera he's bought.

'Mastercard nearly didn't let me have it,' he says, 'but I won in the end.'

'It's tiny.'

'The flash doesn't show, but it takes excellent night-vision shots. I want to record all this business, if it's true.'

'So we're definitely going then?' I stare through the window at the full moon over the sea.

I follow him into the lift, pulling the cap down on my head; it is one of Pete's and it has a strange brand of drum kit, keyboard, or some other kind of musical equipment advertised on the front.

'They're never going to see us,' he pulls at the peak. 'Take it off. You look like an idiot chav.'

I give in and remove it, stuffing the cap in my pocket as he drives us up the road towards the bridle-path intersection.

'We'll park here and walk up.' Guy pats my arm.

'All right. If they kill a cat what are we going to do?'

'Courtney is a lightweight. I'll pin her down, you call the police.'

'Oh my God.'

'No, hang on,' Guy changes his mind, 'that means Claudia gets arrested too. Buggeration. I was always useless at understanding what happened in spy films. I can barely comprehend the plots on *The Bill*.'

I giggle. It's not a normal giggle; it's a slightly breath-less, manic one.

'Shhh.'

'Don't be silly,' he waves me away, 'they can't hear a bloody thing,' he switches his torch on and off experimentally.

'What if we get caught?'

'Three against, four. You, me and Claudia against them. They're all skin and bone anyway.' He sniffs. 'And may I tell you,' he adds, 'they were all hopeless shags.'

We keep walking and I try not to laugh. Despite everything I hate about Guy, he is still the best free entertainment I know.

And then we are there, in the darkness, with only the stars, the moon and some distant lights to guide us.

I see Courtney immediately through the trees, clasp-ing a cat to her shoulder. She is naked.

Guy holds up his camera through the tree branches and steadies his gaze, clicking the shutter. Then he tries it again with his phone camera.

While Courtney walks anti-clockwise around a

circle of candles, Claudia, Deb, Jan and Lou stand to the north, south, east and west of the circle. There's a pile of stuff in the middle – not, I hope, the bloody tissues and used condoms, though I suspect it may be – and there's a cardboard box underneath a tree, which I assume has been the cat's home until now.

Courtney is chanting, but I don't understand what she's chanting.

Then Deb starts pawing at herself and I have to look away.

I look closer and see the knife resting on top of the pile of assorted rubbish in the centre of the circle. If Courtney's knife goes anywhere near the cat's throat, I'm going to have to run out there and stop it. I've never really been a cat person, but I don't think I could stand to watch the knife go in.

In the end, though, it's Guy who decides on an action plan, not me.

'Oh for God's sake,' he shouts, giving up his position in the bushes, 'it's like a bad school play.' Then he grabs my hand, strides out with me and grabs Claudia, holding his coat out for her, so she can cover herself up.

'Really, Courtney,' he confronts her as she turns to face him, 'this is a bit bloody pathetic, isn't it? A bit childish?'

Courtney clutches the cat to her, while Deb, Jan and Lou look on and Claudia covers herself with his coat.

'Nice pussy,' Guy says, taking the struggling animal from Courtney. It's black and white, but its fur has been hacked off from its tail to its neck.

'Nice pussy,' Guy repeats, 'and by the way, ladies,' he says, unable to resist, 'I don't mean yours.'

Guy looks at the pile in the middle of the circle with the kind of disdainful expression he normally reserves for cheap wine in the pub after work.

'For one mad moment', he continues, 'I actually

thought this might make an OK story for the *News of the World*. How wrong I was. It's just sad,' he spits at Jan.

'Prick!' Jan spits in reply while Courtney waves her arms over and over around her head, as if she can't see us any more.

And then Guy nods at me, and I push the struggling cat back into its box, leading the way out of the field with it under my arm, while Claudia hugs Guy's coat around her body as if it's suddenly turned into some magical cloak of protection.

CHAPTER SIXTEEN

The twenty axed jobs were not enough for our management company in London, and the *Brighton & Hove Courier* officially closes down a few days later.

It vanishes with a whimper, rather than a bang, and I'm almost the last to know.

'They've stopped doing it, I think,' the newsagent tells me when I ask her where it is.

I look at the faces of the other people in the shop to see if they're shocked by this news, or if they care at all, but it doesn't seem to have changed their lives in the slightest.

All those years we sweated on deadlines and look, even the fish and chip shops probably won't miss it. Later I'm invited to a gathering of staff in the Merchant Arms by the freelancer who normally works on the Sudoku – the one who realized that Jim's shark prediction was about a Damien Hirst. He isn't worried about losing his job, because he's just spotted an advertisement in *The Guardian* for new staff to join a Sudoku website.

'That was terrible, wasn't it,' he says when I sit down and join him and the other subs, and I realize he means the story on Jim. 'Real gutter stuff.'

'Total crap,' I agree.

'Whatever did Jim Gabriel do to Courtney Creely? She must really hate him.'

'Not sure,' I fudge the truth because I've just remembered I am married to Jim, now, and as his loyal wife must keep some things about his past secret.

'Nice fuzzy photo of you, too,' the sub concludes.

'We're married,' I waggle my finger at him. 'Jim and I got married on Friday. That's one scoop they missed.'

'Oh,' he takes this in. 'Well, congratulations. But . . . living with a psychic,' the sub waves his beer glass around, 'that must be hard. It's bloody difficult enough without that as well.'

I laugh.

Several old staff members are quite drunk now, I see, and one or two of them are even looking teary-eyed. There is anger too. When the *Courier* first ran into trouble two years ago, Molloy oversaw a change of contracts, which meant a lot of people were forced into part-time or freelance work on the paper, losing any chance of a fair redundancy package. The smart ones stood their ground, the less smart ones let him get away with it, and now they have rent to find or mortgages to pay and no money to do it with.

'What am I going to do?' asks someone from our advertising department.

'Get a better-paid job somewhere else,' says one of her colleagues glibly – it turns out she already did a few weeks ago. She lined it up the moment she heard Jennifer George was our new editor.

It goes without saying that neither Jennifer nor Courtney have been invited to the pub.

'Is Jim Gabriel going to be sent back to Australia?' someone asks me.

'Dunno,' I shake my head. In the time that I have gone to the ladies' loo and back again it seems the Sudoku sub-editor has managed to spread the word about my newly-married status.

'Did you marry him so he could stay in the country?' one of the work-experience boys persists.

'Yeah,' I give in. 'Should you really be drinking by the way?'

'Is he really a fake?' he persists.

'No,' I say as rudely as I can. No wonder he wants to be a journalist.

Then I see a familiar face across the room. It's Magic Marky with his hair in an extremely high ponytail, wearing what appears to be a woman's plastic poncho.

'Hello.' He swaggers over.

'Congratulations.' I raise my glass. 'About the song. It's everywhere.'

'Oh yeah, Pete's got his hit,' he remembers as his ponytail bounces up and down. 'That wasn't anything to do with me, though.'

'Still, it's going to help everything else, isn't it?'

'Oh yeah,' Magic Marky looks vague for a moment. Then he remembers what it is that's bothering him. 'You and Pete broke up.'

'Yes. He had sex with Tania.'

Marky laughs nervously.

'It wasn't just that, though,' I say, feeling the wine kick in. 'It was lots of things. I'm not sure we were that good for each other really.'

'Oh you were good for him,' Marky cuts me off.

'Tell Pete I'm married now anyway.'

'Yeah?' Marky looks amazed.

'Tell him I married Jim. I should ring Pete myself, I suppose, but can you tell him? I've been busy. We did it on Friday, so Jim could stay in the country. They were going to deport him.'

'Oh yeah, yeah,' Marky waves a hand. 'I saw all that in the paper. Jim the psychic.' Then he grins at me, showing me the full extent of his gum disease. 'Good call, Katie. Nice one.'

'Thanks.'

Magic Marky drags a chair over and sits down. The ladies' poncho is transparent plastic, so I can see his chest underneath it. I suppose there has been rain, on and off, throughout the day, so it's not such a mad idea. However, he's also wearing sandals that look like they've been stolen from a nun.

'What are you up to anyway?' I make conversation as he's still hanging around. 'Are you still doing that Japanese ringtone thing?'

'Yeah. And I'm doing E-Brighton,' he says.

'Is that a new drug?'

He cackles, showing me his grey teeth again. 'It's a TV station. On the internet. Sort of home-made news, by the people for the people. Everyone's doing it. It's cheap. Broadband. You should have a look.' He nods. 'It's www.e-brighton.co.uk. Oh,' Marky suddenly thinks of something, 'I think you know her – the one who's doing it. She said she knew you anyway. She said she wanted you or the psychic guy to go on it and tell the other side of the story – you know.'

'Who?' God I wish Marky hadn't done so many drugs.

'She's a friend of Linda's. Hang on, I'll get it in a minute. Gwennie.'

'Gwynnie. She was there at Christmas. She was putting on my reindeer-antler headbands,' I suddenly remember, 'and using them as suspender belts.'

'Nice one.'

'Have you got a card?'

Despite the plastic poncho, the vagueness and the whiff of skunk weed about his person, Marky is a dab hand with business cards, and he immediately finds one in his briefcase.

'Just put her name at the front,' he says, indicating his e-mail address, 'it's the same for everyone.'

'Thanks.'

He wanders off.

Then I get drunk with the rest of the staff, leave it somewhere, fail to remember the e-prefix – life is far too full of wwws and e-stuff for me to take in any more – and end up calling Linda for Gwynnie's details instead.

'Oh yes, Gwynnie wants to talk to you,' Linda roars down the phone as I hear loud, ancient punk songs playing in the background. 'About the paper closing. It's really good. Like a proper little TV station. You can say whatever you like, apparently, they don't edit you. You can blog on there, you can send your DVDs in, whatever you fancy. I mean, actually, it's funny that they want to talk to you about the paper, because God knows, in five years' time this will actually be the new paper.'

Then she remembers something else.

'Sue wants to talk to you as well. They want to do that book with you.'

'Aaargh!' I jiggle up and down in my seat.

'Yeah, the BBC is still getting calls about Jim, apparently. And now that stuff's been in the paper about him, they've had even more calls. Sue said the illegal immigrant thing got syndicated everywhere.'

'Sue hasn't been put off him?'

'All she wants to do now is get a book out on him before somebody else does.'

I ring off. Then, as more drinks arrive at our table, I see Magic Marky reappear holding a bottle of beer in one hand and steering Pete towards me with the other.

'You got married,' Pete says, sitting down, while Marky salutes at us, as if he has just completed a mission, and wanders off again. 'Marky said you were too busy to tell me about it.'

'I was. I mean it. It's been mad, Pete. Sorry – I thought you might have got the text I sent out. I sent out one big one to everyone in my address book when we were in the register office.'

'Yeah.'

'Marky just texted me.' He pulls a face. ' I was up the

road with Polly. That was nice of you, getting Jim down the register office so they wouldn't have to send him home.'

There is a look in Pete's eyes that I don't like, and one of them looks lazier than usual – a sure sign that he's back doing huge amounts of drugs, I realize. He looked like that on the first day I interviewed him.

'I saw the paper,' he raises his eyebrows.

'Yeah. Change the subject. Have you been staying with Polly, then?'

'I've been flat broke.' Pete stares hard at me as if this is somehow my fault. 'But I got an advance on me money today, so I could give Polly some rent.' He cheers up. 'The bank even gave me a card. They said, "Oooh, Pete Oram, we've heard of you. 'Beach Boy, Beach Girl'." So I got a silver hologram card.'

'Wow.'

He makes silver hologram card shapes with his fingers, as if he's flashing it in the sun.

'Yeah. Big time credit card, Katie. So me and Polly came down to Brighton. We're staying at the Grand. Polly always wanted to see what it was like. Her mother used to clean there.'

I check my heart for jealousy and realize that it is pulsating nicely. Will I never learn? What on earth is it that makes me resent other women for having what I don't want anyway?

I excuse myself and go to the loo so I can splash water on my face. It's boiling hot in the pub and there is no air-conditioning.

I am over Pete Oram, I tell myself. Over, over, over.

Then I look at the silver ring on my finger, and think, anyway, I'm a married woman now. Well, sham married, anyway. Shmarried. Shammied.

'Let's go for a walk on the beach,' Pete says when I return. 'It's too hot to stay in here.'

So we walk, without talking, as we have done so

often, along Marine Parade, and then down the steps, past the aquarium, onto the seafront. The only difference is that this time we're walking about half a metre apart.

'They've opened all these new shops,' Pete nods at a designer homewares place which has sprung up where a long-forgotten fortune-teller used to be.

I think of Jim and wish he would call me.

'That's new as well,' Pete points out a freshly painted café, selling enormous, piled-up ice-creams. Before he can ask me if I want one, though, he spots Polly, standing side-on to us in the window of another new shop called Bliss.

'Bliss,' Pete half laughs, putting on a Manc accent. 'Yes, I'd say that's an accurate description of it. Look at her. She's only had me new credit card for a minute and she's already peaking. The bank said, would I be the only cardholder? Man,' he shakes his head, 'she had her name on the form before I'd even got the pen out. She's as high as a kite on it.'

Polly's hair looks just as I remember it from the last time I saw her in Brighton. It's bleached, blonde and piled up on her head. She's tanned and thin, wearing a strappy pink dress, and she has her sunglasses pushed up on her forehead. She's wearing a lot of clanking necklaces, too. I'd forgotten about the necklaces.

'She'll see us staring.' I push Pete away. 'Stop looking.'

'She's as blind as a bat.' He pushes me back. 'Come on, let's all have a laugh at Polly going shopping.'

Then I think of something.

'Where's Ben?'

'With his grandma back in York. Me and Polly need, you know –' he makes a face – 'some time.'

'Pete. I think I'll just go.'

'OK then,' he watches Polly through the boutique

window. 'Eh, she says she wants to get back with me.'

'Great.'

'For Ben's sake.'

'Yup.'

'Now I've got money I can be a proper dad.' Pete sounds as if he is trying to convince himself. 'We can try again. She said it was only the money that broke us up before.'

'Really?' I peck him on the cheek. 'I have to go. See you.'

'Give us a call then!' Pete shouts as I make my good-byes and walk away. 'Don't be a stranger, all right? I miss you, nineteen fifties girl.'

'But I don't miss you,' I tell an inflatable plastic crab that's parked outside a nearby fish and chip shop. And then I think, I must go home. If you're so drunk that you're trying to pour your heart out to blow-up crustaceans, it's definitely time for an early night.

The next day, I face the awful truth about my finances. According to the letter on my doormat, I am overdrawn and not keeping up my mortgage repayments. I sit down and face the truth. I am going to have to rent the flat out and move somewhere cheap. Like a tent.

Sue has emailed me the offer for the book on Jim – £5,000 each, before tax. It's barely enough to pay off my credit card, never mind the rest of it, but I forward the good news to him anyway.

'Jim,' I reach him on the phone at last. 'Have you got your bucket with you? I need you to tell my fortune.'

'I'm on the train,' he says, then he laughs at himself. 'God, I'm becoming English,' he says, putting on a whiney accent. 'I'm just on the train, love . . .'

'To Brighton?'

'To see you.'

'How are you?'

'Cool. Good.'

'Are you in disguise?'

'Yeah.' He laughs at himself again. 'Sunglasses. I know how famous people must feel now – every day of their lives.'

'Do you feel like shit?'

'Yeah,' he agrees. 'A bit. I had to pour brandy all over the newspaper in my rubbish bin, then burn it and chuck the ashes down the loo just to get it out of my head. They even heard about the illegal immigrant thing in Australia – my parents rang. But Katie,' he takes a deep breath, 'it's all over now. And you don't have a job.'

'Yeah. I'm skint. I have to rent my flat out.'

'We'll talk,' he promises me. 'I'll see you at your place. Don't worry, Katie. OK?'

When he arrives at my flat he's wearing his dark glasses, as promised, and an orange hat jammed down on his head.

'Sorry, but I'd know you anywhere,' I tell him as we kiss each other politely on the lips. 'You're Jim Gabriel, that psychic bloke off the telly. That terrible Aussie con man and well-known fake who was in the paper.'

Jim sits cross-legged on my floor and starts eating all the apricots in my fruit bowl.

'So we're married,' I hear myself saying.

'Weird.' He nods.

'Just checking to see how you feel.'

'I feel fine.' He turns to face me. 'And you?'

'Same.' I shrug. This is one of the strangest conversations I have ever had in my life.

'Move in with me,' Jim offers. 'I've got the Hastings place until the end of the year. There's still that spare room there. You could even move your bed in.'

'What's the rent?'

'For you, Mrs Gabriel, nothing.'

'Wow.' I think about it. 'Yes, then.'

Jim works his way through a pile of apricots.

'These are good,' he looks up at me. 'Tape,' he produces his cassette and throws it into my hands.

'Oh no,' I put it down on the table. 'It gives me the creeps.'

'No,' he shakes his head again. 'The voices have gone. We can listen if you like. The predictions are still there, but the voices disappeared.'

I take a deep breath and sit down at the table.

'So Andrew's not on there any more?'

'Nope.'

'My grandfather?'

'Gone.'

'Weird. I mean, nothing's weird to me any more, since you, but still.'

'The little girl's voice has gone as well,' Jim says.

'That's one of the things that was scaring me.'

'All gone,' Jim finishes his apricots and gets up to join me at the table.

Then he wanders off to find my old photo albums.

'Show me Andrew,' he says.

'Nothing mad's going to happen?'

'I promise.'

I turn the pages and try to cobble together some information about each of the photos of Andrew and I, although as I tell Jim about each one it feels as if I'm a tour guide explaining a foreign country. Didn't L.P. Hartley say that in *The Go-Between*? The past is a foreign country and they do things differently there?

'Ah, there's the Jaguar,' Jim points to a photograph of Andrew, standing proudly in front of it.

'I can't believe I left this in here. I'm sure I took it out.'

I pick up the photo, which is not mounted like the others, but floating between the pages of the album.

'You did,' Jim smiles.

'Sorry?'

'You did leave it out. Andrew probably put it back for you. It was a nice car. He was a nice guy. Be happy.'

'Jim, you said nothing mad!'

Jim grins and leans back in my kitchen chair. Then he pours himself a glass of water, brings it back, bends down and takes his shoes off.

'You had bare feet when I first met you before Christmas. I thought you were mad. It was freezing.'

He smiles.

'We saw Courtney doing her black magic on the South Downs,' I push the photo album across the table.

'Who's we?'

'Me, and Guy. Claudia told us where they were going to be. I think Courtney was going to kill a cat. But Guy jumped in and stopped it. They were all there at the full moon. Courtney had her knife out, they were naked, the whole thing.'

'Courtney, Deb, Lou and Jan.' Jim clicks his fingers. 'But Claudia's out of it. She's safe.'

'Yes.'

'I have to help Courtney.' Jim frowns.

'Why?'

'Because I can.'

'Can't somebody else?'

Jim shrugs. 'I have to do it.'

'All right. How will you help her?'

'It has to get worse before it gets better, but when the dark energy peaks around Courtney, that's when I have to move in.'

'You mean bad things are going to happen to her?'

'*Really* bad. It's like a wave', Jim tries to explain, 'in the ocean. If you launch a ship you create a swell. The swell hits the opposite shore and then it comes back. The best time for me to work on the darkness that Courtney has created is when the swell's at its biggest.

I have to catch it.' He clicks his fingers again. 'Right before it hits. It's the only time I can stop it.'

Then he takes my hand, staring into his glass of water.

'Look. I can see a girl. She's about four years old.' He stares into the glass. 'She has brown hair and blue eyes. She's calling you her mother.'

'What?'

'That was her on the tape. Your little girl. She's with Andrew. Her father.'

Jim gets up from his chair and holds me.

'I didn't know it was a girl,' I manage to say.

'Yes, she turned out to be a girl.'

'I miscarried.'

'Yes.'

'What else?'

I must not cry. I must not cry.

Jim takes a deep breath. 'I can see you and Andrew driving to the doctor. You're in the Jaguar. You think you're pregnant because you just threw up some scones.'

'Yes. It was scones. A horrible Devonshire tea somewhere.'

'You take a test at the clinic and find out that you're pregnant. But the stork doesn't come in to land.'

Jim finds a tissue and hands it to me.

'Smoking,' he says. 'You argued with Andrew about smoking after you miscarried. He thought that was why.'

'Yes.' I use the tissue.

'It was a bad argument. And then he went into a hole. Depressed.'

'Yes.'

'Do you want me to stop?'

I shake my head.

'Andrew tried to kill himself long before he met you.'

'Did he?'

'He wrote off two cars, didn't he?'

'Yes.'

I remember that, vaguely, though Andrew never made much of it.

'Drinking and driving were his thing when he was depressed.'

Jim stops talking and stares into the distance with his blue, blue eyes.

'Your baby went to spirit,' he tells me, 'and when Andrew went, too, she was the first person he met. She was waiting for him. Trust me. She's growing up there now. He's holding her hand.'

Jim smiles at me, his hand warm and strong in mine as I blow my nose.

Then my phone beeps as a text message arrives.

'Pete.' I pull a face. 'Oh my God. Number one in Japan. It says he's number one in Japan and Parrot are flying him over to do a tour.'

Claudia comes round for a coffee the next day, and tells me Guy has told her she was always his favourite.

'He said I was too nice for him,' she ventures. 'Bit corny, but I thought—'

'Yes. He said that to me, too.'

'Yeah,' she tries not to look too pleased at this news, 'and he said the others weren't anything as good as me in bed, either.'

'Wow.'

'I know it's the usual Guy Booth crap, but it makes me feel better.' Claudia laughs at herself.

'You're you again,' I tell her.

'I know.'

'Phew.'

'Yeah,' she agrees. 'And the cat's all right now.' Claudia changes the subject. 'The vet said its fur will grow back. We put out an advertisement on the lost pets thing on the radio, but nobody rang. So I'm keeping it.'

'That's good.'

'Guy's moving to London to work on some magazine,' Claudia sighs. 'He says I can visit him.'

'I'm sure.'

'Do you think he'll go back to that woman he used to be with? The posh one?'

'Don't know.' I shake my head.

'I've sort of learned about Guy, anyway,' she goes on. 'Freedom's his thing.'

'But it's not yours.'

'I'm finding out anyway.' Claudia nods – then she tells me she's rung the RSPCA about Courtney. 'Someone had to. Guy said not to bother – they've found half the cats now anyway because Lou and Deb just used to dump them back on the street. But I thought I couldn't let it happen again.'

'Did you tell them she killed one of them?'

'No.' Claudia shrinks back in her chair. 'I couldn't do that.'

I've put off going back into work to get my stuff for days, but I'm beginning to miss my old dictionary, my favourite fountain pen and a few other things. I suppose they're still there, in the desk I called home for so many years.

When I go back into the office it looks as if it's been ransacked. Two light fittings are missing, and so is the giant cardboard cut-out of David Beckham, which has been booting a ball in our foyer for ever. Most of the computers have vanished, and I wonder if the place has been broken into, though if I'd been ripped off by the *Courier* the way some of the staff were, I'd steal the equipment too.

Jennifer George's office is completely empty; not even her desk – Molloy's old desk – remains.

And then I see her. Courtney. Rolling up a poster she has just taken down from a wall. Was it *Lord of the Rings*? Or *Harry Potter*? I can't remember now.

'Hello,' she says, across the empty carpet.

I nod.

'Nobody else wants it.' She shrugs, putting a rubber band around the poster.

'Oh they probably do,' I contradict her. The thought of never, ever having to see her face again, or confront her jutting breasts, or listen to her Sarf London vowels fills me with an incredible sense of joy.

'I might have a new job,' she says. 'It would be starting on the seventh of the seventh – that's lucky.'

She hums to herself. It's as if the horrible night on the South Downs had never happened, and I had never seen her throwing her hands up to the sky.

'Is the seventh of the seventh really lucky?' I ask stupidly.

'Oh yeah,' she continues to chew on her gum. 'Seven and seven together is really powerful. And then you add two and five together, for 2005, and you get another seven in the date,' she concludes, looking smug.

'What sort of job?'

'In London,' she says proudly. 'Modelling.'

'Lingerie?'

'In a boutique.' She tosses her head.

I let her roll her poster up and go. And then I see them – dozens and dozens of seagulls, wheeling and crying in front of the windows, as if a gale is blowing them towards us, though it's a sunny day and there is no wind at all.

The BBC2 programme wants to have Jim back on – with his tape, this time. John has suddenly lost his scepticism since his boss has become Jim's biggest fan, and now everyone wants to know the rest of Jim's story.

'Are you sure?' I ask Jim.

'I can trust John. And it's Paul Saxon again. I can trust him, too.'

'But why? It's such a circus, Jim.'

'People need to know. They need to see the truth.'

'Can't we just hide away in Hastings and be normal for a while?'

But I already know the answer to that one.

'Jim, about the immigration department,' I change the subject.

We have already read all the letters from them, and it doesn't look good, despite our newly-married status and his endlessly apologetic calls.

Oh, there's a chance he can stay and make amends, I suppose. But if he gets any more publicity of the weirdo psychic kind, I think – especially on national television – I am sure he'll be shipped back to Australia before I can even get my new wedding ring off.

'I want to do it, Katie,' Jim returns to the subject of his television show. 'I need to explain what's been going on. All the whys and hows. People need to know.'

Then he nags me to go to the BBC studios with him until I give in.

'Oh, and Courtney might have a job in London,' I say, after we have queued for a taxi at Victoria station.

'Courtney,' he says thoughtfully.

'Jim, you're staring into the river. Why?'

'Courtney,' he says again. 'Bugger. I can't get it. It keeps slipping away. Did Guy's photos of the other night come out?'

'Oh. No. He did say something about that. And his phone broke down as well.'

'Yeah. I thought that might happen.'

'And what does that mean?'

'The power's still with her,' he says. 'So it's building.

That means when it all starts to turn on her it'll come back harder.'

'God. Just concentrate on the BBC thing,' I try to steer him back to the present.

'Madonna on a horse, and off a horse,' Jim says automatically, reciting his soundbites for me. 'England are going to win the Ashes. 2005 is like 1987.'

'And if they bring up the immigration stuff, what are you going to do?' I coach him again.

'Snort dismissively,' Jim remembers my instructions.

The Thames is soon behind us, and before I can feel too nervous for Jim, we are at the BBC and he has been taken into make-up.

I sit in the Green Room, fiddling with my hair. At some point this year I promised myself I would get my hair cut, my eyebrows done professionally and my legs waxed. Whatever happened to that?

And whatever happened to my journal? I haven't even looked at it, not since the night it nearly imploded, after I wrote down what I thought about Pete and Tania.

I feel panicky and strange. My body is not obeying me today. The more I tell it to operate normally, the more it speeds up. Jim has been calm since the moment he got up, but I feel nervous and hot.

There are some other people in the Green Room, but I don't even bother to say hello, and neither do they. All of us are transfixed, staring at the television.

Then the theme music for *Lunchtime Forum* blasts through the speakers, and Jim's scrawled messages from the previous programme flash up on screen.

'Fate or free will? Can professional psychic Jim Gabriel give us his insights?' Paul Saxon introduces Jim. It feels strange seeing him on screen while he's only a few rooms away, and then the camera pans across to a man from a Catholic University in Ireland.

He's not Irish, though, he is very English and very middle class.

'Tsunami, Nelson Mandela, local paper, blah, blah, blah,' Paul follows the autocue. I'm not listening. I feel as if I'm going to die from nerves.

'Damien Hirst, destiny, consciousness, blah, blah, meaning, controversy,' I hear.

Then the tape is played with my voice edited out – thank God – over a series of photo library shots. It begins with a picture of a fox hunt, then switches to Dame Alicia Markova, a map of Sri Lanka, a picture of Nelson Mandela, a photograph of Damien Hirst's shark – and the images spin on and on until Camilla and Charles pop up, to be replaced by Tony Blair, grinning and waving at the door of Number Ten.

'We take it very seriously,' says Dr Browning, the Catholic academic.

Suddenly Jim interrupts him.

'What's the date?' he asks.

'July fifth,' Paul answers.

'America's still celebrating the fourth of July, but the money needs to be put aside,' Jim gabbles, staring into the glass of water that someone has placed on the desk next to him. 'Money has to be put aside, a hurricane is coming. America needs to prepare. People are going to die. Some of the poorest and most vulnerable people in the richest country in the world – we have to be there as soon as it happens. Please,' he leans forward as if he's personally asking Paul Saxon to help.

'I believe we also have that on your tape,' Paul quickly fills in. 'You're predicting a hurricane for America.'

Then Jim stands up and faces Dr Browning. He looks as if he's going to cry. My heart aches for him. 'What do you think of me?' he challenges him.

Looking thoroughly alarmed, Dr Browning fluffs his answer, so the camera moves quickly back to Paul Saxon.

311

'Help me,' Jim turns to him. 'You've studied it all. What purpose do you think I serve?'

The camera cuts to Dr Browning, who's now looking seriously rattled, and then pans back to Jim.

'If I can't see it all,' Jim goes on, as if he is having a conversation with himself as much as the other two, 'if half the time nobody listens to me anyway, what purpose do I have? I mean, do I have a date for the hurricane? Can I make them evacuate anybody?'

'Could we go to your stockmarket prediction, perhaps?' the presenter interrupts.

But Jim is already standing up, unclipping his microphone and on his way out of the studio.

'Well exactly,' the academic recovers as he and the presenter watch him go. 'What purpose do people like him serve?'

The next day London wins its Olympics bid. I watch it happen in the pub with Linda, and we get drunk and shouty along with everyone else at the bar.

The morning after that Courtney takes the train from Brighton to Victoria for her job interview. She is in the newsagent at King's Cross station, buying a magazine before her next train, when Jim calls her from our kitchen.

'Go out of the station, cross the road and keep walking as far as you can,' I hear him tell her. 'Don't look back. Stay calm. Keep walking until you're past the British Library. Don't get on a bus, Courtney. Just stay on the street. And whatever you do, just keep walking as fast as you can.'

A pause. She must be arguing with him.

'As fast as you can,' Jim repeats, 'and as far as you can. Don't look back.'

CHAPTER SEVENTEEN

The explosions on the tube keep happening and nobody I know wants to catch the train to London any more. Meanwhile the sun keeps shining in Brighton.

Then on Monday, when I'm packing up my flat ready to move to Hastings with Jim, I receive a lunch invitation from Jennifer.

'I'm preparing myself for a refusal,' she says when she calls, 'but there's a part of me that hopes you'll give me some time.'

'Courtney told you a pack of lies, but you still went ahead and printed it all. They're going to deport him.'

'Courtney misled me.' Her voice drops. 'She's very sorry she did that and so am I.'

'You work in the media, you should check the bloody facts. Or didn't you care?'

I am trembling with rage.

Jennifer pauses, as if she is thinking about hanging up, and then she returns to the phone.

'Courtney has just told me that Jim saved her life. He called her at King's Cross station on the morning of the bombs.'

'She nearly didn't make it. He had to talk her into getting out.'

'It's the most astonishing thing I've ever heard,' she goes on.

'You made Jim look ugly.' Again I feel shaky with anger. 'You called him a fake and everything else under the sun, and then you shopped him to immigration just in case that wasn't enough. And then the paper closed anyway. And nobody cares. But what you did to him, that'll affect him for life.'

'I'm sorry,' Jennifer repeats. 'Wow. I can hear how upset you are. I'm so sorry.'

'Doesn't sound like it.'

'I'm just so sorry,' she tries again. 'And I can understand why you're enraged. But I just wanted to call, to say I'm moving back to London where I've accepted a position with a new media company, and I'm sending flowers to you and Jim. I'm ringing for his address actually. I heard you got married too. Congratulations.'

I give in. I can't be angry with Jennifer for ever.

'Thanks.'

'I've asked Courtney to move out of my flat,' she goes on. 'She owes me money. She's a member of several online gambling sites. Did you know?'

'No.'

'I think she's lost any money she had.'

'I don't want to have lunch with you,' I hear myself saying. 'Sorry. And I don't trust you enough to give you Jim's address. Even for flowers. Sorry again.'

'I understand.'

A long pause.

'So what are your plans now?' Jennifer asks brightly.

'We're doing the book.'

'I look forward to it, but may I say something? The most interesting thing to me is that moment when Jim asked us what his purpose was.'

'Well, he didn't ask us. He asked that Catholic bloke Dr Browning.'

'Still,' Jennifer concludes. 'I wonder if you can answer that question in your book?'

And then she hangs up. I wonder if her home phone is black and white too, like the rest of her.

I meet Guy a few days later for a late breakfast on the seafront.

'I'm enjoying being unemployed,' he says, slapping a pile of newspapers on the table. 'Pity it's not going to last. What about you? Got a job yet?'

'I'm doing a book.' I feel relieved to be able to tell him something. 'With Jim.'

'Got an agent?'

'No.'

'Signed anything?'

'Yes.'

Guy rolls his eyes. 'Hopeless, Katie.' He sighs. 'No agent and you've already signed?'

'Oh well.' I shrug.

'Some psychic he is if he can't even help you get your first million.' He lights a cigarette. 'And by the way, I'm surprised the anti-terrorism squad isn't onto him,' Guy smokes and flicks through the papers. 'Anyone else who'd appeared on national television and said they'd seen all that coming would have been arrested by now.'

'He didn't say he saw the July bombing coming. He just saw London crying tears of blood after a celebration. That's all that was on the tape.'

'Still.' Guy shrugs. Then he stares at me. 'I heard a rumour that Courtney nearly got it,' he said. 'Except Jim rang her up and told her to get out of the station. Is that true?'

'Yup.' I signal to a waitress.

'I almost feel sorry for her,' he says.

'But I bet you haven't rung her to say so. Jennifer's thrown her out, too. She's got debts. She's been experimenting with online casinos.'

Guy shrugs.

'She was doing that when she was with me,' he explains, 'but she was winning back then.'

I watch the gulls in the distance – they appear to be normal seagulls, being themselves for a change. No swooping, no swarming.

'I miss you being my conscience.' Guy offers me a cigarette, and then sits back hard in his chair with his jaw hanging like a ventriloquist's dummy when I refuse it.

'It's amazing,' I say, 'nothing shocks you at all. You worked on that paper for years and nothing ever rattled you, not even when the pier burned down. And now, all I have to do is give up smoking and you practically have a heart attack.'

'Oh don't say that,' Guy pats his chest. 'That's what happened to Molloy. Is that why you've given up?'

'I'm not sure why. Maybe I just felt like it. Now I'm not at the paper every day, I don't really need an excuse for a break.'

'I'm smoking more,' Guy emphasizes.

'I suppose I gave up for Jim.' I smile to myself, realizing that another of his bucket predictions has come true without me realizing it, but Guy isn't listening.

'Do you miss Molloy?' I ask, second-guessing him.

'Absolutely,' Guy takes our menus as the waitress brings them over. 'More than I thought. He was a fabulous old bastard. What about you?'

'No. I don't miss him at all. Sorry.'

'But you were . . .' Guy waves the menu at me, as if this will describe the complicated nature of my professional relationship with Molloy. 'You know, Katie, you were never . . .' He waves the menu again.

'So tell me about *His Stuff*,' I change the subject.

It takes seconds for Guy to produce a copy of the magazine from his bag.

'You'll hate it,' he says cheerfully.

'The girl on the front seems to be holding two portable DVD players over her breasts.'

'I've already enquired.' Guy grins. 'She's married.'

'Oh for God's sake.'

'Actually, is it all right if I make a call?' he apologizes. 'You've just reminded me. I'm supposed to be doing this story for them on leather Vespa covers, and I've got to ring some bloke in Italy.'

'Fine,' I give the waitress our order, remembering what Guy likes. 'A strong double espresso for him, please, and an orange juice for me.'

Guy gives me a silent thumbs-up, as he scrolls through the numbers on his phone.

I lean back in my chair and read *His Stuff*. It still amazes me that some people are so pushed for time and/or so rich that they have to buy a magazine to tell them what's in the shops.

His Stuff isn't really for rich people, though. They're giving away a horrible PVC steering-wheel cover with every subscription, so they can hardly be selling the magazine to the kind of men who can afford leather Vespa covers.

There's an article called 'Double Trouble' in the centre pages, about the wisdom of buying two of everything, in case something goes wrong with the first one. There's an interview with a man in Suffolk who always buys pairs of Armani suits in case one is at the dry-cleaners when he has a hot date – although he looks like the kind of person who nobody would want to date – and there's a piece about a Brixton DJ who owns two identical iPods.

I think about the iPod Pete gave me and feel guilty. I never use it. Maybe I should send it to the DJ in Brixton so he can have three of them.

The 'Double Trouble' feature is illustrated by twin models wearing what Guy once explained to me were hand-bras. It's what happens when the photographer's assistant stands behind the model and cups her breasts. I suppose they had to pay another photographer's assistant to do the job this time. Or maybe the entire staff and management of *His Stuff* queued up to volunteer. I bet Guy wishes he was one of them.

I wonder how Claudia will cope with all this, and decide that she won't.

Then I listen to Guy for ages, droning on to his Italian Vespa cover man. He is having difficulty being understood, which I know he hates. Guy has always had a thing about dastardly Euro-wops, as he calls them. I finish flicking through the magazine, which I am sure he will love working on, with all its hand-bras and expensive cameras, and I scan the masthead.

'I'll be on there soon,' Guy says proudly, as he hangs up on the man who cannot understand him. 'I'm going to be the Features Editor.'

'Does that mean you get to be the hands in a hand-bra picture?'

'Ooh yeah.' Guy slurps his coffee. 'But don't worry. I'm going to be good now. I've already met her,' he emphasizes.

'And who's her?'

'She went to the same school as Princess Anne.' He looks smug.

'Wowee.'

'She's not actually on *His Stuff*; she works for the group. She's their marketing director. Want, want, want.'

'You don't muck around,' I say, knowing that he'll be pleased I've said it.

'No, I don't muck around.' He brushes an imaginary crumb off his trousers.

'What about Claudia?'

'She wants her freedom.' Guy sighs. 'I did ask. I'm not a complete waste of space, Katie. But she said she'd thought about it – and me – and she wanted to be free.'

'Nice.' I think about it.

'She's cut all her hair off, too.' Guy frowns at his magazine. 'Much better.'

Because I have nothing else to do at the moment, I have started watching daytime television. Most of it is endless updates on London's Terror, as they are all calling it, but I cannot bring myself to watch any more. There are three music channels, though, which occasionally run the clip for 'Beach Boy, Beach Girl', so I've become addicted to them instead, willing the station programmer to put the song on.

I am also waiting to hear a news flash telling me that Madonna has come off a horse. As Jim predicted, she has already held hands with Africa – the Live 8 concert footage is on high rotation on all three channels.

My favourite music station of the three has a Hot 100 chart, which is counted down every night at midnight. The day after I have breakfast with Guy, though, there is a disaster. 'Beach Boy, Beach Girl', goes from number 30 to number 94. Highest-ever UK chart position, 12, current UK chart position, nowhere.

I wonder what the protocol is when a hit single is no longer a hit. Is it like a death in the family? Do you just avoid the subject altogether with the bereaved?

When Pete rings me from Manchester, though, he cuts to the chase and tells me the bad news himself.

' "Beach Boy, Beach Girl",' he announces, 'is bombing. Cos of the bombs probably. People don't want to be happy.'

'Oh well.'

'Meanwhile, it's steady at twenty-five in the Japanese chart,' he informs me.

'Do you mind?'

'Do I, feck. We're moving to Manchester, Katie. We're buying a house!'

Then he invites me to lunch. Just like Jennifer. What is it about me and lunch at the moment? Do people just think of me and start thinking about their favourite restaurant?

'I don't like loose ends in me life, Katie. Can we meet up?'

'Didn't we do that?'

'Plus, my stuff's still with your stuff,' he goes on. 'I put all me MP3s in your sock box. The "Song With No Name" is in there. I've got to grab that, if you don't mind.'

'Aha. Now I understand. In the sock box, is it?'

'Yeah, you've definitely still got it, haven't you? The song I did after Jim rang up and did the tra, la, la John Lennon bit with me.'

'Don't worry,' I reassure him. 'It's all still there.'

We agree that Pete can come round on Friday to collect his stuff, and I spend Thursday night packing up the very last of my possessions and furniture, ready for the move to Hastings. I try to speed things up by throwing all Pete's junk on my bed, and when there isn't enough room I clear a space in the middle of the sitting room and lug everything there instead. What amazes me most is the huge number of postcards, books, magazines and folded-up, ripped-up articles he owns. They are everywhere.

Inevitably I find a bag of dope he has forgotten about, too, so I throw that on the pile as well.

I sit on the floor, waiting for him to arrive, and inspect all his idols in turn. Jim Morrison. The Beatles – separately and together. Kurt Cobain. The Boomtown Rats, circa 1978. Moby. Public Enemy. Janis Joplin. Kate Bush. Clint Eastwood. Sharon Osbourne. Noddy Holder. Marc Bolan. Steve Harley. Benjamin

Zephaniah. The Edge. Bono. Jackson Browne. Mark E. Smith. Someone called Salif Keita. Someone called Vashti Bunyan. Doctor Who (but how can he be his role model; he doesn't even exist and there were hundreds of him). Chris Martin. The Clash. Richard Ashcroft. Sid Vicious. Freddie Mercury. Bob Dylan. Charlie Watts. David Bowie. Bruce Springsteen. Ian Curtis. Madness. Elvis Presley (I wondered when I'd find him). Frank Zappa. Johnny Cash. Björk. The Smiths. Sonic Youth. David Byrne. Kermit the Frog (what?). Oh, and Bagpuss (what? What?).

I put them all in a plastic bag, and then I compare the number of famous-people/famous-fictional-creature postcards, photographs and stickers with the number of pictures Pete has of himself, or Polly, or Ben. There is absolutely no comparison. The non-real wins over the real by a landslide.

I pile everything neatly into cardboard boxes. I don't think Pete would expect anything less from his former 1950s girl. I even clean red-wine stains off the Sid Vicious sticker.

'Katie,' he bows when I open the front door.

'Why are you doing that?' I ask as he follows me in.

'Getting ready for Japan.' He shrugs, going straight past me in search of his shoebox of MP3 recordings.

'I wouldn't mind hearing that song with Jim's John Lennon thing on it,' I tell him. 'Could I get a copy? Jim would probably like to hear it, too.'

'You should come to Manchester.' Pete pats the shoebox. 'Then you can listen to it properly. Come and stay. Polly made me buy the biggest feck-off house you've ever seen. There's a music room,' he informs me. 'It's all set up. I can play it to you in there. Then you'll hear it on a proper sound system.' He looks askance at my old stereo, which he has never approved of.

'Well, maybe not stay,' I chicken out.

'Whatever.' He flops down on my floorboards.

Sitting next to him now in this almost-empty flat reminds me of the first time I met him in his flat downstairs, when Polly had cleaned everything out.

And now look. She appears to be piling everything back into his life again.

Pete stretches his legs out on the floor, and I see he is wearing new designer trousers and one of those T-shirts which is so well-cut and simple that you know it must have cost a fortune.

'I put everything in boxes for you,' I say.

'So I see.' He nods. 'Thanks very much.'

'You've got a lot of photos of famous people. I don't think I realized.'

'Who's your favourite?' he asks suddenly.

'What?'

'Out of all of them,' he points to the box on the floor, 'who's the best one?'

'I haven't thought about it.'

'All right then.' Pete wriggles on the flooboards. 'Anyone in the world. Who would you want to be if you could change places with anyone in the world?'

'Well, not Kermit the Frog or Bagpuss.'

'Obviously.' Pete inclines his head.

'Maybe I'm not normal.' I think about it for a minute. 'I've never wanted to be anyone else. I still don't. I wouldn't say I'm happy being me, but it still doesn't mean I want to swap places with . . .' I feel silly saying 'a star'.

'You'd like some of their things, though, wouldn't you?' Pete nods at me. 'Like their country estates and their big mansions, and all that.'

'Oh yeah.' I shake my leg up and down because I'm getting pins and needles. 'I'd have the house, if that's what you mean. And the garden.'

'All you ever wanted was a cottage with roses

around the door,' Pete concludes, looking pleased with himself.

'All right then. I'm guilty. I suppose you're going to say I've blown it now, aren't you, because you're so rich now that you could give it to me.'

He gives a little smile. 'No.' He shakes his head, 'I just wanted to check I was right.'

'My God, Pete!'

'What?' he looks panicked.

'I just realized. You can have everything you want now, can't you? I mean, I know the song's out of the chart, but Japan's an enormous country. There are millions of people there. You must be making a fortune.'

'Yeah.' He shrugs.

'So what do you want, then? I mean, I've never known anyone who's become a squillionaire before. Now that you've got all the money, what do you really, really want?'

'I'm not sure.' Pete looks up at the ceiling.

'Well, you've got the place in Manchester, now, anyway. A new life.'

'Sting's got it right.' Pete suddenly gets up from the floorboards and starts sliding his boxes towards the door. 'Sting and Bob Geldof. They're family men. See, the kids have got to come first.'

I help him move the boxes.

'That's what I want,' he decides, looking relieved.

Suddenly I realize that his new outfit is irrefutably Sting-like.

'Do you think I should cut all me hair off?' is the last question he asks before the taxi driver starts his engine in the driveway behind my flats and takes Pete, the newly-minted, fantasy family man, away.

I go back into the flat, relieved that he has gone, and flop on the bed.

Really. The correct answer to my question should

have been, 'I want to be an imaginary creature. Preferably a glamorous, famous, imaginary creature.'

Pete Oram basically wants to be a unicorn, I think. Or a griffin. A cross between Sting, Bob Geldof and one of those. Why on earth did it take me most of this year to realize?

I fall asleep on top of a pile of rubbish bags on the bed and I dream about Andrew.

'I need to talk to you,' he says in my dream. But it doesn't feel like a dream. It's all very straightforward and simple. Andrew is wearing his work suit and tie, and he's looking in my diary for me. 'You haven't got anything else on,' he says. 'What about tomorrow, at eleven a.m.? Ask Jim to come here. He can pick up a suitcase for you while he's here and take it back to Hastings.'

I wake up, expecting Andrew to be sitting on the side of my bed, as he was in the dream. But the bedroom is empty – all that remains is the wardrobe and a plastic rubbish bag full of my winter shoes.

'Can I see you at my flat tomorrow? At eleven a.m.?' I call Jim.

'Sure.'

'I had a dream about Andrew. He said he wanted to talk to me. I suppose he wants you to do it for him.'

'Yeah. I already had that message. I saw the hands on the clock.'

'In the bucket?'

'In my beer.' He laughs at himself.

'I'm scared.'

'Don't be.'

'The dream was so real. Andrew was really there.'

'It wasn't a dream. I'll see you at eleven o'clock tomorrow. I can take a suitcase of your stuff back with me,' Jim adds.

When he arrives the next day, he takes a step back.

'You're all dressed up,' he says, kissing me on the cheek.

'I know. I couldn't help it.'

'Did Andrew like you in that dress?' he looks at my swirly, pale blue cotton tie-waister.

'Yes. God, I feel stupid. I mean, I really am thinking of this as if it's a date.'

'I know.' Jim rubs my shoulder.

'Sit down.' He arranges a pile of cushions on the floorboards. 'And stop thinking about everything so much.' Then he lifts his head up, as if he has just heard something. 'He's here.' He shivers.

'Why did you do that?'

'He's walked into my energy field. I just got the temperature drop.'

'Oh God. Will I see him?'

'Nope.'

'Will he speak?'

'I promise you, you won't hear anything. Katie, really, what you're talking about is incredibly difficult. For them and for us.'

I try to relax and fail.

'So anyway,' Jim closes his eyes as if he's hearing something in the distance. 'He's saying nice dress and well done for cleaning up the flat.'

'Yes.' I smile, despite my nerves. Then I close my eyes to make it easier to imagine that Andrew is really here with me.

'Andrew says he has to make this short,' Jim goes on. 'Basically, he wants you to tell his parents that it's all right to bury him with the rest of the family.'

'Yes.'

'Andrew says he asked Dad to hang onto the ashes because he thought they couldn't bury him with other people, because it was suicide.'

'*Dan*. Not Dad. He wanted *Dan* to keep the urn. That's what we all had that argument about, with his parents. It was just when I met you. You picked up on it the moment I walked into your office.'

'Think about Andrew,' Jim warns me. 'Concentrate. Keep the connection with him.'

'OK.'

'Andrew says don't cry. All you've done this year is cry.'

'That's just what I said the other day.'

'Too many changes.'

'Yes.'

'Andrew's saying, just make sure my parents know. And tell Dan I want to be buried with the family now. I'm not ashamed any more. They can put me there. And tell them all the truth – tell them I took myself away.'

'Show his parents the note?'

'Talk to Dan about it. But he's saying his parents deserve to know.'

'God. Don't go, Andrew.'

'He says he's always here. You just have to tune in. Oh.'

'What?'

'The baby. She'll come back to you. All right?'

'Our baby?'

'She's coming back. Strange to relate – you're going to have a daughter, and it'll be her.'

Jim sinks back on the sofa, exhausted.

'Those words you used – "Strange to relate" – that's so typically Andrew,' I tell him. 'That's absolutely the way he spoke.'

Jim smiles, eyes closed, with one hand behind his head and the other on his stomach.

'Great energy,' he nods, though the sense of emptiness and disappointment I feel now that Andrew has gone is awful.

'I've got so much to say to him. Can we do it again? When you're up for it? God, do you think it's true about having a baby?'

'Pray if you want to talk to Andrew.'

'I don't believe in God.'

'Lucky you don't. Pray anyway. You don't have to be in a church. Andrew can hear you.'

'Really?'

I wipe my eyes. 2005, the year of the tear. But . . . . I'm smiling too.

'Prayer is telepathy.' Jim shrugs. 'It's how it works. Quiet messages sent with intent. Do it. He'll hear you.'

Jim and I begin writing the book the same evening, working our way through a Thai takeaway, sitting cross-legged on the floor. It is still light outside. I wish it would stay like this for ever.

'Will you be rich from it one day? Will it be a best-seller? Will I be rich?' I push my luck with Jim.

'I'm not a prediction monkey.' He scratches his armpits. 'What else do you want, the winning lottery numbers?'

'Yes please. Overdraft. Credit card. Mortgage,' I remind him.

I drag out my tape-recorder to work on the first chapter with him, and position it between us, wedging it between two cushions.

'So anyway,' he says after I've spooned the contents of three tinfoil containers onto two plates, 'I'm giving it all up. All the psychic stuff. I thought I should let you know.'

I try to listen patiently while he finds the right words.

'The book is a good way to finish.' He sighs. 'A great way to finish. So you might as well put that in chapter one. Once upon a time, a psychic named Jim Gabriel retired. Hey.'

'Yes?'

'Stop looking like that. I'm happy about it. Don't worry.'

I nod.

Then I push the microphone towards him and let him talk.

'When I went into the TV studio the other day,' he sighs, 'the woman in production said they had about five thousand emails to give me. And everyone wants to know the same thing.' Jim clicks his fingers. 'How does Jim do it? Why does Jim do it? Is he a fake? Where do we go when we die? How can I learn how to do it, too? Is there a God? Is there a Hell? Who's right? Hindus, Buddhists or Christians? The Jews, or Chairman Mao? Can Jim Gabriel talk to my wife for me, I can't believe that she's gone. Can Jim Gabriel give me the name of a good chiropodist?'

I laugh.

'I've had enough.'

'Is it because of the bombs?'

'Yeah.'

'I got a thread,' Jim makes a small gesture with his finger and thumb, 'a little thread of the tapestry. Just enough to show people on TV that I wasn't a fake after all. I could see July seventh coming. I saw London celebrating, I saw the blood. Wow. Amazing.'

'But you weren't shown enough to prevent it.'

'Yeah.'

'But you still saved Courtney's life.'

'I didn't manage to save anyone else. Katie,' Jim turns the tape-recorder on because I have forgotten to press the button – another reason why Guy always said I was a crap journalist.

He smiles.

'I really meant what I said when I asked the Catholic guy Dr Browning what he thought I was here for. And look at him – a lifetime studying in God knows how many Vatican libraries and he didn't have one word for me.'

'You help people. Maybe that's what it's for.'

'Do I, really? I haven't found Osama Bin Laden. That would make us both multi-millionaires and save the planet.'

'You've helped me so much,' I say, thinking of Andrew.

'What's the point of helping just some of the people, some of the time, though?' Jim asks. 'Why can I see an English schoolgirl on a beach, but not see the whole of the tsunami? I could have saved people. It wasn't in the bucket.'

'No.'

'Who cares about a Charles and Camilla mug? I could have seen the station the bombers left from. I could have seen the date, the time, the names. I can see names in a phone book, why not that?'

'I know.'

Some of the comment pieces in the London papers have been saying exactly the same thing.

'I was OK with the deal from the spirit world for a while,' Jim says slowly, 'and now I'm not. So ... I think I've done my job. The whole country knows there's more to death than death after they've seen me on TV.'

'The dog who ate the golf tee, Paul Saxon, all of that – he's been singing your praises everywhere.'

'But what's the point? Unless people honestly start to see that the world doesn't actually work the way they think it does, so what?'

I nod and squeeze his hand, just as he's always squeezing mine. I've never seen him so upset.

'What am I good for, if I haven't done that?'

I hug him and hold him as tightly as I can.

'I've had enough,' Jim breaks away from me and holds up the glass of water. 'I want to be able to drink that without seeing Madonna falling off a horse in it.'

I laugh.

'What's going to happen to her?' I ask.

'I have no idea.' Jim rolls his eyes.

'I was going to ask you about that,' I speak into the tape-recorder, 'for the book. Why is everything back to front, or like a puzzle? Like Madonna. Or the shark. Why did Nostradamus have to say everything in riddles? Why do you?'

'Laws of time.' Jim shrugs. 'The spirit world can't create a paradox. If Nostradamus had given the date, time and place of the Kennedy assassination, it wouldn't have happened.'

'But after the fact, anyone could look at what he'd said and see he was right. He said it in a symbolic sort of way, but he was proven right.'

'So he won,' Jim concludes, 'but for what? To be called' – he makes jazz hands – 'uncanny?'

Then he takes the glass of water, holds it steadily in front of his eyes and begins to talk.

'OK. Here's the last thing I ever predict,' he says.

'All right.'

I check the tape-recorder.

'I'm being shown the years to come on a wall calendar,' Jim says, and I move the tape-recorder closer to him. 'Each sheet on the calendar is peeling off. There is an eclipse in Aries and Libra, signs of war and peace in 2006. The seeds sown then will be harvested in 2012 and 2013. Be careful what you sow, in your personal life and globally. Demand better from the people who are your leaders and the people who are under them *right now*.'

He refocuses his gaze on the water.

'In 2008, the first big global corporation crumbles and falls. New ones will be born after 2025. Make sure you know where your pensions are or they'll crumble too. I can see skyscrapers in New York and Tokyo.' Jim peers into the water, 'their names are up in lights – big brand names. Household names. The lights go out one by one from 2008 to 2024.' Jim leans back on his heels.

'New beginnings will follow those endings,' he says. 'Let go when it happens. Don't hold on.'

I move the microphone closer.

'Prince Charles and his brothers and sisters.' Jim nods. 'That's the key to the new order, the new structure – his brothers and sisters. It's time to ask some new questions about who you want to lead you and why. And the new celebrities will be old, too,' he frowns into the water. 'In 2015 all our superstars will be old superstars. The cult of youth dies. And in 2020 you will also see the death of old age.'

'Why?' I interrupt him.

'You will not be old the way your mother is now old,' he looks up from his glass of water.

'Sorry. I stopped your flow. Wow.'

'It's finished.' Jim shrugs, crossing his legs on the floor. Then he rubs his face, blinks hard and looks properly at me, as if he's seeing me for the first time.

'And for my next trick,' he says, taking me in his arms, 'I'd like to try having a relationship with you that unfolds without any interference from a bucket.'

CHAPTER EIGHTEEN

Madonna literally – not symbolically – falls off her horse. The BBC are excited, but Jim won't talk to them.

'I'm retiring,' he says when they ring.

Guy is excited too. 'You've got to get Jim in the Sunday supplements now,' he says when he calls me – he is packing up the remains of his flat, ready for his move to London.

'He doesn't want to do it any more.'

'But you're his wife.' Guy half jokes.

Then he tells me he wants me to accompany him to Molloy's grave so he can pay his respects.

'I didn't do it properly', he explains, 'the first time. Actually, I didn't do it at all.'

'Why me?'

But what can I do? I don't have a job. I don't have any money. There is nothing to do in the Hastings flat except sit around and read library books while Jim is out surfing.

Despite the fact that we have started our relationship – well anyway, at least we're finally sharing a bed – it almost feels the way it was before. We're like friends, not partners. And as for a married couple? Forget it.

'Is he good then?' Linda asked me on the phone the other day.

And I suppose she meant is he good in bed, which she always used to insist he would be. But what does that mean? Pushing the right buttons at the right time?

'Everything's fine,' I told her. 'We're just not a couple, all right? More like . . .' I try to think of the right words, 'ships that pass in the night and occasionally shag.'

'Weird,' she says.

'Weird,' I agree. 'But this is Jim Gabriel. I don't know why I thought it would be normal.'

In the end I let Guy talk me into the trip to see Molloy's grave because I am so bored at home.

When I meet him at the gates I see he has bought a wreath.

'See, this is Brighton & Hove Albion colours,' Guy puts the flowers down on the headstone.

'Aha.'

'Nobody thought about that, when they had the service. Nobody remembered he was a sporting man.'

'No.'

Guy stares at the grave.

It turns out that Molloy not only had a first name, he had a second and a third name as well. And looking around me now I realize he had a mother. And a father. I realize I hardly knew him at all.

Then I worry that he is hovering nearby and try to think nice things.

'Nice,' Guy says, for no reason that I can see. I let him stand at the grave while I wander around, looking at the other headstones.

All of old Brighton must be in here. Newspaper men, barmaids, boozers, minor royals, the lot.

I wonder about the newspapers which have sprung up here and vanished here – not just ours, there must have been dozens of them – and wonder where everyone's ended up.

'Sad,' Guy says when I tell him about E-Brighton,

the website run by Linda's mad friend Gwynnie. 'Because that'll be the future soon enough. No more old pros like us. News for the people, by the people,' he shudders. 'And an absolute bloody nightmare it will be, too.'

I visit Gwynnie for my interview about the closure of the *Courier* at her house one Wednesday afternoon when Jim is at home, writing out everything we've been recording for the book.

When I arrive at Gwynnie's house I realize that she hasn't been joking about the website at all – it is literally run from her sitting room. Magic Marky is in charge of the equipment, and there's another man hovering nearby, who turns out to be her husband. I suppose the cocker spaniel sitting in the corner sells the ads.

'The *Brighton & Hove Courier* was part of local life for most of last century,' Gwynnie says solemnly into the camera while an image of her is relayed through the computer. 'Katie Pickard, and her grandfather Henry Pickard before her, were both long-time staff members. Katie, what are your thoughts on the recent closure of the paper?'

'It's sad,' I say truthfully. Then I realize something strange. I have never been interviewed like this before. And I don't want to tell her anything. I really, really don't want to say a word.

'So, what do you think about E-Brighton then, and the rise of new media?' Gwynnie asks suddenly.

'Well I suppose it's the way it's all going,' I say stupidly. God, I could have come up with a better soundbite than that.

And then Steve Buxted comes into the room. Steve Bastard. I haven't seen him since the day I was creeping around with a photographer trying to squeeze a story out of his best friend's funeral.

Magic Marky is told to cut and we take a break.

'Hello,' Steve says, shaking my hand.

'I thought we could get you two together,' Gwynnie motions at the computer. 'Sort of two sides of the story. How you both feel about the paper closing down.'

'No,' I say.

'Oh,' Gwynnie gets stuck.

'I didn't know you were going to be here,' Steve says, getting up from his chair and opening a window. Then he shoots a look at Gwynnie. 'She didn't tell me.'

'Sorry,' Gwynnie looks embarrassed.

'OK if I smoke out of the window?' he asks.

'Actually, can you go into the garden?' Gwynnie's husband sniffs as the E-Brighton logo takes over the computer screen.

Steve Buxted and I walk outside. I am pretending to smoke so I can follow him out. He is brown, as if he's been on holiday, and his hair has grown since the last time I saw him. And there is something else that's new, too: he is happy.

'I left the paper anyway, before it closed,' I tell him as we sit down at a plastic table and chairs.

'Sorry.' He motions at the house with his cigarette, 'I didn't know they were going to do that – have both of us on. I won't do it if you don't want me to.'

'Free country. You can say what you like about the paper.'

'I had a breakdown.' Steve stares at the flowers in Gwynnie's garden. 'That's what I was going to talk about. After your story came out I had a breakdown.'

I take a cigarette from his pack, then find my willpower again and put it back.

When I look up again I see Gwynnie's husband leaning out of the window, snapping Steve with his camera phone.

'Eh?' Steve gets up from his chair, then he realizes we are being photographed and shouts at him to piss off.

'Let's go.' He taps me on the arm. 'Come on.'

And without a backward look at the suburban E-Brighton nerve centre, that is exactly what we do.

The next time I see Magic Marky, a few days later, coming out of Brighton station, he says that Steve and I let Gwynnie down. Her husband is furious because the reporter/victim piece was his idea.

'They thought it would be, y'know,' he searches for the right words, 'a good thing to talk about. The paper going. What you thought about it. What everyone thought about it, who'd been in the paper.'

I cannot be bothered replying.

Then I see a girl with a suitcase not far behind him. Tania.

'Shit,' she says when she sees me.

'Anyway,' I tell Marky. 'Gotta go.'

Then he remembers something. 'Pete sold the ringtones to the Japanese.'

'Great.'

I leave him and Tania to it. She is still walking like the bow of an 18th-century ship, I see. Jutting out all over the place while Magic Marky walks pathetically behind.

Jim still has no telephone line in his Hastings flat, so whenever I need to check my email I am forced to walk miles to an internet café full of teenage boys hitting each other over the head, or pretending to wipe bogeys on each other's heads, and then photographing it with their phones, loading it and sending it to their friends.

The first email I open when I get there is from Pete. As Magic Marky said, the Japanese company have indeed bought all the animal ringtones, and are now developing animated characters, video blogs, screensavers, e-cards, internet wallpaper, soft toys and stationery to go with them.

THEY LIKED ME MOUSE BEST, Pete lets me know in capital letters, which is his favourite way to write emails. It feels as if he's shouting at me.

I tell Jim all about it when I catch the train back to Hastings.

'Interesting. The real number one he's going to have – the English one – is the long song,' he says, peering into his bottle of lemonade.

'The "Song With No Name".'

'The ringtones and the other thing get him noticed. But that's the proper hit,' Jim nods.

'It's going to take you ages, isn't it,' I tease him, 'to stop looking in a bottle of Sprite and seeing the future.'

'Yeah.' He laughs at himself.

'Think of it like giving up smoking,' I tell him, 'which incidentally, I did do just for you.'

'The bucket wins again.' He smiles back at me.

Then he tells me that he has an appointment to see someone from the Department of Immigration tomorrow, in London. They want me to come, too. He's just had the call, and he's definitely going to be deported now, it's just a question of when, not if.

Jim finds a phone box so he can call his parents in Australia and let them know.

'They asked when my wife was coming over.' He looks embarrassed.

'When she's paid off her debts.' I pull a mock-horrified face. And . . . we leave it there.

Increasingly the entire subject of our man-and-wife status is becoming a no-go area in our relationship. If, indeed, I can call it that.

Instead we try to focus on business, like arguing with the immigration department, and we catch the train to London the following day. It's the first time I've been out of Brighton since the bombs, and I try not to look, when two dark, bearded men get on at South Kensington with over-stuffed suitcases.

Jim shows me the letter from immigration while we bob and sway in the carriage. It's hot and crowded, and if we do get blown up, I wonder where bits of my pants will end up. Not to mention bits of me. I force myself to think about other things and read the letter.

'So much for the wedding, then,' I tell Jim as we get off at our stop and walk towards the office block address on the back of the envelope.

We make our way to the third floor – after our bags are checked by security on the ground floor – and meet Rima, the woman in charge of Jim's case.

'Thanks for coming.' She gets up to shake our hands.

She has clearly done this thousands of times before.

But nothing could have prepared her for this, because as soon as she pours Jim a glass of water, he starts talking to her about her dead father.

'Someone with a P, an L and a T in his name has a message for you,' he says, leaning forward in his chair. 'Male. Close to you. Father?'

'Yes.' She stares at him. 'Yes, yes.'

Please, Jim, I think. Don't do it.

But Rima, it seems, wants nothing more in the world than some kind of communication with her father, because he died of a heart attack in New Delhi two weeks ago and she didn't have a chance to say good-bye. Her brother was there at the end, she tells Jim, but her brother and father never got on, so it doesn't feel right.

'I'm seeing a boxer,' Jim says.

Rima looks puzzled.

'Oh, the dog.'

'Zak? I can see a Z, then an A, then a K in the water.'

'Zak!' She leans forward on the desk. 'Zakky!'

'Your father is showing me a Rubik's Cube. The feeling I get is, it's funny.'

'I threw it at a girl I didn't like.' Rima rolls her eyes. 'My God. He had to see the teacher about me. How

338

can you know this? Are you really speaking to him?'

Jim keeps talking. None of it makes any sense to me, but for Rima it seems to mean everything. He talks about Maltesers rolling down a cinema aisle, and the Eden Project, and Rima's husband's clicking knee, and the time they caught the Mersey Ferry and didn't pay, by mistake. And he gazes into the glass of water and sees holidays in Spain where the plumbing didn't work, and a Manet exhibition in Madrid.

'Your father has survived,' he says when he is finally winding down. 'He has survived from this place to the next place, and that's where he is. I have no other way of knowing this about you, do I?'

Rima is laughing and crying all at the same time.

'Such a stupid thing,' she shakes her head at me when Jim has excused himself to go to the toilet. 'So many stupid things. How did he know?'

We receive a letter from her a few days later, confirming that he will be deported, but giving him the maximum amount of time to leave the UK – another month.

I hug Jim when the letter arrives.

'It's weird,' he agrees later when we go for a walk to get some fish and chips, 'I'm staying, but I'm going. I feel as if I'm on an escalator, going backwards.'

'I know.'

'I've got the lease on the flat until Christmas.' He nods. 'You should stay here.'

'I'm going to have to,' I tell him. 'I'm still waiting for the agency to rent out my flat.'

We sit down on the sea wall and stare at the waves.

'It's great,' Jim says after a while. 'I really think it's over now.'

'The psychic thing?'

'Yeah. Rima and her father were the last things. I'm looking at the water now, and' – he shakes his head – 'nothing. It's gone.'

'Are you sure?'

'Nothing.'

The contracts have now arrived for the book, which should pay my covering rent in Hastings for a while, if nothing else, and help Jim with his first few months in Australia.

We have developed a routine at home. Jim gets up at dawn and goes for a swim or a surf if the weather's right, and I wake up after him, just in time to make breakfast for us on his return.

Then we work, with the tape-recorder between us on the sofa, until it's time for lunch, when Jim makes one of his impressive range of salads.

Sometimes we sleep together, sometimes we don't. Jim, I am beginning to realize, needs his space.

But . . . I like it. No matter how strange it seems, after life with Pete – those mad, lovestruck early stages with Pete – I'm becoming . . . accustomed to it, I suppose.

Pete and Andrew were like electrical storms. This is like an endless sunny day. Calm weather, calm waters.

Jim and I dangle our legs on the sea wall. I am already trying to work out how I can get to Australia, of course. As soon as I saw the letter from Rima, I was already calculating the airfares in my head.

I once heard Pete say that the bond between the musicians in his band was so good, apparently, that it felt like great sex. What a wanker – Great sex, man! I expect he was talking about Tania, in hindsight. But now I understand what he meant.

When Jim and I work together it feels as if we're flowing, as if we're joined at the hip. I know what he's going to say before he says it, and I hardly ever have to explain my questions.

And then on warm summer evenings, when we're finishing one side of a tape and drinking a glass of white wine together, it's all I can do not to ask him if we can be husband and wife properly.

I stare at the waves while Jim breathes in the sea air.

I don't want to be in a sham marriage. I've never been in a sham anything, why should I make an exception for this?

I look at the cheap silver ring on my finger. Rima wasn't fooled by it for a second. And the reason it's cheap is because Jim has always known we are meant for other people. So have I.

Look at us. We're side by side on the sea wall and not even touching.

We have had all year to get to know each other, I realize. If something was going to happen between us, it would have happened by now. And if Jim had ever felt anything at all for me – properly – we wouldn't have rushed to a register office, we would have booked somewhere nice and invited my parents and his parents from Australia, and all the rest of it.

'What are you thinking about?' Jim looks at me.

'Nothing.'

Later on I go to the internet café while Jim goes home.

There's an email from Beverley at the RSPCA, telling me that Courtney Creely will face charges of animal cruelty, following evidence given by Claudia, Jan, Lou and Deb about the stolen cats. They will be fined, too, Beverley tells me, but the RSPCA is planning to throw the book at Courtney.

Then there's an email from Guy, telling me that Courtney has been trying to borrow money from him.

And she's ill, he says. Courtney has contracted cat scratch disease. He thinks one of the cats she stole has transmitted the virus to her, and when she rang him she said she was covered in cotton wool and sticking plasters.

'She said a scratch or an insect bite turns into an

open wound in a few hours,' Guy writes. 'And it doesn't heal. It stays open, so she has to wear the plasters. She says she'll have scars.'

Neither of us can think of anything to say about that.

Some teenage boys in the internet café are waving phone cameras at each other now and shouting.

'Shut,' I tell one of them, 'up.'

Guy goes on to say that he has rented out his flat in Brighton, found somewhere new to live in Richmond and is about to go out to dinner this weekend with Claudia.

Claudia?

I read it again. He is about to go out to dinner with Claudia. He has decided that she needs a break from Brighton after all she's been through, so he's invited her to stay. Just as friends, of course . . .

Yeah, right.

I wonder what happened to the glamorous woman in marketing that Guy was in love with, the one who went to Princess Anne's old school, and decide that she probably told him to go away after discovering how much he wanted to be a human hand-bra.

And then I think about Claudia and her newfound love of freedom. I fully expect that to last about ten nanoseconds – just until Guy opens the wine, in fact.

After I've finished with my email, I walk home, past empty amusement arcades and antiques shops which have closed for the day.

Jim has made dinner – an enormous salad full of avocado, tomato and some sauce with red peppers and chillies in it.

'Aussie recipe,' he says, as I pour the wine and turn the lights on.

'Yes, I like these salads. And you'll be there soon,' I say pointlessly.

He nods and puts his fork down.

'I am going to miss you like hell.' He sighs. 'Say

you'll come over to live for a while. When you've paid off everything and sorted it all out.'

'Yes, of course.' I listen to myself and sound oddly polite. 'Soon.'

'Bugger it. Come now.'

'I don't have a job. I can't afford it.'

'You can stay with a friend of mine,' he offers, 'at the beach near Hungry Head. She's going travelling. If you look after her dog you won't have to pay any rent. She grows her own veggies. You can eat those. Easy.'

'I can't live like that.'

And I am hurt, I suppose, that he hasn't suggested I move in properly with him when he goes over there. He wants me, but he's pushing me away, too. Oh, I know he says he's going to miss me, but we are already in this flat together and it feels like we're miles apart.

A few days ago it felt as if I was getting somewhere. Every day that we worked together it felt as if we were on the edge of something.

Now he's drifted away again. It's just like watching him surf.

I wonder why he's never been with any woman for more than a few months, and decide he's commitment-phobic. He's had me fooled all along, of course, but he's nothing more, nothing less.

It's so ordinary, I think. But it feels like the truth.

Jim pours me some more wine.

'I bet you miss Australia.' I make conversation.

He leans back in his chair and locks his fingers behind his head.

'I miss the light.' He nods. 'Everyone and everything looks good in that light. They say it's harsh, but it's beautiful. You see it as soon as you step off the plane. And the water. Where I come from, you wash your hair in rainwater, from tanks. You can taste it when you brush your teeth in the morning.'

I let him talk.

'I miss the space, too.' He nods. 'There's nobody in the bush, nobody on the beach. You don't queue, you don't have a hundred people coming at you on the pavement. There's no crap in the water. No crap on the streets. I miss the sound of the whip birds in the morning, and the kookaburras on the wires. I miss the cicadas, and the tree frogs on the windows, and the way you can chuck a tomato in the compost and have a tomato plant two weeks later.'

Then he squeezes my hand.

'And I'll miss your lipstick, because you never put it on right, and I'll miss the way you sound so *reasonable*. I'll miss the way you sing to yourself when you're cooking, and I'll miss the way you put your hair up when you can't be bothered to wash it. I'll miss the way you cross off things on your shopping list, and the way you never, ever give up.' He smiles at me. 'I'll miss that most of all. You're so tenacious. You hang onto your dreams like, grrr.' He makes dog teeth.

'Sort of.' I suddenly feel embarrassed. 'A bit.'

'You're my best friend,' he finishes.

Ah. Best friend, then.

'Do you miss Pete?' he asks suddenly.

'Pete used to want to be other people all the time. So now, when I look back, I wonder who I was actually with. I think he wants to be Sting now.'

Jim laughs.

'Anyway. You never talk about your ex-girlfriends,' I mock complain.

'Not worth it.'

'Yes it is.'

And then he laughs at some private thought and I feel as if he's shut me out again.

Later on, when I'm washing up, I look at the calendar. Jim's flight is booked for 6 September. That gives us about three weeks, if we're ever going to get married. Again.

I dry the dishes. I could go to Australia for a few months while I live rent-free in someone's house, and eat their vegetables, and walk their dog, and then I could come back here. But so what?

I think about my journal, which I have left alone for weeks. My dream cottage, with my dream family waving from the windows, is still in there. It's never left me. Don't I owe myself that much?

My head hurts. Wine and warm rooms never mix – I should have remembered that from all those blurry winter days with the radiators turned on at full-strength, with Pete in my bed and endless bottles of red on the kitchen table.

I can hear Jim in the bathroom now, running a shower.

He belongs to the summer, I think. No wonder he wants to go back.

Then I give up and go to bed, with a pillow tucked next to me under the sheet. In Japan, apparently, they make them with arms.

CHAPTER NINETEEN

Sue rings a few days later, fizzing with excitement. A famous writer has been blasted into the sky and a famous actor paid for it. Johnny Depp has organized fireworks at a wake for Hunter S. Thompson.

'But how could Jim have known?' she keeps saying when she rings. 'I mean, I know it's the question we're always asking, but we're absolutely gobsmacked here. Can you ask him? He made that prediction almost nine months ago.'

'It'll be in the book,' I promise. 'The way time works. The way Jim works. All of that.'

Guy remembers the prediction too and he emails Jim to ask him for a reading.

'What?' I cannot believe it when Jim tells me.

'It's OK. I told him I don't do it any more.'

We're having breakfast, on a rainy late summer day when he tells me.

'He probably wants to know about Claudia,' I decide.

'Oh that,' Jim waves a hand, 'I saw that before. That's a done deal.'

'Is it?'

'Hard work, but a done deal.'

'Don't. I don't want to know about them not being happy. I've had enough of people not being happy this year.'

346

'Molloy set up the job on the magazine for him, by the way,' Jim goes on, pouring more muesli into his bowl.

'In London? Do you mean Molloy set it up for him after he was *dead*?'

'Don't be like that.' Jim laughs. 'Not dead. Molloy's on the other side. Yes, I saw it in the water a while ago. They've got karma together, those two.'

'But how', I insist 'did Molloy do it? I mean, you say that to me all the time. Spirit people did this, spirit people did that. What happens? How can you get someone a job if you're made of thin air?'

'Save it for chapter twelve,' Jim teases me.

I wonder if Guy will stay at the magazine and decide that he won't. His pride is immense, but I know *His Stuff* is too far down the food chain for Guy to stay there long. If it's true that Molloy engineered the job for him, though, then he definitely did the right thing. Guy's job in London has saved him.

I remember what Jim said about him months ago on the pier. Guy Booth is a desperate guy. I wonder how things would have been in his life if he'd never been so desperate?

Maybe he would have ended up at a proper newspaper, I think. One his parents would have been proud of.

It reminds me of a chapter Jim and I have been working on about choices. Forks in the road – free will, fate and all that.

We are high up on the hill, near the old Hastings Caves, when I ask him about it again.

'Can't you just look in your bucket for a teensy, weensy second and show me the choices I've got?' I plead.

'Nope.' He turns round and smiles at me.

'But I don't know what to do. Stay here? Go to

347

Australia? Move to London and hope that Guy can get me a job somewhere? Move back to Brighton?'

'Don't worry about work,' Jim sits down on the grass. We are near a fairy ring of mushrooms which, impressively, the locals have managed to avoid treading on.

'I can't help worrying,' I say.

'Cheque.' Jim hands me a piece of folded paper from his pocket. It's for £20,000 and it is made out to me.

I stare.

'For the book?' I say stupidly.

'I sold the beach hut. You can live on that for a while. Find out what you really want to do.'

'Oh my God.'

'I'm going to a real beach,' Jim shrugs. 'I don't need the hut any more.'

'Thank you so much. But I can't.' I hand the cheque back.

'Please take it.'

I take a deep breath and put it in my pocket.

'Thank you.'

'Good.' Jim stretches out on the grass with his hands behind his head. Then I lie down, too, and watch him staring at the clouds.

'I can't believe it,' I begin to thank him again, but he holds up his hand, like a policeman stopping traffic.

I give in and watch the clouds, too. Then I sit bolt upright again.

'I can come to Australia now.'

'Yep.'

'I can go there with you.'

'If you want.'

'Well, I do want. I mean, is that all right?'

'Sure,' Jim closes his eyes and I see that that is all I'm going to get out of him.

I had another email from Pete this morning. He told

me that he and Polly have decided to get married in Japan.

They will spend their honeymoon in Tokyo, which is Polly's favourite place in the world, although she's never been there.

And – I am jealous. Not of Polly. No, not that. But I am jealous of the fact that after all this time and struggle, they are finally engaged and set for a proper wedding. And then, all being well, they will be together for the rest of their lives.

I am a legally married woman who is jealous of other people's weddings, and I know it's pathetic, but it's true.

I think about Pete and Polly growing old and grey together, while people wander up to Hastings Castle in the distance.

Ben's parents have made Ben happy at last. And I expect he will make them happy as well when he stops his child-monster phase.

I wonder if Ben will remember me at all when he is grown up, and decide that I will be one of a chain of names in his father's life. I never wanted to be a commercial break in the continuing drama that is Pete and Polly, and look, it turns out I was an entire chocolate ad.

I find myself speculating about how long it will take for Pete to switch from fly agaric mushrooms to E to cocaine. Probably about five minutes, as soon as he and Polly hit their first Tokyo nightclub.

There are so many things that keep couples together. With me and Andrew it was country pubs and stupid jokes and the constant dream of the cottage with the roses around the door. For Pete and Polly it's drugs, Ben, money and maybe fame.

I can't think badly of them for that. I can't resent Polly, even though I now know that my suspicions were right and she was sleeping with Pete the whole time we were living together.

It was in one of the dozens of emails Pete has been sending lately. I suppose now he has confessed everything the torrent of emails will stop. I hope so. I don't think I can stand looking at any more capital letters.

He can't spell Tokyo either. I laugh to myself, and Jim rolls over on the grass and smiles back at me.

'Pete's releasing the "Song With No Name",' I remember another piece of his news.

'That's the big number one. The proper one.'

'Well, if that's what you saw in your bucket . . .'

We get up and walk to the café, looking out over Hastings.

'He said he's going to release it on the internet and charge people fifty pence to download it. He says nobody needs record companies any more.'

'Nope,' Jim agrees.

'It's like the news. There won't ever be just one news again, will there?'

'Millions of angles, instead,' Jim agrees. 'Home podcasts, mobile phone photographs and blogs – that's the new news.'

'Like the bomb in London.'

'We might even get something approximating the truth about the world one day.' Jim smiles.

'If I have to go back and work on a newspaper, I think I'll throw up.' I link my arm with his.

'Find out what you love and do it,' Jim interrupts.

'I can't take your money.'

'This is the last conversation I am going to have with you about it.'

'You're going to need it.'

'Like I said.' Jim shrugs.

I bank the cheque a few days later, and Jim makes me promise to buy a surfboard.

'Learn here and it won't be so scary when you get to Australia,' he emphasizes.

'So I'm going, then?'

'Well, you don't have to.'

'No, I want to. I mean, is that what you want me to do?'

'It's up to you. You don't have to come with me. Just because we'll have finished the book soon doesn't mean you need to be . . .' He clicks his fingers.

'What?'

'With me.' He can barely get the words out.

'But I am with you.' And then I say the dreaded words. 'I'm married to you. You're my husband.'

'Yes, but I'm the husband who can never come back to England, too,' he points out.

'You're just thinking of me. Is that what this is all about?'

'I know it's driving you mad, Katie, but I need to give you the choice. After all you've done for me. I'm going back there to teach surfing, to do a bit of diving, all of that. That's the new life. Is that what you want?'

'Don't know until I get there.'

'The rules might change one day, but if we go out there doing the marriage thing, you can't come back to England. At least not with me.'

'Not for long anyway.'

'Exactly. What if you miss it.'

'Anyway,' I say politely, 'thank you for offering me so many choices.'

And then, yet again, we go home to separate beds and our weird together-apart lives.

A few days later I draw out some of Jim's money and buy a surfboard, under Jim's instructions, from a shop in Brighton.

'You won't feel a thing in a wetsuit,' he says, once I've purchased my kit and we've headed back to Hastings for my first lesson.

'But just look at it out there,' I say, scanning the

351

waves in front of us. It's cold and windy, and I don't even want to think about the temperature of the water.

'Nice short waves. If you can get up on them you'll be OK by the time you get to Bondi.' Jim laughs as we crunch across the pebbles and reach the road. It's beginning to rain, now, and not just any kind of rain, the fierce, freezing, needling kind that always hits the back of your neck first.

'OK, OK,' Jim comforts me, seeing my face, 'we'll go out there tomorrow.' He points at the waves. 'It'll be milder tomorrow. All right?'

And then I kiss him.

And he kisses me back.

And then we stand under the awning of a sweet shop, with sticks of rock and huge twists of marshmallow in the window – and hearts, too, great big red toffee hearts – and we hold each other until people come out of the shop and we are forced to move.

'I've been trying, really trying,' I manage to say once he's taken my hand and led me across the road again to the pier. 'I mean, I've been trying to choose. And I can't. I need you to choose.'

'We're so *unsuitable* together.' He half smiles at me. 'I don't think I can.'

'Are you scared?'

'Yes.'

'Because you can't see into your bucket any more. You can't see what's going to happen to us if we stay together properly.'

'It's not that.'

'You should listen to that Kate Bush song, "The Hounds of Love".' I think of the song Pete put on my iPod months before.

He sighs and pulls me towards him.

'I know it well.' He smiles, and then he spots an

352

electronic fortune-teller, next to all the fruit machines just inside the pier.

The electronic fortune-teller has only a head and no body, but if you put £1 in the slot she will apparently tell you everything.

'See, that's what we need,' I tell Jim. 'She can fix it for us. "Dear Jim and Katie, you will live happily ever after in a cottage by the sea with loads of good surf and eight wonderful children. The end."'

Jim laughs. 'That voice you're putting on,' he says, 'is that how you think psychic ladies talk?'

And then he suddenly remembers that we cannot take our first surfing lesson tomorrow morning after all, because he's promised to exorcize Courtney.

'Say that again?'

'Maybe not exorcize, so much. More like give her a new start. Get her away from all that occult stuff.'

'Really?'

'We're going to do it in the sea at Brighton. She asked me. Don't look like that.'

Jim takes my hand and puts it in his pocket as we leave the amusement arcade and walk back.

'She has scars from the cat scratch disease,' he says. 'She's better now, but she says she has too many marks on her skin. She can't model any more. And Cornucopia closed down. They reckon they'll make more money selling coffee out of there.'

'Oh.'

'Courtney can't get her hair done at the salon any more, either – the girls won't have anything to do with her. So she dyed her own hair and had an allergic reaction. It burned her. Half her hair's come out.'

'God.'

'This is between me and her,' Jim says after he has kissed me again and we have had enough of the pier. 'I have to do it. It's a Buddhist ceremony someone showed me once. I'm sort of adapting it.'

'Yes.'

'OK?'

'Yes, yes. So is Courtney all right?'

'She'll be OK. And the energy is peaking now. It's the right time.'

'What about her family?'

'This much I know about Courtney.' Jim shrugs. 'Don't even ask.'

Later that evening I ring Guy.

'Courtney is pretty bad,' I say.

'Katie, I'm not interested.'

'Can you turn the TV down a bit?'

'All right then.'

He's gone for a few minutes, and when he comes back he tells me again that he is definitely, positively not interested in Courtney Creely.

'She's lucky I didn't have her up on charges.'

'She's burned her scalp. She used some hair dye, because Jan won't colour her hair any more, and Jim said her hair's come out.'

'I don't want anything to do with it.'

'Forgive her.'

'Why?'

'Because it will help her. Jim's going to do something with her tomorrow.'

'What sort of something?' Guy asks suspiciously.

'I know you think it's all rubbish, but he has a Buddhist ceremony he wants to do. To get rid of all the nasty stuff.'

'Nasty stuff,' Guy says thoughtfully.

'He wants her to throw the knife away as part of the ceremony.'

'Too weird for me.'

'She was stupid. Not evil, just stupid. She got into something she didn't understand. You saw what happened. She's got no money, nobody to help her, nowhere to live. It's rebounded on her, and it's not

354

stopping. It's almost as if the thing she tapped into to help her wants to get its own back.'

'Too weird for me,' Guy says again. 'Anyway, where is she living?'

'Jim says she's sleeping on the sofa at her mother's in Newcastle.'

'Ah yes. Her barking mad mother,' Guy emphasizes.

'Will you forgive her?' I persist.

'How can I do something I don't feel like doing?' Guy snaps.

But the following morning, after Jim has taken Courtney into the sea and thrown rose petals over her head, and said Buddhist words, and called on the Buddhist goddesses Green Tara and White Tara to protect her, Courtney turns on her phone to find a one-line text from him.

It says nothing more than take care, but Jim says, it's all she needs to get better.

I have trouble going near Jim afterwards, and I feel guilty but I can't do it.

'Come here,' he says, pulling me towards him on the sofa that evening, when we're back in the flat. We are surrounded by tea-light candles in metal containers because of a power cut.

'It just feels odd, you and Courtney this morning. I need a bit of time to think.'

'OK, OK.'

'I'm not jealous or anything.'

'No.'

'But what you did was – intimate. No, that's the wrong word.'

'Could be the right word.'

'Is she all right now?'

'She's fine.' Jim lights more candles.

'What about the knife?'

'Buried it. Washed it in the sea and then buried it, where nobody will ever find it. Hey. Come here,' Jim

355

pulls me into his side again, and I lie like that, not moving, but thinking about Courtney, as we both watch the news.

'What do you think she'll do now?' I ask him.

'I don't know. But the darkness has gone,' Jim says, and at the moment he says the words, all the lights in the flat come on again.

Later on we go to bed – together – and Jim scoops up all the candles.

'What are you doing?'

'Decorating the room.' He shrugs. 'We never did have a honeymoon.'

And then at last, at last, he tells me that when we go to Australia everything will feel different and we can make a new start, just the way Courtney did in the ocean this morning.

'Sleeping in the sand dunes,' he says before he pulls my nightie off – it's the silly, spriggy, demure 1950s nightie that always made Pete laugh.

'I bet sand gets everywhere.' I give in and throw the nightie on the floor, as the candles double the light in the room, and for the first time since our wedding I let myself feel like Jim Gabriel's wife.

CHAPTER TWENTY

When Hurricane Katrina hits, I have to keep reminding myself that I do not work on a newsaper any more, and so does Guy.

'Old habits die hard,' he confides when we're having lunch in Brighton one Saturday. 'Two of the rescue workers from here who've gone over are from Hove.'

'I heard.'

'They tried to cover it on the radio.' He waves a dismissive hand.

'Yes, I heard that, too.'

'Rubbish. And what about that E-Brighton thing?'

'Hmmm.'

Then Guy tells me his good news. He is doing so well at *His Stuff* that he's already been taken aside and asked by the editor if he would like his job.

The editor plans to go back to television, which is where he started, and it seems the management are unanimous – Guy Booth is the man for them.

'I think I'm going to tell them to forget it,' Guy complains, swirling his wine around in the glass. 'They only offered me three thou more than I'm getting now.'

'Oh well.'

'I'm working on a magazine about buying things, but with the money they pay me, the only thing I can afford to buy is the bloody subscription they advertise at the back.'

I laugh.

'Tell me what it's like in Australia when you get over there,' Guy says as he looks at the pudding menu. 'I might come and join you.'

'Yes.'

'Claudia's got a new job.' He puts the menu down again. 'They're launching a new title.' He waggles his eyebrows at me. 'I bet you can't guess what it's called.'

'Not *Her Stuff*?'

'Full marks to you.' Guy grins.

Then I show him my ticket to Sydney and he fans himself with it.

'Oh to be gainfully unemployed,' he moans. 'How the other half live.'

'It's just until Christmas. Then I'll come back here.'

'You don't have a plan.' Guy is amazed. 'Katie, I can't believe you're functioning without a plan.'

'No. I mean, we're married. That's probably enough of a plan, isn't it?'

'Oh?' Guy stares. 'Married now, are we? As opposed to' – he shrugs and makes a bored face – 'married.'

'Maybe you can get a job out there, Guy.'

'Maybe.'

'Would you work on a paper again, Katie, eh?'

'No.'

But that is a touchy subject: the fact that I will never, ever work on a newspaper again, so we leave it alone and concentrate on the summer pudding which Guy has just ordered, instead.

After lunch I buy a guidebook on Australia. I have already tried to do this several times, in Jim's presence, and he hasn't let me.

'I can tell you everything,' he keeps saying. 'What do you want to know?'

Sue went on her honeymoon and she keeps

telling me about all the childrens' school uniforms.

'They make them wear these hats,' she says, 'like Lawrence of Arabia. They have these flaps that hang down at the back to keep the sun off. It's incredibly sweet.'

'Yes.' I know I will probably notice nothing else when I finally land in Sydney.

'I'm pregnant, by the way,' she says. 'And we're so glad we didn't buy that awful house with the cart-wheel. Apparently, the other guy who got it has done nothing but throw money at it. So can you tell Jim he was right?'

Aha. Another bucket vision to haunt my husband. I buy the Australia guidebook and take it on the bus with me, glued to photographs of the Opera House and the Sydney Harbour Bridge, while the last of Brighton's summer days turns into drizzle.

Pete sends me a late wedding present. It is a boomerang.

'Made in China,' Jim inspects the sticker on the back. 'I thought so.'

'Oh well.'

'Are you going to send him anything?'

'Yeah,' I suddenly think. 'This. I'll just stand on the M23 and chuck it in the direction of Manchester, see what happens.'

'Wait until you see a real boomerang.' Jim pulls my legs onto his lap.

We are lying on the sofa, watching a documentary on Hurricane Katrina, and it's the first time he has laughed since it happened.

Then I notice something.

'That's Pete's music.'

'Yeah?' Jim turns the volume up on the remote control.

'That's the "Song With No Name". They just played a bit of it then. On the bit about the relief fund.'

'It's good.' Jim nods.

'Sad.'

'Right for the times.'

'Pete sent me an email. He and Marky have done an extended version of the song, and one of the aid agencies is putting it out as a single. They already think they can make a million quid for emergency housing off the back of it.'

I return to my guidebook on Australia and Jim goes back to a surfing magazine.

Since Katrina he has lost all interest in the other book – the one we are supposed to be writing about his life.

'The thing is,' he says, getting up to put the kettle on, 'I'd like to get married again. To you, obviously. You know what I mean.'

'As in, married, married, *married* to me?'

'I've heard that's the best kind,' Jim agrees.

'So who'll propose then?' I ask him.

'Oh, probably me,' he says. 'Or, you know, surprise me.'

And that's where we leave it, at least until the next time.

The following day I go to Brighton to find Pete and Polly a proper wedding present. He can have the boomerang back as well, because I can't resist the joke, but I want to find something for Ben, too.

I walk around the Lanes, exploring toy shops and gift shops, and then I see it. Cornucopia. The sign is still there, but the shop has been gutted and the windows are covered with crossed gaffer tape. There's a notice outside, promising a coffee shop called Sparkles. Honestly.

I keep walking. The place still gives me the creeps. I'll never buy a coffee when Sparkles opens, even if it's the only available coffee in Brighton.

A seagull is tossing a McDonalds container around behind some bins at the end of one of the Lanes. I watch it for a while, thinking about Courtney.

Jim says she's moving in with her mother permanently in Newcastle. She's found a job working in a boutique.

I do the seagull a favour and pick up the container, emptying bits of hamburger onto the ground. Soon it's joined by other birds – sparrows, pigeons and much larger gulls. They don't scare me any more.

I keep walking, and then I find the perfect wedding present for Pete, Polly and Ben. An inflatable life-size Elvis.

'It's what you give people who've got everything, isn't it,' the man behind the counter says.

'Strangely enough, I think he has. Or he's about to,' I correct myself. Then – I can't resist it: 'It's for Pete Oram.'

'Ah, Pete,' says the man, and we both swap knowing smiles of local I-know-him-too smugness.

After this I get a call from Claudia.

'I'm thinking about leaving Guy,' she says as I take the phone into a quiet doorway, with Elvis tucked under my arm.

'Oh.'

'He's too hard.'

'Yeah.'

'He didn't even tell me he was seeing you this weekend.'

'Oh.'

'I could have come, too, he knows we're friends.'

'Sorry. He told me you were busy.'

'No I wasn't.' Claudia sounds tired and fed-up.

'Jim said, ages ago, you'd be together.'

'Really?' she cheers up.

'Yes. He said it would be hard work, but he said it was destiny.'

'Did he?'

'He remembered it the other day. Don't give up, Claudia. Guy just needs to sort himself out, that's all.'

'Bastard.' She manages to laugh.

It's nice being married to Jim Gabriel, as in married, married, married.

He gives me massages, which he learned in Thailand, and he's patient with me when I fall off my surfboard. He makes dinner in exchange for me washing up. He is like no other man I have ever met, the more I get to know him – but then that's probably the reason it took me so long to fall in love with him.

There.

I'm besotted.

And, now that I'm sure, I can finally tell my parents.

'The psychic?' Dad says when I go round for Sunday lunch. 'But aren't you married already?'

'Jim who was on the television?' Mum asks. 'How can you marry him again?'

I feel guilty. I've only just hit them with the news that I'm going to Australia, and now I'm telling them about a wedding as well.

'Come over here and do it,' Mum says. 'A French wedding would be lovely.'

'Well, we think you should come to Australia,' I suggest.

'Did he see it coming?' my father makes a bad joke.

'He did, actually. A long time ago. In a bucket. Though it didn't really happen the way I thought it would.'

Jim left the bucket on the beach at Hastings, deliberately, so a child could find it and take it away. Before then, it was under the kitchen sink. I'm glad someone else has got it now.

'I suppose I should give you a wedding present,' I

say to Jim one evening when we are doing the dishes and listening to the radio.

'Do English people do that?'

'I don't think so, but it doesn't really matter. I just want to give you a present. And . . . I've been wondering if I could give some of that twenty thousand you gave me to those people in New Orleans.'

'Right.' Jim lights a candle.

'But I thought – tell me if this is wrong – I could put the money on a bet. At Ladbrokes or somewhere. On England to win the Ashes.'

Jim nods, watching the flame finally take hold.

'What are the odds?' he asks.

'If England win I'll treble my money.'

'They will.' Jim grins at me. 'Genius, Katie.'

'Yeah?'

'Genius.'

'Do you like that idea as a wedding present?'

'Love it.'

'Right. Well I don't know anything about cricket, so tell me, when is the fifth Test?'

'It starts in a few days.'

'I'll go with you to Ladbrokes.' Jim grins again. 'I want to see their faces when you place the bet.'

Jim's wedding present to me, in the light of all this, turns out to be a prediction that would have shamed Nostradamus.

On 12 September, the bails are removed at The Oval, and the Ashes return to England for the first time since 1987.

'Keep the twenty thousand I gave you.' Jim forces a promise from me as we celebrate at the pub, along with the rest of Hastings. 'But you can give away the rest.'

A drunk man next to us overhears Jim's Australian accent.

'Sorry, mate,' he grins, giving him a thumbs up.

But Jim just replies, 'Best news I've had all year,' and raises his beer glass.

And then he makes me promise something else: that I'll buy myself a proper wedding ring at last, in Sydney, when Ladbrokes finally pay up.

THE END

SINGLE WHITE E-MAIL
Jessica Adams

'SEXY, FUNNY, SMART. FOR ANY WOMAN WHO HAS
EVER BEEN SINGLE'
Cosmopolitan

Dumped on her 30th birthday by the man she thought she
would marry, Victoria Shepworth – known as Victoria
'Total Bloody Relationships Disaster' Shepworth to her
friends – is feeling desperate.

So desperate that she cuts her hair, contemplates becoming
a born-again lesbian and evens throws herself into internet
dating. Armed with a new computer and an anonymous
nickname, she soon starts to feel human again – especially
when she starts receiving e-mails from a fantastic
Frenchman in Paris who claims to be a single white male
seeking single white e-mail.

Soon, everything else in Victoria's life begins to seem
boring, from her job in advertising, to her old friends and
neighbours. It's only when tragedy strikes that her potential
Monsieur Right is finally unmasked, though, and Victoria
realizes that her love life will never be the same again.

'*SINGLE WHITE E-MAIL* HAS AN INNATE HONESTY
ABOUT IT THAT KEEPS YOU ENTERTAINED TO THE
END. AT TIMES DISARMINGLY HARSH AND DECIDEDLY
CANDID, ADAMS' DÉBUT INTO THE LITERARY WORLD
IS FRESH, FRENETIC AND FUN'
Elle

0 552 77278 X

BLACK SWAN

TOM, DICK AND DEBBIE HARRY
Jessica Adams

'THOROUGHLY GRIPPING, YOU MUST READ THIS'
Heat

When Sarah – known to her friends as London's most
romantic singleton – decides to move to Australia to marry
a country vet, her future seems certain. But when she falls
in love with the best man, and out of love with her
husband, she realizes exactly what her romantic principles
are about to cost her.

The best man, Tom, is also about to face facts, as his secret
affair with Sarah starts to affect his relationship with Annie
– who is almost twice his age – and shatters every dream
they shared about their unconventional relationship.

As the Australian summer heats up, so do Sarah and
Annie's feelings. And then Bronte arrives. Tough, funny,
divorced and single, she is determined to hang on to her
dreams as well – and freedom is high on her list. But then
she tangles with gawky Harry, whose lifelong obsession
with Blondie is about to be replaced with something far
more seductive.

'A QUIRKY ROMANTIC COMEDY ABOUT LIFE, LOVE
AND BLONDIE – WITH A TWIST IN THE TALE'
Red

0 552 77279 8

BLACK SWAN

I'M A BELIEVER
Jessica Adams

'AN ORIGINAL AND ENTERTAINING NOVEL ABOUT
LIFE AFTER DEATH'
The Times

Mark Buckle thinks he's an ordinary bloke. He teaches
science at a junior school in south London. He'd rather
read Stephen Hawking than his horoscope, he's highly
suspicious of Uri Geller, Mystic Meg and feng shui, and he
wouldn't be seen dead at a séance. Most importantly, he
absolutely, positively doesn't believe in life after death.
Then, one terrible night, Mark's girlfriend Catherine dies
in a car accident, and even worse, starts communicating
with him in the middle of her own funeral.

While Mark forces himself to the doctor for checks on his
mental health, Catherine continues to find new ways to get
her message through. But the biggest message of all must
be from Tess – the last woman in the world Mark thinks he
should be with.

'A HEART-WARMING, FUNNY BOOK WITH
A SERIOUS CORE'
Glamour

0 552 77280 1

BLACK SWAN

COOL FOR CATS
Jessica Adams

'AN ELOQUENT LOOK AT THE BITTERSWEET NATURE
OF SUCCESS'
Glamour

It's 1979 and Linda Tyler is an assistant cook, engaged to a
bank clerk in a sleepy town called Withingdean, when she
answers an ad in a music paper. Suddenly, she gets the job
that everyone else in England wants.

Within weeks, her life changes beyond recognition. She
finds herself in London, working as a journalist on *NWW*, a
punk and new wave music magazine. Free records by
Blondie, Squeeze and The Clash land on her desk, and her
name is permanently on the guest list.

Before the year is out she will be propositioned by four
members of staff (including her work experience boy) and
meet some rising stars (and occasionally spill
Knickerbocker Glory on them). Along the way, though,
Linda Tyler will also discover who and what she loves
most – and make the most important decision of her life.

'ADAMS' LATEST NOVEL IS HUGELY TOUCHING, WITH
A STOICAL AND FUNNY HEROINE'
Marie Claire

0 552 77084 1

BLACK SWAN